To Sh

enjoy ,

The Haunting of Harriet

Jennifer Button

Jennifer Button

WITHDRAWN

Grosvenor House
Publishing Limited

This book is published by
Grosvenor House Publishing Ltd
28-30 High Street, Guildford, Surrey, GU1 3EL.
www.grosvenorhousepublishing.co.uk

A CIP record for this book
is available from the British Library

ISBN 978-1-908447-85-2

In memory of Peter

Prologue

O nly *angels and saints have the ability to view life from a wider perspective than us. Their elevated position allows them to peer around corners unimpeded by the obstacles that obscure our selfish, limited vision. They predict which paths we will take; while we simply blunder on, blindly relying on the odd signpost or an occasional flash of instinct. As mere mortals the scene from our own little window on the world is restricted to a personal, petty frame of reference. Still we plod along, placing one foot ahead of the other, and nod to those we encounter along the way, forgetting that their lives are what they are focused on. They are at the centre of their own unique universe and to them we are the outsider.*

So, fixed on our own journey, we live out our short span between life and death using only the cards we have been dealt. On occasion we recognize a rare quality in a fellow traveller; one who appears to be holding all the aces; and we call them "special". Whether we believe in Destiny, Divine Decree or the luck of the cards is of little account. All we can do is play the game, even if this means our sole purpose on earth is to serve as catalysts and enablers for those "special" people who are destined to achieve great things.

At least that is what some say......

CHAPTER 1

Harriet felt old and she hated it. Fate had played cruel tricks on her and left her wanting, without love and alone. Now, although still tall and upright, she used her father's cane from necessity rather than style. The silver handle matched her silver hair; that mass of tangled ginger frizz at last drained of pigment and free will. At times she wondered why she clung with such tenacity to this empty life. Was it her stubborn nature or the burning conviction that she had not yet fulfilled her destiny? Fate would have to get a move on. She could not have much longer. Besides she was tired. She longed to lie down and slip away unnoticed and un-mourned. But not yet – not today. She must wait just a bit longer, after all waiting wasn't hard and she had plenty of practice.

*

Liz believed in luck, especially good luck and why shouldn't she with life spread out before her like a smorgasbord of tasty morsels, hers for the picking? The millennium evening belonged to her as she stood surrounded by the people she loved most in the world. She just knew something momentous was about to happen. She was on the brink of a new adventure. It was exhilarating and a bit scary but the night air was crisp and vital. Breathing it in, she filled her lungs and offered herself to the future. She had never before felt so alive, so receptive; every cell, every fibre of her body tingled. Edward let go of her hand and smiled at her, before disappearing into the night, laughing and chatting in his easy-going way.

She had met Edward on a blind date, an evening planned by her old school friend, Carol. It was supposed to be a foursome but Carol failed to turn up, having gone off with Liz's prospective date. So the two rejects, dumped, feeling unwanted and rather stupid, decided to make the best of it and go it alone. By the end of the evening they were in love. Whether this was the hand of fate or a stroke of luck is debatable. Either way, just one week later Edward and Liz moved in together and were married the following month. The Jessops, as they were now known, bought a modest flat on the sort of South London estate that was aimed at first-time buyers, and began to build their nest. They both earned good money and Liz's inheritance from the sale of her parents' house enabled them to move quickly up the ladder to a smart three-bedroomed house suitable to accommodate a family. Edward's determination to succeed was literally paying dividends and propelled him into the high-earning echelons of the money market. Now, several lucrative years on, another substantial move up the property ladder was on the cards.

They had been on the lookout for the ideal house, but so far nothing matching their requirements had turned up. Liz wanted to replicate the home she had been raised in: a solid Edwardian house filled with solid old-fashioned furniture and extolling solid old-fashioned values. Edward dreamed of a modern architect-designed showpiece in which to parade the outward signs of his success. Confident that the perfect property was out there somewhere Liz was content to wait for luck to play its part; but when a nasty bout of food poisoning turned out to be a well advanced pregnancy she panicked.

At first, the idea of a baby put the fear of God in her. But once her natural confidence took hold she began to look forward to motherhood. This confidence ended abruptly when it was announced that she was carrying twins. One baby was manageable but two together! She knew she would fail; the babies would die and Edward would hate her forever. Convinced that she was woefully inadequate to cope she began to sink into a state of anxiety-led depression. House-hunting was put on the back burner until more pressing issues were resolved.

It was then that she hit on her brilliant plan. She bought a puppy. To her hormone-crazed brain it made perfect sense: try everything out on the dog first. If it survived then it would probably be safe for the babies. Of course, if the pup died she would have to rethink her strategy. Luckily, the acquisition of a puppy proved a stroke of genius. It was another case of love at first sight. The tiny creature thrived. Her experiment worked. From day one the guinea pig ruled the house with a paw of iron, earning him the title of The Potentate; Supreme Ruler: The Pote for short.

Caring for the puppy came so naturally to Liz that she convinced herself once again that motherhood would be a doddle. By the time the twins arrived she was ready for anything life could throw at her. Her career was shelved and she became a full-time housewife and mother, which to everyone's amazement suited her really well. Edward relaxed, content that his wife was happy. Secretly he was delighted to have his woman where she belonged; not exactly barefoot and pregnant but at home, a fixed nucleus at the centre of their lives. Suddenly the only problem in their otherwise ideal lives was the house. It shrank overnight. They had to move on up the ladder and soon.

It was over breakfast one Sunday that Edward spotted the advert in the paper. He thought it sounded nice, Liz thought it sounded perfect. According to the ad, the house boasted a mature garden with a lake, a boathouse and a beck, whatever that was and "a wealth of original features". It sounded intriguing: "Beckmans. A grade two listed building. Originally a timber framed Tudor house dating from 1540; the main part of the existing house being late Georgian. The house boasts a wealth of original features. Situated on the side of the Kentish Weald; sheltered to the north by woodland and facing south to the river Medway this is an outstanding property. Having been unoccupied for some time it is in need of some repair."

The idea of living in a really old house had not occurred to either of them. However, Liz's curiosity was more than aroused and being a creature of impulse she had to investigate further. *This is the way luck works*, she thought. *You have to recognize an opportunity, then grasp it.* So she did just that. Now, three months one week and two days later, she was living in her perfect house, about to embark on a whole new adventure. How lucky was that?

*

The evening of the millennium brought with it a new beginning in a new home. They were all standing on the bank of the little lake that dominated the lower part of the gardens at Beckmans. In front of them was what

4

remained of a small wooden bridge that would once have offered passage across the water to the old boathouse, whose shadowy ruin loomed to their left. Behind them at some distance stood the rear of the house itself, the light from the French windows flooding out across the lawn. Upstairs the twins and Robert, Brenda's and Donald's son were (hopefully) sleeping, with The Pote babysitting in tandem with Sue's daughter Emily. Their closest friends, Mel, Bob, David and Sue, were staying for a few days and Liz had invited some of their neighbours to join the celebrations and watch the firework display. Edward had thought this an odd mix but it had worked well. The discovery of new friendships and the solidifying of old ones added to the air of expectancy that buzzed and fizzed around them like the champagne they guzzled down. They could feel it. It was as potent as the sound of laughter.

From somewhere beyond her safe warm cocoon it began to call her. An uneasy feeling wrapped around her; someone was watching her, watching her and willing her not to ask questions, to let the past rest. She had seen it lying on the bottom of the stream on the first day she had explored the garden and she could feel it now although she could not see it from where she was standing. It was there, though, just beneath the water, as it had been then. "It's always been there." The words tumbled out of Liz's mouth by themselves. They made no sense; and why she had said them was a complete mystery. She knew she was referring to the old boat but why should the pathetic image of a sunken rowing boat haunt her? Why did she feel such a connection to it? It was puzzling. Someone was questioning her. What was she talking about?

"The boathouse…no one knows when it was built. It seems it has always been there!"

The lie hung heavily on her lips and she washed it down with a gulp of champagne. Her mind flashed back over the events of the last few months. Everything had happened so quickly. She smiled as she remembered it all. The very next day after reading the ad Edward had to go to the city as usual so she had dumped the twins with her best friend Mel and set off with The Pote on her intrepid journey south, to darkest Kent.

It was one of those bright October mornings when the sky is clear blue and the trees are just beginning to turn. On leaving the motorway Liz followed the directions in the agent's letter. She recalled how happy and carefree she had been, actually enjoying driving for a change. After her parents were killed in a stupid accident Liz had become a bit of a car phobic. But that was long ago; it was time to put it behind her. This was her chance to prove to Edward she could do things on her own; and she was finding asserting her independence pleasurable.

The estate agents had written apologizing for not having anyone free to show her around the property; however, the keys were held at Watermere Post Office and she was welcome to view it on her own. They explained that although the house itself was safe the boathouse was unsound and advised that for reasons of health and safety it be viewed from a sensible distance. They took care to stress that they would accept no responsibility for any accidents should this warning go unheeded. The keys were to be returned to the postmistress by six pm. They had included a map to help her locate the property.

Delighted to have the chance to nose around at leisure, Liz decided to make a day of it and brought a packed lunch with her. The village of Watermere was compact and practical rather than picturesque, and the post office was just where it should be, on the main street by the traffic lights. The postmistress gave her the third degree and told her with smug pleasure that she was one of a long list of potential buyers who had never returned. "Funny old place, I shall be interested to hear what you think of it." She handed Liz an enormous bunch of keys and smiled knowingly. Liz smiled politely and left, her sense of wellbeing somewhat deflated. But when she turned her car into the drive at Beckmans any feelings of impending disappointment vanished, to be replaced by hundreds of butterflies flying around in her tummy, churning out an excited anticipation she had not felt since she was a child.

*

The chattering of her friends brought her back to the party, back to the garden beside the lake overlooking the boathouse; her boathouse. Here she was, living the dream. Those magical keys were in her keeping, unlocking the home she had always dreamed of. Hidden by the darkness Liz smiled to herself, remembering that first time she had held the jangling bunch in her hands; the sheer weight of them had taken her by surprise. Just touching them had linked her to an intriguing history; connecting her to generations of past guardians who had amassed them over the years. History was literally in her grasp. Until that moment her whole world had been secured with one ordinary Yale handed to her on the day she moved in with Edward. By adding a secure modern mortice to the motley bunch she proudly joined the long unseen line of custodians. Held together by a strong iron ring, the keys belonged to the house and the house belonged to itself, not to anybody, living or dead. How exciting was that!

"Come on, you lot, fill up. It's almost time." Liz smiled at her husband, watching him weave among their guests, playfully chiding as he filled their glasses. "Is everyone loaded? It's the witching hour any second now." He raised his glass to the group, who lifted theirs, eyeing one another with anticipation. Monitoring his watch he began: "Ten, nine, eight..." She could hear his childish excitement as his voice got louder with each second until:

"One!" He kissed her, then stepped back, startled by an explosion of sound and light.

He heard Liz whisper "Did the earth move for you?"

He shouted back: "It knocked me off my fucking feet!"

Liz took a sip of her champagne and closed her eyes to recapture the delight she had felt that moment when she first saw Beckmans. It had knocked her off her feet too.

*

Watermere was friendly, a sensible village, a good place to raise a family, and she was pleased that the house, which sat on the outskirts, was still within the community. As she stepped out of the car her feeling of euphoria dipped. Her heart sank. In front of the house was a nasty modern wall, totally out of keeping with the property. It stated the boundary but detracted from the allure that should surround a property of such stature. Builders' rubble littered the entire forecourt, making the journey from car to front door a hazardous task that had to be undertaken with one's eyes fixed on the ground.

Looking up once she reached the steps, she saw the porch towering before her. It was quite splendid, Georgian, wide and welcoming. Its large Doric pillars were imposing even now, bereft of the original door that once stood between them. A tacky modern monstrosity stood there offering nothing but a sad apology. It looked incongruous and embarrassed and Liz felt sorry for it. There was no bell or knocker, just the ruined mechanism of a pulley hanging from the wall, long deprived of its pull-bar and bell. As Liz tapped on the ugly board her leather-gloved knuckles barely made a sound. She knew the house was empty but it seemed discourteous to enter without permission. Examining the weighty bunch she selected a shiny, but uninspiring modern Yale. With one half-turn the door swung open and she stepped over the threshold followed by The Pote, who was pleasantly surprised to be greeted by a tall, elderly woman. It was Harriet.

Harriet believed in Fate, so it came as both a surprise and a disappointment that in her long, at times overlong life, her own destiny had not yet revealed itself. She had been waiting for today. It was an auspicious day. At last something was about to happen. Life had been depressingly tedious with only memories as companions. Many of these unwanted memories had, for reasons of sanity, to be kept locked away. On long, cold nights she would release them in the vain hope that familiarity would grant her immunity from them. But they only brought distress and guilt and it alarmed her that the passing years were taking their toll on her own strength. Meanwhile her furies got even stronger, making it harder to contain and control them. These were her very own ghosts who crowded into the walls of the old house along with all the others that had left their vibrations behind when they went wherever it is ghosts go. Harriet's spectres were always too eager to emerge and crowd her space and it was only a profound sense of loneliness that drove her to release them in the first place.

On this October day she was experiencing something rare, a feeling she had not had for many years. It was hope. The sound of a leathered glove rapping on the door startled Harriet into spilling her morning tea. As she rose from the table she was filled with an excited and pleasant expectancy. Her slippers made no sound as she crossed the tiled floor before placing her ear close to the door to listen, snorting in disgust at the smell of the ugly cheap pine that had replaced mahogany and stained glass. Harriet pressed her ear to the offensive wood but she heard no voices; nothing that filled her with alarm. Surprised by the ease with which they moved, she slipped the bolts free and stepped back into the shadows, while outside a key turned slowly in the lock. A young, slim woman crossed the threshold followed by what at first she thought was a rat. The rat sniffed at her and she recognized it as one of those funny German sausage dogs. She patted it on the head and listened to her house. It approved of these visitors and so did she. She opened her arms and the young woman accepted the embrace with a natural familiarity and courtesy of manner that both house and mistress found endearing.

"Welcome to Beckmans," Harriet said.

"Thank you." The reply came with mirrored courtesy and warmth. The young woman spoke softly with a pleasant, cultured accent. Harriet studied her at some length, liked what she saw and so together they set off, the one to guide and the other to explore yet both with a mutual feeling of belonging. Harriet felt no intrusion had taken place. She welcomed this person into her house and took delight in showing her around. Together they covered every inch of the house, with Harriet chatting away as she used to when she was a child, perfectly relaxed and happy to be sharing her love of Beckmans with another after all these years.

She had lost count of how many "viewers" there had been over the years. Not one of them had proved worthy of admittance, let alone a welcome. They had all been sent packing in no uncertain terms. Many years of practice at making people feel uneasy had paid off; she was an expert at it now and considered it a rather amusing pastime. This young lady was different. She fitted the bill nicely. There was a familiarity and a similarity that pleased them both. Harriet was delighted to show Liz her house. But she would show it through her own bright amber eyes, and only the parts that were filled with light, laughter and music. Not the other; not yet. Beckmans deserved nothing less than to be displayed in all its glory.

Although the entrance hall was shabby and smelt of decay, Liz felt warm arms envelope her. A comfortable feeling of coming home embraced her as she took her first tentative steps onto barely recognizable black-and-white marble floor tiles. Beckmans was making her welcome, which deserved a polite acknowledgement. Saying a courteous "Thank you" she opened the inner door, stopped in her tracks and let her mouth fall open. She was standing on years of dust and debris but beneath this demeaning layer of grime she could determine solid parquet flooring, herring-boned blocks of beech covering a magnificent circular hall that could swallow the entire first floor of their present house. The outside of the house belied these internal dimensions. The sense of space the architect had created was phenomenal. It was like entering the Tardis. Liz stood rooted to the spot but the house was drawing her in, oblivious to its present dilapidated state.

"Come in," a voice said. "See Beckmans in all its glory."

*

An explosion of lights shocked the millennium sky. For a split second Liz was lost, suspended between the past and the present. Her fingers stroked the rough wooden rail that ran the length of the little bridge, while her mind adjusted to the time change. A breeze moved her hair and she saw her own face gazing back at her beside the ruins of the old boathouse, both mirrored in the night-dark water. The second volley dashed her thoughts as the reflected fireworks sent illuminated litter scattering over the unbroken surface. In that moment Liz saw the faces of her friends next to her own, childlike, smiling out from the water. She looked up and caught their true faces pointing upwards as they waited in anticipation for the next burst, eclipsing the stars with their brilliance before they too burnt out and faded to a familiar rosy glow. The air was full of the acrid smell of saltpetre, and the rosy pink took her back to that unforgettable day when she first fell under Beckmans' spell. It was the same colour as the morning light that flooded through the rose window. She easily willed herself back to the moment when she had first seen that window.

*

She was bathed in that light. Looking up she saw it. Large and round, it dominated the hall, even though partially boarded up for reasons of security or safety. She knew instinctively how it must once have looked. There was no need for Harriet's description, Liz's imagination filled in the gaps. It depicted a Tudor rose. Intricate black lead lines held the petals of glass, which deepened from blush-pink to rose-madder as they neared the heart of the flower. Liz took hold of the curved banister beside the staircase and a thick covering of dust parted as she ran her hand along the Georgian mahogany. Removing her glove, she let her bare skin touch the wood and slide sensuously along the curve of the rail. The wood was smooth-polished by years of hands doing exactly what she was doing now. Led on by Harriet, she climbed the first flight of stairs that swept up through the heart of the house before dividing on either side of a wide landing, which was dominated by the great window.

The landing was about the size of their present bedroom and from here the hall looked even more enormous. Liz counted seven doors. Where did they all lead? There was so much to explore, too much. She resolved to make a quick tour today to get the feel of the place; if it was what she wanted she could come back and peruse it at leisure. If? There was no "if". She knew she would return. There was no doubt she was meant to live in this house.

The ceiling showed some signs of damp. She remembered watching Mel's husband Bob tap walls with his knuckles when he was assessing a job, so she did the same; as nothing appeared to fall or crumble she deemed the property pretty sound. Already seductive colour charts were appearing before her eyes, tempting her with their subtle shades. Her feet imagined the luxurious pile of antique carpets as they carried her along the bare boards westward to a large Tudor room. The room was full of beams: oaken, straight, curved, thick and thin, all steeped in a shared history, part of the original house. Large beams forming a cross divided the high ceiling into four. Though deprived for the moment of its grand full-tester bed with acanthus carved pillars and goose-feather pillows, this was a masterful bedroom fit for a husband and wife: perfect for Edward and Liz.

Harriet smiled. This woman needed no guide. She was at one with the house. The old woman knew their destinies were inextricably linked. At last here was someone she could trust.

Together they explored the whole of the first floor, one discovering each new room, the other releasing memories that had remained buried for too long. In the smaller eastern wing Liz discovered a vast joke of a bathroom. A Heath Robinson geyser and the remains of three cast-iron baths of different sizes stood marooned in the centre, conjuring the image of children at bath-time, the splashes and giggles so vivid the soap almost stung her eyes. Harriet had memories exactly like that from so long ago. She laughed at Liz, who had clambered into the largest of the bath tubs. The three baths shared nine legs between them, which was not quite enough as Goldilocks was to discover when the daddy bath collapsed under her weight, evicting an army of spiders that scurried for cover. Horrified by the scuff mark left by her boot, Liz looked around for a cloth to remove it. Then, realizing that the meagre amount of remaining enamel would scarcely coat a bedpan, she laughed at her over-developed sense of domesticity. The baths were rusted through beyond repair and to Liz's delight a small mouse had nested in the down pipe of the baby one. So much for the plumbing!

Harriet was enjoying the company. It had been so long since she had found anything to laugh at. Life had become a tedious round of monotonous tasks; were it not for the knowledge that she had not fulfilled her purpose, her destined task, she would have packed it all in long ago. She felt the old house coming back to life, responding to the vitality this young visitor had brought with her. Maybe she was the person who could unlock the past that had trapped her for so long; although in her heart Harriet did not believe there was a key to fit.

Still chuckling, Liz climbed the last flight of stairs. "It's quite safe. Trust me. Go on. This is the children's room; I really want you to see it." Shamed for pausing before gingerly testing the first step, Liz apologized. Such lack of trust was out of place. With renewed verve and scant regard for safety she bounded up the last ten stairs that led to the attic. Enormous, cavernous, a great cathedral of a room containing the huge beams that supported the house, it astounded her. It dwarfed her. Spurred on by an unseen energy, Liz ran into the centre. She spread her arms wide, threw her head back and began to spin like a top. With each rotation her laughing upturned face and long blonde hair caught the sunlight that shot through the missing peg tiles. Reliving her youth, Harriet spun with her, laughing heartily, until exhausted they collapsed to the floor, having retraced the steps of children long gone or yet to come. This haven echoed with the sound of youngsters playing and she wanted the Jessop twins to share it. The floor was hidden beneath a sea of nutshells, which scrunched and slipped beneath her feet. There were holes where squirrels, mice and rats had nested, and brown marks where rain and snow had got in. The Pote had found his Paradise. The enticing smells sent him into a frenzy of barking as he charged about intent on catching at least one of the squatters.

Fortunately the house appeared to be as solid as a rock. The framework existed. The core, the heart was healthy. She could hear the sarcasm in Edward's voice as he had muttered: "Nothing throwing money at it can't solve." Suddenly she no longer cared how much it was going to cost. She only knew she had to have it. Luckily most of her inheritance was untouched and Beckmans was the perfect project to spend it on. This house was a part of her, just as if she was heir to it. She belonged here. She resolved to restore Beckmans to its former glory and she laughed at the thought of her own impudence and indulgent extravagance. Harriet applauded her astuteness.

*

"Aren't you going to share the joke?" Edward slipped his arm around Liz's waist.

"Sorry, what was that?"

"You were chuckling away at something."

"It's because I'm so happy – and a bit giddy," she said, throwing her head back to catch the latest rocket burst.

"It's from looking up so much. Great, isn't it? Like being a kid again!"

"Yes, isn't it just!" Liz chuckled some more and returned to her nutshells.

*

With amazement, she noticed it was already one o'clock and she had not touched the ground floor or the garden, with that intriguing boathouse. She counted six double bedrooms and plenty of space for shower-rooms and bathrooms. If they took it one project at a time it was quite feasible. She could talk to Bob about doing the building work. All they needed was a kitchen, a bathroom, a nursery and a bedroom for now. The rest they could do at their leisure. Her mind was frantically calculating how fast they would have to move to be in there ready to celebrate the millennium when something made her turn again to the east wing. At the end of the corridor was a second staircase, smaller, utilitarian, the servants' stairs. Down and round she went, stepping carefully over the last tread. It was loose and needed fixing.

The servants' stairs brought her out in the business end of the house: sculleries, washrooms, bottle stores and cook-houses reeking of hams and coal, soap and ale, the memory of smells lingering in the fusty air. Liz moved from room to room, poking her fingers into the scars of vanished sinks, kitchen ranges, ovens and stoves wrenched from their homes; appliances that would have been state-of-the-art to past generations. A history lesson in domestic life stretched before her. Combining the space would make ample room for a dream kitchen, a utility room and, most importantly, a family room, a breakfast-room like the one from her childhood: a comfortable, informal, welcoming heart to the house. Harriet was exhausted but content. Liz was ecstatic. She had come home.

*

Crashing back to reality, her conscience hit her. *Home!* Beckmans was her home now, occupied by her children and her dog, poor Pote! How could she have been so thoughtless? She had visions of him cringing beneath the table or shivering dejectedly in a corner. Or, far more likely, reverting to his full title of The Potentate: he who must be obeyed, terrorizing the children, furious at having been forgotten. She hoisted her dress, ready to dash to his rescue, when a pair of firm hands caught her by the shoulders.

"They're fine. The babies are safe as houses, so is that wretched hound. Sue just peeped in to check. So relax and enjoy the show." Edward's reassurance was convincing enough to let Liz slip back into her reverie with a clear conscience.

*

The door ahead brought her back into the hall. She remembered the echo of her leather shoes on the wooden floor as she walked across, like the sound of hands clapping: the house applauding. It welcomed newness as much as it revered the past. That was how it had survived for so long, through armadas, wars, plagues and revolution. It had endured everything time threw at it: storm, flood, fire and tempest; it had witnessed births, deaths, adultery and passion, heartbreak, joy, love and hate. It would surely cope with two babies and a dachshund.

Liz remembered sitting on the wide curve of the bottom stair, oblivious to the dirt and grime surrounding her. She was hungry and took out her sandwiches. Her teeth sank into the soft bread and she realized she knew this house. She had been here before. Somewhere in her subconscious she was familiar with every nook and cranny. This awareness was comforting and not in the least alarming. A pigeon flapped above her head, startling her for a moment, but when she got up to guide it out it knew its way. It too was familiar with this remarkable old house. As she chewed, she caught the whisper of a perfume. A scent her mother had worn? What was it called, something to do with Paris? She recalled dark blue glass, a silver Cinderella's slipper, an Eiffel Tower. "Evening in Paris"; she smiled at the memory. It had been all the rage then. Now it would be considered naff. Poor Mummy, she'd have thought this place far too big and dilapidated. Would she approve of her money being used to do it up? The sum total of her parents' lives used up to supply a kitchen and a couple of bathrooms seemed obscene when put like that. Why was everything so temporary? Beckmans must have born witness to countless fashions. How it must cringe at each fresh fad inflicted on it. Guiltily she retrieved her sandwich wrapper from the floor and pocketed it. This house had been neglected for too long. It needed TLC, not litter. She felt an approving acknowledgement; as if her mother was watching. But it was Harriet.

Lunch over, she resumed her tour. There were five more doors. Methodically, she took them clockwise. The first opened onto a perfect study for Edward. She closed her eyes and breathed the sweetness of pipe tobacco. As a rule she hated smoking in any form but this smelled delicious. Asking herself why, Liz realized that she was speaking aloud. Was she talking to herself or the house? Harriet listened, bemused, as Liz chided herself for her stupidity and moved on to the next room. It was Tudor; grand and oak. It would easily accommodate a table to seat twenty. She saw candles gutter, wax drip, garden flowers grace the centre. She heard the chatter of friends as they sat talking into the small hours putting the world to rights. Liz had found her dining-room.

All that was missing was a lounge large enough to be called a drawing-room, somewhere to entertain. There were two doors left. The fourth was considerably lower than all the others but wider and made of a heavy oak, carved in scrolled panels that had over the years darkened to a dense black. The fifth was an impressive pair of doors, at least ten feet tall, leading to the main reception room. Longing to find her lounge but sticking to her clockwise routine, Liz returned to the fourth door. Harriet retreated to the shadows, her face showing displeasure and her body trembling with emotion. As Liz turned the large iron ring of the handle she experienced a distinct feeling that she was in the wrong place. The catch did not respond to her first attempt or her second. The door remained firmly closed. She moved on to the large double doors, which towered above her.

Harriet pushed them gently and the great doors swung wide. Liz had hardly touched them. "Wow!" The exclamation escaped through a wide O of a mouth that remained open long after the sound had faded. Harriet stepped aside for Liz to enter.

"This was Mama's drawing-room. It's beautiful, isn't it? She loved this room because it complemented her so well. She was a very beautiful woman." For a brief moment Harriet was a child again, sitting behind the banisters with her brother watching as the guests arrived. The miscellaneous perfumes and the sound of servants bearing trays of tinkling glasses, musicians tuning up, the jazz and the colours all brought back a longing for a childhood that never really happened. As a child she assumed a mother's duty was to look beautiful and throw parties. That was all, and as such her Mama was brilliant. Her mother's lust for life was prodigious and her propensity for entertaining boundless. She was always giving parties, always extravagant affairs, to the delight of her guests. At these events Harriet's mother, Alice, would circulate, ensuring she took centre-stage. Meanwhile her father, George, having mingled enough for politeness' sake, would retire to his study, leaving Alice's vivacity to carry her from guest to guest: a bewitching butterfly, leaving a trail of smiling, happily flattered people in her wake. There was always a young man to hand should her cigarette need lighting. Another was ready to serve when a cushion needed to be placed in the small of her back as she arranged herself on the *chaise longue*, while engaging yet some other young man in conversation. With some of them she would touch hands briefly as they happened to pass, and sly smiles would be exchanged discreetly, indicating the sharing of a delicious secret.

The parties became famous. Beckmans was "the place" to meet people and to be seen doing so. Music always featured, a small jazz band by the boathouse, a dance combo on the terrace or the piano playing in the drawing-room with Alice singing Cole Porter or Noel Coward. Harriet would peek through the French windows to watch her lovely Mama, her left arm resting on the Spanish shawl that protected the rosewood piano, her emerald ring glistening on her long, slim finger, as she sang and flirted shamelessly with all the men. The couple's popularity grew, not merely because of their splendid hospitality, but because they were "good sorts".

Throughout those carefree days before the war they, or rather she, entertained, lavishly and generously. She loved company and loved being admired, as did the house.

Liz remembered the agent's leaflet had boasted a grand drawing-room measuring thirty-four feet square and had mentioned elegance and grandeur in the blurb but it had failed to convey the perfection of this room. It was Georgian architecture at its most graceful. Ignoring the four sorry lightbulbs dangling from the ceiling, Liz saw opulent crystal chandeliers scattering the flames of a hundred candles. The plaster roses and cornicing were missing but they could be replaced. As Liz gazed up, her feet instinctively took her across the room to the heavy shutters covering the tall windows. She pulled them back and the western sun streamed in. It fell in shafts that sent the resident dust dancing and whirling in suspension. Freeing the shutters on the south-facing windows allowed their light to flood in and puddle on the bare floorboards. Liz's feet performed a crazy quickstep to an unheard band. Harriet closed her eyes as she guided her partner and together they joined the past. With each turn and twist the two dancers saw the white-veined marble of the handsome fireplace, flames dancing around the orchard logs. Harriet saw them both reflected in the large mirror that hung above the mantle. Liz saw only a darkened patch where a mirror had once hung. The shadow of a grand piano stood in the centre of the sprung floor, its melody spinning in the air along with the dust. Angostura and gin perfumed the atmosphere and the brush of silk chiffon touched her skin as she danced.

Liz danced back to the French windows, where Harriet was now standing, and pressed her face against the cold glass. The lake shimmered in the distance and the soft outline of a building caught her breath. A gothic apparition standing at the water's edge; the boathouse was waiting. As she watched, the light began to change until all that remained was a silhouette against the early setting sun. Checking her watch she gasped; it had already gone four o'clock. How long had she been standing there? She still had another room to see and had not even touched the gardens, with the lake and that tantalizing folly. She had entered a forgotten world. She spun around for the last time and gently drew the doors behind her. Again there was the faintest hint of a forgotten perfume, the aroma of cocktail cigarettes; the smoke from their scented tobacco curling up to the high ceiling as it spiralled and reeled with her senses, and cobwebs brushed her cheek with the delicacy of a feather boa. Reluctant to lose her dream, she rested her back against the towering doors. Her senses had never felt so alive and there was still the Fourth Room left to explore.

*

Edward nudged her arm. He was recharging the glasses and she swigged hers back greedily before holding it out for a refill. Taking her champagne with her she closed her eyes and stood tall. She moved away from the great doors. She remembered her feeling of urgency, the need to get a move on. It was getting late. In a business-like manner she crossed the hall and returned to the heavy door of the elusive Fourth Room. It was covered in thick sticky cobwebs encrusted with dust and the remains of the victims caught in their lethal traps. Spiders did not bother Liz so she reached through and twisted the iron ring, pushing against the door at the same time. It did not budge. Taking the ring in both hands she pushed hard.

"You can't go in there. It's private. I keep it locked." Harriet hissed the words at Liz, who was busy studying her bunch of keys.

"Well, I can be as stubborn as you," she shouted as she hurled herself at the door. It did not give an inch but her shoulder hurt. The door might be locked but she had the keys. The front door, back door, garden door and cellar door were all clearly labelled. The lounge, dining-room, inner hall, master bedroom, the attic: each had a key; even the boathouse had one. This room had no name and no key. Was it just a cupboard? Where was that damned leaflet from the agent? Harriet lifted the paper from Liz's bag and secured it in her own pocket, watching as the young woman rummaged frantically in her black hole of a handbag. In final desperation Liz tipped the entire contents onto the floor, before turning out the pockets of her coat. She had lost it.

"God, I'm such an idiot!"

Remorse made Harriet blush. This was not the way to encourage this young woman to feel at home. "I do apologize. That was extremely discourteous of me. Here, let me show you."

Liz returned to the breakfast-room, where her hand reached up to a concealed ledge above the garden door. Tucked at the back of the ledge was a large iron key. It was at least eight inches in length and the head was wrought in the shape of a fabulous beast. She approached the door again. Harriet closed her eyes and sighed. She had of course promised the house would hold no secrets for Liz but she had not reckoned with this. Both their hearts were beating fast and Liz's hand shook as she offered the key to the lock. The tumblers turned with a heavy unwillingness. Strands of cobwebs grabbed at her face. They stuck to her coat and her gloves, clinging the tighter as she attempted to brush them away. The sticky threads mixed with her hair and a gossamer veil covered her face. She was cold and frightened. She shook her head in a frantic attempt to rid herself of the hideous stuff. She was beginning to panic.

*

Mel was standing beside her friend, watching her beat the air with flaying arms, fighting frantically as though her life depended on it. "What on earth is the matter?" Mel took Liz's arm, holding it still. "God, you're frozen. Here, take this. I'm warm as toast." She placed the shawl around her friend's shoulders. Mad Mel was Liz's dearest friend, wild and impetuous, her head surrounded by clouds of magenta curls; an eccentric in touch with angels and spirits, in complete contrast to cool, smooth Liz. Mel was never further than a handbag away from her Tarot cards. Irreverent about all matters religious and with a wicked lust for life, Mel stuck two fingers up to the establishment and went with the flow. Liz adored her. Mel filled Liz's life with colour. But tonight even her closest friend could not persuade Liz to abandon her memories. She continued brushing vigorously at her hair, her glass spilling its contents as she did so. She muttered some words of thanks and pulled the borrowed wrap closer around her but it did nothing to prevent the chill that gripped her. She closed her eyes, ignored her friend and embraced the cold.

*

Calming herself with deep breaths, she reluctantly entered the fourth and final room. Harriet remained outside. She did not have on her side the courage that came from ignorance. Covering her eyes with her cloak she waited for the young woman to return to her. The warmth of welcome had gone and it was as an intruder that Liz entered. Two steep wooden steps took her by surprise and as she ducked low to avoid hitting her head on the door frame she stumbled. It was dark and her eyes took time adjusting to the change in light. The room's only window was boarded up, letting only a thin inadequate glimmer enter the gloom. Cold and uncomfortable, Liz fumbled around feeling for a light switch. What an idiot to go house-hunting in late October without a torch. Slowly her hand inched along the wall until she found one. She flicked it, nothing happened. She flicked it again and it crashed to the ground leaving its lethal old wires reaching out. Liz was freezing by now. Her resolve was leaving her. It was getting late and she wanted to catch the estate agents before they closed. Anyway, she ought to get those keys back. It was time to leave. Something stronger than fear was pushing her, directing her back to the hall and she was in no mood to stay and find out what it was.

Anxious to get back out her foot slipped on the top step then as she reached out to save herself from falling the heavy door slammed shut, barring her exit and blocking out the only real source of light. Blinded by panic and tears she scrambled about in the dark convinced she would be locked in this awful place forever. Harriet reached out opening the door from the outside. How could she have been so unkind slamming it shut like that! She twisted the handle, just as Liz discovered the clasp. Together they managed to turn it and force the door to release her. Liz fell through the opening, landing back in the hall. Shaking and gasping for air, her eyes closed tight, Liz crouched like a baby scared of what might face her when she opened them. Bending forward, Harriet kissed her softly and whispered an apology in her ear.

*

Liz felt Edward's kiss land on her cheek. With a long sigh of relief she realized she was back beside him at the lake. The fireworks display was banging away in full force. However much had he spent? After all, they still had only half a kitchen, a nursery and one bathroom. There was a mass of work to do before their home was complete. Liz felt petty-minded. They had all the time in the world to do the house up and anyway she would be content to live here just as it was, or even as it had appeared to her on that first visit. But she was not prepared to let Edward know that. Some things were best kept secret, which was why she had not told him about the Fourth Room. What would have been the point? He would only have laughed and told her she was being silly. Why on earth had she let herself get so het up about what probably was nothing? She recalled how stupid she had felt then when she had finally opened her eyes.

*

The hall was filled with the light of early evening and the air was warm. With a sigh of relief Liz sat down on the bottom stair and searched in her handbag for her mirror and comb. As she combed the last of the cobwebs from her hair she tried to make sense of that Fourth Room. It was an empty, neglected room like the others. Darker maybe, but then there was no natural light. The electrics were something else, but at least they matched the plumbing. Anyway, what had she been thinking of? The electricity was not even turned on, foolish girl! Liz chastised herself again. She felt normal once more, the intensity of the fear she had been feeling now forgotten. She just remembered a cold, forbidding room, strange as the rest of the house was so welcoming. This room wanted to be left alone. It was a sad room. It did not want her intruding on its private sorrow. She picked herself up and dusted off her coat.

A quick glance at her watch told her it was five past six. The clocks had just gone back and the light seeping in was moonlight. What had happened to the last two hours? She fumbled in her bag for her mobile. The paper the agent had given her was right there, folded and pristine, exactly where she had put it that morning. How annoying. How could she have missed it before? She heard herself laugh, a loud short snort of a laugh. It took her completely by surprise and she followed it with a more characteristic giggle, which echoed through the hall. There was no reply when she rang the agents. They had very wisely gone home.

Before leaving Liz glanced back at the Fourth Room. Walking resolutely over to the door she pulled it shut and turned the key. She returned the key to its hiding place on the ledge in the kitchen, telling herself it was just a room, one among many; it should in no way cloud her judgement. After checking that she had left the house securely locked, she climbed into her car, started the engine, but before driving off she took a long last look at Beckmans. The moon was full and hung in the clear October sky directly above the property. All its defects were washed away, bathed clean in milky moonlight. It was beautiful. Yes, it needed a lot of work, of course it did, but beneath the dust and decay, grime and neglect was a rare building. This house was more than just a house, it was home. As she pulled out of the drive she was whistling a tune, the sort that keeps going round and round in your head. She tried Edward's mobile and left a message on his voice-mail. "It's perfect." By now she was singing, "If happy little bluebirds fly...." She was still chirruping away when, an hour later, she picked the twins up from Mel.

*

"You'll have to shout, Lizard. I can't hear you above all this racket." Edward was shouting at her, trying to bring her back to the party, but she was not ready to leave her dream. Harriet kept in the shadows watching and silent. She too was full of memories. She smiled at Liz's reply:

"I was singing." The words came from somewhere between two worlds. Liz chose to travel back in time to that second day when she had returned to Beckmans as she knew she would.

*

She remembered that Mel had agreed to come with her this time. Mel had found her friend's account fascinating and was keen to feel the vibrations of the house for herself. If Liz's story was anything to go by there was something intriguing going on in Kent. The peculiar familiarity, the almost prior knowledge Liz had described, convinced Mel that the house had a presence. Of course she had not voiced this suspicion. Well, not in so many words. Liz was pretty much a sceptic when it came to the paranormal. Mel had learned to play things coolly where Liz was concerned and decided not to pass judgement until she had sussed things out for herself. Liz simply wanted her friend to see the house where she knew she would be spending the rest of her life. As luck had it, Mel took to her bed the next day with a streaming cold. A quick phone call secured the services of a reliable baby-sitter and Liz set off bright and early, undaunted and secretly relieved at not having to contend with the terrible twins and an over-inquisitive dachshund. A flask of hot soup was stowed in the boot along with a powerful torch and a spare pair of shoes. The extra footwear just seemed like a good idea.

She arranged to meet Edward and the estate agent at Beckmans at three o'clock, before the light changed. That way she had a chance to explore the grounds alone while still leaving ample time for Edward to see the house at its best. He was not pleased at the prospect of having to leave work early, but Liz was determined and there was a lot of money at stake.

She was met by the same feeling of welcome when she let herself in. If anything, it was stronger, more positive than before. Everything was just as she remembered and she fell in love with the old property all over again. Wrinkling her nose, she had to admit that the house did smell a bit stale and fusty though she saw no signs of serious rot, just dampness where the elements had found their way in, which was only to be expected.

Liz decided to seize the bull by the horns. Lifting the griffin-headed key from its hiding place, she entered the Fourth Room first. This time she met with no resistance. Harriet had felt ashamed of her churlish behaviour and believing fervently that this young woman was

"The One" did not wish to test Fate by frightening her off. Keeping a foot in the door in case it slammed shut, as it was prone to do, the old woman remained outside, anxious to see her guest's reaction. With her torch at the ready Liz was pleasantly surprised to find she did not need it: the room was quite light enough with the hall door left wide. She sighed with relief to enter an empty room that simply needed a good airing.

It was several degrees colder than the rest of the house but this was easily accounted for by its north-facing aspect. She was drawn to the fine oak fireplace, the more remarkable for having survived the avaricious plundering of the salvagers. Harriet remained by the door and waited with uncharacteristic patience while Liz ran her hand down the acanthus carving on the left-hand side of the inglenook. Her fingers rested on a small embossed hook. Close examination revealed it to be shaped like a tiny bird. Black and hardly visible against the darkness of the oak, it was exquisite. Liz wondered what treasure had hung there. Such a charming hook must have been chosen to hold something precious. She began to realize that in another life this room had been a very private place, a room that had witnessed a great deal of love and possibly heartache. But she was getting sentimental and that would never do. She had promised Edward that today she would be rational and objective in her assessment of the house, which was hard; the place was growing on her and detachment was no longer possible. Harriet tossed a loose strand of hair from her eyes and brushed it back behind her left ear. Liz mirrored the action, making Harriet smile. Characteristically Harriet emitted a spontaneous laugh, almost a snort, before leading the young woman on to explore the rest of her property.

It was with a sense of achievement, tinged slightly by a reluctant admission to having played the drama queen the day before, that she climbed the wooden steps out of the room. As she stepped into the hall she sniffed loudly and found she had tears streaming down her face. "Damn," she thought, "I've caught Mel's cold." Blowing her nose in one of her mother's lacy handkerchiefs, she looked straight at Harriet, who averted her own tear-stained eyes.

The fresh air was a welcome relief as Liz emerged from the back door into the garden. There was a lot of undergrowth. The expanse of once-manicured lawn sloped down from the terrace to a fast-flowing beck, which fed into the lake before gurgling on to the River Medway. The grass was long and wet and the fallen leaves stuck to her shoes. Liz stood on the weathered York flagstones, ignoring the multitude of weeds, and breathed in the crisp autumn air.

The garden was large and derelict, yet even at its worst it was stunning. Harriet painted her a picture of it in summer, asking her to imagine the trees lush and full, a mown, groomed lawn of regimented green stripes sweeping down to the lake.

Liz saw herself in a wide-brimmed straw hat, her children playing on the grass, happy and healthy. A large wooden table groaned with jugs of lemonade, sandwiches and cake beneath the spread of the cobnut tree, which she identified by the wealth of nuts littering the ground. Edward lay asleep in a comfortable wicker chair, face buried beneath the gently fluttering *Financial Times*. It was all so English, so idyllic, and hers for the asking. A movement in the undergrowth startled her and she regretted not having brought The Pote along. She imagined him baying excitedly, his tongue and ears flying out, his long sleek body close to the ground, propelled by short but powerful legs, exulting at being a hound as he rampaged through this perfect world.

By the lake stood a large weeping willow with a reach long enough to dip into the water. Its leaves had mostly dropped and formed a yellow carpet at its base. Stepping-stones led temptingly across the beck, from which the house took its name. The small lake lay to the right of this stream, which flowed eagerly in at the northern side and bubbled out again southwards.

And there it stood; the boathouse. It was on the far side of the lake, the mysterious building she had seen yesterday from the house. Was that really only yesterday? Although always referred to as "the boathouse", it had not been designed to house boats. It was more of a summerhouse, with its dovecot on the turret and the high-pitched fancy barge boarding on its southern face. A vestige of this was still visible but, sadly, much had vanished over the years. A safety rail, no longer fit for purpose, ran along this side. Another smaller window ran along on the right and it was this eastern aspect that overlooked the adjacent stream. Ivy and woodbine had grown in through the low windows that stood to the left of the door. It was little more than a blackened outline of what must have been. Here it was in full daylight, yet it still took the form of the alluring silhouette that had so captured Liz's heart when she first saw it through the cold glass of the French windows. At some point it had suffered a serious fire.

Years ago this had been Harriet's favourite place. Originally built by a wealthy Victorian industrialist, it had been lovingly rebuilt by Harriet's father for his young bride, who had seldom set foot in the place, considering it too small to entertain in. "What on earth could one do in such a remote, dreary place?" she would ask without any understanding of the fact that some people sought solitude and took pleasure in their own company.

Harriet paused by the bridge and Liz paused with her. The danger signs were clear enough. In fact they screamed out, conspicuously written in lurid yellow and black; but they had nothing to do with Harriet's reluctance to cross; she had her own private reasons for withdrawing. Liz, however, heeded the warnings and opted to walk around the lake to view the boathouse from a safe distance. She was beginning to feel inexplicably frustrated and twitchy. The temptation to investigate was overpowering. It could not be that dangerous or the agent would not have let her come here alone. The temporary obstacles put there to deter trespassers proved no match for her and she climbed past them with ease. Normally she was horribly righteous, always obeyed orders and never broke the law. This flirtation with risk was exhilarating and gave her a new-found confidence. Being a rebel was a novel experience and she loved the buzz.

Slowly, trying to appear gung-ho, she inched her way across until she stood on the walkway that surrounded three-quarters of the folly. The last few planks by the entrance were missing, leaving a gaping hole above the water. On closer inspection of the main shell, the signs of the fire that had consumed much of the vulnerable structure were more apparent. This was presumably why it had been left to rot. It explained the blackness of the wood. Even so, it was straight out of a spooky dream, standing desolate in its sorry state of disrepair. All the windows were obscured, covered with the thick twisted stems that had become a part of the old building as the plants claimed it for themselves. Her gentle attempt at parting them proved futile, so she braced herself and gave the main stem an almighty yank. The ivy gave way, taking the window frame with it. Falling backwards, Liz screamed as her left foot disappeared between the rotted struts. A searing pain shot up her leg, and for a moment she could not move. Once the shock had subsided she looked down at her leg. Blood was pouring out from a long gash and as she tried to extricate her foot from the jagged planks her shoe plopped into the water.

*

"Ouch!" The shock of her own voice took her by surprise. Someone was standing beside her and caught her before she pitched forward into the water. It was Sue.

"What's wrong? Have you hurt yourself?"

"I'm fine. I just caught my heel" She looked down at her leg and gave it a brisk rub. Her stockings were intact, so was her skin. There was nothing to see now, only the memory of pain. She was cold and was back in the present. Screwing up her eyes tightly she returned to that October afternoon just over a year ago.

*

She recalled that weird sensation of being watched. The knowledge of someone looking at you, the feeling that makes you turn around had been there from the moment she entered the garden, an awareness that eyes were fixed on her. Was it her guilty conscience? She had been recklessly stupid. Thank goodness she had not brought the twins with her. They could have drowned. It did not bear thinking about. She opened her eyes and looked down to her right.

It was then that she saw it. Beneath the water a small dinghy lay on the bottom where the stream cut deep into the lake. It was a simple little rowing boat. The wooden hull was green with algae and fish swam around it obviously used to its presence. It was as if it had always been there; a small wreck with no history of service. As Liz stared down at her discovery she felt a strong desire to lie beside it, to drift for ever in a submerged half-world of oblivion.

Harriet threw her cloak around Liz and placed one of her large hands on the young woman's shoulder. She looked straight into Liz's eyes. "It's always been there." Her voice rang with authority as if giving an order, some sort of edict. *Do not ask questions. It is none of your business* was implicit in the single-repeated phrase: "It's always been there."

*

"So you keep saying. What's always been where?" Mel asked the question for the umpteenth time. The question and the persistence of the questioner caught Liz off-guard. She felt stupid and confused. Where was she? What was she talking about? The coldness of the night air hit her and she realized exactly where she was. Had she missed a whole conversation? How embarrassing. She tried to remember what she had been thinking about. The boat, yes that was it! Surely they must have seen it too? Was she the only one who cared about it?

"That boat!" she said, pointing to the far side of the lake beside the boathouse. "It's always been there. Well, for as long as I've known anyway." She looked around at the puzzled expressions. This was not the Liz they knew.

"Well, I don't see any boat. Can anyone see a boat? Do I sense a touch of Manderley?" Sue was using her English teacher's voice, throwing a rhetorical question into the ether as she did with her students. Liz caught it. But her answer was not in the least convincing.

"Of course you can't see it from here… You have to cross the bridge and walk to the other side." The crassness of her remark made her squirm. "Sorry, I, um, I was miles away! You must think me crazy!" She emitted an atypical snort by way of a laugh, which took everyone including herself by surprise then, with a brisk shake of her head she tossed aside both the remark and a stray lock of blonde hair. Harriet sighed with relief. She did not like intruders.

"Don't worry. One day I shall tell you," she said.

Liz looked around at her guests, realizing she really did not know most of them at all. Which one had spoken to her? It was a woman's voice, a pleasant comforting voice, musical and rich with a depth of tone, and rather posh. The neighbours would surely know some of the history of the house. All would be explained in the fullness of time. But the insistence of it gnawed away at her. Why had she made such a stupid remark? Of what possible significance could a rotten old dinghy be? Why should she care? It was absolutely nothing to do with her. For Heaven's sake, she had only lived here a few months. The wretched wreck must have been there for donkey's years. She told herself not to be so bloody silly. But she could not shift it from her mind.

Fireworks were still thundering overhead, only now they hurt her ears, confusing her thoughts, which were in the silent water below with the little boat. "Edward, that boat..."

"Oh, for Heaven's sake not now, Liz, you're obsessed." He withdrew his arm from his wife's waist and gave David's shoulder a manly squeeze. Then he threw his head back and bellowed: "Two thousand effing years!" He howled like a wolf at the moon.

It was getting cold. January was not the right time to be in a garden beside a lake at midnight. Taking Ed's face in her hands she kissed him. The show had finished to a round of applause. Suddenly there was stillness, the bellicose symphony having fizzled out, leaving that nostalgic smell of potassium nitrate heavy in the air. The party had fallen silent, their eyes still turned skyward. All that could be heard was the slopping of the water against the little jetty that led from the ruins of the old boathouse. Once again Liz had the eerie feeling of being observed, but it was not unpleasant, more being watched over than spied on. It contained too much warmth to be in any way sinister. She felt protected.

CHAPTER 2

Over the years Harriet had convinced herself that the life of a recluse was her choice. Now in two short months she began to think that Fate had chosen it in spite of her. Changes were occurring, not only to her surroundings but to her herself. What amazed this solitary, private woman was that she welcomed the change. The thought of a life she could share thrilled her. Beckmans had also registered these imminent changes without sounding an alarm. As usual, she took her signal from the house so she was content to go with the flow. She had been right. A few weeks before the millennium she had allowed the Jessops to move in and so far she had no regrets.

The arrival of such a vibrant young family proved far more of an upheaval than Harriet could ever have imagined. The house had burst into life catapulting Harriet into the twenty-first century. Mrs Jessop's taste was immaculate; a mixture of traditional and modern. Boilers and bathrooms; kitchens and gadgets; paint, plaster, tiles and fabrics the like of which she had never seen, kept arriving. The house was lifted out of the past and plopped beautifully into the present. Old cloth-coated electrical wires were wrenched out and replaced, consumer boxes stood where fuse boxes had lived for years. Miles of new copper pipes were concealed beneath the flooring in place of the lead monstrosities that had previously taken the scenic route, meandering around the house, gurgling and spluttering as they spewed out their contents. Computers and televisions, videos and DVD players, game's consoles and laptops were installed and consulted at every move. Cookers that told the time, sinks which gobbled up waste, machines to chop, shred, mix, heat, cool or freeze all became part of the exciting new world that was now Beckmans.

Harriet marvelled at these modern miracles. Had the world moved so far away from her? How long had she been living her isolated existence? This energetic young family exuded a vibrancy that energized her. The house was beginning to look stunning in its new clothes, and the layering of love that permeated the whole structure warmed Harriet's heart. She felt safe and completely at home. Of course, she was now sharing it. To a great extent she was living her life through others. At first she had been content to act solely as advisor. Someone had to explain the complicated layout of the house, or the angle at which the sun entered each room at each season or various times of day. She needed to advise on suitable deployment for all the rooms, to explain how they had been previously used. Their potential for a modern twenty-first century family and the choice of decoration she left up to Liz. Once her task was complete she would adopt a lower profile, to avoid the unpleasant sensation of eavesdropping that she was already experiencing. This was a family starting out in life and they needed their own privacy and space. The house was bursting with activity. Visitors came and went in a constant flow, bringing gifts and flowers and a fellowship that Harriet loved to share but had no wish to abuse. She would keep herself to herself unless needed. Tonight was an exception.

Harriet had been content to take a back seat until now. She did not want to spoil the party. She was considerably older than the rest of the guests, almost from another world. She sidled up to her new friend and slipped an arm around her. She was smiling in the dark where no one could see her. She began to whisper in Liz's ear, cupping a hand around her mouth as if telling a secret. But it was Liz who began to speak.

"I've always loved fireworks. Mind you, when I was a child we never had anything like this, just a few sparklers and bangers on bonfire night itself. *Remember, remember the fifth of November, gunpowder, treason and plot.* We always had a huge fire. Tom said it got rid of all the rotten orchard stuff. It was quite dangerous, I suppose." She let out a short uncharacteristic laugh, almost a snort. "Every year, without fail, a Catherine wheel, those wonderful whirling things, would spin into a wobble then go shooting off its nail at a tangent. We had to run for our lives, not knowing which way it would shoot next. Or a rocket would fall out of its bottle and Tom would kick it into action before it launched into space. No one got hurt; well, not badly, and of course it was only once a year. Sorry, did I just say that? Come to think of it, I only remember one year when we actually had fireworks. How strange! Mama didn't approve of them. And I suppose one couldn't get fireworks during the war."

"What are you rabbiting on about? You weren't even born when the bloody war was on. And who on earth is Tom when he's at home?" Edward looked at his young wife and waited for an explanation but she ignored him. She appeared detached, as if in a dream, and she spoke slowly, her voice deeper and softer than usual. It was as though she was speaking to herself.

"Do children still make a guy and collect pennies for him? 'A penny for the guy, Gov?' We always wanted to but Mummy would never let us. She didn't approve of that either. She said it was common, like begging. We'd put great big unpeeled potatoes in the fire... we thought they tasted wonderful but they were always quite raw in the middle, though charcoal-black on the outside. Of course we didn't care. Life was much simpler then. We were so happy. Ashes and charcoal... and wet wool from our gloves... such memories! I can taste those potatoes now." She licked her lips as she listened to the explosions around her. An extra-loud crack brought her crashing back to the twenty-first century.

"Are you all right, Liz? You're spouting a load of rubbish." Edward was gripping her arms, almost shaking her.

"Sorry, darling. Sorry. Gosh. I was thinking... I don't really know what I was thinking of.... Mummy, I think. She used to tell me about bonfire night when she was a little girl. I must have had too much champagne. Sorry. I'm fine." She gave a little giggle. It probably was the champagne, Edward thought, although usually Liz could drink most people under the table. "Thank you for buying this house. I love it so much." Liz tucked her arm through his.

Edward laughed. "Do you remember what a mess it was? God, it was a total tip! Only you could have seen through all that crap."

Liz could only remember falling in love. The first time she walked through the house she could feel the very soul of the place. It was organic, alive, created by the laying down of centuries of time. The rambling lay-out; the quirky adjoining rooms; the two staircases and many different floor levels held no mystery for Liz. She had found her way around with faultless confidence, guided by a familiarity that neither startled nor surprised her. She already knew this house and she knew she would live in it. She knew how to decorate it and what furniture it needed. This house was meant for her. It wanted her to nurture it. How lucky that they had spotted it in the paper. She smiled as she remembered telling the agent they would buy it. It was only the second time she had seen it. But she just knew it was meant. She remembered how she shook the agent's hand and watched as he left. She felt her legs buckling beneath her as she punched the air with excitement. Never before had she spent so much money in such a short time. The thought of it still made her weak at the knees. Then she had had to tell Edward. How do you tell your husband you have been so recklessly extravagant? It had actually been quite easy as she recalled.

*

"Hello, darling, I'm at the house. It's perfect. I've made them an offer. You'll love it, Ed. It has such a friendly feel about it; just the place to raise a family." Liz's enthusiasm had gushed forth, leaving Edward little choice but to comply. His business self was less compliant.

"OK, I hear you. You like it, love it even. But, and this is a big but, if it's so perfect how come it's been left empty, sitting on the market all these years? How many is it, thirty, forty, maybe more? It could be riddled with dry rot, wet rot, all sorts of rot we've never heard of. There has to be a good reason why it hasn't sold." He felt Liz's hackles rising with each word he spoke. "I don't want to squash your dreams, Liz, but what reason did the agents give? They must have offered some explanation when you asked? You did ask, didn't you?"

"Of course I did. I'm not completely stupid. Apparently there was some complication with a will, a mix-up that took years to sort. Then the developers who bought it in the sixties had some wrangles with the listed buildings people. Anyway, it sort of got put on the shelf and forgotten. The rest of the estate was developed but Beckmans, the house, was forgotten. Don't you see? It was meant for us. It was waiting, as if it knew I would find it. Mel thinks it's fate."

"Well, she would, wouldn't she? Mel's a lovely girl, and all that, but she's barking. How can a house 'know' anything? And, what's more, you don't believe in fate, any more than I do. Come off it, Liz. Be honest. You want the house and that's that!"

"Yes, I do. So please just come and see it – feel it – you have to feel it for yourself. I don't know, maybe Mel is talking rubbish, but you have to agree, it is odd – all those years just waiting.…" Her voice was pleading with him. How could he refuse to go and see the place, even if every financial bone in his body told him it was a foolhardy deal?

"OK. I'll come to see it tomorrow. Happy now?"

"Just wait, you'll love it. Bye."

She remembered her shock when, on viewing the house the next day, Edward announced that he did not like it. In fact he hated it. Liz had stuck out her chin and said, simply and finally: "Tough, because I've already bought it."

Edward returned her unflinching stare. "That doesn't mean I have to like it. Anyway, nothing is signed yet. Look at it, Liz. It's falling down. It's dilapidated as hell.

It smells to high heaven and... how shall I put it? It's a wreck! It's the pits!" He paused, then added: "What the hell. I've always wanted to live in a pit. Well, what are you waiting for? You'd better get another key cut before I change my mind. There's nothing here throwing money at won't solve."

*

Now here they were living the dream. Liz gave her husband's arm a squeeze and pinched herself to make sure she was not dreaming. No, it was all real. He had told her later that he had agreed to buy the place because he could not bring himself to disappoint her since she obviously loved it so much. But he had been convinced they were being extremely foolish. Edward gave Liz's arm a squeeze back. "Love you. And I love this place too, even though it eats money." Liz let her head rest on Edward's shoulder and thought about those first busy months at Beckmans.

Everyone had been amazed at Liz's apparent ability to see through walls, her uncanny knack of knowing exactly where windows had previously been sited or where stairs had originally begun and finished. It came as no surprise to psychic Mel, of course, and Liz was too busy to question it. She was inspired, a woman with a mission; and as soon as was possible, before even the sale was complete, work was in progress.

Edward's prediction also came true. Money was indeed thrown in all directions but the aim proved true and Beckmans became a fitting reflection of its latest custodians. From the first day, Liz had known that a house with such a legacy could never be owned. One merely, and humbly, became a trustee whose task was to ensure survival and continuity. Liz took her commitment seriously and proudly joined the long ranks of former custodians. She swore that under her care Beckmans would prosper and thrive. The house reciprocated by surrendering itself to the changes heaped on it by hands it both recognized and trusted. Liz and the house had found the perfect balance; a partnership of minds. Except for the Fourth Room, it no longer frightened her but it stood apart, as if waiting to give its permission to be used. She agreed to accept this rule but said nothing to anyone. The following December Edward carried his wife over the threshold, saying: "Welcome to our new house."

To which she had replied: "Home, darling. This is our home."

*

Liz shook herself back to reality. This was her home but tonight it was full of guests who deserved her total attention. Fortunately no one other than Edward had been aware of Liz's funny five minutes. The rest of the group were too intent on talking about the fireworks. Liz held her husband's arm and kissed his cheek.

Harriet felt a pang of jealousy. This was the first time in her long existence that she had been able to share her thoughts, feelings and needs with anyone and now she was being ignored. But she realized it would not do to overwhelm her new friend with too much gushing attention. It was a new beginning and she too tingled with a renewed sense of purpose. All she needed to concentrate on was the wonderful fact that she had a family again. This time it would work out. It had to.

Meanwhile the neighbours were making their various ways home. The Circus was retreating to the house, where the warm glow of a log fire and candlelight beckoned through the French windows and out across the lawn. Liz had lingered behind, savouring the last of the night air. She pushed at the stray blonde lock with her fingers, willing it to stay in place. On letting go, the hair slid back; she secured it firmly with her ivory comb. She began to run, overcome by a desperate need to see her children. A sense of dread swept over her. An unaccountable ache lay in her belly. The twins were so vulnerable, so dependent on her; what if she failed in her duty to protect them? Then she stopped. She stood very still. The ache and the cold were replaced by the warmth of a hug and a kiss on her cheek. She turned to say thank you but she was alone. The others were already at the house.

*

Edward and David were the first to enter the lounge. The two had been friends since school but were as different as chalk and cheese. Being a lecturer in English at a modest college David seldom had occasion to wear a dinner suit and took little interest in fashion. So, pleasantly surprised on catching his reflection in the large mirror above the fireplace, he was glad he had gone to the bother of dressing up. Edward was just thinking his mate's suit had seen better days when David spoke. "That was something else, like setting fire to a wad of fivers!"

David had often wondered at Edward's profligate attitude to money. He found the money market boring and, to be frank, downright immoral. Obviously it paid better than academia but did it merit the sort of rewards Edward was currently reaping? No doubt Edward was good at his job, whatever that was. The commodity market had proved a real money-spinner in his hands. Was that because they were a safe pair of hands or dextrous to the point of sleight? David did not possess a jealous bone in his body so was merely stating fact when he said: "I could no more afford this lot than fly out the window... unless, of course, I chuck it all in and write a bestseller." He chuckled at the thought but inside there was a desperate itch to scratch.

Edward had been poking the fire. He threw on another log and watched flames lick around it, giving off a satisfying sizzle. His success in the money market was never a source of embarrassment for him. He took pleasure in sharing his good fortune with his friends, but his insensitivity meant that it never occurred to him this might be construed as showing off.

"You should. God knows you've been threatening to for long enough. And don't forget your friends when the film rights roll in. I've just been bloody lucky, mate; and let's face it, you can't take it with you, Dave, so enjoy." He refilled their whisky glasses and raised his. "Here's to you, old friend, Happy New Year. The twenty-first century! Who'd have thought it!" Then as a flippant aside: "Of course, I could be tapping you for a bob or two if the dreaded millennium bug hits and wipes the whole shebang!"

As the others burst into the room, the men's moment of intimacy was gone. Liz, desperate to see her children, had already reached the first landing when Edward, hearing her voice, turned and saw her framed against the rose window. Elegant and tall, she could have been carved from ivory except for that vital spark of light that shone out of deep emerald eyes. The soft light of the candles gave her the appearance of a young girl rather than a mother of two-year-old twins. Liz saw him watching her and blew him a kiss; then seeing Donald she blew one to him, turned on her heels and was gone, effortlessly running up the next flight.

Donald turned to look at his own wife. Brenda was slumped inelegantly in an armchair by the fire. Letting out a slight snore she slumped further into the voluminous chair and let her head fall back, surrendering to the irrepressible spinning of the room. Her legs splayed in front of her, one of her sensible brown shoes abandoned beneath the chair. Donald looked at his semi-conscious wife and for a brief moment contrasted her to the willowy figure on the stairs,

"She's gone! One glass and she's had it."

"Night, night, darlings…" The words might have come from Brenda's mouth but her mind was already lost to the ether of the night.

The rest of "the Circus", the name adopted by this close group of friends, was sitting around the fire when Liz re-joined them. They were munching thick doorsteps of sandwiches that Mel had obviously thrown together without the refined removal of crusts that Liz would have insisted on. Donald rose and sidled up to her, sliding his solid arm around her waist.

"Thanks," he said. "I assume it's all quiet on the Western front?"

Good old Donald, at least he showed some sense of responsibility towards his son. David had shown no concern about young Emily. But then she was thirteen and had been left in charge of the other three. He probably assumed that being so dependable, a clone of her mother, she needed no checking on. And Edward…

well, he was the host and far too busy to play concerned father. She gave Donald a peck on the cheek and answered his question.

"They're fine, all 'snuggly-buggly', including the dog. Even your Robert's fast asleep, bless him. Get me a drink, there's an angel."

Donald filled a clean glass with champagne. "I hope Ed realizes what a lucky sod he is."

Liz threw him a wry look and grabbed the last of the sandwiches: "Mine, I think," she said, sinking her teeth into the thick crusty bread. She groaned with ecstasy as her fingers crammed the crust into her mouth. After dinner she had vowed never to eat again but now she was famished. *Well,* she thought, *this is another century, the start of a new millennium.* She tore off another chunk and was suddenly filled with an overpowering sense of guilt. *How mean of me to criticize Mel's sandwiches. They're deliciously decadent. Why have I so much? This world is such a hell hole for some, survival dependent on a global post-code lottery? Maybe Mel's right. We will all have to come back to live other lives until we've been through the whole gamut of experience, before we get to rest in peace? How many of those who stood here before me asked the same questions? Maybe they had lost children in dreadful epidemics or been struck down by hideous plagues. Thank God for modern medicine. I'm a lucky cow.* With that final thought she unceremoniously stuffed the last morsel into her mouth.

Edward was whispering obscenities in Mel's unabashed ear. Chewing with an over-full mouth, Liz slipped her arm around her husband's waist and then foolishly attempted to speak. What came out was a jumble of words and crumbs that sprayed incoherently over Mel.

"Hey, didn't your mother teach you not to talk with your mouth full? I assume you want your husband back. Here, he's all yours but don't believe a word he says; he's a cad!" She pushed him towards Liz, whom he literally swept off her feet, lifting her into his arms. Liz threw her head back and laughed as he kissed her greedily, stealing the remains of the sandwich in the process.

"Hey, you, that's my supper. You are disgusting. You're a disgusting...." Between choking and laughing Liz found the right word: "A disgusting husband!" she exclaimed. "But you are my disgusting husband and I love you, Mr Edward Anthony Jessop."

"And I love you, Mrs Edward Anthony Jessop." Now he was waltzing her around and around. "I love you. I love you. I love you. I love the twins, I love my friends. I love this house. My God, tonight I even love the fucking dog!" Edward threw back his head and let loose his infectious, natural laugh, which tonight came from the core of his being.

Edward stopped spinning and placed Liz gently onto her stocking feet; holding her close until her balance returned. For a moment she was spinning alone in an empty room, the piano just a shadow and the grandeur still a dream with the lake and the boathouse waiting for her... and that boat. The drawing-room was filled with candles, their scented heat mingling with the delicious smoke from the apple logs. This was how it had been that first time she saw it. The house was perfect as she had known it would be. Everything she had wanted to do she had done. She opened her eyes and remembered they still had a lot of work to do before the restoration was complete. But this was definitely the home they were meant to find and now it was extending hospitality to their closest friends. What more could she possibly want? She shut her eyes tight so that she might burn the image on her mind. She wanted to hold on to it forever.

As the night drew on, the group grew quiet. They stood by the open windows and watched the millennium dawn. From somewhere in the distance came the sound of a woman singing in French, her contralto voice trained and mature. In that moment Liz was at peace. Subliminally she understood that we never know the true reason for our existence, our reason for being. And for that brief moment she was content to remain in a state of ignorance. She was on the brink. The future called to her and she was excited, keen even, to visit it, but not if it meant leaving this present time. *It should be possible to bottle moments of your life like rare perfume, so that you could relive them by the simple unscrewing of a cork*, she thought. *Imagine all those bottles lined up each one filled with a fabulous memory, their magic contents as fresh as new, just waiting to be released. Better than photographs or souvenirs, the essence of a moment waiting to emerge like a genie to transport you back to the past, to brighten up dark future days. Like this haunting song. I'll never hear it again in such a perfect setting, at such a magic time. If only I could capture it and hear it again whenever my soul wants to fly?* She did not realize she was the only one who had heard it.

CHAPTER 3

George Alfred Marchant had been wounded during the First World War; he was hit by the door of a moving train while standing on the platform at Tonbridge station on his way to join his regiment. He never fully recovered from the ignominy of these injuries, which were severe enough to prevent him ever reaching the front. His shame grew with each published list of the fallen and honourably wounded. By way of atonement, he threw himself into his work at the Foreign Office with every fibre of his being. As a result of this diligence, when war ended he was still a young man of twenty-three but with considerable standing in the department.

A pipe-smoking, slow-thinking man, George was quiet by nature, old before his time in some ways, much of which was due to his disability. He lived his life through others, never begrudgingly, because he chose to observe, not participate. He was a private, modest man: a natural bachelor who, at the age of forty-five, was amazed to find himself knocked off his feet again, this time by a tiny redhead. He was literally bowled over. They were both at a formal party when, enjoying being watched rather than watching where she was going, Alice had crashed into this tall, awkward man. For him it was love at first sight, for her it was a novel experience. He was twenty-five years her senior and as shy as she was forward; so when she proposed he found himself accepting before he realized what was happening. Friends warned him it was folly to consider marrying a woman as strong and attractive as Alice, but he could not resist. The unlikely pair married with a great deal of pomp and ceremony just three months later.

Alice had been born ornamental rather than useful. She was a perfectionist used to being spoiled and indulged. Her Papa, the main cause of her spoiling, gave Beckmans to her as a wedding present. It would have been far more diplomatic to have presented it to the couple but diplomacy was not in his autocratic makeup. It never occurred to him that such an action could be the cause of future dissent. The gift had been accepted with some disdain. Looking at the large, unwieldy bunch of keys that came with the property, Alice declared them ugly, overweight and hideously old-fashioned, just like the house.

In fairness, the house had not been touched since 1869 and the Victorian stamp had been heavily applied. No one had wielded a paintbrush or repapered an inch of wall since then. It was a brown house: walls, ceilings, woodwork, floors. Alice had never seen so many shades of the same, sad colour, ranging from mousey biscuit beiges to the darkest burnt umbers. This was not the Art Deco dream in which she pictured herself, all glass and crisp; frightfully modern and bright. But once she overcame her sulks and conducted a thorough inspection of the old place its potential began to speak to her. She took it upon herself to modernize it, determined to turn it into the perfect country house for entertaining her many friends. George loved the quiet thought-provoking duns and bays. To satisfy his undemanding taste Beckmans needed nothing more than a gentle spring clean. He felt comfortable in it just as it was. But, characteristically, with no consideration for her unfortunate husband, Alice set to letting her creative genius loose.

Her extravagance knew no bounds; the house was taken apart and put together again. Once the task was completed to her exacting standards she gave it her stamp of approval. She engaged a housekeeper, a cook, a team of gardeners, maids, a chauffeur, and a handyman to maintain this state of perfection. Everything had its place and Alice insisted that nothing was out by so much as an inch. The rugs had to lie with their fringes immaculately combed and each ornament knew it must face the window or the door at precisely the right angle or the staff would bear witness to an embarrassing display of childish tantrums. Of course such behaviour was never experienced by the multitude of guests and revellers with which the house was constantly buzzing but it was only ever a closed door away. Behind another closed door her husband could be found continuing his solitary existence in his wife's house. When things were going smoothly and when displaying her public face, Alice was sweetness and light, convinced that running a large house was simplicity itself. It was obviously one of her many natural talents.

Natural was not a word to associate with Alice Emily Marchant, born Alice Weatherby. Her life was one long artifice. She spent hours daily preparing herself before surfacing from her cocoon of a bedroom, bathed, oiled and buffed, crimson nails lacquered smooth, the white moons shining, face powdered and rouged, lips sculpted in scarlet. Such was her daily ritual. Her hair was the colour of copper and it was brushed every day until the burnished metal was moulded into an intricate series of swirls and coils secured by combs and pins of tortoiseshell. Life was an art form to be practised until faultless perfection was achieved and a flawless butterfly emerged.

Thoughts of motherhood had never entered her immaculately coiffed head. The couple had not discussed having babies. Being only five-foot three and extremely proud of her slim figure Alice had no intention of giving birth, deeming the whole process barbaric, primitive and unhygienic. After a year of marriage she removed her husband from the marital bed, having found sex to be an uncomfortable, messy business. As his subsequent visits to her boudoir had proved both depressingly unsatisfactory while thankfully infrequent, she had abandoned any fear of conception. So when in 1929 the Marchants discovered they were expecting their first child, interviews for the post of full-time nanny began. Alice was incandescent with rage, considering her pregnancy to be a hideous deformity that she blamed on her husband. She remained out of public view for the duration and made life a living hell for everyone around her. Her sainted husband kept his distance but secretly he was delighted. This marriage suited him. It was almost as though he were still a bachelor with the wonderful bonus of fatherhood.

Their first-born was a boy, David, who arrived without fuss and relatively painlessly in a short labour. Ten hours later Harriet arrived. Her birth was totally unexpected and agonizingly difficult. The doctor was surprised and exhausted, the midwife alarmed and scared; and Alice was all of these. She was also furious. She never forgave her daughter for those ten hours of hell during which they both very nearly died. Her instinctive favouritism was confirmed when the babies were finally displayed side by side. David was small, beautiful and feminine whereas Harriet was over-large, plain ugly and decidedly hairy. The general consensus was that the two had been born into the wrong bodies although no one was brave enough to say so within earshot of the mother. This anomaly became increasingly apparent as the children grew. David's hair shone with the same bright cinnamon as his Mama's, he could win the most reluctant onlookers with his radiant smile, and although he did not share her natural centre-stage flair, his beauty gained him all the attention, which did not please his jealous mother.

Harriet was tall - not long and graceful but large and ungainly. From birth she shunned the limelight, being happiest unnoticed beside her beautiful brother, or better still when her father sang to her, which he only ever did when no one else was near. She shared his solitary manner, the air of a watcher rather than a doer. She was obviously her father's daughter and he spent as much time as he could with his beloved baby girl. Together they kept to the shadows, leaving front of stage to Davy and his Mama, who basked in the reflected light of the son. Although ten hours younger, Harriet was by far the stronger twin and took on the role of protector as if she knew she was destined to watch over her little brother throughout his life.

Alice took scant interest in the children. Her son's resemblance to herself made him a rival. She thought him beautiful and enjoyed the reflection of the praise that was lavished on him. When she looked at Harriet she could see nothing of beauty. Secretly this changeling child frightened her. It was those eyes. They were in fact mirror images of her own but Alice could not see it. The only time she saw her own amber eyes was when they shone back from the one of the many mirrors she consulted, always with a gleam of approval. Her daughter's eyes peered disapprovingly into her soul, exposing her shallowness. One looked into mother's or daughter's eyes at one's peril; to do so was to fall instantly under a spell. George was smitten; first by the mother, then by these disparate children. He doted on them, much to Alice's chagrin. David was his first-born, his son and heir, but Harriet was his sunshine and his joy.

*

By the time the Marchant twins were eight, Harriet towered over Davy. Never destined to be a diminutive stunner like her mother, she dwarfed the pair of them and her Mama was often heard referring to her as a freak. She grew faster than Tom the gardener's runner beans and was as thin as one of the bamboo poles that supported them although she could eat the entire pantry at one sitting. She moved with an ungainly, lolloping gait, as if her brain was too far from her feet for any message to get through. And she knew only two speeds: flat-out or stop. Her thoughts travelled even faster than her feet, so when she spoke her words tumbled out in such rapid succession that the sense of them was lost in the delivery.

The child had a mind of her own, as did her hair. From day one it was thick and coarse, unlike her mother's silken, Titian tresses. The red mass that was Harriet's crowning shame grew in unruly chunks that did not so much frame her face as imprison it, sticking out in different directions, depending on their mood.

Attempts to tame it by cutting a fringe failed: the horrid stuff refused to lie flat, preferring to protrude at a right-angle, giving the appearance of a shelf, which took several hair slides and grips to hold back. The only way to control this mane was to plait it while it was still wet, which worked well enough until Harriet, who loathed ribbons or dresses or anything feminine, would wrench it free, letting it bounce back with a vengeance and explode into wild corkscrews resembling a barley-sugar twist.

Whereas most redheads have pale, transparent skin, Harriet's radiated health. The sun only had to look at her to turn her natural olive tone an even bronze glow, which continued to darken to the colour of a conker. Her eyes were her truly redeeming feature. They were pure amber, translucent honey weapons that she deployed with total ignorance as to their potency. Unlike her mother's, they were filled with kindness and mischief. Tough, independent and fiercely loyal as she was, her brother adored her and willingly accepted her as his leader. She was wilful, with a stubbornness that matched her mother's. Alice, to her horror, had given birth to an out-and-out tomboy. The two had not yet reached a point of conflict but the meagre foundations that lay beneath them were shaky.

Young Harriet's most extraordinary attribute was her voice. She could hold a tune and deliver a song with a mellow full-throated quality that seemed to come from deep in her stomach. Strong and mature, it had a richness of tone not usually associated with one so young. Her father's failing eyesight was compensated by the sound of this voice. She would sit on his lap on his old wicker chair by the boathouse, lost in their own secret world:

two songbirds warbling for the sheer joy it. And Harriet could whistle as well as any man; much of the day was spent with her hands thrust deep into her pockets, whistling or humming to herself, as she strode about, her brother in her wake, running full pelt to keep up.

George was invalided out of service with early retirement in January 1939. His accidental collision with the seven-twenty, all those years ago, had not only fractured his skull, impairing his eyesight, but he had evidently also suffered severe damage to his cranial and optic nerve. An epileptic fit while at work had cost him his job, the use of his right eye and a second opportunity to serve King and country in the war that he had known for some time was inevitable. He arrived back in Kent broken and depressed. Life without his work to go to was a strange, alien thing, an increasingly difficult journey leading nowhere. Tom encouraged him to help in the garden but his fits came more and more frequently, which made working outside dangerous and difficult. Lack of employment left him with an inclination to do nothing in which he began to indulge. His depressions deepened. He would sink into pits of self-loathing and despair that terrified Alice, who had little empathy with her husband's affliction and saw him as a liability.

His "little nightingale" was his salvation. Her patience was infinite, her devotion total. They would start each day walking together around the garden, her right hand gripped tightly in his left, his black cane in service in the other. With his stick he would point to items at random - a bud, a leaf, an insect - and Harriet would run to them, kneeling to examine them more closely; then placing them in her canvas bag she would run back to the comfort of that large hand while chattering non-stop about the latest amazing treasure, which they would examine later under a magnifying glass. The bond being cemented daily between father and child was to be for the child a powerful force in a strange, lonely life.

So far Harriet's life had been fine. She had a few troubles but adopted the philosophy that there was no point worrying about something if you could not do anything about it. Her relationship with her mother fell into this category. Although Alice was an abysmal parent, Harriet taught herself to accept her or ignore her. Her love for her brother came naturally and was mutually rewarding. Her love for her father was absolute. Watching him slip away cut her to the quick. His dependence on her, however, turned her into a fiercely independent creature, old for her age and proud of her role as a carer. She had been born stubborn and now she was growing up, her individualism was surfacing with a vengeance. So when her father suffered his first stroke Harriet was ready to become his "nightingale" in more ways than one. Given the choice, she would have been constantly at his side, nursing him in her own earnest way.

George's concentration diminished daily. But Harriet never moaned. When she was not wiping the stream of dribble from the corner of his lop-sided mouth or packing his pipe and puffing on it to get it started before handing it over for him to take a few feeble sucks, she was content simply to sit and sing to him, knowing that the days when he could walk with her or carry her aloft on his shoulders were over. She had to accept that their precious days together were numbered. When his face contorted with pain or he became insensible to her presence, she wondered where he went but she never gave up on him. Sitting in silence was hard for Harriet and she tried to read quietly beside him. She even attempted sewing and produced a pathetic sampler that he hung beside his chair in the Tudor room. There was little she could do other than love him. For the child, that was enough but for the man it caused a deep ache, a yearning to gather her into his arms and fly away with her beyond all the pain and cruelty this world afforded. There were times when Harriet's presence served as a hideous reminder of his inadequacy as a father. His depression crippled him. He would be lost without her and afraid of leaving her. Locked inside his unresponsive frame was a loving father desperate to escape by any means. The telepathy between them was so strong that the child began to sense the pain her presence caused him. Reluctantly she limited the time she spent with him to such times when she could see it was helping him. The prison that trapped him became a two-way barrier blocking her on the outside, unable to reach through to him while he could find no release from the pain.

Alice remained oblivious to all this. She was starring in a drama of her own. She had discovered the joy of sex with almost anyone but George. The war delighted her. London became even more enticing with its constantly changing supply of handsome uniformed officers to admire her. The blacked-out streets, the knowledge that at any moment it could all end, that any kiss could be the last, was irresistible. War had brought an excitement, an added frisson of danger that fed her addiction and exaggerated the glitz behind the dark exteriors of the nightclubs she frequented. She was hooked on being "naughty" and this war was the perfect excuse to indulge her bad behaviour. A car would call each night and whisk her away to her secret life.

Harriet took to hiding on the corner of the landing, out of her mother's view, watching for her to make her appearance. She was still a very beautiful woman and to see her in all her glory was like being at the cinema. Her long evening gown, a fox fur draped over wide, padded shoulders, sleek, cinnamon hair caught up in combs and braids and those long red talons flashing as she placed a black Sobranie in its holder. The click of the small silver lighter before its bright orange flame leapt up to meet it, catching the watcher in the spell that was Alice. Seeing those wonderful sculpted lips purse as they sucked hard and long; the practised tilt of the head before the thin coil was released from a perfect oval to begin its long journey around the elegant head, lingering for a moment before continuing on up to the top of the staircase, growing weaker as it climbed higher and higher. It was straight out of the movies. At the bottom of the stairs the cigarette was stubbed out. Long gloves were pulled on and with a final pout of reflective approval she was gone. As the front door closed Harriet would sneak into the temple, stand before her mother's altar and mimic the sensuous action she had witnessed so many times. First she ran her tongue along her teeth to remove any trace of red then a quick flick at each corner of her mouth with the fourth finger of each hand to ensure a perfect finish. Next, ignoring her well chewed rather grubby nails, she would balance her pencil between her first and second fingers and adopting an affected pose would blow a kiss at her reflection, before sweeping onto the landing and beginning her descent to the ring of rapturous applause from her "audience".

Not that Harriet had ever seen a film. Her mother considered all picture palaces dirty flea-ridden places that decent people did not frequent. But as Harriet only ever viewed her mother from this unnatural distance she may as well have been made of celluloid. She observed her without the warmth of physical contact. She just watched, the image of her mother's ritual etching itself into her memory. The brushing of the hair, the drenching of the spray from the fascinating array of bottles displayed on the dressing-table would stay with Harriet for the rest of her life, enabling her to recall the smell of her mother. Simply by closing her eyes, she could conjure up the exact sensation of silk or fur against her skin. Nobody ever saw her creep into her mother's room and pull cinnamon threads from that ivory brush to hold against and compare with her own. Jabbing at her freckles with a loaded powder puff she watched them vanish beneath a thick layer of fine white dust. This caress by proxy was the closest she got to actually touching her mother. She never felt the warmth of her mother's skin. She judged by appearance. In winter it was as cold and forbidding as alabaster and in the summer that pale golden sheen was far too exquisite to be touched, defiled by dirty fingermarks.

Harriet dreamed of being beautiful. She too wanted to be sculpted out of polished marble. Her mother was precious, valuable; a rare object to be worshipped from afar or at least at arm's length. She was like the Chinese vase on the hall table, beautiful, expensive but breakable. Where this creature disappeared to each night or at what time she staggered back was never questioned. George must have known about his wife's escapades but her nocturnal shenanigans were of little interest to him. It suited both parties admirably for him to turn a blind eye. For her part, Harriet needed the love of her father. At night in her dreams he was strong again, kissing her goodnight and stroking her tangle of hair as if it were spun from the purest of silk. He would lift her onto his shoulders, calling her his "little nightingale" while laughing at her funny face as she twisted round to meet his eyes. As long as he was there she was content to live this strange half-life with him. The thought of life without her father was unbearable. Without her brother it would be hell.

CHAPTER 4

That summer of 1940 was heaven, a glorious season of continuous sunshine. War was raging over Europe but in this tiny pocket of Kent life was blissful. The twins watched the planes with old Tom, who would abandon his digging to wave at the tiny Spitfires and the great Lancasters that flew past on missions, having taken off from the nearby airfield at West Malling. Tom said they were "off to bomb the bloody Hun" and taught them to count them out then count them back again, saying a quiet prayer for any brave pilot who failed to return. The Hun was far away; an unknown monster in a funny-shaped helmet. To the children, war was an exciting but distant adventure. To Mrs P, the stalwart rotund housekeeper, it was a great excuse to deny any request they made with the stock answer, "Don't you know there's a war on?" To their poor father it was an added burden of shame, sending him deeper into his miserable shell.

Old Tom was too old to be called up but suffered none of his employer's guilt. He had done his bit in the last war. Once was enough. He never wanted to go through "that lot" again. He had tried rather half-heartedly to enlist for this second lot but age was against him. He was turned down. To avoid feeling useless he dug for England. He grew it and his wife, the indomitable Mrs P pickled, preserved, potted or embalmed it. They would certainly not starve while she was in charge. Beckmans became a production line with chickens pecking round the orchard and ducks inhabiting the small island in the centre of the lake. No one minded or noticed if the Pritchard's meagre income was supplemented with the occasional clutch of eggs or a freshly plucked chicken.

Old Tom could never deny the children anything, especially his time, and they loved him for it. His resourcefulness knew no bounds but he excelled himself when he came home with a dilapidated old dinghy. He presented it to the ecstatic children, who with his help, made her sea-worthy in no time. They christened her the *Jolly Roger* and she was launched at precisely midday with a shot from David's toy cannon and a bottle of ginger beer smashed across her bow. Tom had also acquired a boat hook, long and wooden with a large brass hook on the end. Best of all was the fact that he had taken the time to carve their initials into the end of the long shaft, which made it theirs alone. It was the best present the twins had ever had. From the moment she was launched the boat became the centre of their lives. Harriet did most of the rowing, being the stronger, but David's keen eyes made him a great navigator. He could spot a shark or an enemy vessel long before anyone else. By the end of summer their father was confined to a wheelchair but on a good day Tom would wheel him down the garden to watch the buccaneers in action. No pleasure registered on his distorted face yet his daughter knew that he was smiling inside.

Mama had taken to lying in her solitary bed, seldom rising before two in the afternoon, when she would waft downstairs clad in her silk kimono and clouds of perfume and smoke. Gliding into the drawing-room, she would pour herself a drink, then stand at the long French windows gazing out across the lawn, her black cigarette firmly planted in its holder, smoke billowing from her red lips. She had a perfect view of the lake from this vantage point. She must have seen the little boat and its crew merrily cavorting around the island but she never mentioned it. She appeared disinterested in anything to do with her family or the house. She had become disconnected, a celluloid shadow without weight or form.

*

Harriet practised the art of self-sufficiency to a degree that was unnatural for someone of her age. Brother and sister had learned to lean on each other in times of crisis, although David did most of the leaning. Having no other friends, they spent a great deal of time together. The dinghy rendered them inseparable, made them a team: a crew. Messing about in the boat was their passion. When Mama threw one of her increasingly frequent tantrums they would grab a chunk of bread, some fruit and a bottle of water and take to the high seas. That whole summer the sun shone down on them and the skull and crossbones fluttered rebelliously above the *Jolly Roger*.

On the odd occasion when they were deemed too noisy they were banished to the loft. Their mother thought this an effective way to make them repent. The loft space at Beckmans ran the entire length of the house and this had been their territory long before they conquered the lake. This vast empty room was almost as magical as the water. It was their private universe. Ritual demanded that they stand stock-still in the centre until at an agreed signal the spinning would start. Throwing their heads back, their arms held straight out to each side, they become human planets, whirling dervishes, rotating and spinning, slowly at first then gathering momentum with each twist. All this was accompanied by a low moan, which like a dynamo increased at each turn, building up in a deafening crescendo that emptied their lungs and turned them the colour of Mrs P's boiled beetroot. The sky winked at them through the missing peg tiles until, giddy and exhausted, they fell to the floor in a disorientated heap, laughing and gasping, waiting for their heads to catch up with their bodies. They were invincible, whether in their planetarium or on the high seas. They were the two musketeers and Harriet vowed to keep it that way for ever…however long that was.

*

Two days after the twins' tenth birthday David was sent away to school. No warning was given, no time for goodbyes. A trunk was packed, a car arrived and David was gone. Harriet rowed herself to the middle of the lake and howled like a dog. The house was full of emptiness. Father's nurse was bathing him, which meant no one was to disturb them. Mama had gone out and Harriet found herself alone. She did not dislike her own company but this was different. For the first time she felt lonely. Returning to the house she climbed up the main stairs. She examined the first floor, room by room, finding them boring and unused; even the bathroom echoed with nothingness. She slammed each door behind her, hoping to find some comfort in the angry noise. The attic too was empty. There were no moons or stars, just a large hollow room smelling of damp. Returning down the back stairs she inspected the sculleries and kitchen.

Nothing bubbled on the stoves and the wet garments on the clothes-horse draped there abandoned. She too had been hung out to dry. The world was stuffed full of nothing. What was she going to do without her brother? London was being bombed every night and the fear that his life was endangered clung to her like a cobweb. She dragged her heavy feet back across the hall, the rubber soles of her sandals leaving long scuff marks on the polished wood.

Selecting a favourite book, she mooched off down to the boathouse, forcing the most mournful tune she could think of through her pursed lips in a thin wailing whistle. She had so much time, too much time; time to kill, time to be killed. Boring winter days stretched out before her. She had been given a prison sentence to be spent in solitary confinement. She had to learn to be alone. She must teach herself to be self-sufficient. The boathouse was cold and the September sun was too low to reach its windows. Spiders were spinning, ready to take over for the winter. She did not want to stay here. Harriet took off her shorts and shirt, kicking off her shoes at the same time, and stood there in her navy knickers, back straight and chest flat, her book clutched in her hand. Stepping out into the sunshine she climbed down into the *Jolly Roger*. With one oar she pushed the boat free of the jetty; securing the oar, she lay flat and gave herself up to the gentle movement of the drifting dinghy with the warmth of the sun on her skin.

She must have dozed off and she woke up with goose bumps. The sun was setting behind her as she took up the oars and rowed back to the jetty. Her fingers were cold as she tied the little boat to its post. Someone stepped over her grave and she shuddered, but not in an uncomfortable way. She wondered how it would feel to have someone actually walk over you when you were dead. How would you know when you were dead? She had just stepped into the boathouse when she heard a voice talking loudly and excitedly, the words slurred, the way her father had sounded after his stroke. But this was her mother's voice; had she been struck too?

Harriet grabbed her clothes as the door opened and a stranger entered. He was not as tall as her father and considerably younger. His hair was slicked back with grease, suiting his cocky attitude. A smell of whisky combined with the sickly stale smell of tobacco came in with him. She watched a curl of yellow smoke leave his nostrils and weave itself into his hair. His mouth was smiling but not the sort of smile that encouraged you to join in. The cigarette dangling from his lips dropped its heavy ash on the boathouse floor and he spoke from between half-closed teeth. Harriet dived under the window seat, still clutching her bundle of clothes.

From her hiding place she could see her mother and the strange man clearly. They stood very close, kissing. He had his arms about her waist and was pulling at her skirt, easing it up over her hips, revealing her stocking-tops and suspenders. Harriet could see those fascinating black French knickers she had tried on so often when her mother had been out. Now this man was touching them, tearing at them, at the same time as slobbering over her mother's face and neck. The sound of saliva as he covered her face with his open mouth made Harriet want to vomit. The ivory statue was transforming into a vulgar woman tugging at the man's belt buckle. She was undoing his trousers. Harriet recoiled as she watched the frantic woman sink to her knees and kiss him, down there. She pressed her hand tightly over her mouth and hid her face in her clothes. A burning acrid liquid filled her mouth and she swallowed hard before looking out again.

They were on the floor. The man was on top, forcing the woman's legs apart with his body. Her thighs spread wide, she gripped her legs around his bare buttocks as he pushed against her with strong thrusts. The woman made strange, pathetic moaning noises and scratched at his back with long crimson nails. She pulled him over so that she was astride him, riding him obscenely and hungrily, like an animal, her head tossing back and forth with each grotesque rise and fall. Harriet buried her face and ears in her clothes as the noises reached a crescendo. Then suddenly it was over and with a loud ugly shudder the man rolled off the woman.

When Harriet looked again they were lying quietly side by side. The man was lighting two cigarettes. Harriet inched back further into the shadows, frightened of being seen in the light of the flame. Her mother was staring up at the ceiling dragging hard and noisily on her cigarette, the tip surged brightly as the oxygen coursed through the tobacco. The man got up, his cigarette dangling from his lips. "You are amazing. You look like some sacred goddess but you fuck like a damned whore." He adjusted his pants before he sleeked back his short greasy hair with his fingers, then tucked his shirt back into his trousers. He stood awkwardly leaning to one side as his did up the buttons of his flies. Her mother was pouting into her mirror reapplying her mask.

"And you, my darling, are a fucking bastard." Her fingers wiped the scarlet grease from the corners of her beautiful mouth then she too adjusted her clothes. She smoothed her hair and patted it fondly. The marble statue was restored.

*

That night Harriet dreamed she was at sea and her tiny boat was pitching and tossing on mountainous waves. A dense mist rose from the surface, making it impossible to navigate. Icebergs the size of cathedrals loomed, towering over her craft, threatening to sink her and drown her crew. Her father was standing unaided in the bow; his strong arm pointed out to sea but she could not see what he was looking at. She strained to hear him but his voice was drowned out by the wind and the roar of waves. As she steered a path between the icebergs, she watched them melt and reshape into ice carvings of mythical proportions: goddesses who ruled the frozen wastes with a terrifying all-powerful authority. Clouds of frozen vapour poured from their blue-painted mouths as they threw back their expressionless heads and laughed.

When Harriet awoke she was soaked in sweat and was shivering. Her bedclothes lay in a heap on the floor and she felt as if she had been fighting for her life against armies of giants. Wrapping her eiderdown tightly around her she stole down the back stairs, taking care to avoid the bottom one, which creaked. The house was silent as she crept into her father's room and lay beside him. Her mind was filled with images of Mama and that awful man. She did not understand what she had witnessed but knew it was wrong and dirty. She had no natural love for her mother but the awe in which she had held her had until now been an adequate substitute. No longer. Softly crying while rocking herself for comfort, she willed herself into a shallow, dreamless sleep, having vowed never to set foot in the boathouse again, as long as she lived. As for telling anyone what she had seen.... No. The fall of the sacred statue was her secret.

She stuffed it away in the back of her mind as if it were a conker stowed in the pocket of her knickers. Instinct told her that she now had the edge on her mother. She possessed the means to destroy her should she want to. This knowledge; this power made the whole hideous experience tolerable. In one single treacherous act the roles had been reversed. The statue had fallen and no one could put it back on its pedestal.

CHAPTER 5

Young David came home each Christmas and for the summer holidays. These days were the highlights of Harriet's life. During the months apart long scrawling letters kept them in touch but Harriet read with increasing horror just how miserable her brother was in this overtly masculine environment. He was bullied constantly, not only by the other pupils, but it seemed the staff had an aversion to a boy who avoided cricket or rugby and hid his considerable academic abilities in a cloak of shyness and natural modesty. His letters revealed a sad, damaged child not so much a fish out of water as a bird caged underwater. Harriet had no one to appeal to on his behalf. A series of rapid severe strokes had rendered their father senseless; a creature trapped in a body that no longer functioned. He never left the Tudor room, where he lived a bed-bound existence with a washstand, a commode and a full-time nurse. His daughter spent as much time as possible with him, singing or reading him items from the newspaper, hoping that by some miracle he would respond. In the main it was a thankless task and at times she began to doubt that he knew she was there. The dream of her going to school remained just that, and she gave up even thinking about it. Anyway, by now it was much too late. She consoled herself with the knowledge that she was needed here with her father. Who else would show him he was loved and wanted? Certainly not Mama! No, any thoughts of a proper education had to be abandoned but she resented never having been offered the opportunity.

She longed to learn the things her brother talked about and she pounced on the books he brought home in the holidays. They were different from anything she could get in the library and she devoured them with her voracious appetite for knowledge. She read copiously and taught herself the humanities and sciences up to a point. She loved to fill her scrapbooks and play the piano and of course she had her singing. She never met children of her own age, or indeed of any age, which left her without many social skills. Those she had were at times precocious and often eccentric but, as she never ventured into society, this was not a severe disadvantage. Her ability to keep herself occupied was a credit to her resourcefulness and determination of will but it was nevertheless the foundation course for a reclusive adulthood.

Beneath the surface the tension between mother and daughter was building to a dangerous level. Harriet had little respect for her "dear Mama" and after witnessing the incident in the boathouse what little there was had turned to contempt. When she unwittingly overheard a phone-call obviously not meant for her ears, her disdain switched to loathing. It was apparent from the obsequious tone her mother adopted that she was talking to someone in authority, but not someone she held in high regard. She was playing the distraught wife, and she was a good actress. Her poor, dear husband was in desperate need of full-time care and the only solution was to find a suitable nursing home that could lavish the same level of attention on him that he received at home.

Harriet listened in silence as the melodrama unfolded: the loving wife exhausted by years of selfless devotion. The reluctant decision that they must live apart after many blissful years together was very convincingly expressed.

Harriet ran outside to the lavatory and was sick.

*

On 19th December 1942 David came home for Christmas. The two siblings were thrilled at the prospect of a whole month together. Mama said hello, patted him on the head and went out. Harriet was itching to discuss her father's future with her brother. She had to find a way of telling him just what sort of mother they had, but she could not share any graphic details for she had made a vow of silence. Harriet never reneged on a promise. Anyway, telling her brother the whole truth would be cruel, and would inflict pain far outweighing any relief the unburdening might bring. It was obvious that David still loved their mother. When the time was right she would know. For now she could wait. They deserved to enjoy some free time together. To "lark about", as Mrs P called it. Once free of his horrid uniform the two of them set off clad in thick Fair-Isle sweaters, duffel coats and Wellington boots. They cast off from the little jetty and set out "to sea". Beckmans had not heard the laughter of children for so long.

David had hardly grown since they had last met but he was glowing with pride as he took the oars and rowed his sister around the lake and back again, without having to stop for breath. Harriet sat in the stern dangling her hand in the water. It was freezing cold but she was so happy she did not care. David rested the oars and let the boat drift. Above them the winter sky was blue and the birds drifted overhead as aimlessly as the boat. There was no distance between them. It was as if they had been together all year. It was David that finally broke the silence.

"I'm not going back to school, Harry. I've run away. I can't take it anymore. Now I'm in the senior school it's getting worse, not better. I can't face it. I'm scared. God, I'd rather die than go back. Do you think I'm a coward? You do, don't you?"

"No, of course I don't. Have you told anyone else – about running away, I mean?"

"Good God, no! Only you…. Will you tell Mama for me? She'll listen to you."

Harriet released a short contemptuous snort. "She never listens to anyone – least of all me. I don't think she knows I exist. We'll have to think of something else. Don't worry and don't cry. I promise we'll think of something. We've got a whole month; that's an eternity."

David picked up the oars and rowed them around the lake once more. By the time they moored at the jetty he wore a thin smile, offering it to Harriet as they climbed ashore.

"You're the best sister a chap could have. Let's go in the boathouse and light a fire, like old times."

"I'm never going in that place again, and don't ever ask me why." Then, trying to appear as if it did not matter if he knew or not, Harriet asked: "David, what does 'hoar' mean?"

"Noun or adjective? If you're spelling it H-O-A-R, it's a type of frost. I think it means white. Then of course there's the noun W-H-O-R-E. But you obviously don't mean that."

"I think, actually, I do."

"Crumbs! Well, a whore is a woman of the night, a prostitute. A bad sort, who sells herself for money. Why on earth do you want to know that?"

"Just curious… oh, and I don't suppose you know what 'fuck' means, do you?"

David's pale face turned ashen. "Good God, Harry, where in blazes did you hear that? It's a dreadful word: taboo and all that. One of the prefects was expelled for saying that last Michaelmas and he must have been at least eighteen."

"Expelled… crumbs," was all Harriet said.

*

The next morning David was woken by the heavy thump of Harriet crash-landing on his bed.

"For God's sake, Harry, get off, you great lump. I can't breathe."

"Listen, my sweet little brother, I have a simply brilliant plan…."

The plan was so simple that it was indeed brilliant. David would return to school, swear at one of the masters and get himself thrown out. Having been dismissed in shameful disgrace he would be sent to another school where his exploits would give him huge kudos with the other lads. Anyway, if the horrific stories of bullying were only half true, nowhere could be worse than the present school he was in. Besides, he was stronger now and they had a whole month to toughen him up some more. He had to agree, the plan was brilliant. Christmas and the New Year stretched out ahead of them like a never-ending adventure. If they spent a little time now, planning it in detail, they could enjoy the rest of the holiday at leisure. Harriet said nothing about their mother's scheming. Once their plan was foolproof there would be plenty of time for that.

After a few tortuous hours of trying to get David to swear convincingly, the plan to get him expelled was complete. It was Christmas Eve, the staff had gone to church, Mother was out and Father was already settled for the night in his room. Harriet had confided in David that she had something of enormous importance and the utmost secrecy to discuss. David told her that for reasons of security, meetings concerning great affairs of state often took place at sea. Where better to convene their conference than aboard the *Jolly Roger*? They would not be overheard or interrupted and there was nothing to distract them.

Armed with torches, hot-water bottles, paper, pencils, some mince pies and a flask of hot lemon squash, they donned their woollen scarves, gloves and duffel coats and set off across the garden. It had been snowing and Harriet prayed that the lake was not frozen. The water was still flowing freely as she rowed the boat to the centre of the lake and pulled the heavy oars on board. Removing her woolly mitten she rummaged in her pocket and produced an official-looking manila envelope; all the while she was re-enacting what she had overheard on the telephone. Telling him to hold out his hand and open his mouth, she thrust the envelope into David's gloved hand and a mince pie into his mouth. They drifted and bobbed as he read and re-read the letter. Harriet had spent days lying in wait for the postman and her vigilance had paid off when she managed to intercept the tell-tale missive before her mother could get her manicured hands on it.

"What it means, if you cut out the gibberish, is that she's going to put Father in a home."

"Maybe that would be for the best." As soon as he had said it he knew it was a mistake.

Harriet exploded: "Best, my foot! Best for who?"

"Whom… best for whom."

"For her! That lazy, selfish cow, our beloved Mama! You do realize what they'll do, don't you? They'll stick him in a corner and forget about him." Harriet was seething. "I hate her. I hate her! And that's not all. You know what she'll do next? She'll split us up, put us into separate homes or farm us out to horrid, boring old families so we'll never see each other again." She was shaking, spilling hot tears of fear and anger from a heart that ached with dread for the future.

"They can't split us up. Not if we don't want it. Can they? I couldn't bear life without you." The awful reality of the situation was dawning on him. "We could run away together."

"Mother's the one who should go. They should put her in the nuthouse with all the other whores. She's a fucking whore!"

"Stop it, stop it…. Don't say that…. I won't let you." David's brain was spinning. His loyalties were divided and he hit out at the thing nearest to him. The sickening thud as her head hit the deck was the last thing she remembered for a very long time.

Chapter 6

"What is the point of having a large house if you don't intend to fill it?" This had been Liz's philosophy since they had moved in to Beckmans. Time had flown by and this was their fifth Christmas. The house buzzed with the noise of friends at one with their own company and surroundings. The tree groaned beneath its weight of tinsel, baubles and fairy lights; enough, according to Edward, to confound the National Grid. Lights flickered and danced among the myriad new and familiar decorations below the ancient Christmas fairy, who balanced precariously on top, just as she had when Liz was a child. She was much too old to be performing such death-defying feats but Liz was too sentimental to think of ever replacing her.

Harriet brushed her fingers along the prickly pine, releasing a pungent scent that took her back to her childhood. She smiled as she wondered what Mama would think of her now. As children they had been forbidden to touch the tree in case they damaged it. The tree would appear in the hall on Christmas Eve morning, tall and proud and dressed, so for many years she had assumed it came fully decorated. This family let the twins choose each bauble and hang it exactly where they wanted, creating a spontaneous display that made up for any loss of designer elegance with originality and enthusiasm; so different from the totem pole Harriet remembered.

Sue, Mel and Brenda scuttled to and fro, ushered by Liz. They emerged from the steamy kitchen laden with an apparently endless stream of dishes. Crispy buttery parsnips, roasted potatoes, sprouts with lardons and chestnuts, red cabbage gleaming with butter and smelling of spice, along with gravies, sauces, sausages and bacon rolls, all the paraphernalia of a traditional English Christmas blow-out were paraded for the feast. This was a time for excess and Liz was in her element: entertaining. The house had proved to be everything she had wanted and then some. It suited her. It suited them all. They belonged here, safely wrapped in that warm embrace that had first greeted her all those years ago, and what better time than Christmas to share it?

The Jessop twins, Jenny and James, were now mischievous eight-year-olds who knew exactly what Christmas was about. They leant across the table, egged on by the older and wiser Robert and Emily, pulling more and more crackers, squealing with delight at the rubbishy treasures that spilled out after each bang. The men opened bottles, oblivious to the mountain of litter the children were creating. They were being boys again, resplendent in the stupid, ill-fitting paper hats the children foisted on them, laughing at appalling jokes, while consuming rather than tasting the various wines.

*

Harriet watched from a distance. She was thinking of her father, before he was confined to the Tudor room, seated in his dinner suit at the end of the long polished table, with her mother, exquisitely dressed, so far away at the other. She and her brother sat somewhere in between. Mama considered crackers to be vulgar and untidy, an attitude that cast a formal, stiff shadow over the whole festival. An ostentatious wreath hung on the front door, lying to the world that this was a house of festive cheer. Then there was the tree, which had given up its life to stand all alone in the cold hall for a few miserable days. Harriet remembered crying one year when, shortly after Boxing Day, Tom dragged it off to the bonfire to be burned before its needles could drop and cause unnecessary mess. Christmas was a time of painful memories and increased loneliness, so for most of her life she had chosen to ignore it, overshadowed as it had become with ghosts and demons. Anyway, that was all so long ago. It no longer mattered. Christmas was indeed a festive season now; she did not want old memories spoiling things.

So much had changed. For one thing, no one smoked anymore. Everyone smoked then, that wonderful aroma of exotic tobaccos filling the air, while adding a degree of decadence and devil-may-care nonchalance to the atmosphere. The elegance of long cigarette holders and the sight of gentlemen leaning over to light their ladies' Russian or Turkish cigarettes had all gone. Time had relaxed everything. No one followed the rituals. Manners were ignored to the point of non-existence and children mixed with the adults displaying a natural ease and assurance that amused and delighted Harriet. The women lingered at the dining-table long after the meal was over and the gentlemen left them to attend to their own chairs without so much as rising from theirs. Harriet wished she was beginning her own life as a young adult in this emancipated, free age, with fewer rules and the company of such bright young people as these surrounding her now.

The women carted the dishes, now stacked and empty, back into the kitchen, laughing and joking about their lazy men. Harriet noticed that it was still the women, working together, making light of their work. Some things never change. But stacking, that was another thing. Her mother never let the servants stack dishes. Nor would she ever actually touch one herself. How she would have disapproved. But tonight the clearing-up provided a source of fun for the four friends as they bustled about, filling dishwashers, sorting glassware and yelling at Brenda to get out of the way. In time, the exhausted twins were settled upstairs and the teenagers, Emily and Robert sloped off to listen to their new CDs, allowing the Circus to settle around the fire that crackled in the great marble fireplace in the lounge. Candles shone from every surface and eventually the women joined their men. Everyone was merry with the atmosphere and the wine.

Mel took out her Tarot pack. Donald groaned and Brenda sniffed her disapproval, David and Edward feigned indifference, but Bob smiled. He knew it was pointless to try to stop his wife. Liz and Sue were with Mel, eagerly clearing a space on the floor for her to spread the deck. The air was heavy with expectancy. Even those who did not share Mel's beliefs were gripped by a certain thrill of anticipation, that possible glimpse into the future. Deftly she shuffled her well-worn cards, her dark eyes shining with mischief as they glanced in turn at each of the friends. Suddenly, as if she had been told where to go, the cards were handed to Liz, who cut the pack before handing them back. Overcome by an inexplicable sense of foreboding Harriet removed herself to the back of the room.

*

Mel's thick hair mimicked the flames as it caught their light with each movement of her head. She spread the cards face-down in a horseshoe. This was her preferred method of giving a reading. If all went well she would be given a clear insight into the past and the present, making any predictions about the future far more plausible and acceptable to whosoever the reading was for. Slowly and deliberately her black-painted fingernails rapped on the first card. This was her trade and she was good at it. There was more than a touch of the showman about Mel, which was what kept her in popular demand as a psychic.

Mel tapped on the card at the apex of the horseshoe, the one furthest from her. Her long, dramatic nail hesitated before moving on to rest on the card nearest to her. This she turned slowly to reveal the picture of a tall woman seated on a throne: a queen with blonde hair piled beneath a crown and holding a sword. Mel stroked the card, then flipped the next one. This contained the image of a dark-haired king. He too was seated on an elaborate throne but in his hands held a simple staff. The two figures sat passively facing each other. Mel mused, "This is the Queen of Swords – it is you, blonde, strong-minded. This card is strength. Swords are air signs. This," her finger pushed at the second card, "is fire. The King of Wands; he has strength too, energy: businesslike, dependable. Edward. You're facing each other, communicating. Or it could mean conflict; air and fire, interesting. Now let's see." She smiled at Liz, another mischievous little grin as she turned the next card. Mel was enjoying herself.

The next card showed the picture of a large man standing in a small boat. He held a long pole in his hands with which he steered the little craft.

"This is the boatman. The Six of Swords," said Mel. "Remember, swords are strength. Look, there are two smaller figures in the boat. He is steering them and see, the water this side is smooth, but on the other side it's rough."

"But what does it mean?" Liz was getting impatient and Mel reprimanded her.

"All in good time; you mustn't hurry the cards." She tut-tutted to herself as her fingers drummed on the upturned face of the fourth card.

Mel spent her life reading the Tarot. To her the cards were simply a tool; a thing to be respected, but used. To Liz they were beginning to represent a window into a whole new world; a world of the unknown, the mystical world of spirits. Or they could be rubbish. This fourth card looked to Liz like two figures quarrelling but Mel had seen far more. She announced:

"Cups are emotions. This is a very emotionally charged card. The Six of Cups is a family card. Bringing together or moving apart; it means either a separation or a connection."

"Who are the two figures?"

"Children, probably yours; but look, there's a third one, much smaller, in the background. Let's see if we can find out who they are. Are you okay with this?" Mel looked at Liz, her smile asking for permission to continue.

"Yes. This is fascinating. What's next?"

The Knight of Pentacles followed: a dark youth on a black-spirited steed, bright, alert, ready for action. Mel described him as a young man going places. His horse was raring to go, the reins held firmly in the young man's grip. He held a pentacle, the sign of money. He was riding towards wealth and achievement. Liz thought of James. This was so like him, self-assured and positive about his life. How could Mel see so much in a simple picture? Liz was hooked.

The next card sent Liz into a fit of the giggles. It was Jenny, there was no mistaking her. The Page of Swords looked more like a girl than a boy, a Joan of Arc figure standing on sturdy legs, holding a heavy sword above her head. "Swords are for mind and thought," Mel said and described this as a younger version of the first card; strong-minded, a free spirit, a sign of the air. Primed and ready for action, this was a brave figure at the beginning of a remarkable life. Nothing would deter her but she was not too proud to serve. Yes, this was Jenny all right, lion-hearted and valiant, always steadfast and firm on her strong long legs as she took her familiar resolute stance. Was she destined for great things? Liz was excited. Here before her was her family, her life and it looked wonderful.

The next cards brought change, challenges, suspicion and betrayal. Liz began to feel uneasy. Mel was telling her she held the sword, the strength was in her hands, but what did that mean? Her mother always told her to be strong when something awful was about to happen. Was she going to split up with Edward? Was this a warning? Was her luck running out? Was her life about to take a turn for the worse? Mel sensed that Liz was getting edgy. She needed to lighten the mood. Harriet too was unhappy at the way Mel was interpreting the cards. She crept closer with each revelation, bridling at each fresh pronouncement. Now the stupid woman was telling Liz she had inherited her mother's voice. She'd be telling her to take up singing next!

"No, no, no, that's all wrong. The gift has skipped a generation." Harriet was trying to be discreet as she whispered in Mel's ear. Mel rubbed her ear; it was burning hot. As she moved away from the fire she tossed her head and her hair fell across Harriet's face. Harriet and Liz snorted in unison, that short, sharp dismissive laugh they now both affected.

"Jenny's the only one in the family who can sing. I'm tone deaf."

Harriet sighed with relief. Liz was laughing again and at last someone was on the right wave-length. She drew closer to Mel and hissed, "You see, at least someone is listening. Liz has a voice like a fog-horn. But she can paint a bit and I'm going to teach her to be really good."

Mel rubbed her ear again. "Well, I can't change what the cards tell me. We can't always choose what we want in life. This is telling me you need to stand on your own two feet. You are not using your talent. Don't be afraid to follow your star, and I'm convinced it involves singing."

Harriet pressed her mouth right up against Mel's ear, so close she could have bitten the long crystal pendant that dangled from it. This time she shouted her message loud and clear.

"Yes, that's Jenny. Liz is going to PAINT! Are you deaf as well as stupid?"

Exasperation got the better of Harriet. Resorting to a less orthodox method of communication, she pushed Mel so hard that she pitched forward, hands splaying out on the carpet in a vain effort to save herself. The entire pack of cards shot up in the air, landing in a confused heap beneath an equally confused Mel. When she righted herself it was obvious that the reading was ruined. Mel rubbed her back. "I'm getting too old for this scrabbling about on the floor. Oh, well; not to worry. We can start again if you like. There must be a reason for this. Everything has a reason." She rubbed at her sore back. It felt as if she had been kicked by a mule.

The mood was broken and the group decided to call it a day; all but Liz, who sat rigidly holding onto the only card to have survived the tumble. People were chatting about the cards and the evening, but all these words meant nothing to Liz. She saw only a tall figure dressed in a long black cloak, standing beside a stretch of water. On the ground were five cups. Two stood upright but the nearest three were spilled over at the foot of the tall figure. It was the last card Mel had turned over and something had compelled her to stretch out and save it. The colour drained from her already-pale face and her voice shook with emotion as she demanded: "What does this card mean? No, don't tell me. Oh, my God! Someone's going to die. It's the death card, isn't it?"

The group froze. They were staring at Liz. She had flipped, turning from the cool, calm creature who was always in control to a demented fury scrabbling about on the floor, scraping up the fallen cards as though her life depended on it. Having gathered them she hurled them across the room, letting out a loud scream as she did so: "Stupid bloody things!" She was shouting and literally spitting as she spoke. She paused to wipe the spittle from her chin then continued in a quieter but still ferocious mumble, "How the hell can bits of card tell anything about anything? It's a load of rubbish. They're probably made in bloody China or somewhere, factories of them, churned out by the thousands by poor bloody peasants paid in peanuts. And we're meant to believe they can tell the future. Crap!" She sat back on her heels and took a large swig of wine. "Crap!" she repeated loudly and with conviction.

"Feel better now?" Mel was calmly collecting her precious cards. She put all but one back in their box and placed the box in her bag. "There," she said, "they've gone. And for your information the Five of Cups is not a death card. It's the mourning card, an emotional card, a card for reflection, a card that demands time be granted to adjust to whatever changes are to take place. The whole sequence of cards was good. They were exciting, promising fresh challenges; a clearing out of the redundant past to make way for the new...."

Liz cut her off. "How can you believe in such...?" she searched for the right word.

"Crap?" Mel offered. "Listen, if it is only crap, then why get so aerated? Yes, you're right the cards are just that – cards, bits of paper, so relax. Don't get your knickers in a twist."

Liz crawled on all-fours until she was beside Mel. She knew she had been out of order. Mel was a respected psychic and a close friend; it was unkind and unfair to insult her in such a cruel way. She attempted an apology: "I didn't mean to undermine your work, Mel. I know you believe in what you do. I've no right to put it down...."

Mel jumped in before Liz could finish: "You can't undermine what I do. I know what I know, so say what you like it won't affect that. No, Liz, what you won't do is accept what's staring you in your beautiful, blinkered face. It was all there in the cards but you couldn't take it.

Great when they're telling you what you want to hear. But woe betide anyone who dares to rock your boat. You, Liz Jessop, you have the power. The sword is in your hand. OK, there are a few challenges ahead of you and some may not be that pleasant. Goodness, your life has been pretty plain sailing up to now. None of us gets off Scot-free in this life. Just don't let any traumas that are coming wreck what you've built with Edward. You can crumble and give in to what you saw in those crappy bits of card or you can use your bloody sword to protect your kids and your home. I'm telling you, it's in your hands. Your fate is yours to mould. The Tarot can only show you the likely outcome. It's up to you whether you choose to continue on the same path. Pick a path, any path, have an affair, shoot someone, jump off a cliff; it's your choice. Life isn't wonderfully easy. Nothing is written, only the possibilities. The rest is a blank page. I suggest you grow up, Liz. Take responsibility for your own action – or inaction. I'm going to bed."

The others, whether for reasons of diplomacy or out of sheer embarrassment, had quietly taken themselves off, leaving Liz all alone, stunned and hurt. Her future lay scattered around her like so many pieces of paper. Maybe Mel had got it wrong. All that rubbish about singing was way off. Anyway, how dare Mel talk to her like that? What did she know about her life and her frustrations? What could betrayal mean other than Edward proving to be unfaithful? There was no way he would be so cruel. Anyway they were very happy. There was no need for him to look at another woman. They were the ideal team. He liked the fact that she needed him, leant on him. It flattered his manhood. He was after all an old-fashioned man who liked to be the breadwinner. Maybe she did rely on him a bit too much, but why not? Suddenly the cold realization of a truth she had never before been brave enough to face dawned on her. She was nothing on her own. But her future was in her hands. She could control it. She resolved to face her fears and wield her sword. She wrote an apology to Mel and thanked her for being a friend. On her way up she slipped the note under Mel and Bob's door and took herself off to bed.

She did not sleep. That last card was always staring at her; she could not shake it from her mind. Was the figure in the foreground male or female? What on earth could it mean? Was someone going to die; Edward, the children or possibly even herself? Mel had said no. Well, she could hardly have said: *yes, death is staring you in the face. Tough, just get on with it.* Liz closed her eyes so tightly that they hurt but the image on the card remained burned into her brain. A tall figure dressed in a long black cloak, that was all she had seen, but its presence was around her. This long dark spectre was vivid in her mind's eye but try as she would she could not see its face. Mentally she turned the card over again and again, trying to see it afresh. Slowly the figure turned its back on her. Her body shuddered. She was so cold. She was drifting in a fragment of a boat. The children came and went until they were rowed out to sea by a faceless boatman. She was left on the shore, her cloak offering no warmth from the cold mist rising from the sea. On the far bank stood a tall figure, silently calling to her from the jetty by the old boathouse. Edward grunted as she pulled the duvet from him and wrapped it closely around her thin nightdress.

At four o'clock she awoke and walked back downstairs. She went to the Fourth Room. Opening the door she peered in and looked around. It was peaceful and dark: a junk room. Whatever had been present earlier was gone. Liz closed the door as carefully as if on a sleeping child and, despising herself as she did so, turned the key in the lock before replacing it on the secret ledge in the kitchen. As her fingers withdrew from the now familiar-shaped key she knew she could not contain it. She was too late; something significant had happened that night. She also knew The Five of Cups was an image that would haunt her for the rest of her life.

CHAPTER 7

The incident with the Tarot was not revisited. Convincing herself that it was just superstitious nonsense, Liz told Mel in no uncertain terms that the whole thing was a load of crap. After an exhausting night of tossing and turning she had woken with a closed throat and swollen eyes. A stubborn virus that was doing the rounds put an abrupt end to the celebrations; the merry season had fizzled out. Liz's continued poor health made the New Year a subdued affair and it was not until late spring that Liz felt her spirits lifting. She was still suffering nights of broken sleep and although she never said anything it was the face on that wretched card that she saw as she closed her eyes, and again when she woke. It was haunting her.

But by summer Liz announced to Edward that she was out of the doldrums and raring to go. It was the night of the summer solstice and they had been enjoying a quiet dinner for two. Edward had braved Marks & Spencer's and prepared a surprisingly professional meal. The sight of his slender wife steadily reducing to an anorexic waif had really scared him. Tonight she had eaten well and drunk a considerable amount of alcohol. So, when after dinner Liz suggested that they took their brandies down to the lake, he was confident that she was fully recovered.

The silence of the water was hypnotic. When its surface was broken for a second by a lazy trout gulping a late-night snack, they both jumped. They raised their glasses to each other. The old boathouse was directly beneath the moon, the dovecote and tower silhouetted against it.

"You're right," Edward said, "it is quite beautiful. I don't think I've ever really noticed it before. It's very dramatic, isn't it?"

"It's perfect!" Liz replied. They stood watching the shadows change as the clouds obscured the enormous moon, only to make it seem brighter than ever when it reappeared. This was the summer solstice, when at noon the sun reaches its highest point in the sky giving the longest day: a day when magical things can happen.

"Darling," Liz spoke softly, using the spell of the scene as a prop. As she only used the "D" word when she wanted something, Edward braced himself. "Do you remember what you said the first time you saw Beckmans?"

"No, but I'm sure you are going to tell me."

"You hated it. You said it smelt of rot and was totally uninhabitable."

"Did I?"

"Yes. You called it a money-pit and said the agent must have seen me coming."

"Really!"

"Yes. Then you said there must be a good reason why it had been empty for thirty years and that you wouldn't touch it with a barge pole."

"Did I?"

"Then you said that if I really wanted it I could have it, and anyway there was nothing that throwing money at couldn't solve."

"And I've been throwing money at it ever since!"

"You don't regret it though, do you, darling?"

There it was again, the dreaded "D" word. "Not yet, but why do I think I might any minute now?"

"Well, I just wanted to thank you for trusting me. I love this house and I love you and I know you'll love the new boathouse too."

Edward swallowed hard. He had enjoyed teasing Liz. He liked hearing how selfless and generous he was. And he had to admit he had grown to love the old house nearly as much as Liz did. It suited them well. It was probably the perfect home for them and Liz had done a great job restoring it. But it had cost a lot of money and the money market was getting pretty tough with all the indicators pointing to a worse drop before they recovered. Now was not a good time to start spending vast sums of money rebuilding a useless folly. That itself would be folly. The school fees were the next major expense and would take a considerable outlay. No, he had to be firm.

"Hang on – you just said it was perfect. Now you want to pull it down. Anyway, I like it just as it is, all Romantic and Gothic and in ruins."

"You did say we should do it up."

"I did not. When did I say that?"

"Just now... It was your idea. Anyway, we have to do something, and soon, it's an accident waiting to happen. I mean, just suppose, God forbid, that something happened to the twins.... I mean, it's completely rotten. It could collapse at any moment. I dread to think what might happen if their little school friends come round and, well... Their parents could sue us for millions. Anyway, it'll look fabulous. I can see it..." She was weaving her magic, casting her spells. He felt doomed.

He knew he did not stand a chance. "Say something, darling."

"You're obviously feeling much better." This was not the reply she wanted. Edward looked at her standing there in the moonlight. She was quite lovely once she got the bit between her teeth. She was right, of course. The building in front of them was extremely dangerous. A rush of guilt shot through him. Something stronger than his conscience dared him to refuse her.

"Listen, I'll think about it. OK? No promises. And I never agreed to anything before; I simply said it was beautiful. It is beautiful. I like it just as it is."

Liz was disappointed but not defeated. She had thought the argument was won. Now she realized she had more work to do. The first thing was to lighten the tone. If they rowed about it the cause could be set back for months.

"Of course it's beautiful, it's in the bloody dark! Even I look good in the dark!"

"Ah, but only from the left. Your right side's a bit dodgy and your bum looks... ouch!"

Liz's slap hit home, catching him sharply across his upper arm.

He raised his hands to ward off any more blows. "Convince me, and I may... I said *may* just make some enquiries. But can we please go in now? It's getting bloody cold and I feel a lengthy debate coming on. You are going to have to be pretty convincing, young lady. Of course, you could resort to other means of persuasion."

Grabbing his wife he drew her to him, kissing her passionately and fully on the lips. They still had the ability to excite each other and were it not for the small, aggressive dog pulling jealously at his left trouser leg he might well have taken Liz there and then. Leaving their glasses, they ran back to the house together, with the tenacious hound snapping at Edward's heels. Taking the stairs two at a time he closed the door on the disgruntled animal, threw his wife on the bed and the subject of the boathouse was forgotten… for the moment.

That night they both slept well, which came as a welcome change for Liz. Since her illness her nights had been filled with a succession of vivid dreams, some of which woke her and repeated with a disturbing regularity. Lately she was experiencing a bout of quite raunchy, erotic dreams. Often she would wake Edward by talking to him in her sleep. He never told her that she was "talking dirty", for he knew she would be embarrassed. Liz was no prude but she was no wanton hussy either. Some of the things she said would have mortified her. She claimed not to remember what she had been dreaming about when she awoke sweating and breathless in the middle of the night. But their sex life was definitely benefiting from whatever her nocturnal exploits were so he decided to keep quiet and enjoy the ride. Liz genuinely could not recall the substance of these dreams, but there was a great deal of uninhibited sex involved.

Then one morning after a night of particularly vivid and obviously illicit passion, Liz awoke obsessed with a strange compulsion. The boathouse had to be razed to the ground. There was no recognizable connection between this burning conviction and her illusive dream. She only knew that what remained of the boathouse must be destroyed before they could think about rebuilding it. Once she had acknowledged this, she felt a strange peace. She pulled on her jeans and the first sweater that came to hand, scooped up her bowl of cornflakes and set off to take a closer look at the doomed building.

Seated on the bench under the willow, she gazed across the water at the derelict shell. There was something very sad about it, something that was intrinsically linked with the old submerged dinghy. An involuntary shudder took her by surprise and for a split second she felt decidedly cold. Liz tried not to think about the boat. Somehow it was forbidden territory; some sort of taboo hung over it. She never went to look at it but often at night it rose up to feature in her dreams and always associated with the black figure. Sometimes it stood in the boat, at others it merely watched as the dinghy sailed by. The most fearful dreams were when they stood side by side and watched as the boat capsized. Then Liz would wake with a feeling of utter powerlessness. Even now the merest thought of it brought her out in goose pimples. Something linked the sunken boat to the fire; that much she knew. And something linked it all to her, although she still knew precisely nothing. How had it sunk? Was anyone drowned? How had the boathouse caught fire? Was it deliberately set alight? She had quizzed the neighbours, but even the oldest inhabitants of the village had not been around long enough to know, though this did not stop them offering theories. The stories ranged from murder to witchcraft, but it was mostly spiced-up speculation. Liz was convinced that some personal tragedy had happened here and it could not have been that long ago. The archives at the local library and the church records were the logical places to start, but her confidence in her skills as a researcher was woefully lacking and as often as she resolved to make it her next major project she never quite got round to it.

The ruined building was quite something. If only she could paint it as it was now: romantic, dilapidated, beautifully melancholic. It was a ridiculous idea, of course. How could anyone hope to capture the mystery of such a place? Liz had not painted since school, and then she had only shown mediocre talent. This was too ambitious for an amateur to attempt. *Why not try?* As the thought struck her it was accompanied by the weird sensation that she was not alone. She looked around. There was no one there, just the gentle sound of the water lapping against the bank. Something brushed her hand; when she looked down, The Pote was sitting by her side, looking up at her. She ruffled his ears and eased herself out of the chair, pausing long enough to take one last look at the boathouse before they wandered back to the house together.

Turning the griffin key in its lock Liz entered what was still referred to as the Fourth Room. No longer an unwelcoming room, it had nevertheless remained in a sort of limbo for five years. Liz had never quite decided what to do with it, so it had become the place where all those potentially useful things not yet allocated a permanent home languished: old cricket pads and odd golf clubs; an unused sewing-machine; a dressmaker's dummy whose proportions fitted no one and never had; piles of those awful plastic storage boxes that, once filled and shut, were never opened again. Rummaging in one of the children's boxes, Liz dug out an old paint-box. The palette required only a quick spit and a rub with her finger to restore its true colours. The brush was well past its sell-by date, but with a little TLC it would do. Adding to this a sketchpad, a pencil and a jam-jar, she set off back across the lawn. Using the bench as a table she laid out her trappings, then with her sketchpad propped on her knees finally settled down to work.

After an hour she had amassed a pile of litter, which lay scattered around her exactly where thrown down in disgust. On the brink of giving up, she made one last stab at it. Suddenly there it was. The boathouse was there on the page. Somehow she had drawn a pretty good likeness. Exchanging her pencil for a brush she sloshed it in the water and began to paint. At first everything came out too opaque. The transparency of the water and the magic of the light playing on its surface eluded her ability. How did painters like Turner capture such luminosity? Well, she conceded that involved sheer genius; but how did they keep the colours clean and clear?

Frustrated at her own incompetence, she threw her hands up in despair. This sudden serendipitous movement knocked over the jam-jar. The water spilled out, slowly covering the paper and forming an annoying puddle. Still she carried on, painting wet on wet. She loved it. Losing all sense of time, she played with her new toys, no longer afraid of the results, simply enjoying the process. Her inhibitions had flown. She was free to experiment and have fun. She was still engrossed in her work when the twins burst into the garden, making it time to return to being a mother. But before packing her stuff away she could not resist taking a photo of the boathouse, to serve as a memory of a perfect afternoon. She emptied the jam-jar into the lake, disturbing a nearby trout that had been watching her progress. Apologizing to the basking fish, she returned to the house, grinning from ear to ear and feeling restored to health.

*

Liz's painting of the boathouse was hung in the hall at Beckmans. Framed and mounted, it did look extremely accomplished, not at all like a first effort; maybe not a work of genius but certainly that of a competent amateur. She had captured some of the ethereal quality of her subject: the way the light played through the broken timbers, sending shafts down into the dark reed-filled water. The process of painting had completely absorbed her. She had been suspended in time. Her hand moved unaided, mixing colours from unlikely combinations, finding greens and blues she never knew existed. There was sufficient detail to define, yet obscurity enough to allow for a romantic, almost spiritual vision of the beautiful old ruin. It was a remarkably good painting and, of course, Harriet had had a hand in it.

Harriet was delighted at her pupil's progress. As a young woman she herself had been well taught and now could pass on everything she knew. She had never before felt such a sense of pride. Her patience had been well rewarded. But she knew there was a price to pay. Liz's painting reopened the question of the boathouse, sparking off some alarmingly heated discussions about the future of the folly. Its survival hung in the balance. Harriet wished the whole thing would go away but, try as she did, she failed to convince Liz it was a doomed project.

Liz recognized she had a real battle on her hands to win Edward around. She attempted to explain to him how she felt about the old building, without sounding too dramatic. Edward had no wish to be enlightened to the more spiritual side of the argument. Frankly, he thought Liz was becoming obsessive. He guessed it was Mel's psychic hand behind all this and was not too happy about that. All that ridiculous palaver at Christmas had played on Liz's mind and definitely delayed her recovery from what should have been a simple virus.

It was Bob who brought common sense to bear. His matter-of-fact approach could not be argued with. "Let's face it mate, the place is a death trap. You have no choice but to pull it down. What you do after that is up to you two to sort out. If you want to rebuild it, I'm your man. I could do a modern state-of-the-art job, I can even build a replica of the Taj Mahal; but I warn you, Indian palaces don't come cheap. No, as I see it, it's very simple. Just ask yourself: do I want a peaceful life? Then, what sort of bonus am I going to get this year?"

Edward's bonus was of an obscenely generous nature. He had planned to take the family to Disney World but certain comments Jenny had dropped along the way made him realize he was not altogether in touch with the likes and dislikes of his children. He decided instead to offer them a *carte blanche* holiday cruise. Anywhere they liked as long as it did not include the Bombay slums, which seemed Jenny's preference. She had abandoned all thoughts of becoming a vet and was now hell-bent on being the next Mother Teresa. Life was never simple with Jenny, who was an extremely determined young woman. James was the complete opposite. He knew exactly where he was going, but was always going to take the easy route. His father had been disappointed that he showed little interest or aptitude for sports, but it was some consolation that his enthusiasm for maths and his facility with figures implied he would follow in his father's footsteps. He was a great kid, which was the main thing. Everybody loved James.

Bob's entry into the discussion about the future of the boathouse was a clear indication to Liz that Edward had at last come round to her way of thinking; after a few minor discussions about the old versus the new they agreed that demolition work should begin that summer. Faced with a blank canvas, Liz began to get carried away. Greek temples, a ruined Gothic folly, even a Japanese pagoda flashed through her mind. Harriet was constantly on hand to keep this fertile young imagination in check. Eventually a decision was reached. It was to be rebuilt to look exactly as it must have done before the fire. Liz was ecstatic and Harriet was exhausted. She took herself off to what she still called the Tudor room to rest and recuperate.

Exhaustion took Harriet to that pleasant state halfway between consciousness and sleep. In her mind she could see the old boathouse when she still thought it beautiful, before the fire. She could not remember when it had burnt down or if she had ever painted it before the fire ravaged it. It hardly seemed to matter now which came as a complete surprise to her.

CHAPTER 8

Harriet's love of painting had taken a long and at times difficult route. Sometime after that fateful Christmas Eve on the lake Harriet had woken up to find she was in hospital. Once she was no longer confined to bed but still receiving a considerable amount of medication, always under the watchful eye of the terrifying ward sister, she was sent to a unit where she was given treatment that they called occupational therapy. She knew it as painting and when first presented with paints, paper and brushes she withdrew further into herself, stubbornly refusing to co-operate. Then one day, as if a switch had been thrown, she began to emerge. At first she produced violent explosions of black and red, the paint applied in vicious stabbing gestures, ripping the paper, which substituted for her flesh and exorcised her pain as though some macabre blood-letting ritual were taking place. A destructive rage ate away at her, breaking out in sudden uncontrollable bursts of violence that left her exhausted, crippled with remorse and shame. Gradually, over the months, she developed more control until she discovered she could command her moods as well as her paint. The work that poured from her was still, however, profoundly disturbed and belied the fact that she was still a young child. But her love of painting had begun and was never to leave her.

During her entire stay in the hospital she received no visitors and although she wrote to her brother every day without fail, no post came back. Her memory of that day aboard the *Jolly Roger* had been almost wiped from her fragile mind, leaving her with scant knowledge of what had happened. Wild speculation and hideous imaginings crowded in on her until eventually she created a safe world of her own making where she could take control, secure in the knowledge that all would be restored to normal as soon as she got home to her father and brother.

After a long difficult six months she was deemed well enough to be discharged. The same large car that had taken David away came to collect her and it was only as it pulled out through the gateway that she knew exactly where she had been living. The words written above the gates read, "St Luke's Asylum for the Insane and the Incurable". Her eyes fixed on the huge metal letters until long after they had disappeared from sight. That heavy iron arch was to hang over her for much of her life, reminding her that she would never be whole or normal again. The car was expensive and black and smelt of leather. The driver did not speak to her, not even when she asked where they were going, so she kept quiet during the journey. After about an hour they drove in through another pair of similarly ominous iron gates. But above these were the wonderful words: "Bletchley Academy for Girls". She was going to school.

*

The next day she received her first and only visitor: dear Mama. It was the last time that mother and daughter were to meet. She recalled how all eyes had been drawn toward this tiny but elegant figure in a close-fitting black costume, a small black, feathered hat perched on that cinnamon coiffure, and a dead fox draped across her wide, padded shoulders. The grotesque sight of that dead creature, its tortured eyes looking straight at her, made Harriet retch. It hung there pleading with her to stop its cruel humiliation, its tail held cynically in its own mouth as its empty legs dangled and swayed in time with her mother's elegant gestures. She did not remember anything her mother said to her, so fixated was she with the dead animal, nor did she utter a single word in reply. She did remember watching her mother leave, the sound of her high suede heels clacking against the stone floor, and the image of her mother's skirt pulled up, caught in those ridiculous black French knickers, revealing her stocking-tops and her shame. As a snort of derision left Harriet's lips her mother turned on her and challenged those moist amber eyes for the last time. Only this time the hatred was returned with equal venom.

She had begun to paint as therapy at St Luke's, but here at school she learned the joy of painting for itself, taught by an enthusiastic young woman called Miss Wright, whose energetic approach encouraged Harriet to enjoy herself, while working hard at an often frustrating but always absorbing process. The acquisition of new skills was a joy for the child, whose life until now had not had too many things to feel happy about. It was this knowledge and love of art that she had been given by Miss Wright that she wanted to pass on to Liz. Harriet recalled her first completed picture and the satisfaction it had given her when her teacher had praised it. Now Liz too was experiencing the thrill that came with doing something new, achieving something one did not know was within one's reach. To teach and encourage Liz might not be Harriet's true destiny, but in the meantime it was a mutually rewarding way to while away the hours.

*

Revisiting the past was not something Harriet often chose to do. Life here with the Jessops suited her well, but lately connections were emerging. She could see a pattern, pieces of a jigsaw that began to fit together, leading her to understand who she was and where she was going. Was she ready to examine parts of her past that she had intentionally kept buried? Things that she had not thought about for many years began to surface. They had played a significant part in moulding her character and now at last she recognized that she was strong enough to face them.

The months she had spent in hospital were still painful to recall and having already given them a cursory glance, it seemed unnecessary to explore them in depth. Her time at school, however, was different. She was amazed that she could recall it with something akin to affection. During these years she had learned not only how to paint and enjoy the process of painting, but how glorious it was to sing. It was here that she discovered that she had been given a rare voice. The Academy had a large music department and the head of music, a rather strict woman, took this awkward young prodigy under her large wing. Harriet learnt how to develop her voice, to respect it and use it correctly. She learned how to stand, how to breathe and how to control this amazing talent. She was forever grateful to the stern, overlarge lady, Miss Bunting, for having faith in her and pushing her to the limit of her ability. It was years since she had thought of her two mentors, but their names came back to her in a flash. They were etched in her memory, with love, in the case of Miss Wright, but with respect and gratitude for Miss Bunting. Recollection of her formidable authority was enough to make Harriet leap to attention in anticipation of an hour's hard work, receiving little in the way of praise other than a brief nod of the head, which was satisfaction enough.

For five years Harriet lived at Bletchley without ever seeing her father, brother or mother. Peace broke out, but it made little difference to Harriet. Other girls' fathers returned from the Front, to ecstatic reunions, while some tear-stained girls were given black armbands and sent home on unofficial leave. Harriet had become immune to the emotions of other people and no one insisted that she get involved. The school protected its girls, and its detached method of caring suited her. It became her home, a place where she was safe.

Her unruly hair was cut into a neat bob so, for the first time in her life, she could forget about it. Her height had levelled out, so that although still tall, she was no longer head and shoulders above the other girls. Uniformly dressed, she was the same as everyone else so she no longer stood out in the crowd. She kept herself to herself, forging no friendships but making no enemies. The other girls speculated as to why she received no visitors and stayed at school alone during the many, often long, holidays. Rumours abounded that she was the love child of an aristocrat, or that her father was a spy. None of this worried her. She loved to learn and at last her voracious appetite was being satisfied. She had brought her own enclosed world with her, a place to live where she felt safe, untouched by the outside and the unknown. Bletchley had wrapped a second layer around her; deepening her cocoon. She had, of course, become totally institutionalized, but she would happily have remained at Bletchley for the rest of her life.

Her determination to know why David had not come to see her and to find out how her poor father was had always remained uppermost in her mind, although it sat awkwardly juxtaposed with an overpowering conviction that she was alone in the world. So when, one day in the winter of 1947, she was ushered into the headmistress's study and a callow young man who introduced himself as Mr Ernest Kepple informed her that, regretfully, all her family were dead she was stunned but not altogether surprised. She remembered this awkward young man. He wore a black jacket and pinstriped trousers and had a stutter not unlike her brother's. Throughout the interview his bony hand fidgeted with a bowler hat that looked far too large for his pointed head, which was far too bald for a man of his age. He was from the firm of Kepple, Kepple & Cross, family solicitors. He spoke slowly, not unsympathetically, but in staccato and never relaying the exact circumstances of the deaths of Harriet's relatives. His formal manner did not solicit questions. So when she was told that her brother had been killed that awful night in 1942 and her father had died of a stroke shortly afterwards she merely accepted it as fact. Her mother had apparently withheld this information from her daughter to save her any distress. But then just two days ago the widow and grieving mother, having survived this devastating compound tragedy was to fall victim to a tragic accident of her own, when the car she was travelling in slid on black ice at the top of Wrotham Hill killing its two occupants outright. How cruel of Fate. Her father and her brother were dead and her dear mother had avoided any revenge that Harriet might have hoped to visit her with.

To Harriet it was obvious. Her brother had taken his own life. The fact that she had not been there to stop him was a burden of guilt that Harriet was prepared to carry for the rest of her life. The bullies had won. She had no memory after hitting her head. He must have thought he had killed her. His gentle nature would never have let him forgive himself. He was not strong and without her could not have gone through with their plan. Faced with such a dreadful future, disappearing into the cold water must have seemed the only solution. There was no doubt that all the blame belonged at her mother's door, but it had been her responsibility to protect her brother. Nothing could ease her own crippling sense of guilt.

How convenient her mother's death had been. Where was that natural justice the philosophers talked about? A quick, clean car crash was too small a price to pay for all the misery that wretched woman had heaped on them. The circumstance of her father's death was different. In many ways it could be seen as a blessing. His health was never going to improve, rendering his life progressively meaningless. At least the end had come while he was still in his beloved Beckmans. She hoped it had been swift and painless and that he was now over the rainbow with the bluebirds, waiting for her to join him. But, and it was a very big but, she should have been with him. He must have called out for her just as she had called to him over the years.

In the few days before her homecoming Harriet wrapped herself in a further layer of cynicism and bitterness, which cast her as a lonely spinster, not yet eighteen years of age. She had been away five years. All she had ever owned was a school uniform, three pairs of knickers, three vests and a small black-and-white photograph. Now Beckmans was hers. She was going home.

Slowly, as she approached the front door, she looked up at the twin pillars standing either side of her. They were not as high as she remembered, but there they stood, proud sentinels, and she thanked them for being so solid and dependable. This was her real home. It would make her welcome, she knew that. Her fingers closed around the bunch of keys forming a fist, which she lifted to her lips and kissed before knocking gently on the glass. "Open it, Miss Marchant. There is no need to knock. Beckmans belongs to you now." Mr Kepple had driven her back to Watermere and followed her into the house, unnecessarily but courteously carrying her small half-empty case for her. He was wondering what this tall, rather odd young woman was going to do with such a large forbidding property. He did not feel the house embracing her. He could not see the tears of joy she cried from behind her unblinking amber eyes as they acknowledged the welcome. He could not know that Beckmans belonged to itself. None of this registered on Harriet's face so that when he turned to leave he felt guilty and ashamed to be abandoning such a young girl. But, as Harriet turned the key in the lock behind him, she smiled. She was home. No one could tell her how to live her life, not now and not ever. She was mistress of her own destiny.

The first thing she did was to strip out her mother's belongings, which she parcelled up and sent to the vicarage. The funeral was arranged for the day after she arrived home. The kind man in the pinstriped trousers attended and so did the sexton and the vicar. That was all. The small coffin containing her mother's body was lowered into the family grave and Harriet placed a posy of snowdrops, a bag of bull's eyes and a model spitfire alongside it. These were for her father and her brother. Then she turned her back on her dead Mama and returned home.

Mr Kepple, accompanied Harriet back to Beckmans for the reading of the will. It turned out that Miss Harriet Marchant was now a wealthy young woman. Her independence was assured and she intended to keep it that way. He agreed that the firm of Kepple, Kepple & Cross would continue to handle all her affairs. At her request, post was to be sent to their premises in London and dealt with by them. She did not wish to be bothered by any of life's minutiae and once she had written a cheque for a considerable amount of money to be sent to Tom and Ada Pritchard, she held out her hand to shake that of Mr Kepple and seal the transaction.

That was the last time Harriet touched another human being. Her groceries were delivered weekly and left in a box on the front doorstep. Her laundry was collected and returned by a delivery service. Apart from a telephone that stood unused on the hall table she closed off contact with the outside world. As the door shut behind Mr Kepple, a sense of relief flooded over her. At last, she could be herself. There was no one to answer to, no one to peer into her soul and see her shortcomings. She took the large iron key-ring that came with the house and examined each key in turn. As a child she coveted this amazing collection, watching and listening as it swung suspended by a chain from the belt of the skinny, uptight housekeeper, whose hand constantly dropped to silence the jingly bunch with a firm reprimand. Later they were imprisoned in Mrs P.'s voluminous apron pocket where they tore at the starched cotton in an attempt to escape the heat of her round, sweaty body. Now they were hers. First, she removed the front door key and placed it in the keyhole inside the hallway. Then she removed the smaller back door key and repeated the procedure. She no longer needed the rest of them, except for one.

Removing the large iron key with the griffin's head, she entered her father's room and positioned the key in the lock behind her. Turning it with both hands she felt its powerful resistance before it gave way, releasing the heavy tumbler, which clunked as it fell into place. Leaving the key in the door she crossed the room to her father's small desk. She laid the rest of the keys in the drawer beside his watch and his pipe. She stepped over to the fireplace, where her sampler still hung on the hook her father had hammered into the solid Tudor oak. The letters of the alphabet, both upper- and lower-case, some birds, recognizable as bluebirds by their colour, a rainbow with a few too many colours and in the wrong order and the words "Happy little bluebirds" had been lovingly embroidered on a bluish-grey background. The whole was worked in a wobbly version of cross-stitch and had taken her months of sweat and tears. She had signed it "*H.M. 1939*" and thought she would burst with pride when her father insisted it be framed, and hung it in his room on a pretty little hook in the shape of a bluebird. Her fingers reached out to touch it briefly before she sank back in the leather armchair and wept.

The next morning she wrapped her cloak around her shoulders more for comfort than warmth. She knew what she must do if she was to live here with any semblance of peace. Her long legs propelled her swiftly across the lawn to the beck, where she stopped beside the little bridge that led to the boathouse. The *Jolly Roger* lay at its berth beside the jetty, its mooring ropes worn but still clinging tightly to its secret. She stared at it, willing it to tell her the truth. It refused to divulge any of the mystery. Any facts that might help her piece together the last moments of David's life remained an enigma. Suddenly what she had to do was so blindingly apparent she almost laughed with relief. Taking a deep breath, she marched over the bridge. Steeling herself to visit it again, she marched straight into the boathouse and grabbed the boat hook. As she lifted it a shudder went through her and she knew that it too was withholding evidence from her. Outside again, she breathed in the fresh air. So far, so good! Motivated by an overwhelming sense of purpose she untied the little boat and pulled it round to the far side of the building before striking at it with the unwieldy hook. It took several strikes, using all her strength, to penetrate the hull, but eventually she saw the water begin to seep in and spread. She had pierced its heart. Their beautiful boat was sinking. The ties that held them were severed. They shared no history. The boat was no longer connected to her. It was just an old wreck that had always been there and she would tell anyone who asked that: "It has always been there."

Next she cast the boat hook into the lake along with the submerging dinghy, but not before she let her fingers touch the lovingly carved initials *H* and *D*. She said a silent prayer for old Tom as she watched the murky water close over her past. Then, throwing her cloak around her in preparation for her grand finale, she strode back into the boathouse. Inside it was dark and cold. The smell of damp was everywhere, but she could also smell the stench of sex. Even when she closed her eyes she could see her mother writhing on the floor with that horrible stranger. Selecting some kindling wood and paper from the log box by the grate, she proceeded to set them in a small pyramid right in the centre of the floor. It was the exact spot where she had seen them perform. She struck the match and stood back to watch the flames greedily consume the paper. They weakened as they attacked the kindling, crackling as they bit into the dried wood. Then as they gathered strength the fascination of the fire took hold of her. Nothing could stop it now. She was a natural arsonist. The fire took on a life of its own, way beyond her control. The force of the blaze both horrified and thrilled her. She backed out of the boathouse and turned her back on the inferno. Its hold on her was loosening as the hungry flames licked at her, washing her clean.

She awoke to find herself in a new millennium, sitting alone in the Tudor room, her memories still burning in her mind's eye. Forcing the past to retreat, she wrapped her faithful cloak about her once more, crossed the hall and marched through the breakfast-room into the garden. Liz was standing on the near bank. It was dusk and the silhouette of the boathouse stood out against the darkening sky. She pinched her arm to remind herself that this was the twenty-first century and she was here with her friend. Memories still crowded in on her. She had opened the floodgates and nothing would hold them back now. Thoughts and images she had suppressed for a lifetime were flying free. Well, let them do their worst.

They no longer filled her with hatred nor had the power to destroy her. She let loose an alarmingly loud, defiant laugh that dared her furies to show their ugly faces one last time. All the dark trappings of her early life melted. Life was about to begin again, charged by the energy usually reserved for the young. The future held no fears; in fact, she welcomed it.

Harriet turned to look at the young woman standing beside her. This was her friend and it was fate that had thrown them together. Through this vital young woman she could reach out and touch life, free to follow its twists and turns, no longer afraid of what lay around the next bend. Together the two women watched the old boathouse, one seeing it consumed in flames the other rebuilding it in her mind's eye.

They turned and walked back to the house, Harriet at last ready to face her fate, Liz thanking her lucky stars she had been dealt such a fabulous hand. Harriet wrapped her cloak around Liz's shoulders as together they watched some tiny birds flying high in the sky overhead. Liz thought they might be bluebirds and wondered why she suddenly felt so deliciously warm.

CHAPTER 9

The first of August was deemed an apposite day for the actual building work to begin. It happened to be Liz's thirty-fifth birthday and as it was her pet project what better choice of day could there be? Bob wanted to remove the old structure, clean out the lake and clear the site thoroughly well before that date. He estimated it would take two or three weeks. If they started now that allowed enough time to draw up the plans and steer them through any bureaucratic hiccups. They all prayed for an Indian summer so that the really messy work would be over before the wet winter the forecasters had promised began in earnest. The enthusiasm to get started gripped everyone, except poor Liz. The old boat was in the way of any future construction work and her fears were staring her in the face.

She knew the first thing the men intended to do was raise the wreck. The very thought of this apparently trivial act filled her with a dreadful foreboding that could reduce her to tears. Telling herself that she was getting things out of proportion – it was just an old dinghy - did nothing to lift her anxiety. Why the mystery? Vivid memories of how violently she had reacted on the night of the millennium would leap out of nowhere, still with the power to terrify her. It was all linked to a feeling of complicity. Guilt pressed down on her whenever she thought of it, making it difficult to breathe, her chest hurt so much. Now she had to go through it all again. What they were about to do was an act of desecration. Hoping it would lessen the strain she had persuaded them to complete the salvage work on the day before her birthday, but now the day had arrived she was not sure she could go through with it.

If she shouted to them to stop they would have to listen to her. After all, it had been her idea to pull down the boathouse; she could simply say she had changed her mind, it was a ridiculous waste of money and they should call it a day. Before she could speak, her head began to swim and she felt herself swaying. A slight nausea crept over her as she struggled to stay upright. The light-headedness spread through her body. It was as though she were floating a few inches above the ground. Her senses functioned; she could hear and see, but nothing felt normal. When she tried to move she could not. Something was raising her up, lifting her to a point where she could see without the limitations of perspective and reality.

She had distanced herself from the others by standing on the near bank beneath the willow. The boat was not visible from here, but she preferred that. Harriet placed herself behind Liz; they could see Mel standing with the twins on the far bank where they had a good view of the proceedings. Liz was no longer shaking with fear. She was paralysed. Harriet moved closer until they were standing shoulder to shoulder. Outwardly they appeared calm and composed. Inside their shared feelings were complex. Neither wanted to face what was about to surface.

Bob, clad only in his shorts and a huge grin, lowered himself into the water shuddering at the unexpected chill as it reached his nether regions. They watched as he tied various lengths of rope around the rotting hull before instructing Edward to haul it in. The twins rushed forward to help their struggling father until with a loud crack the first plank broke loose and crashed on to the bank. The three fell backwards in a heap, to be met by a rousing cheer from Mel. Sliver by sliver, plank by rotten plank it was wrenched free, no longer held together by knotted reeds and years of compacted mud. Gradually what remained of the little boat was laid out on the bank, like a giant half-eaten jigsaw. It was hardly recognizable as a boat, just fragments of wood caked with mud, algae and lichen. It smelt rank.

"Look at this!" Bob exclaimed, holding aloft a length of hull with a jagged hole at its centre. "Pierced through the heart, looks like she was scuppered... what d'ye think, me 'earties?" He pulled a face with one eye closed, the other opened wide, and he hopped around ridiculously on one leg. James and Mel took up the pirate theme but Jenny was too busy. She was examining a piece of wood with a thoroughness which would have met with the approval of Sherlock Holmes himself. They were barely visible, but fragments of red paint had not escaped Jenny's eagle eyes. After close scrutiny she exclaimed the strange words: "*olly Ro.*"

"The *Olly Ro*," squealed James. "Wow, what a cool name."

Jenny, who was still examining the remains, corrected him. "No, look, the 'o' is small but the 'R' is a capital letter. I do believe you are right, Captain Bob, we have a pirate vessel here. I present *The Jolly Roger*. God bless her and all who sail in her!"

Mel was kneeling beside her God-daughter. Edward scratched his head. Whose daughter was this? She never failed to amaze him. Jenny winked at Mel before pulling her brother down onto the grass beside her, holding him in an arm-lock akin to a half-Nelson.

"*Olly Ro, Olly Ro, Olly Ro*," he chanted until she too took up the cry and they found themselves in a shouting competition. The Pote joined in, barking at full voice and trying to nip the odd ankle as it presented itself. Bob was still waist-deep in the water. "Someone fetch a rake. There's something else buried in the mud down here. I need something long to pull it out."

"No! Leave that where it is." Liz's command stopped the men in their tracks.

Throughout the whole salvage procedure Liz and Harriet had been standing at the far bank beneath the willow, lost in their own strange world. It was a hot July day yet Liz felt chilled through to the marrow. Her body ached with an inexplicable overwhelming sadness. Tears streamed from her eyes as she wrapped her arms around herself and rocked to and fro.

"It's a boat hook," she said. Her voice was deep, and detached. As the company turned to look at her she remained rooted to the spot, staring into the depths of the lake. Her face was drained of colour and tears poured down her cheeks. Her hand rose to push back the stray lock of hair that was stuck to her face with hot pain-filled tears.

"Leave it there! Leave it alone!" Liz was hysterical. Abruptly, she turned and marched across the lawn to the house. Mel clambered up from her kneeling position beside the salvaged wreck, signalling for the others to stay put while she followed her friend inside. Blinking against the sudden darkness, Liz crossed through the kitchen, pausing to collect the iron key from its secret ledge. Crossing the hall she stopped outside the Fourth Room, then opened the oak door and stepped inside. She was sobbing uncontrollably, each sob taking her closer to hysterics, until she was shouting and ranting at the room, "What do you want from me? Tell me, for Christ's sake tell me or leave me alone. I can't take much more."

Mel caught up with her and followed her into the room. "It's all right, Liz, I'm here."

"Nothing's bloody well all right. Can't you feel it? You're supposed to be a psychic, so tell me what's going on. What's happening to me?"

Mel moved into the centre of the room. She was unfamiliar with this place. Liz tended to keep it locked, referring to it merely as "the Fourth Room", undesignated and undecorated. Mel peered around her in the gloom. The room was square, with a large oak fireplace on one wall and a deep bay window, with leaded diamond panes, on another. The ceiling was lower than in the other reception rooms, and covered with oak beams, giving the room a claustrophobic atmosphere. There were no nooks or crannies, no pretence, just four honest corners and one very wide door to enter and leave by; a straightforward Tudor room: a waiting-room.

The two women stood together in the middle. Like this room, they too were in limbo. Mel stretched out her arms, palms upturned, and took long deliberate breaths through her nose. Her eyes were gently closed and she lifted her head to face the ceiling. The lack of natural light in the room dulled her normally bright hair to a deep matt brown. It was not yet dusk, but she left the lights off, preferring to let the room grow dark with the evening and blend in with the gathering shadows. Liz's head was pounding. Blood was coursing through her ears and she raised her hands to block out the sound. Mel lowered her arms and moved across to an old sofa that stood in the window bay. Removing a pair of cricket pads and a pile of old curtains she sat in the middle of the seat, patting the cushion beside her. Liz crossed the room to join her. Harriet was already seated. Her patience was growing thin and she wondered why this was taking them so long.

All three women closed their eyes. Their breath was regular and deep, the only sound in the room. Liz had no thoughts and no memory. She was entering a place without time and where self no longer existed; a place she would never describe and would not remember. She was poised on the brink of somewhere she had never been before, but a place that she knew intimately. She was entering a trance and Harriet was her guide. Together they went back through those happy early childhood days, days destroyed by the loss of a brother and a father. They felt the absence of a mother's love, the isolation of a child cut off from all warmth and security until, abandoned, it is forced to create a world in which it can survive. Harriet showed her the pain of being exposed to the cold, the enduring pain of a long life lived alone and the bitterness this left in one's soul. Then she shared the redemptive joy that came from being welcomed into a new family. The warmth that filled her now and her determination to repay their generosity was laid bare as Harriet poured out her heart and soul. By the time she had finished she was weeping and kneeling on the floor, too drained to speak or stand.

The trance began to lift. Physically Liz had remained unaltered but her spirit had travelled from child to adolescent through adulthood to old age. The strange thing was that none of it came as a revelation to her. With each new twist and turn of the story she was ahead of the narrator, she had seen it all before; lived it all before, but without any conscious knowledge of it. She was a long way away, far away in time and space, in a place where no one lived but everyone had lived and would live again. It was a place where now did not exist. It was neither the future nor the past, it just was, and while she was there it was familiar.

Liz heard a voice calling her. It came from far away. As it drew nearer, the space she had been occupying sped backward, sucked down a long light shaft. Cold air carried her back along the duct until the tunnel itself began to recede. The air around her grew still and the temperature returned to normal. Once more silence became the strongest presence in the room... the room? Yes, of course, she was in the Fourth Room. She heard her own breath entering and leaving her body. Then she heard Mel exhale a laborious sigh. Mel looked anxiously at Liz, willing her to open her eyes. Harriet had already opened hers and was staring at Mel with disbelief.

Reluctantly Liz returned to the room. She had been a long way off, out of her own body, drifting in an ethereal world where she did not need weight or substance. Lifting her head, she opened her eyes and the shock of reality hit her hard.

"OK?" asked Mel.

"Yeah, I think so... a bit spaced out. I feel as though... I don't know what I feel... actually I don't feel too good." Liz was shaking violently and tears streamed down her face. Taking a hanky from her pocket she blew her nose loudly.

"Well done. That was quite amazing." Mel had opened the door enough to let a crack of light in. She peered at her watch. "How long would you say we've been here?"

"I've no idea... five, maybe ten minutes," Liz said.

"It's nine o'clock," said Mel triumphantly.

"You're joking! Did I fall asleep? Good grief, it's dark already!"

"You have just experienced your very first trance, Mrs Jessop!" Mel was excited. This was her friend's spiritual awakening and could cement the already strong bond they shared. Liz had never totally accepted this "other" world. Without actually denying it she dismissed it as fascinating and rather scary. Mel was desperate to question Liz: to discover how much she could remember of the séance, but she had to approach it carefully. It was highly likely that Liz would recall nothing of the experience. Mel's experience told her to tread cautiously.

Harriet had little or no respect for Mel and her so-called psychic powers. If that previous fiasco with those ridiculous picture cards was anything to go by, Liz needed to be protected from this woman. She had just poured out her inner-most secrets to her friend, a task she found both difficult and painful. She did not want them relayed to this idiot. It had been no mean feat on Harriet's part to share her very private past with another, so her resentment of it being passed on to yet another was justified. However, more than a little jealousy was at play. Sharing Liz's friendship did not come easily to Harriet, having being starved of intimacy all her life. Their relationship was based on mutual trust and she did not appreciate this interfering drama queen stealing her thunder. Besides, Mel was filling Liz's head with nonsense and scaring her to boot. Harriet determined not to let Mel gain the upper hand.

"What happened? I can't remember a thing. Is it that late? Tell me what happened, was it good?" Liz was talking quickly and excitedly; she was as high as a kite. Mel realized she ought to bring her back down slowly, so she spoke in a calm professional voice:

"We'll have a post-mortem later. Let's get some water first. I don't know about you, but I'm thirsty. Are you all right, kiddo? OK, let's find the others. They'll have given up on us."

Liz began to ease back into reality. The bright light of the hall made her pause until her eyes grew accustomed to the glare. Three hours had been lost. What possible explanation could she give? Her only recollection was of having been away somewhere very different and exciting. A delicious smell of bacon and eggs guided her across the hall to the breakfast-room.

Harriet remained behind, smarting from what felt like rejection. No recognition as to her contribution had been given. *A thank-you would have been nice*, she thought as she sat in the armchair. The Pote crept in and settled himself noisily on her lap. She stroked his cold, silky ears. "Well, at least you appreciate me," she said, and they both fell asleep.

Edward, Bob and the children were sitting around the table. The children were unwashed but relaxed about it.

"Where have you two been? We looked everywhere. I was beginning to think about getting worried." Edward's forced frown brought Liz back to earth with a bang. She had no idea what to say. Mel was less reticent.

"We were in the Fourth Room. Poor Liz had a nasty attack of hay-fever so I gave her some healing. It was so deliciously cool in there we just sat on that old sofa and we were goners. Too many gins and all that sun. She's been telling me her plans for that room. I hadn't realized it was so lovely. I've not actually been in there before." Mel lied beautifully. Liz was impressed and grateful to have such a clever accomplice. She smiled across at her and Mel winked back.

Bob had been quietly munching on his food while looking intently at Liz.

"That thing I found buried in the mud. It was a boat hook, but how the heck did you know? You couldn't possibly have seen. Even a blooming giraffe couldn't have spotted it from where you were." He shovelled another forkful into his mouth and waited for Liz's answer.

"What boat hook?"

"How many boat hooks are there round here? The one you told me to leave alone."

"I don't remember any boat hooks, sorry. So what did you do with it?"

"Left it alone, mate, I recognize an order when I hear one! I'm married to her, remember." Bob nodded towards his wife and laughed his relaxed down-to-earth laugh. For the first time that day Liz felt completely normal. The mention of a boat hook rang no bells and it hardly seemed worth pursuing so late in the day. Soon the twins would be bathed and in bed, stories read, books put away. The men would have retired to the lounge with full bellies and large whiskies, settling down to watch some sport, leaving Mel and her alone to indulge themselves. Maybe at last she would begin to understand what had happened to her. It was not a day she wanted to repeat but she needed to make sense of it.

At eleven the men went off to bed, worn out by the combination of hard labour, fresh air, children and whisky. Glad that her friend was staying the night, Liz took another bottle of Pinot from the fridge and the two women sat down at the breakfast table ready for a long session. Mel, who was shuffling her beloved Tarot cards, began by asking questions of a frustrated Liz, who was bursting with questions of her own. She needed answers, not more damned questions.

"So, what happened to you down by the lake?" Mel asked.

"I've no idea."

"Think. Take it step by step. Not why, just what."

Casting her mind back, Liz tried to recapture her feelings. "I knew something important was going to happen."

"How?"

"I just knew."

"When you first woke up?"

"Yes, the day felt special."

"Nice special or nasty special?"

"Nasty. I had butterflies in my stomach. More like anticipation, dread, definitely not nice. I'd been dreading today for a long time."

"Why?"

"That wretched boat… I can't explain." Liz knew it was all connected to that card – the Five of Cups. She shuddered at the thought of it. Part of her wanted Mel to know. Maybe another reading was what she needed, but it was the last thing she wanted.

"Close your eyes, Liz, let yourself go back to the lake."

Liz was not sure she wanted to go back over everything that had happened. This had not been one of her better days. She laughed a small hollow laugh, trying to understate her feeling of foreboding. "It was like standing on the edge of a cliff, you know? Frightening, dangerous, somewhere you really don't want to be... but riveting."

Mel nodded. "Now think, when did you first feel frightened?"

"Oh, by the lake, before they even started to raise the boat. It was anxiety at first, then it turned to pure fear. My hair stood on end, I was bitterly cold and my heart was pounding so hard I thought you could all hear it. I wanted to scream...or cry...or both, but I was paralysed. My body did not seem to be in my control. That sounds so stupid." Liz's eyes pleaded with her friend. Hopefully this madness would prove to be temporary. Normally calm and in control as she was, to have been overtaken by some unknown force terrified her. "It was as if I wasn't actually there. No... It was more as if I'd stopped being me. Help me out here I'm talking rubbish."

Mel responded with yet another question. "Who were you?"

Liz sighed. "I don't know. I was under the willow. It was so odd because I could see everything, which isn't possible, not from there. I must have imagined it."

Mel shook her head, "Now you're being rational. Don't. You said it wasn't you. What made you say that?"

Harriet had been woken abruptly by the dog scrabbling at the door to get out. Her ears were burning hot; someone was talking about her. She found the two women in the breakfast-room and was horrified to hear Mel's line of questioning. Standing directly behind Mel she began tapping her foot impatiently on the floor. She was getting very angry indeed. How could Liz be so disloyal? Everything she had told her had been in confidence and here was her friend betraying her by telling tales to this awful woman. She listened to Mel's constant questioning. How typical of a damned psychic to keep nibbling away until she got the answer she wanted: the one that fitted her theory. Harriet was convinced the woman was a charlatan.

"I was watching me. I was outside my body watching myself." Liz frowned and shook her head while holding out her glass for Mel to refill it. "I'm so confused. Maybe it's the menopause, I am thirty-five tomorrow." She attempted to laugh but could not quite manage it, so she took a large swig and thumped the glass down onto the table. "Have you ever felt like that, Mel?"

"What? That I'm getting old, or have I had an out-of-body experience? Listen, ducky, this is par for the course for me," retorted Mel with a sly wink.

"So which me was on the bank, the real me or another one?" Poor Liz was looking straight into Mel's eyes as she asked her question. Surely the answer would be reflected in those purple pools of mystery.

"Spirits sometimes use our bodies, take us over. They have to. They have no physical power of their own. I think that might be what happened to you."

"Utter claptrap!" Harriet was incensed. "There is only one you, Liz. No one took you over. That's ridiculous. I was there, I should know, I was right there with you." It was time to explain a few things. Filling her powerful lungs with a deep breath Harriet faced her foe and took her position, centre-stage. "Why don't you ask me what I was feeling, eh? If you had asked me I might have told you too, but you don't listen, do you? You don't even acknowledge my existence. Well, madam, this is just for you; Liz has heard it all before, but for you I'll take it from the top, as young Jenny says. But you'd better listen because I shall never say it again."

Mel paused. She knew there was a presence in the room and it did not feel friendly. It was addressing her, but for some reason she could not tune in to it. This was taking her way out of her comfort zone and it was more than a little alarming.

"Liz, I'm not sure what's going on here, but shall we just go with the flow?"

Liz nodded. Mel sat back and Harriet punched the air emphatically just as she had seen the Jessop twins do in a moment of triumph.

Harriet began to pour out her story. It came in an often obscure stream of consciousness. Much of it made little sense. It was so personal and had been lost in the twists and turns of time, but the essence was there. Talking to Liz had been so natural. It was as if their souls could meet and share experiences. There was no need to externalize everything into words. Words had always proved inadequate. The sad little girl who still lived in Harriet was ready to release her pain, but she only had a child's vocabulary. How could she describe the horrid scene in the boathouse that had scarred her early life? Who but Liz would understand the awfulness of not knowing what had happened to her brother David? Only Liz need know the wonderful potential contained in her daughter. It was all so private. But Harriet had started and once the floodgates were open, the flow could not be staunched; not until the last drop of emotion had poured out. It was harrowing for them all. When she finally drew breath and fell silent, they were totally spent.

The three of them sat in silence for a long time. Eventually Harriet gave Liz a hug before she slipped away back to her sanctuary where she collapsed into her chair by the fire. Back in the breakfast-room the atmosphere was so intense one could have cut it with a knife. It wove itself around the room holding the two women in its grip, unable to move or speak.

It was Liz who suddenly broke the spell by leaping into action.

"That was incredible, Mel. What you said made such sense. It explains so much. What does it feel like to be taken over like that? Doesn't it drain you? You must be knackered."

Mel stared at Liz, whose face was radiant: her eyes shone with such clarity and brilliance it was hard to believe she had been talking for nearly four hours. Liz was fresh as a daisy.

"Sorry. Would you rather have a cup of tea? It appears to be morning. God, it's simply ages since we sat up all night like this. You must be shattered with all that talking. Was that your guide talking through you? I felt as though I could reach out and touch them it was so vivid."

Mel got up and took the bottle from Liz, pouring a generous refill for herself. "I wasn't talking. You were. It was you. How much do you remember, Liz?"

"Don't be silly. I was listening to you. Anyway all this will have to wait. I'm shattered. I think I'll grab a few hours' shut-eye before the hooligans descend." Halfway through the door she stopped and added mid-yawn, "By the way, your idea for the Fourth Room…. it's brilliant. I can't wait to get started. Try and get forty winks. Sleep well."

"Liz?"

"Yes, Mel?"

"Happy birthday!"

Alone, Mel poured another drink. The events of that night were a complete puzzle. It had been Liz, not her, who had done all the talking, with her tales of marble statues, rainbows and knickers. She was shocked to hear how cruel Liz's mother had been; she remembered her as a pleasant gentlewoman who would not say boo to a goose. As for the harrowing story of the child that might have drowned, who could that have been? Liz was obviously picking up vibrations from this poor little soul. But there was so much confusion. Was this all muddled information about someone else? Had they or had she inadvertently let in some malign mischief-making force? How much would Liz remember of the evening? How much should she tell her?

While Mel was debating these various possibilities Harriet, refreshed from her nap, had come back to see what was going on in the breakfast-room. The buzz connected to this evening's strange events was exhilarating. She stood in the corner by the dresser, smiling to herself as she caught the end of Mel's lament. Should she be mean and spin Mel a tale or two? She was toying with dropping hints about a bearded man on the landing or a ravished parlour maid in the pantry when she was brought up short. Suddenly the tables were turned as Mel addressed her directly.

"I don't know who you are, but I know you are there."

Harriet looked about. There was no one else. This crazy woman obviously meant her.

"I can help you if you'll let me." Mel could feel a strong presence in the room. All her training, and a little of her prejudice, led her to conclude it was a disturbed spirit, trapped between the physical and the spiritual world. If she could just contact it she knew she could guide it to the light and let it rest in peace.

Harriet could not make up her mind. Should she put Mel out of her misery and explain the precise nature of the situation to her or let her carry on with her "exorcism" and have some fun while teaching her a lesson? But before she had decided, something Mel was saying caught her attention. Mel was describing feelings of loneliness and isolation, a life of strict routine and self-imposed privation. Then out of the blue came a pronouncement that brought Harriet to her knees: Mel was describing a fall, her fall. Now how on earth did she know about that?

CHAPTER 10

Mel's words resonated deep within Harriet. All those years ago, all that empty wasted time another life ago. She was stunned. She had just been informed that she had died on 1st August 1971. She had fallen down two stupid steps and died. She gave one of her loudest "humphs" and sat down beside Mel with a resounding thump. Being told that you were dead was not something that happened every day. It came as a huge shock. It had never occurred to her that she was anything other than a normal living being. She certainly did not feel dead. Why was she even listening to that ridiculous charlatan? That deluded woman had got it wrong. It would not be the first time. Harriet felt her hackles rise, recalling the fiasco with those stupid cards. Reluctantly she admitted Mel was right in mentioning a fall. She had taken a tumble, but it was an insignificant slip, not a life-ending drama. She composed her thoughts before willing herself back to 1971, when she had lived here all alone, to see for herself what had happened.

*

Life was one long routine to be endured with superstitious regularity. Every day, without fail, she completed the tour-of-duty that took her around the kitchen garden and the orchards, past the hives, through the little wall by Tom's shed and past the greenhouse full of tomatoes, before returning to the house via the front door. A tall upright figure dressed in a long black cloak and clutching a silver-handled cane. Each time she crossed the threshold, the old house put out its arms to welcome her; each time she thanked it for providing her with a sanctuary and a home while wondering: *Is it today?*

A few hours spent painting or day-dreaming followed, then a cup of cocoa and an early night. Harriet lived the life of a hermit. The postman never called. Any letters - legal, business or pesky circulars - were redirected by the post office to Mr Kepple's London office. Each week the village shop delivered a box of groceries and each week took away the empty. It was always the same order; it never varied and was never missed. A half-pound of Cheddar cheese, a large bloomer, half a pound of butter, a tin of condensed milk, a small jar of honey, two tins of sardines, a tin of corned beef, a packet of cocoa and one of tea. A cheque was left out with the box. No doctor was summoned, no vicar called. There were no friends to visit. Any childhood ideas of friendship had long been abandoned, recognized as deceptive falsehoods from the unreliable world of fiction. People played no part in her life. Relationships always ended in pain. She wanted no more separations. She was fine with being alone. The past was the past; gone. As for tomorrow, tomorrow was another world. It had nothing to do with Harriet Marchant.

And for many years tomorrow never did come. Each today became a replica of the day before. Her life was punctuated only by the changing seasons and the weekly grocery delivery. For the next twenty-four years Harriet lived this life. It never occurred to her to question whether she was enjoying it; she just got on with it. On occasions she would question the very purpose of life itself but in truth she had long been of the opinion that fate had passed her by.

On 1st August 1971 she woke with a profound sense that fate had remembered her. Something portentous was about to happen. Having completed her ritual tour she stood in the porch and pulled off her outdoor shoes. She heard the latest in a long succession of delivery boys tinkle on his bicycle bell as he pulled up to the front door, and a similar signal as he peddled off, closing the iron gates behind him. Why should she have butterflies in her stomach, that strange mixture of pleasure and fear?

She had run out of bread and was hungry for her breakfast. Her slippers were still in the Tudor room and she ran across the hall in stockinged feet. She was chuckling to herself as she heard Mrs P.'s voice from the past warning her to "Slow down, My Lady, before you go arse-over-tip!" The next thing she remembered was her heart in her mouth as her foot slid from beneath her on the slippery wooden step. Headlong she pitched, reaching out in the hope of steadying herself. There was nothing to grab hold of. No one heard her cry out or the loud thud as the full force of her body hit the floor.

The next thing she could remember was sitting at the kitchen table eating toast and drinking tea. She felt a bit shaken, but she appeared unharmed. She remembered voices. Was that possible? Had she seen people in the hall? It was a miracle she had not been hurt. It occurred to her that if she had died she would have lain there for weeks until her body was found. Would it have mattered? Who would miss a lonely, middle-aged spinster? She was nothing in the overall scheme of things; nothing special in the grand plan. This sparing of her life was hardly proof that she had a mission to complete – a role in life specific to her. It was simply a fluke. Yet her sense of fate was back. Something had changed. Something of significance had taken place. Life would be different from now.

For years Harriet had rattled around Beckmans like a forgotten pea in a discarded pod. Now she was filled with renewed energy. Her life had purpose; all that pain and disappointment had been leading to this moment. Her belief in fate was restored with a conviction that was hardly the mind-set of a dead woman. Her sights were firmly set on the completion of some as yet undisclosed task and she vowed to fulfil it, however hard it proved. She recalled the inspirational force, the lightning bolt that had surged through her body; one thing she knew for sure was that in order to meet her future destiny, she needed life.

So, there was no way that Mel was going to convince Harriet she was dead. She had never felt so alive. She shrugged off Mel's preposterous claims. She could remember each day of life after the fall with startling clarity. Admittedly she had forgotten the temporary disappointment when things did not change immediately. In fact for some time life had continued to be as boring as always, far too boring to be a new beginning in a new dimension. Life after Death must surely offer more than the predictable continuation of the humdrum.

What made her cling to her lonely existence with such stubborn tenacity? She no longer took life for granted. Every day threw another question at her. Where did her irrational sense of destiny originate? Did everyone have their own personal reason for living or was it just a chosen few? If so, why her, a reclusive old spinster with nothing to show for her life so far? Harriet battled with these questions. Why her? What was it she still had to do? Who could explain it to her and grant her the peace to let her life reach its natural conclusion, whatever that was? There had been no "natural conclusion" for her brother or father. Why should her life be different? She always came back to the same unanswered question. Why in God's name was she still here?

What Harriet did not know was that one week after her fall the delivery boy discovered her box of groceries untouched on the door step. Harriet saw only the shadows of the police man and the agitated boy as they broke down the door to gain access to the house. She did not hear the commotion caused by the ambulance and police car when they arrived with their sirens blaring. Unbeknown to her, they took her body to the local morgue. Poor Mr Kepple tried hard to locate any living relatives but at last he gave up and signed the forms granting permission for Harriet May Marchant's body to be released for burial. She was laid alongside her father, mother and brother in the family grave in Watermere churchyard. Harriet had not visited this place since the day she had buried her mother, so she never saw her own name carved beside the others already listed on the headstones. She did not see Mr Kepple and the vicar standing alone under a large black umbrella, silently paying their respects as the rain fell. As far as she was concerned she was at home eating toast and sipping tea.

Disappointingly for Harriet, things carried on as normal. In spite of her inspirational certainty that fate had at last summoned her, the boring aspects of her life continued unaltered. Until one drab drizzly day, a day that started like any other, something unpredictable happened and things would never be the same again. She had returned from her tour-of-duty to discover two cars in the driveway. They did not resemble her mother's Bentley or Tom's old Riley, nor even the little Austin with which Matron terrorized the poor people who lived near Bletchley Academy. These were vehicles from outer space, reminiscent of pictures in David's comic-strip books. The iron gates had been thrown wide and the front door was open to the elements. But what terrified Harriet was the sound of voices coming from the hall. Lifting her walking-stick above her head like a weapon, she took a deep breath and stepped resolutely into the unknown. Two men, one in a dark suit, the other taller and younger, wearing blue jeans and a leather jacket, stood at the bottom of the stairs. Deep in conversation, they did not see Harriet enter. One held a metal measure in his hand; the other, the suited one, held a large blueprint, which he stabbed at with a gold pen, impatiently emphasizing his point. Harriet watched in utter disbelief as the young man took a stump of white chalk from his pocket and proceeded to draw a cross on the hall panelling. His fingers, already coated with chalkdust, gained another layer as he turned the stump over and over, fidgeting with it between thumb and forefinger.

The presence of men unnerved Harriet; the fact that they were strangers made their presence even more alarming. However, that she was by now a woman of a certain age afforded her some protection. Chivalry could not be that dead. As her fear began to subside, so righteous anger rose to take its place. This violation of her private space, her sanctuary, was unforgivable.

Raising herself to her full height, and still holding her father's cane aloft, she marched over to the intruders and challenged the older man to explain himself.

"What are you doing in my house?" she asked.

He ignored her. Worse, he pushed past her, pointing to the front door with his pen.

"And that, I'll have that stained glass before the bloody vandals get it. That's early Victorian, possibly Regency; but I don't expect you to care one way or the other. Just make sure they treat it with respect when they remove it. Better take the whole bloody door to be safe." He was addressing the younger man: "And make sure the place is properly secured. I could get in here with a tart's hairpin."

"Yeah, yeah, is that all?" The young man chalked a large cross on the mahogany door then measured it with his tape, writing the measurements in a notebook.

The older man glanced around. "Yep, that just about covers it," he said. "Oh, apart from that room." He jerked his pen towards the Tudor room. "No one seems to have the key." He studied his blueprint, refolding it and placing his pen back into his inside pocket. "Nice-sized room; not as large as some, but part of the original Tudor house. There'll be some nice bits in there. Maybe even an inglenook. When did you last see a place like this that hadn't been stripped bare? Good old oak fetches a fair whack on the antique market. We're going to make a killing."

"Don't be too greedy, Colin." The taller man smiled in an unpleasant manner. Harriet wanted to smack him, but his next words turned her blood to ice: "Don't forget you're putting it on the market as a listed building. You've got to leave some original features or you'll seriously devalue it. Even if it ends up as flats it'll need a few original bits to pull in the quality punters."

The suited man was smirking. Harriet recoiled as he removed a none too clean hanky from his pocket, shook it and blew his nose loudly. "Bloody dust," he said sneezing. "That's the trouble with these old places, always full of bleeding dust." He blew his nose again. Inspected the handkerchief briefly, then shook it again, ensuring the germs escaped, before screwing it up and thrusting it back into his trouser pocket. In a voice puffed up with self-satisfaction he said, "Anyhow, I've already made sure of a handsome profit, whatever this old house fetches. That orchard bit and the field... what did they call it - "the meadow"? Well, we'll get six four-bed luxury detacheds in there. Then there's that so-called boathouse. Imagine a lovely block of maisonettes overlooking that pond. We could even drain half and double our money. If I can get the woods at the back and put a road through here we'll be millionaires by Christmas!" He chortled, took out his disgusting handkerchief, shook it and blew his nose again.

Harriet retched. Had she heard this horrid little man, correctly? They were plotting to sell her property, her home, divide it up and desecrate it. Over her dead body!

"Excuse me." Harriet pushed between them, brandishing her stick in what she hoped was a threatening manner. "I don't know if you are aware of the fact that this is private property. My private property, and I should like you to leave, *now*." She placed herself between them and the front door, which she held wide. The men stared at the door as it swung open until it hit the wall. "Out, now, this instant or I shall call the police. Do you hear me? Out! Now!" She was shouting at the top of her voice, waving her stick above her head like a demented banshee. She lunged at the little man with her weapon. Thrusting it between his ribs she began to push him towards the door. He staggered for a second, then turned to look straight at her. Harriet gave him her most withering look, her amber eyes narrowing into slits.

"What's up? You look like you've seen a ghost. Now that would be a good selling point."

The little man was nursing his ribs where he had knocked himself against the door knob.

"Let's get out of here. It's giving me the creeps. The best thing to do with a dump like this is to tear it down and start again."

"Get out! Get out!" Harriet screamed at the top of her powerful voice, while still waving her cane above her head of wild white hair. Seemingly unflummoxed the men laughed, shook hands as if clinching a deal and left by the door Harriet was holding open. She slammed the door, locking it behind them and listened with distain to them as, laughing and chatting they walked across the drive, climbed into their cars and drove out. Then, to Harriet's amazement, the younger of the two returned, pulled the heavy iron gates together and proceeded to secure them with a large padlock and chain. She listened for the sound of their cars to fade into the distance before running across the gravel to the gates. She tugged at the chain with all her might, but it would not budge. She was locked into her own property.

Shaken, she returned to the kitchen and took a large cloth from beneath the sink. Still clad in her outer shoes and cloak she stomped off around the house. Each time she found a white cross she wiped it out, releasing a snort of disgust as she did so. How dare they trespass on her land, enter her beloved Beckmans and proceed to vandalize it? At least they had left when she ordered them out; but how rude of them not to introduce themselves, or even acknowledge her existence. That was discourteous in the extreme. On returning to the hall, having erased thirty-two of the offensive crosses, she made sure the front door was locked and bolted top and bottom. If she could not get out then surely no one could get in. She entered the security of her kitchen and put on the kettle and the radio.

*

After the "invasion", Harriet moved all her personal possessions downstairs. She had grown nervous of stairs since her fall and it seemed logical to restrict herself to the kitchen and the Tudor room, from where she could monitor any activity at the main entrance. The unwanted visitors had unnerved her. As a precaution, a new ritual was added to the twice-daily tour of the house, involving checking and re-checking the locks. She reclaimed the keys from the drawer and carried them in a large noisy bunch clipped to her belt. She slept with them beneath her pillow, checking on them several times each night. Often when passing through the kitchen to embark on her garden patrol her eyes strayed to the ledge above the door and she thought of the great iron key that protected the Tudor room. A smile would creep across her face as she relished the knowledge of having thwarted those two horrid men by denying them access to her private world.

The next morning Harriet tried to slot back into her simple routine of gentle walks around the house and garden, frugal meals, painting and, of course, music. Her voice was still good, still rich in those dark tones developed during her brief training at school. Harriet took no pride in her voice. To her it was a gift involving neither fame nor fortune. To the outside world her life might well be deemed a failure. "Promising, talented, young woman turns into sad, solitary recluse." She never let herself think in this way, not seeing herself as special but one who shared a unique importance with every other human being. This marvellous, common yet exclusive attribute equipped her to fulfil her role, her destiny. Even those painful black days in the past had combined to make her who she was today: a stubborn tenacious woman, with a formidable character that had borne her through such a tragic and traumatic childhood and would equip her to deal with whatever future lay in store.

Then one night she dreamed the strangest dream. Having fallen down a rabbit hole she was confronted by Tweedledum and Tweedledee bearing a remarkable resemblance to the two discourteous developers. Grabbing a croquet mallet she proceeded to batter the two idiots about their over-large heads. With each strike they bowled over, only to bounce back, until all that remained were two enormous heads rolling around in the hall while she rode on the back of an iron hobby-horse with the head of a griffin, singing at the top of her considerable voice. The noise of her whacking, and their shrieks as each blow struck home woke her.

From outside the whirring and droning of a generator combined with the general din of heavy machinery and men's voices. The view from her window revealed that the gates had been swung open. Hurriedly dressing, she rushed to the kitchen, muttering to herself as she went, "Keep calm, Harriet. There is nothing to be afraid of. Take a deep breath. You have right on your side." She grabbed her cloak and armed with her father's cane marched into the garden.

As she approached the orchard the light summer rain was turning into an unseasonably heavy storm. By now her blood was up and she was impervious to the weather, feeling ready for a fight. The wind lashing against her face was stimulating and the wild conditions presented a fittingly dramatic backdrop. She thought of lying low and conducting a recce, but shrugged this off as the behaviour of wimps. So her tall, black figure strode on, carried by determined legs. On reaching the red-brick wall encircling the orchard she was brought to an abrupt halt. Part of the wall was still standing but close against it stretched a hideous length of plastic-coated chain-link. The sturdy metal posts had been cruelly driven in with no thought for the roots of the old espalier peach trees that Tom Pritchard had so loving planted in the shelter of the warm bricks. The archway that for centuries had served as the entrance, covered by the reddest of scented roses, had been reduced to a heap of rubble, the petals of the flowers mixing in the mud with the ancient dust of the red Pluckley Stock and the ghastly metal barrier that stood in their place.

"Who has done this? I dare you to show yourselves, you cowards!" Harriet cried, as she tugged at the intransient posts. No amount of wrenching or kicking would move the monsters. She glared about her, amber eyes alive with the fire of betrayal. "I know who you are. It's you two horrid little men: Tweedledum and Tweedledee. This has your handiwork written all over it. It's the white cross syndrome again. Well, this time you've gone too far." She turned and, throwing her cloak around herself in a dramatic gesture, strode back to the house.

After a soothing cup of Earl Grey she was quieter but no less angry. Each determined step back had sent her anger deep inside her. The dreaded chain-link stretched from the coach-house, around the front of the orchards, then ran the full length of the garden until it reached the old boundary across the beck. Her garden was being divided up into plots. They had paid no heed to the natural lines of the planting. Bushes and shrubs were randomly left on either side of the straight divide; some were actually cut in half as the unbending monster claimed its passage.

"They must have been here all night. They are stealing my home right under my nose, inch by inch," she said. "This is harassment. They want me out so they can take the lot. Well, they don't know what they have taken on."

Underlying her defiance was a fear that she was losing her once-sharp mind. Could she have signed something without reading it properly? She would have remembered a visit from Mr Kepple. Her short-term memory was getting bad lately but not that bad. What if she was suffering from Alzheimer's, how would she know? Women like her were preyed on by unscrupulous developers. Was it possible that she had signed away her land?

"Never!" Harriet spat out the word. She paced around the kitchen, picking up pots and pans, only to bang them down again in a temper. As she began to calm down, the thought occurred to her that it might be time to think about reducing her responsibilities. Would it be so awful if she only had access to the rear garden? She was telling herself only the other day that it was getting too much to walk around the whole estate every day, twice a day. Maybe selling off part of the land was the sensible thing to do, the rational approach.

That night Harriet retired exhausted from hours of reflecting on her situation. Should she fight to keep the house as it was? Should she sell off part of the land? Or should she consider moving out altogether? Was fate telling her to move on? Had the time arrived when she should hand over to the future generations? With all this swirling around in her thoughts she fell into a fitful sleep that left her feeling more exhausted than when she had gone to bed. Dreams began to float in and out of her head too quickly to take form, evaporating before she could recall them in the exasperating way that dreams do. Something was telling her to stay. In her dream it had been so obvious. It worried her that she could not recall it. "Hark at me, stupid old fool. It was a dream, for God's sake, just a stupid dream!" Telling herself off in her usual way she dismissed the thoughts with a short laugh and prepared for her constitutional.

Although just a dream, or fragments of a dream, the notion of purpose was renewed in Harriet. Having to defend it, to justify and explain her belief in her as yet incomplete destiny, somehow restored her fervour. Her determination to cling on to her house went far deeper than her love for the property. This sense of mission, ridiculous and grandiose as it seemed, was compelling. It was her duty to maintain Beckmans for future custodians, who should inherit it in all its glory, not reduced to a shadowy apology. That was part of her purpose and on its own was enough. Now that she had interpreted her dream to her own satisfaction, Harriet's resolve to fight on was unshakable. Having even so much as entertained the notion of moving made her laugh. No, she would never surrender her home. Re-development? Ha! She was having none of it.

"So they think I'm losing it, do they? Well, there is nothing wrong with my mind. This is my land, Beckmans land, and no one is going to carve it up like a Christmas goose. I won't sit back and watch them wreck the place. Over my dead body! I never signed anything over to anyone. Huh, as if I would, barmy or not!" She snorted with indignation and flounced off to the sanctuary of her room. Soon the sound of Harriet singing at the top of her remarkable voice resounded through the much relieved house.

The property had indeed been sold, all legally overseen by Harriet's solicitors. For the time being work was being done only on the surrounding land. Each morning at some ungodly hour, Harriet was woken by the din of earth-moving equipment knocking down walls and causing general havoc. Bulldozers crashed through regardless of the destruction left in their wake and teams of rowdy men with their jeans hanging down below the point of decency dug, hacked and laboured, creating a mud-bath out of Eden.

At first Harriet hid away in wilful ignorance of what was happening to her beloved home. Then one night she retaliated. Armed with a pair of stout wire-cutters she attacked the invidious chain-link and discovered the sweet taste of revenge. Each night she ran her one-woman vigilante army to halt their progress. She became expert in sabotage, destroying engines, slashing tyres and siphoning diesel, generally impeding the building work. Deep down she knew she was no more than an irritant, a flea on the back of the animal she wanted to destroy; but after a few months it became a game that

Harriet enjoyed playing. The original reason for the war was forgotten and she became immersed in the battle to outwit her main protagonists. Tweedledum and Tweedledee arrived regularly to survey and assess the damage. Harriet derived great satisfaction from witnessing their frustration and distress. They assumed it was down to local vandalism, which it was. The police quickly lost interest, leaving Harriet free to continue her wrecking game unimpeded. It was when matters became personal with the tyres of his Jaguar being slashed that Tweedledum opted not to appear on site in person, which rather took the fun out of it for Harriet.

*

Despite nearly a year of intensive battle, the development was completed. All was quiet once more. The coach house and the orchards had given way to six detached mock-Georgian houses, and new families moved in, unaware of what had vanished to make way for them. Harriet adjusted remarkably well and quickly. She never left by the front door these days, so the only difference was that her daily tour of the garden was considerably shorter. The perimeter shrubbery had gone, devoured by the new gardens next door. Now as a survival technique she saw only what she chose to see. In her mind's eye Tom's handiwork was all around. She did not notice the grass was knee-high and the terrace covered in moss and weed. The nut tree had grown enormous and saplings grew unchallenged where the squirrels had planted their hoard. All the paths had vanished, covered by thick green moss and grass and the wisteria occupied half of the side terrace and much of the upstairs rooms. The red brick wall with its arch was covered in summer with scented roses. She did not see the withered vines in the greenhouses because to her they were full of the ripeness of summer and the hives still buzzed with activity and sweetness. The lawn swept down to the lake in straight stripes of light and dark and the ruin of the burnt out boathouse stared back complete across the water.

Then a simple knock on the door changed everything. Her reason for clinging on so tenaciously made sense. The entry of the Jessops had transformed Harriet's life, propelling her into the twenty-first century, where she had been living life in their slipstream ever since. It had never been so vibrant, so full of shared joy. So why, even now at the age of seventy-five, was she still asking the same questions? If fate had not finished with her, it had better get a move on. She was not getting any younger. She laughed at the thought of being asked to question her own existence. Was she really being told she had not lived all those years of emptiness? All that battling to protect Beckmans from destruction, was that a figment of her imagination? How dare anyone suggest such a thing? According to Mel she had ceased to exist thirty-five years ago. Harriet threw back her head and laughed. Life was many things but it was real, of that she was certain. Harriet took herself off to the Tudor room. It had been a funny old day, a busy day full of memories and surprises. Tomorrow was Liz's birthday and work would start on the boathouse. "Ah, well, life goes on," she said out loud and guffawed as she realized the irony of her remark.

Chapter 11

Liz had gone up to bed oblivious of the drama unfolding downstairs. She fell into a delicious, dreamless sleep the moment her head hit the pillow. Being woken by hefty twins landing on her stomach a few hours later did not stop her from feeling fully refreshed and raring to go. Questions that had plagued her for years no longer hovered around her brain nagging her for answers. She knew where she was going and her journey was charged with a sense of purpose. It was the same feeling she had felt on the night of the millennium, only this time it came with an urgency that had been absent then. This was her time. She was on the brink of something new. The twins were nearly ten now and the main house was complete. The garden was looking good and was at last under control. Today work was about to start on the boathouse and hopefully by the end of the summer it would be finished. That just left the Fourth Room, which no longer confused her. It was her room now, it had accepted her at last and she would do it proud.

Edward cooked a birthday breakfast comprising mainly toast, as all the bacon and eggs had been scoffed the night before. Next on the agenda was the ceremonial opening of the presents. Jenny was particularly excited about hers, but insisted it be opened last. James gave his mother a sable paintbrush as usual and The Pote half-presented her with a bone, which he immediately snatched back. There were theatre tickets from Edward and a book on famous gardens from Mel. At last it was Jenny's turn. She had been hunting for months for a suitable and affordable gift. Her diligence had paid off: in the back of an antique-cum-junk shop she had found exactly what she wanted. Liz held the flat oblong package in front of her. She shook it, sniffed at it and prodded it, before carefully unwrapping it.

"The lady in the shop said she had some others that were much better and older. One was dated 1670, imagine. But it was a bit scruffy and very expensive. Anyway, I liked this one best. It's that song you're always humming so I knew you'd like it. And it was a lot cheaper. Look, it's signed 1939 so it's still an antique." Jenny leant over the arm of Liz's chair, waiting for her mother to open her present. Liz tore at the wrapping. Inside the purple paper was a framed picture. Liz took it to the light for a closer look. The simple wooden frame held a small sample of stitchwork. The letters of the alphabet, both upper and lower case, had been embroidered around the text "Happy little bluebirds" and it was illustrated with an enormous rainbow whose abundant colours were upside-down and over which small, blue-coloured birds were flitting. It was not very accomplished but had enormous charm and a quirky quality that made it unique. Liz loved it immediately. "It's perfect, Jenny, and I know exactly where it should live."

"But that's not the best bit, Mummy. Take the back off. You'll never believe it!" Jenny dashed forward to help speed things up.

Tucked between the backing card and the sampler was a small black-and-white snapshot of a shy-looking man and a little girl. The child's smile lit up the picture. Her cheeky beaming face, surrounded by a halo of wild thick hair, exuded utter happiness as it grinned from ear to ear and peered into the upturned face of the man on whose shoulders she was perched. The age difference implied that it was grandfather and granddaughter, but something told Liz it was a father and his child. Its tatty crumpled state left no doubt that this was a much loved image, one that had been visited time and time again. As she replaced the treasure she remembered a small picture of herself and her own father taken at Brighton. They were not dissimilar.

"Goodness, Jenny, has this been hidden there all this time? Do you think this is the little girl who embroidered it? Look, there's something written on the back: 'To my little nightingale'. She must have sung this to him. Oh, Jenny. You are so clever to have found it."

"You haven't spotted it yet, have you?" Jenny's impatience was laced with incredulity.

"What am I supposed to be looking at?" her mother asked.

"You'll have to find it yourself." Jenny smiled that infuriating crooked smile of hers. "It's truly amazing!" She was bouncing up and down, beside herself with excitement.

Liz scoured the photo but all she could see was a dog-eared picture of a man and a child. The two figures were obviously in a garden. The man held the child high on his shoulders and they were laughing, looking into each other's eyes, oblivious to anything around them. The photo was hardly bigger than an inch and a half by two. Liz held it close and peered hard. This time she looked beyond the main subject. The figures took up most of the shot, but behind them one could just see a stretch of immaculately striped lawn sweeping down to some water. On the far side of the water was a building. It was tiny, but there was no mistaking it. It was the boathouse.

Everybody agreed it was an incredible find. Liz was overjoyed. Since last night she felt as though all the cares and doubts she had been harbouring had been blown away. Now this amazing coincidence confirmed her belief that everything was about to fall into place. It was such a stroke of luck. Jenny could have picked up any old sampler from any old shop, but to find this particular one was a miracle. Clutching her treasure, Liz marched across the hall to the Fourth Room. Pushing a pile of junk to one side she cleared a space in front of the inglenook then with great care she hung her precious sampler where it belonged; on the bird-shaped hook. This was just the beginning. While work was going on outside she would clear this room of its clutter and transform it into a quiet sanctuary; a place in which to dream.

Harriet slipped her arm around Jenny. "Thank you, my darling. How can I repay you?"

"You can teach me to sing!" was the child's reply. Harriet had two pupils and two friends. At last her destiny had a nucleus: Jenny was taking centre-stage.

*

Until now, Jenny had been content to explore and discover the physical world, a world filled with doing. The earth, the sky, everything around her, not to mention her own body, this had been more than enough to contend with. Now in her tenth year her receptive mind was developing as rapidly and noticeably as her physical self. Her young brain was ripe to explore abstract thoughts; to perform mental gymnastics, which were proving equally exciting as running, climbing or swimming. At school everything was labelled and divided into boxes, which frustrated her. Maths, History, Geography, Science, they were all treated as separate subjects, yet they had to be connected if her world was to make any sense.

One night she lay awake with the thread of an alarming dilemma unravelling in her head. She was trying to imagine what it would be like to have been born without a birthday. She imagined being told she would have to wait to be born because there was no time slot for her. With this conundrum tying her brain in knots she burst into her parents' room.

"If this is now, when does it become then?" she asked. Liz pretended she was still asleep. Once Jenny got hold of an abstract idea she worried at it like The Pote with a bone.

"Not now, darling, please. It's the middle of the night. Come back in the morning."

"But that will be the future and I need to know now, while it is still now. Right now, before it's the past." She was shaking her mother in an attempt to wake her.

"Go to sleep, kid." Edward's foot pushed at her from beneath the duvet. "Go! Now! Or you won't have a future." He turned over and tried to ignore her.

"So what's the difference between the past and the future? Do they swap places if you turn around?" Jenny waited. She was standing on the bed now, looming over her father, with her hands placed firmly on her hips. "Daddy, I really need to know. Are they fixed like West and East? Is there a magnetic time pole?" She was tugging at the duvet now.

"I don't know. Go and Google it or something!" Edward pulled the duvet over his head. Jenny turned on her mother, placing her face on top of Liz's so that her hot, angry breath hit her.

"Mothers and fathers are supposed to know these things. They're supposed to impart knowledge to their offspring." Her jaw was set firm. The terrier was challenging.

"Most mummies and daddies don't have a terrier for a daughter. Now go to bed. Go! That is an order! Go!" Edward made the last word long and drawn out to emphasize his point.

Jenny slid off the bed onto the floor. She got to the door, turned and said, accusingly,

"If I die in my sleep, still floundering in ignorance, you'll be sorry."

"Don't you be so sure!" replied Edward without moving.

*

The next day Jenny was up at crack of dawn Googling time zones. She had already printed off several pages before her father's dressing-gowned figure appeared.

"Daddy," she said. His heart sank at the prospect of a cross-examination before his first shot of coffee. He thought of retreating from the study, but decided to mount an attack and hopefully gain the high ground.

"You didn't die then?"

"I decided not to." She was deadly serious: "Daddy?"

"Yes, my little terrier?"

"Did you know that right now it's a completely different time in New York? They are five hours behind us. We're in their future, they are in our past. Isn't that fascinating?"

"Fascinating," he said, with that tone of disinterest that children hate. Edward was still asleep. His body was crying out for caffeine and his daughter's logic sent his thoughts spinning. How he had fathered such a child baffled him.

"Listen, poppet," he said trying to sound extremely interested, "that is so profound I shall have to give it some thought. Let's talk about it later?" He raised his eyebrows and nodded at the child, hoping she would shrug her shoulders and agree. Sometimes it worked. Today it did not.

"You see, you're already putting it off till the future. If we all did that the whole world would grind to a halt." The urgency in her voice was appropriate. "So stop procrastinating and get on with things!" She added a quick nod of her head as an emphatic punctuation mark.

Edward's pride did not take kindly to being beaten by a nine-year-old, even when it was his own child. "Now I'm really confused, Jen."

Jenny was standing with her strong legs apart, her hands on her hips, reminding him of a picture he had seen of Joan of Arc: the young warrior faced her foe and demanded to know why.

"Well, because I'm not sure if that was an order or a request," he explained.

Jenny, quite unfazed, looked straight at her father and declared, "I should take it as advice, Daddy." And she stomped off into the garden.

Liz had been watching from the hall and remembered the young page on the Tarot card. It was so like Jenny, it was almost frightening.

*

Time and the concept of time remained Jenny's main obsession and school did little to encourage or explore such fascinatingly abstract ideas. She had conquered the concept of timelines. Man-made time was easy. It was the nagging question of when did the past become the past that sent her mind spinning out of control. If the future became now before it too became the past, when was now? Did it have time to exist or was it over before we realized it was here? Then there was the big question. Did the future ever change before becoming now, or was it fixed? Did it actually exist or was it an excuse to allow life to continue? Which led to the big question: was any time real or was it all man-made?

The Pote was the only one that would listen to her for any length of time when she tried to externalize these difficult theories. On this November day they were sitting on the solid, new walkway that ran round the new boathouse. The rain had stopped and to Jenny the smell of the wet leaves contained the whole of spring, summer and autumn. She picked out some of the brightest, the crimson maple and acid-yellow sycamore, and laid them on the decking. She carefully moved them in formation, using them to illustrate her theory to a dog whose interest was being diverted by a pair of mallards. She was about to demand his attention when a short, sharp laugh made her stop the seminar. Embarrassed at being caught talking to herself, she shuffled the leaves and began humming. When she looked up it was not after all her mother who met her gaze but the lady from the Fourth Room: the lady who was going to teach her to sing.

The first time the two of them had met was when Jenny was no more than a baby and had developed a dreadful fear of the dark. One night Harriet had listened long enough to the dreadful noises the child was making and had taken it upon herself to pacify her with a song. It had worked like a dream. The child fell asleep instantly and remained peaceful for the rest of the night. No one minded, in fact they seemed grateful, so Harriet had continued the practice until the child was no longer afraid of the night. Jenny had always been aware of this strange but kind person, although she did not know her name. She had never mentioned her to anyone else. It had not seemed relevant. The subject never came up for discussion so it had remained, albeit unintentionally, Jenny's secret.

The lady was tall and a lot older than Jenny's mother. She wore a distinctive dark cloak draped over her shoulders. It was not fashionable but suited her well. In her hand she carried an ebony walking-stick with a silver handle. She looked rather arty and reassuringly familiar as she smiled at Jenny from a respectable distance. She was imposing, her crown of thick white hair held back by an ivory comb. Her eyes were liquid amber and although she looked ancient to a nine-year-old, her hypnotic gaze shone with the eagerness of youth.

"Hello. I was eavesdropping. It's unforgivable, I know, but it's a hobby of mine. I hope you don't think that was rude of me?"

"I was only talking to my dog. Actually, I was talking to myself. It's a bad habit."

"But enjoyable. I do it all the time." The woman's voice was rich, quite deep and made you want to listen to her. "I like your dog. He's a dachshund, isn't he? While she spoke The Pote sat calmly wagging his tail and looking straight at her.

"This is The Pote. He really likes you. Normally he barks like crazy at strangers."

"That's a good name. The Potentate: the omnipotent ruler."

"How did you know that?" Jenny was astounded. Nobody had ever guessed that before.

"I often wonder about the concept of time myself," she said, ignoring the child's question.

"Cool. Most grown-ups think I'm a pain. I do go on a bit."

"One has to go on if one is to get anywhere," said the lady. "What is more, I think you've almost arrived."

"Have I? I'm still a bit muddled in here." Jenny pointed to her head and laughed.

The woman laughed with her. "Oh, I know that feeling only too well. But you are right. You were debating how long now lasts? I believe that now is all we have. Dream of it and it is yet to be; think about it and it is gone."

"It's the past!"

"Quite. So however fleeting life is we must live it, not waste it, and certainly never worry about the 'now' that is yet to come."

"That's the future!" Jenny liked the way this woman thought. "That's it exactly. Now is *now* and nothing else exists. I've got it," said Jenny. "It makes perfect sense. Time doesn't really exist. I knew it. Or, rather, I thought as much."

The lady got up and leaned against the wooden railing to stare out across the water. She began to sing. When she finished Jenny said, "That's from the *Wizard of Oz*, isn't it?"

"I miss having someone to sing with. My father used to sing with me when I was a lot younger than you are now." As the woman spoke, her face grew quite lovely and it was at that moment that Jenny recognized her as the little girl in the photograph.

"Will you really teach me?" Jenny asked.

"You're a twin, aren't you? I had a twin brother but he died." She gestured for Jenny to join her and showed her how to stand tall and how to breathe, filling her lungs with air before turning it into sound. They spent the next hour standing tall and looking out over the lake singing together; the dark contralto weaving around the thin untrained soprano. Their voices carried across the water, across the lawn to the house, stirring distant warming memories as the sound soaked into the stone fabric of the old building.

Suddenly the lady turned to Jenny. "I have to go now. It's time for my nap. We shall meet again soon," she said. "Tell your mother I love the room and the boathouse."

"My name is…."

"Jenny. Yes, I know. Goodbye. Come along, Pote."

The little dog abandoned Jenny and waddled off behind the black cloak. She watched them cross the lawn, the dog's dwarf legs trying to keep up with Harriet's enormous strides. Jenny checked her watch. At precisely five o'clock the two of them settled in the small armchair by the inglenook of the Fourth Room, where they slept for exactly fifteen minutes.

*

After that first singing lesson Jenny and Harriet met regularly down by the boathouse. Unlike most adults Jenny had met, her new friend never dismissed ideas simply because they came from a child. They met on the same level. She told her pupil that to have lived longer was no guarantee of superior wisdom; and any knowledge was worthless unless applied with prudence and understanding. This was exactly the teacher Jenny had been waiting for. Their relationship was alive with the promise of things to come. Singing was the icing on an already rich cake.

Jenny had always been able to hold a tune and had the gift of perfect pitch. Her voice was high and pure and called out for the discipline of a good teacher. Harriet was just such a teacher. She worked her pupil hard, and Jenny rose to the challenge. She loved singing and the more proficient she became the more she realized it was in her destiny to sing. Harriet knew this too. Those rare qualities she had possessed in her own voice were here in Jenny's. With the right training and guidance she could reach the pinnacle of success. Already she poured her heart and soul into everything she sang, giving her voice a spiritual dimension that sets great singers apart from merely good ones. Her own career had not been meant to happen, but this young woman would not be thwarted in the same cruel way. It was not jealousy and not a desire to live her unfulfilled life through another that motivated Harriet. No, this young girl was linked to Harriet's destiny, and the part she was to play in it was every bit as important to her as her own life.

Jenny had never thought about fate. There was only the excitement of learning to sing. She was also delighted to have found a friend who not only knew much more than her, but was happy to discuss those profound puzzling questions that everyone else dismissed as irrelevant or tedious. So, later that same month, when Jenny sat on the jetty in her duffel coat kicking her heels against the post, she hoped her friend would join her as she had an important matter to discuss. As she swung her legs she began to sing, her feet beating time to her song as they skimmed above the high November waterline.

"If happy little bluebirds fly..."

"Beyond the rainbow..." Harriet joined in,

"Why, oh, why, can't I?" they finished in unison. The lady looked at the eager little face in front of her. The Jessop twins were both beautiful, but this one was special.

"I think today you are in search of answers rather than tuition."

How did this woman always know just what to say? This lady never chastised Jenny for asking too many questions. Her mother did, and her teachers often ignored her because she shot her hand up so often, desperately in need of an answer. They all accused her of asking too many questions. But this lady understood that she needed the answers so as to move on to examine the next intriguing question. Jenny knew the questions instinctively yet although her vocabulary was remarkable for a child her age it was often too hard to put the thoughts into words. With Harriet there was no need. This remarkable woman, tall and quiet, leaning against her cane, her long, black cloak falling almost to the ground, simply read her mind. Words, although delicious, were not essential between them. But in this instance it was words that Jenny wanted to discuss:

"I've been trying to establish the difference between transparent and invisible."

"Ah. Let's see. Transparent comes from the Latin *transparere*. It literally means 'shining through'; so light can shine through and let you see what is behind it."

The lady spoke so clearly, she made it seem obvious. "Like glass and water?"

"Invisible, that's also from the Latin: *invisibilis*. It means not visible, which just means we cannot see it."

"Like air?" asked Jenny tentatively.

"It cannot be seen. But that pre-supposes it is really there. "

"Unlike something imaginary?" Jenny was not yet satisfied. "I have a friend at school with an imaginary friend. Mummy says she's imaginary and only exists in my friend's head, but I think she's actually there but no one else can see her. Doesn't that make her invisible but real?"

"We'll sing now," was all Harriet said.

Jenny took her coat off and straightened her sweater, taking care to remember what she had been taught about stance and breathing.

"Reality is relative; like time. Are you really here? Am I here? Who is to say we are? But who is to say we are not? We are certainly having a conversation so I would see that as a pretty good indication that we are both real to one another. Wouldn't you?"

"Absolutely!" exclaimed Jenny. "Can I ask you one more thing? Am I transparent?"

"Remember your breathing. I'm going to teach you a French song."

With that, the lesson began. When it ended the teacher looked at Jenny and smiled. "Your mother is right. The light shines through you. You are a jewel."

Jenny smiled back. "I like your hair; it's like thick snow. I've got my father's hair but grandpa Jessop had invisible hair on top when he died. Do you look like your mother or father?"

"Practise your breathing. That music is by Fauré and is not easy."

"You never actually answer a question, do you?"

"When you sing it must come from the top of your head and through the eyes. That is where the true voice lives, not in the throat. That simply holds the mechanical parts. Listen to me, Jenny, it isn't until you know the pain of loss that you will really be able to sing. A great singer learns to use their pain. You, my little one, are destined to be a great singer one day."

"I want to learn everything you know," Jenny said.

"When you get as old as me you will realize that all we ever know is the depth of our ignorance." And she was gone.

*

Jenny thought hard about what had just been said. She wanted more than anything to be a truly great singer. Was her voice good enough, and what was all that stuff about pain? Was something awful about to happen? She sat on the jetty dangling her legs, humming the Canticle to Jean Racine, which she was trying to memorize. The melody pulled at her insides until they hurt. Was that the pain her friend had been talking about, the pain of beautiful things? Jenny had already learnt that great music, fine paintings and especially nature could reduce her to tears. The common denominator she could recognize was love. But surely love should make you happy. In *The Lives of the Saints*, which her Aunty Brenda had given her for Christmas, all the saints had experienced a state of "ecstasy". The dictionary described that as a state of supreme happiness; but it was always associated with agonizing torments, visions, or even death, which did not match her concept of being happy. Since she had given up the thought of being a vet she had been toying with the idea of becoming a saint, but suddenly it did not seem such a good idea. She abandoned all thoughts of ecstasy and set her sights a bit lower. She would be an opera singer of world renown: happy rather than ecstatic. Content to have reached such a satisfactory solution, she performed a near-perfect somersault and skipped back across the bridge to the house.

CHAPTER 12

2007 was meant to be an auspicious year. Edward would hit forty in March and the twins would make double figures in May. It was destined to be a year of celebrations. Edward was the first to display any doubts. His family and friends seemed to think it amusing that he was about to reach "a sensible age". He was not quite so amused. He joked about it and expected to receive the odd walking-stick or Zimmer frame as presents, along with some incontinence pants and a few Viagra pills. But his laugh was growing thin, like his hair; he dreaded the changes that the passing years would bring. Was it time to take stock and settle down to a quieter life with a little less cricket and a little more gardening? Time to take up bird-watching, perhaps, or learn to play bridge?

These doubts and fears had not gone unnoticed by Liz. Edward looked tired and drained. He was snappy and touchy with the children and she found herself treading on eggshells whenever they were alone. At first she put it down to stress of work. His working hours seemed to be getting longer all the time. Sometimes he stayed in London at a friend's flat to save himself the journey from Kent to the birdcage, as he called Canary Wharf. Liz felt sorry for him but she hated those empty nights when he was away. The gulf between them was growing and was in danger of becoming wider than the distance between Beckmans and London. She was worried that a heart attack was never far away and she wished there was someone he would talk to. She decided to ask David if he could find out what was going on. Maybe at the next rugby match he could do a bit of casual detective work. David agreed to do some digging, but in truth Liz knew it was pointless. For all his bravado Edward was a very private man who seldom shared his inner-most thoughts. He never discussed his work except to brag about his mega-deals. If things were going wrong there was no way he would let on. He had always loved his job, thriving on the stress and the challenge. The financial world was in crisis, but that was exactly what he thrived on most. Liz knew better than to question him. He would never tell her anything anyway, certainly not if things got really bad. She would be the last to know. So when night after night he ate dinner in comparative silence before disappearing into his study, and the level in the scotch decanter fell at an alarming rate, she bit her tongue rather than have her head bitten off.

This sorry state of affairs came to a head at Christmas: that fixed star in the heavens was shaken badly when Sue and David announced they would not be coming to Beckmans this year; or any other year. They were divorcing. David was going to France to write his novel and Sue was off to the West Country to live with her newly married daughter, the indomitable Emily. They were all devastated. Edward took it particularly badly. He was secretly furious that his best mate had not confided in him. How dare he leave him in the lurch just when he needed a friend? Who would he play cricket with now? Like a wounded animal he lashed out. Instead of sympathizing with David he was cruelly flippant. He accused him of pursuing infantile fantasies and dared him to return without a bloody bestseller. He challenged him to lavish the proceeds of it around as a token repayment for all the times they had accepted his generosity. He upset the whole crowd by declaring that the only recognition David would get was an OBE for sticking it out with such a miserably dull wife for so long and that Emily was as stupid as her mother for even thinking they could survive more than a week of each other's boring company. These remarks were dismissed as bad jokes or possibly drunken slips, but they seriously wounded his friendship with David and Sue, and shocked the rest of the group with their callousness.

Bad moods were catching. An epidemic of tetchiness was in the air and Edward did not curb his barbed tongue throughout the rest of the festivities. The season of good will was tested to its limits. Normally Mel would have shrugged off Edward's rudeness with a cutting but witty quip or two and contained the whole thing before it bubbled out of control. But recently she had not been her usual self. She was edgy and impatient with everyone. Even phlegmatic Bob did not escape the sharp end of her tongue when, more than once, she lashed out at him. Her usual go-with-the-flow attitude had gone and it took only the slightest thing to send her into a temper. Edward rose to the bait and they sparked each other off throughout the holiday. As Edward was carving the turkey, he started on again about how selfish and excruciatingly dull Sue had always been, and Mel exploded. For a while it was touch and go, with Edward brandishing the carving knife and Mel goading him across the table; but miraculously common sense prevailed. The Circus survived Christmas, more secure though smaller, having aired several unpleasant truths.

*

The survival of the Circus was one thing; Liz and Edward were another. They were anything but secure in their relationship. Edward was spending more and more time at work. He left early in the morning and arrived back later and later at night. Often he stayed in town. When Liz accused him of caring more about work than family the rows began in earnest. He had been experiencing a new game-play in his wonderful world of finance. This once-benign territory had grown dangerously unpredictable. Signs that had used to be legible to him were suddenly hard to read. Investors were unsure whom to trust and had begun to flee the market altogether. He had never been afraid of competition, but he was now living through a famine where every scrap of food was fought over; you secured it or went under. His own investments were shrinking rapidly and for once his bonus was a mere drop in the proverbial rather than the tsunami of excess to which he had become accustomed. He had not shared any of this before because he did not want anyone to accuse him of failure. Being a natural optimist he believed it to be just a blip, a short down-turn of fortune. The market, in which he had total faith, would right itself given time. That market forces fluctuate was the fun of the game. One had to keep one's head until they bottomed out and let supply-and-demand sort it. Market economy would flourish once more.

At least they owned their house. Yes, property prices were falling dramatically but, as they had no intention of selling, that had little effect on their lives. Some prudent management and they would not even notice this dip in circumstances. However, things were not improving as quickly as he had planned. All the money he had put aside was in the form of stocks and shares and was hardly worth the paper it was written on. To sell now would be crazy. They had to ride out the storm and hope for the best. But it was his job. He should have seen it coming. He was beginning to hate his job; it was making more and more demands on him, and his hair was receding at an alarming rate.

Edward stared at the man staring back at him from the bathroom mirror. It was his father. He checked his teeth. Not bad: a few crowns and a small bridge - pretty lucky after all those years of rugby. *Should I invest in veneers?*, he wondered. Placing his hands against his jaw he pulled the skin back towards his ears. *Maybe a small nip-and-tuck?* His hands slid to his hairline. He could get something to cover the grey, *but what do I do about this?* His fingers teased his hair back over his receding hairline. His father had gone bald at fifty; did the same fate await him? He turned his body sideways and breathed in. "Not bad," he said aloud. He flexed his bicep and pulled a manly pose. Putting his face close to the mirror he caught the reflection of his wife's eyes smiling back at him. "God, Liz. I look just like my dad," he uttered despairingly.

"So what's wrong with that? I liked your dad," she said.

That flippant remark cut like a knife. Edward was used to being the best-looking guy in the room. Women always flirted with him and he flirted back, but that was about as far as it went. He had never actually been unfaithful, but had on occasions come close to the odd dalliance. Now a young woman who had just joined the firm was giving him signals that she wanted to get involved. He had played along with her, enjoying the game, and had even wondered what would happen if he had a fling. In his imaginings he was already being unfaithful, but he did not realize how short the distance was to the real thing. The next day at work he took that fatal step.

Now he had real guilt to contend with and he began to twist the truth to fit his newly-acquired perspective. Edward had little or no perception of how Liz viewed the world. He worked all the days God gave him and he worked hard. The money he earned was generously spent to keep his wife and family in luxury. She had a cleaner, a woman to do the ironing, a full-time gardener, a plastic card for the house and a platinum card for her personal indulgences. What more could any woman want? It was true that until this latest deal was completed he would have to work very late and maybe give up some Saturdays too, which meant giving up his sport. For the life of him he did not understand why Liz was incapable of recognizing the sacrifices he made for her. A couple more bonuses, even as feeble as the last one, would secure the children's schooling at whatever establishments they chose. It would even cover a large chunk of their university fees. Surely that was worth forgoing a few dinners at a posh restaurant. Most sensible women would recognize that all this luxury could stop as quickly as it had started. The financial climate was decidedly sticky and in the City there was talk of a general slump, even a depression. This was no time to take things easy. Was it too much to expect some gratitude, some appreciation for the effort he was making? So what if he took a little something for himself? Who wouldn't? And, if that something meant a bit on the side, so what? He viewed his indulgence in a little extra-marital fling as harmless and forgivable, even inevitable, in the circumstances. He was still a young man with appetites. His work was placing more and more demands on him and he was exhausted. What he wanted was a woman who supported him, not one that nagged all the time. But instead of gratitude or sympathetic understanding Liz was deliberately creating this awful chasm, separating them both physically and emotionally.

When Liz accused him of caring more about his work than his family, the rows began again, in earnest. When a woman reaches her mid-thirties life revolving around a house, a garden, young children and a dog can be claustrophobic and stifling; the beginning of the end; a sentence of repetitive service. If seen as a constant round of drudgery and sacrifice any resentment it might foster could, understandably, be justified. If survival depends on such sacrifice then the hard balancing act of keeping the wolf from the door becomes a worthy struggle, bringing a sense of pride and achievement with it. But a woman who feels trapped in domestic servitude, for no obvious reason, can become angry and resentful. To exist solely as the means of supporting a husband's career is both demeaning and demoralizing, and this was where Liz now perceived herself to be. She felt dispensable and undervalued. Her life of domestic responsibilities, punctuated by coffee mornings and lunches, bored her rigid. So she took her resentment out on Edward. His immediate reaction was to match aggression with aggression.

His attitude to David and Sue at Christmas had frightened her. Was it shock and disappointment that made him let rip like that? Or did he harbour a secret callous streak? If so he had certainly hidden it well. What if his true feelings for her were equally well disguised? There was no longer any passion and neither party seemed eager to rekindle it. She was letting herself grow cold towards him and he did nothing to reverse the trend. Edward had never forgotten a birthday and his gifts were always generous to a fault. She began to wonder if they were a little too generous. Did they hide a guilty secret? Take those earrings he had given her for Christmas, they must have cost a small fortune but jewellery was an easy gift. Had his PA chosen them? They had not given her a feeling of being cherished. Nor did they elicit the hoped for response. Liz had thanked him, acknowledged that they were beautiful but that was that.

She began to check his mobile and go through his pockets. She fostered wild thoughts of turning up at his office unannounced and checking the hours he had actually been working. An affair would explain all those late nights and the odd weekends when he had stopped over in town. Expensive gifts could be a way to salve a troubled conscience. Their love-making had ground to a virtual halt; when they had sex it was a hurried affair that left Liz wet and resentful. Surely these were classic signs of infidelity? She began to reject his advances, making excuses, sometimes out of spite, but mostly to avoid the hurt she felt when he rolled off her and fell into a deep satisfied coma, leaving her to angry tears as she washed herself between her legs and sat sleepless on the side of the bath, wondering: "Is this it?" Liz and Edward were on a collision course. One of them would have to give way, but they were both being equally stubborn.

When the phone rang and Edward explained he would not be home that night, Liz was prepared for outright war. Just as she was about to let rip, a sudden pain gripped her arm, forcing her to drop the phone and send it crashing to the floor with a resounding bang. As she cradled her arm she could hear Edward calling to her from the floor.

"Liz, what's happened? Are you all right?" She bent to pick up the phone. Her eyes filled with tears and she fumbled with the wretched machine, almost dropping it again.

Harriet was stroking her arm where she had pinched it, trying to calm Liz down before she said something she might regret. "Sorry, Liz. I didn't mean to hurt you. I just wanted to stop you doing anything rash. Give him the benefit of the doubt." She was pleading for clemency thinking of the innocent children and hating herself for defending such a man.

Edward was in bed with the beautiful Sophie when he heard the crash, followed by a long silence. "What's happened? God, Liz, speak to me!" His concern was genuine and as guilt swept over him so remorse flooded over her. She gathered herself and the telephone together. His voice was telling her he was coming home, now, immediately. She must not worry, he would be home soon. He was panicking and scared.

"Sorry. I dropped the phone." Her words were cool and distant and as soon as she said them the magic melted.

"Christ, Liz, I thought you'd died or something. I didn't know you could be so cruel. How long does it take to pick up an effing telephone? Anyway, in case you're bothered I shan't be home tonight so don't wait up. Not that you ever do. Say goodnight to the kids." He hung up abruptly, leaving Liz feeling as if she too had been hung on a hook.

Liz stood in the hall, speechless and seething with anger. She inspected her arm; although sore it seemed perfectly all right. As she straightened up, her eyes fell on the very first painting she had done. It was of the boathouse. She remembered how she had felt on first seeing this house. Now it was her home. She remembered Edward's immediate reaction to the house. He had hated it. Yet he had not tried to talk her out of it. He had simply bought it and given it to her with his love. Where had that love gone? Harriet's heart wept for Liz but all she could do was suggest they have a nice cup of tea.

*

What neither Harriet nor Edward knew was that Liz had been gathering evidence. She had been sorting his jackets for the dry cleaners when she found exactly what she was hoping not to find. It was a receipt for a diamond pendant on a gold chain. Liz already had one of a considerably superior quality. She therefore deduced that this trinket was not meant for her. There were no credit-card accounts to be found anywhere in his study, which was in itself suspicious. Edward was not the tidiest or most organized of men so their absence suggested a deliberate act of concealment. Feeling horribly devious, she phoned the number on the receipt. Posing as Mr Jessop's personal assistant she apologized for the inconvenience, but explained that she had lost the originals and would be grateful if they could send her copies to cover the last six months.

The next day several incriminating documents arrived. She was mortified. Edward was either an extremely generous boss or he had another woman. That evening she waited nervously for him to come home. She had thought hard and long about her approach and had decided to play it cool, to give him the benefit of the doubt and let him explain what was really going on. In fact she had already tried him, found him guilty and wanted to watch him wriggle on the hook and see how he liked it. The moment he closed the door behind him Liz pounced.

"I know, Edward." She aimed the words like daggers.

Edward held his arms wide as he raised his shoulders in a gesture of blamelessness. "Know what?"

"About your affair," Liz spat out the bitter-tasting words.

Edward laughed a bit too loudly. He put down his briefcase, hoping he appeared calm, an innocent victim. He needed to turn the argument to his advantage before it went any further.

"Can I get through the door first? Can I pour myself a drink? Do you want one? Oh, I see you're ahead of me there." He threw his jacket on the back of the chair, poured a large Scotch and sat down heavily at the table. There was no sign of dinner and the atmosphere was hostile.

"So where is all this coming from? I have no idea what you are on about."

"I know you are screwing someone else."

"Come off it, sweetheart, when do I have time to have an affair? I'm working my effing balls off!" As he said it he knew this was not the best approach.

"Oh, I know!" Liz replied with a coldness of tone he had never heard before. "Who is she, this ball-breaking tart? Anyone I know? Should I put her on my Christmas card list, or is she already on it? Now there's a thought."

It was too late for tactics; the slanging match was on. For an hour they slogged it out, playing a rapid point-scoring, hard-hitting tournament of emotional squash. She called him an ageing Lothario; an absentee parent who cared more about cricket than his children. What sort of father didn't even know his children's favourite food, or which books and films they like best? Liz was accused of being a parasite, contributing nothing while living a dilettante lifestyle, watching him wear himself out in the cut-and-thrust of the financial world. He called her empty-headed with no idea how tough it was to earn the sort of money he brought home. She retaliated that he had not a clue how much effort it took to manage and maintain a house of this size to the standards he demanded, raising two small children into the bargain, children he did not deserve.

Edward had been leaning back, balancing his chair on its back legs, his arms behind his head, trying to appear calm and in control, an infuriatingly smug smile on his face throughout the row while Liz had been pacing up and down, opening and slamming drawers with frustration. Suddenly, he sprang up. His chair crashed forwards as he slammed his fist on the table. "Right, that's it," he shouted, then quietly he added: "I'm going to bed. We shall discuss this tomorrow, when your hormones aren't so rampantly out of control."

While he spoke Liz was rummaging in her bag trying to find the evidence. Triumphantly she threw the receipt on the table in front of him. She even smoothed it out for him to read. Then she screamed at him, "Hormones! I'll give you hormones - a thousand pounds' worth of bloody hormones." She stood up tall as Edward sank back in his chair. His mind was racing. How the hell had she got hold of this? His face wore a mask of innocence as he spoke:

"Is this what all this has been about?" He waved his arm as he looked around indicating the row that was still hovering in the room. He moved towards Liz, the receipt in his hand. She backed away. "This was meant to be a surprise," he said, waving the paper in her face.

"Oh, it was that all right!" Liz was seething. Let him try and talk his way out of this one.

"In case it has slipped your mind, there is a certain day coming up - sometime in February - the fourteenth, I think? Correct me if I'm wrong, but isn't that Valentine's day?" He paused. "Ring any bells yet? It's something to do with love…" He looked horribly smug and his voice had an ugly sound to it. "I stupidly thought it might be nice to buy something special for my wife - my beautiful, tolerant wife - as a small thank-you for being so understanding. But if you don't want it," he looked at Liz in a supercilious, patronizing way, waiting for her to capitulate.

Icily Liz snatched back the receipt and placed it in her bag. She looked hard at Edward. She wanted to believe him but could not. He had hurt her; the things he had said had been so cruel. They had both said things that could never be unsaid. Words had crashed into the very walls of the house, to stay there as lasting stains and scars. Her brain was spinning and she felt her body ache from tension. It was way past midnight. She needed sleep; time to re-focus. Realizing the danger of saying more while she was so angry she simply said,

"You're right. I am over-tired. I need to sleep. It's best left until morning. Tomorrow is another day and we have the whole weekend to discuss this." As she left the room she looked over her shoulder to where her husband was sitting and added: "You'll find sheets for the green room in the airing cupboard. Try not to leave it in a mess. Oh, the other receipts are on the sideboard. I look forward to hearing how you explain those. Good night."

It hung in the night air, unresolved and threatening. Liz hardly slept. She tried to imagine always lying in a bed with a duvet to herself and an empty space beside her. The thought filled her with horror. She had started something that had to be seen through, and it tasted bitter.

CHAPTER 13

It was with considerable resentment that Liz found herself planning Edward's fortieth birthday celebrations. No one really wanted to come to the party except the twins. Even the sun declined the offer. All morning it rained and it rained even harder all afternoon. The guests arrived at seven, damp and unenthusiastic. It was a small affair: the remnants of the Circus, a few mates from Edward's office and the next-door neighbours. The dreadful weather cast a dark cloud over an already gloomy occasion. Liz supplied a splendid buffet and the wine flowed freely, but the mix of people was not quite right for the party to gel. The children sensed the brittle atmosphere and wisely took themselves off to the attic as soon as they could. In fact after the meal everyone split, some to watch a video and some to play cards. Mel agreed to give a Tarot reading to Liz's neighbour and was settling herself opposite the rather large woman at the occasional table between the two long windows facing the lake. Her heart was not in the cards and she looked around for inspiration. Desperate to focus her drifting thoughts, she found herself gazing at the window, tracing the patterns of the raindrops that ran down the glass. When she looked through the glass she caught sight of a couple heading across the lawn.

It was Edward with another woman. Mel scanned the room. There was one noticeable absence in the shapely form of Edward's personal assistant. It was her struggling across the wet grass in four-inch heels, balancing a large golf umbrella. In spite of the heavy rain the couple were heading down the garden towards the bridge. Sophie, the sexy PA, had appeared for the first time that evening and Mel's psychic antenna had picked up danger signals. There was an insincere niceness about the creature, something unhealthy about the way she looked at Edward; she seldom took her eyes off him, which did little to allay Mel's suspicious thoughts. Mel's concentration was broken, having been diverted by shadowy figures outside. Making an excuse to the neighbour, she checked the room to establish Liz's whereabouts and was relieved to find her engrossed in a game of poker and likely to be occupied for some time.

Mel slipped on Liz's gumboots and grabbed a Barbour from the back door. Making sure she was not being watched, she followed the escapees. They had covered the last few yards in record time and were already at the door of the boathouse as Mel positioned herself behind the willow. They were holding hands and giggling and presumably kissing behind the brolly. The girl slipped inside. Edward cast a furtive eye around, followed her and closed the door. It was straight out of a Noel Coward play and Mel was not sure whether to laugh or puke. Instead she crossed the bridge and crept to the far side of the building.

The only light came from the moon and a few timid solar lamps scattered around the jetty. She welcomed the cover of the deep shadow. The sight that greeted her as she peered in through the window was predictable. The couple were embracing passionately. There was no doubt that this was not the first time those lips had met and there was every sign that they knew exactly where their actions were heading. As she had no wish to play the voyeur and had already seen far more than she wanted to she tried to devise a possible plan of action. Determined to spoil their fun, she was assessing her best means of attack when she inadvertently collided with an extremely large terracotta pot. Instinct made her grab the main stem of the camellia it contained and she managed to steady it, before restoring it to its secure resting place on the decking, miraculously preventing the almighty crash that would surely have given her away. She wanted to catch them in the act. She intended to shame them. Inevitably the lovers were too preoccupied with one another to notice the muffled sounds outside.

Mel patted the shaken plant and steadied herself, patting her own trembling legs. It was then that she caught sight of Jenny running from the house towards the stream. There was no mistaking those long athletic legs that were carrying her with increasing speed towards the scene of the crime. Mel had to act quickly. Her brain was racing unproductively when she heard Liz's voice calling to her daughter. The voice came from the house and as quickly as she had appeared Jenny stopped, turned and ran back. Mel sent up a prayer of thanks to her guardian angel. Another second and the poor child would have witnessed the whole sordid thing. The idea of bursting in on Edward and his "bit of stuff" was one thing, but she had no wish to involve Jenny. Time was short. Direct action was needed before the culprits could prepare their defence. Throwing open the door of the boathouse, she walked calmly over to the table and picked up a book that was lying there. She turned, said good evening to the somewhat dishevelled couple and simply walked out, taking care to leave the door wide open behind her.

Later, out of earshot of Liz or the others, Edward accosted Mel. "It isn't what you think. It's all perfectly innocent. For Christ sake, don't tell Liz. Can we keep this between the two of us? Please, Mel, I'm begging you. I really love Liz. It would destroy her. You know that. Please don't tell her." Mel's look was enough to let Edward know what she thought of him. She was tempted to keep him dangling, let him suffer.

Eventually she said, "You pathetic bastard, of course I won't tell her. But if you ever hurt Liz or those kids I'll kill you."

"OK. Message received." As he spoke Edward doubled over, clutching his stomach.

Harriet could no longer restrain herself. She punched him hard in the solar plexus and felt much better for it. She had of course played her own part in the drama. She knew that Jenny's book was in the boathouse and that at some point she would want to retrieve it. She too had seen the guilty couple slip away in the dark and she was determined to put an end to any shenanigans that could jeopardize her family's happiness. She had been racking her brains to find a way to expose the couple, but everything she came up with involved the rest of the guests or the family finding out. She did not want to see Liz humiliated and especially did not want to confront Jenny with her father's infidelity. It was that stupid woman tripping over the pot that gave Harriet the idea. She had called Jenny back to the house. As for that psychic, she had proved herself quite useful after all. Maybe she was not all bad. Harriet decided to reserve judgment.

The confrontation between Mel and Edward was cut short by Jenny grabbing Mel around the waist. "Oh, great, you found my book. Where was it? I searched everywhere."

"It was in the boathouse." Mel was drying her hair on the kitchen towel and praying that Jenny had not over heard her conversation with Edward.

"I knew that's where I'd left it. I ran all the way down there in the rain, but Mummy called me back, saying she'd got it, then a few minutes later denied all knowledge of it. Can you believe that? She's getting old, you know. How old do you have to be to get Alzheimer's? Are you all right, Dad? You look as if someone punched you in the guts!"

Jenny gave Mel a kiss and took the book from her. Mel stood for a while watching the girl attack the stairs two at a time. She was growing up fast, turning into an amazing young woman. Jenny paused on the landing to smile back and Mel saw her as a grown woman, centre-stage surrounded by thunderous applause, a standing ovation. It was La Scala, The Met, Covent Garden.... Mel's vision ended abruptly, stopped by someone patting her on the back. When she turned around the hall was empty. *Maybe she is a bit psychic after all*, thought Harriet,

The party was over and the last of the guests had gone. The final dregs of clearing up were almost done. Throwing her tea towel onto the draining-board Liz looked at her husband in the stainless-steely light of the kitchen. His once luxurious brown hair was greying at the temples. It was noticeably thinner and had begun to recede. Liz studied the face. Tell-tale signs of crow's feet where his blue eyes had narrowed against the sun were already quite pronounced. He looked tired and strained. She could have got it horribly wrong. She did tend to jump to conclusions. There was so much at stake here. Would it be so difficult to draw a line under it all and chalk it up to mid-life crisis? As soon as she resolved to be magnanimous she felt a surge of relief, as though she were purged. Was this how saints felt when they forgave sinners? Things took on a different perspective for her, one that would let them move on together, which was what she wanted more than any of the other hideous alternatives.

This was the man she loved, whom she had vowed to spend her life standing beside, for better or worse. If this was the worst, it was not that bad. Was she greedy to want more? How could she have been so horrible to him? She kissed him and he pulled away. When he kissed her back it was just a peck.

"You made me jump. Sorry, Liz."

She wondered if he shared her thoughts. They were still capable of being happy, weren't they? Did he still love her?

"That was a lovely evening, wasn't it? There was a fantastic sunset, did you see it? Don't you love the way the sun goes to sleep each night? Mummy used to say it was so that he'd wake up refreshed and ready to fill tomorrow with sunshine."

"God, Liz, you do talk crap sometimes. It's just a star; a spectral-type G star, that's a yellow one, if you really want to know. It can't make decisions."

Liz sighed and took her own face in her hands. "I'm getting old, aren't I?"

"You look stunning. You always do."

"Let's go to bed. Whisk me away from all this and have your wicked way with me." Liz tilted her head and looked sideways at Edward. She was flirting shamelessly and actually enjoying it. She felt young and, yes, stunning. Why not? That was his word and it fitted.

"Not tonight, Liz, I'm knackered. Nice party, well done." He yawned, another noisy unromantic yawn, and throwing his sweater round his shoulders he made his way upstairs.

Liz stayed downstairs. She curled up in the armchair in the Fourth Room with The Pote on her lap and together they watched the dying embers until they grew cold. Miserable and dejected, she pulled herself up to go to bed. Seeing Jenny's sampler hanging on the bird-shaped hook Liz reached out to touch it. A tidal wave of emotions washed over her, sapping her strength as it dragged back taking her feet from under her. Steadying herself she moved to the centre of the room. The small black-and-white photograph filled her thoughts. Who had hidden it there? She knew it was connected to the little boat. "I will find out what happened, one day you will keep your promise and tell me everything you know." The Pote scuttled off, alarmed by his mistress's raised voice, and she followed him out, feeling guilty for upsetting him. It was hardly his fault that she felt so dreadful. As she locked the door behind her it was to keep something in rather than locking anyone out. She put the griffin key back on its secret ledge then marched back across the hall and on upstairs. Throwing her clothes on the floor she climbed noisily into bed, pulled the duvet off her snoring spouse and masturbated herself to sleep.

*

Desperate for a solution, Liz decided to consult Mel. Mel actually laughed in Liz's astonished face. Then she got extremely angry. She accused her friend of taking Edward for granted: of being a spoilt brat. Didn't she recognize a good husband when she saw one? If his behaviour was harming the family and the marriage it was certainly not intentional. Didn't she realize by now that men do not see the obvious? They go through life in blinkers and it is women who have to steer the course if they want to change direction. If Liz perceived a problem then it was up to her to tackle it. She should either confront him head-on or try a more subtle approach to win back his attention. It was her opinion that most men had affairs because they were feeling scared or trapped. Women attacked the same problem by becoming profligate with money, whereas men reverted to other more physically basic means. She did not believe Edward was having an affair, or at least so she told Liz. He might have been tempted, or even have dipped his toe in the water. But it was nothing that could not be reversed or forgiven. She acknowledged that he could be selfish and vain, but basically he was a committed family man. A few over-generous and misplaced gifts did not constitute grounds for divorce. No, Mel sounded convinced that the problem was mostly of Liz's doing and therefore the solution must be hers too. Anyway it was always the woman's job to put things right. Men were so pathetically hopeless at saying sorry.

When Mel had finished her onslaught Liz was cross and hurt. She felt betrayed. This was not the first time Mel had hurt her. She had been expecting a sympathetic, girly chat, not an unwarranted full-on attack. For some reason Mel was taking Edward's side. As Mel left there was a tangible hostility between the two women. The hugs and kisses were absent from their parting and no future meeting was planned. Liz was desolate. Why could no one see her point of view? She had been more than generous, ignoring those blasted receipts. Letting Edward off the hook had not been easy. She spent the rest of the day banging doors shut and stomping up and down the stairs cursing. The feeling of betrayal filled her brain with vacuous thoughts, which, in turn, were creating voids for more invidious thoughts to seep in. Was Mel having an affair with Edward? Was she the other woman trying to cover her tracks by throwing Liz off the scent? Of course the thought was ludicrous. Or was it? Once sown, the seed began to germinate. There had always been an attraction between the two of them. Liz knew that Edward found Mel exotic and fascinating. What red-bloodied male wouldn't? It would explain a lot of things.

Liz's head swam with absurd, hateful, imagined horrors, then her stomach began to contract. A rush of hot liquid filled her mouth. She swallowed hard and felt the acid burn her throat as the liquid rose up again. Reaching the sink, she threw up. When the spasms finished she stood upright and breathed in. Her head began to clear and she left the cold tap running as she splashed her face with handfuls of the icy water, willing each fresh shock to wash her mind clean of the obscene thoughts that had possessed her. How could she have entertained such ridiculous ideas? Maybe Mel was right and she had grown into a spoilt bitch who expected life to be handed her on a plate, and only after all the rotten bits had been consumed by someone else.

After a long, hot bath with plenty of time to reflect, Liz had reached some conclusions. She agreed with Mel that she was a shallow creature who took without giving. Her life was full of blessings if only she could stop moaning long enough to count them. Edward was a fantastic husband; a good man who had made one silly forgivable mistake. He just needed a bit of pampering. Becoming forty was hard for him. She had to make him feel loved and special, not expect him always to be the giver. After all, one of her main talents was as a home-maker. That was one of the reasons Edward had fallen in love with her. It was nothing to be ashamed of. She should take pride in her ability to create a beautiful home. She was lucky enough to have been born with a wealth of talents and it was up to her to use them to the full. If she did not like what life was offering then it was her job to turn it around. Her just desserts could be very palatable, delicious even. But it was up to her to change. Even a spoilt, selfish bitch could change. By the time Liz went to bed she was washed clean of all bodily impurities and her soul felt cleansed and chaste. Apart from a distinct air of smugness, she was perfect.

*

The next day, in her manufactured state of bliss, Liz began taking things into her own hands. She had her hair restyled and her nails French polished. Silky underwear and nightwear by the car load took her platinum card to melting point. A pair of four inch Calvin Klein's and shiny stockings completed the new look. Having made sure that Edward would be home for the weekend and having secured a babysitting service she made a reservation for dinner and booked the Bridal Suite at the Hotel du Vin. Dressed in a new black velvet figure-hugging mini-dress with long pearl earrings and a discreet row of pearls at her neck, she surveyed herself in the mirror. She approved. Not too virginal, but not too tarty. She was ready to do battle and was determined to enjoy it. When her man arrived home, their bags were packed, ready and in the car. She was not taking no for an answer.

The strategy worked. They were young and falling in love all over again. Edward was attentive and charming. He flattered and flirted with her and the more attractive he found her, the more attractive she became. This was what she had missed, the feeling that she was the only woman in his world. The next morning as their eyes met over their breakfast orange juice she had a desperate urge to go home. By eleven they were back. Liz felt the house welcome them, as if it knew the separation was over. The house exuded warmth and love, as it always did if you let it. This was more than returning from a short break. This was significant. It was a homecoming. Harriet watched, sighed with relief, but she had by no means finished with Edward. Not yet.

*

Of course Mel had gone straight home and told Bob of her row with Liz, having already told him about the incident at the boathouse. She suggested that he should talk to Edward "man to man", and to keep her sweet he arranged to meet Edward for a pint the next Saturday. Assuming that Bob had a problem with cash-flow or something business-related, Edward was keen to prove that in spite of the general consensus he was a good listener. He knew it would get back to Liz via Mel, it always did and a few more Brownie points would not go amiss. Bob got the beers and carried them to a table in the corner rather than their preferred stools at the bar.

"OK, mate." Bob's voice did not sound like that of a man seeking advice. "What the fuck do you think you're playing at?"

Edward's jaw dropped. Bob rarely swore. His attitude meant business of a different kind from what Edward was expecting.

"I'm not with you, mate," he said.

"This bimbo, you know who I mean - is she worth it?" He waited for an answer.

"Are you accusing me of something? If so, spit it out, Bob." Edward's gaze met Bob's full-on without flinching.

"OK. Sophie. Does the name ring a bell? Wednesdays, Strand Palace Hotel; Mondays, Inn on the Park; cosy dinners for two in Magdalene's... Shall I go on?"

Edward pushed his beer away from him. He put his hand under the collar of his polo-neck sweater and eased it around his neck. He coughed a couple of times, clearing his throat. All the time his kept his eyes fixed on Bob. Neither man averted their gaze. Suddenly Edward's face twisted into a smirk, he looked away, took a long draught of beer and returned his gaze to Bob. But he knew he had lost the battle.

"OK, so I've been having some fun. Christ almighty, man, I'm forty. Don't tell me you've never had a bit on the side? I'll bet..."

"No, I bloody haven't," Bob butted in, "and I'm not interested in the sordid details. This is the only time I'll mention it - her... whatever... but I'd be failing you and Liz if I didn't speak my mind. I've always considered you a decent guy. Don't throw it all away for a quick shag!"

Analysing emotions was unfamiliar territory for Edward. He felt abused by Bob, who he thought was behaving like an over-pious prick. However, beneath that thought lurked an unpleasant sickness in the pit of his stomach. His groin ached and he recognized the sensation from his childhood. It was the feeling of being caught out. He could see the reproving eyes of his headmaster and that snivelling, little sneak Brown; Brown's look of outright triumph when he, Jessop, the school captain, had been exposed as a thief. All he had done was borrow a pair of crummy rugby shorts from Brown's locker to cover for forgetting his own. It was having lied that got him the cane and lost him his captaincy. Edward swallowed hard.

"OK, maybe it was stupid. But that's just what it was: a quick shag. It meant nothing." Edward's lies were unconvincing even to himself.

"I'm not that interested. You're obviously going through some kind of mid-life crisis, I don't particularly care. I do, however, care about Liz and the kids. I won't judge you, but I will say my piece. Stop it now while it still means nothing. Recognize what you've got and count your blessings." He took a swig of beer, then clinked his glass against Edward's in a gesture of continuing friendship.

They drank together in silence until Bob added, almost as a postscript: "Oh, Mel says if Liz gets wind of this she'll cut your fucking balls off. OK?"

CHAPTER 14

Liz's feelings of elation did not last long. She was not depressed, yet she was definitely not happy. She considered herself to be a good wife and mother, but where was her own life going? Was the dissatisfaction she was now experiencing the price to pay for taking an easy ride as a passenger through life? When she married she became Mrs Jessop; she had laughed at the fact it was also her mother-in-law's name. What had happened to Elizabeth Prior? Where had her dreams gone? That young woman had aspired to so many things in life, but they had all been subsumed by stronger forces. She was not in control of her own life and began to think she never had been. Someone else always held the wheel or trimmed the sails. It was not so much a case of drifting aimlessly, more a feeling of being a companion traveller on someone else's voyage.

Her husband held the purse strings when it came to the mega decisions. Or did he? She had chosen Beckmans, and he never denied her anything, in the end. She played the major role in building their home. She had put some of her inheritance in the pot as well, but was well aware that did not count for much in the overall scheme of things. But then Edward earned phenomenal money. There was no way any career path she might have pursued would have come anywhere near that sort of financial reward. Just one of his many bonuses eclipsed her entire life's earnings, so giving up her job when the twins were born made sense.

But it was not a lack of monetary independence that niggled. It went deeper than that. It was more a question of identity. Was this a woman thing or just her? Sue had her teaching, Brenda had her nursing, neither of which paid particularly well but gave them a title. Mel had her "mystic Meg business", which was actually quite lucrative. Did she envy them? Sue had spent a large part of their friendship moaning about the difficulty of juggling motherhood with a demanding job. David was hardly a male chauvinist and they had always seemed to share out the routine tasks involved in parenting. She could not remember him ever getting involved in nest-building; he was no great DIY merchant or interior designer, but then neither was Sue. Their house was always regimentally tidy, but sterile and contrived, which while irritating Liz's sensibilities seemed to be what they wanted. As for Brenda and Donald, their lives were totally opposite to hers. They were content to be slipping into middle age; they willingly embraced the comfort of letting go. Brenda never coloured or restyled her hair, or went on a mad shopping spree or even splashed out on a new ironing board and Donald was so careful with money, he could have been the prototype for the stereotypically cautious Scot. They seemed content to lead rather boring, empty lives. But they did seem content. Mel and Bob led such different lives it was hard to compare them. Mel was always so out of control, in a controlled way. It was she that led Bob, not the other way around. She always claimed to be going with the flow but Liz watched her control the sluice gates with a frightening dexterity. Was that what she wanted for herself? Control? Yes, that was the itch that needed scratching.

The twins were at school and Edward was off making more money. Liz picked up her coffee, smiled at the slogan on the mug and made her way across the hall towards the Fourth Room. As she passed the staircase she noted one of the pictures was askew. Putting her mug on the curved bottom stair she reached up to straighten it. She chuckled as she thought of Sue's house, where everything stood to attention, far too terrified to step or slip out of place. Mel always called her anally retentive when she got so aerated about trivial details. In Brenda's house no painting had a line to step out of, though she could not remember seeing any paintings at Brenda's, apart from the one she had done for them last Christmas. She had presented them with a small watercolour of their house and had found it hard to paint such an unkempt garden without doing a little virtual pruning and mowing. She remembered feeling naughty when she had lopped off a branch or two, taking artistic licence to enhance the scene. As she adjusted her own picture back into alignment it began to dawn on her what it was that was bothering her.

The children had grown up to the point where they no longer needed her fussing around them twenty-four seven, a fact that they were not shy in repeatedly telling her. Edward had to be allowed his own space in order to manage his demanding work and hopefully keep him on the straight and narrow. That meant time out to pursue his sports and the odd visit to the pub with his mates. The house which had demanded so much of her time pretty well looked after itself, with the help of a cleaner. The garden was in Terry's capable hands and he now worked three days a week, which kept it looking well groomed. So what was her role? *Housekeeper, housewife, lady of leisure?* Surely she had not become one of those awful *"ladies that lunch"* or, worse, *a kept woman?* That was what Mel had called her. The title hurt but that was a simple case of wounded pride. It did not touch the real problem. The fact was, she was bored.

As her hands straightened the gilded frame, the answer became obvious. It was staring her in the face. She was holding it in her hands: her painting. Liz had been painting for several years now. It suited her temperament to have periods when she could be solitary and silent, with the added bonus of an end result that solicited praise. A local frame-maker helped her select the exact colour and size of mount to compliment her work, which now adorned the stairwell, spilling over to the corridor above. The walls of many of her dear friends also displayed an original Liz Jessop. Edward said they were taking over the world, but was secretly proud of his wife's achievements.

She would mount an exhibition of her work, nothing too grand – just enough to launch herself as a local artist. Surely she could get a few commissions and the frame-maker would, no doubt, be glad of the extra work. The objective was not to make loads of money, although that would be nice as an indicator of her work's worth. Nor was it to become famous, although that too would be fun. No, this was to establish her identity; to reclaim herself from the role of wife and mother and establish herself as a person in her own right. And it wouldn't hurt to show Mel that she still had it in her! Should she revert to her maiden name or would that be too obvious a statement? The realization that she had already signed her work with her married name came as a slight annoyance. She convinced herself that it really did not matter which name she used. It was not a name that decided who she was inside. There would be no more moaning or bleating about her empty life. From now on she would fill it. Mel had accused her of complacency and self-pity. Well, no more wallowing. These paintings would sell, everybody loved them and goodness knows she could well afford to mount an exhibition. She had enough contacts to fill a private viewing and drown the punters in vintage Champagne. Yes, as dear, mad Mel had so eloquently put it, she should get off her effing butt and do something.

Harriet had been listening to Liz's soliloquy with great excitement. It had occurred to her before now that Liz was wasting her talents merely producing the odd Christmas present or two. Her painting was becoming more and more accomplished and should be displayed where it would be appreciated by a wider public. She also craved the chance to bask in Liz's glory. All her life she had painted, and her paintings were good. But who had seen them? Now they were all destroyed or lost. Only that pathetic sampler remained to show her artistic talents. It had been crafted with love and had taken weeks of concentration, her poor little fingers pricked to pieces by needles that refused to behave. She could not think why she had not done a painting for her father. Then she remembered. Mama disapproved of paints. They were messy things and she would not allow them in the house. So, this was her chance too. She would paint through Liz and take revenge on her hateful Mama at the same time. What could be better than that?

Liz set to work immediately. She contacted several small galleries in Tunbridge Wells and one agreed to look at samples of her work. If they liked it and she was prepared to fund her own show they saw no reason why she should not mount an exhibition in the autumn. She had selected ten of her favourite pictures and reckoned she could produce a further ten before her show. She had started on the design for a catalogue and had some business cards printed. She had even drafted a letter of invitation to send to a few watercolour dealers informing them of the private viewing. Her greatest achievement to date was that she had managed to keep the whole thing a secret from everybody, apart from Jenny, who seemed to know everything that was going on without being told.

When Liz finally told Mel, the reaction she received was not what she hoped for nor expected. Mel was decidedly indifferent. Her usual wild enthusiasm was painfully absent. She was not against the idea, just not interested. Worse, she did not seem to care. Liz was baffled. The venture had been Mel's idea; at least it was Mel who had motivated her into action. Now she did not want to know. When Liz suggested that Mel should be in charge of the private view she was horrified to hear her friend announce that she would probably not be there. Liz was perplexed and mortified. She had not realized she had offended Mel so deeply, but each time she broached the subject Mel ducked out, barely offering an excuse.

Doubts began to rise once more as to Mel's relationship with Edward. Had the attack on her inadequacy been a cleverly concocted smoke screen behind which she had been taken for a complete fool? Liz had already choked on a large portion of humble pie. She was not ready for desserts just yet, but she knew that if she wanted to keep Mel's friendship she had to hold her tongue and let things be or bite the bullet and wait for the fireworks. There was no one to confide in. The one person she would have talked to was in the centre of the intrigue. Just as she was despairing, help came from an unexpected but close source.

Jenny had known about her mother's plans from the off. Harriet had been so excited that she had confided in the child. She had told her that her mother was going to need her support. Jenny proved amazingly expert when it came to choosing what went into the exhibition and what was needed to supplement the existing work. She identified the prospective market, and James then researched into the estimated price her paintings could hope to achieve. Their combined resourcefulness left Liz speechless. Nothing was beyond their grasp. As James explained, it was only a mouse's click away. While she had been busy dealing with her own problems these incredible youngsters were growing into fully functioning people with skills and talents she had not dreamed they possessed. They were also caring people who were interested in her as a person. They did not see her as just a mother; someone who washed their clothes and put food in their stomachs. When she attempted to express this pride to them, James knocked the whole thing into perspective by exclaiming that he never realized anyone actually washed his clothes. He had put it down to the soap Fairy. It was not until Jenny pointed out that James had never heard of Fairy as a washing product that Liz realized he was not being intentionally witty. He really had never considered laundry before. It simply did not feature on his agenda. There was so much she had to find out about her twins and so much for them to discover about her. She felt lucky to have been given such a fabulous chance to get to know them, but she could not help wishing Mel was sharing it too. She was missing her friend badly.

*

By mid-March Mel looked positively ill. "It's cancer." She said it without ceremony or drama. The two women were drinking coffee in the breakfast-room. Liz had managed to persuade Mel to spend some time with her. They had planned to grab some lunch out in Tunbridge Wells when Mel announced she would prefer a quiet lunch at Beckmans. Cancer! The word hit Liz in the pit of her stomach. Her coffee cup spilled over, covering the table top with a dark brown slick that dripped on to the floor. The Pote rushed to lap it up, but retreated as the hot bitter coffee burned his tongue. Questions churned through Liz's brain, turning it to mush. Where? What sort? And, worst of all, how long? They all sounded so negative and she must be positive.

"Are they sure?"

"Yes, I'm afraid so." Mel had got up and was wiping the table and floor with liberal amounts of kitchen paper. She tossed the soggy mess in the bin and picked up the peeved dog. He lay in her arms like a baby, flat on his back shamelessly displaying those precious private bits he had retained. His tongue reached out to lick Mel's hands and she buried her nose in his warm coat. "I've been having tests since November," she said.

"You knew all over Christmas! Why on earth didn't you tell me?" Liz was hurt.

"Because first there was all that business with David and Sue, then there was my unholy row with the sacred

Brenda. Then what with the damned recession and Bob's business taking a nose-dive, well... and actually this was to do with me, not you." Mel was rocking the dog as if it were a sleeping child. She nuzzled his fur again. "I love that biscuity smell. It's like toast. Poor old Pote, he must be getting on now. Sometimes I wish I'd had a baby."

"He's nearly ten, but I wish you'd told me sooner. I'm your friend Mel."

"I know. But I had to deal with this. I didn't want to confuse things by having to deal with other people's reactions too. It's been hard enough coping with my own."

"I'm not 'other people'. I'm me." Liz's hurt came through loud and clear.

"That's exactly what I mean. This is about me. It's my problem. I had to decide when and if I was ready to share it. Nothing was definite before. The first biopsies were inconclusive. Why should a whole bunch of people worry about nothing? Anyway, I'm telling you now because now I know what I'm facing, and I need your support." Mel smiled.

Liz was a good friend, but she tended to judge everything from her own narrow standpoint. Her view of life radiated from that central fixed position. It never occurred to her that perspectives change radically with a shift of vantage point, informed by observation, reflection and the exchange of ideas. Liz was a great jumper to conclusions. She got up and walked over to Mel. She wanted to find something clever and profound to say to show that she understood, but she could not. She felt rage and impotency. So instead she wrapped her arms around her friend and the two women held each other close. "You'll be fine," Liz said, but behind Mel she sensed a tall figure in a long black cloak staring back at her with tears in its shrouded eyes.

Mel's cancer was in her left breast. She had already had a lumpectomy and this procedure had revealed a malignant tumour requiring further, urgent surgery. This was to be followed up with radiotherapy and possible chemo. She told Liz that she was booked in for the following day and would probably be in hospital for five or six days, maximum.

"I'm a tough old bird, you know," laughed Mel.

"I know, but… oh, Mel, I don't know what to say."

"My guardian angel is feeling very positive so don't worry. I want a daily supply of expensive chocolates, and balloons. They don't let you have flowers, the rotten sods. So I'll have those when I get out, bucket loads of exotic blooms. I've bought the most gorgeous silk pyjamas and dressing-gown, so I'll be wowing them in Maidstone hospital and if I don't catch some god-awful bug I shall be out demanding champagne before you even miss me." Mel was rummaging in the kitchen fridge. "Where does your mean bastard of a husband hide the booze?"

"In the drinks fridge, as you should know!" said Liz. "What happened between you and Brenda? I must have missed that. What happened? What are you looking for?"

"Champagne." Mel's hunt had proved productive and she was removing the wire from a bottle of Moet as she spoke. "Let's celebrate. I have no intention of dying just yet." She laughed as the bubbles forced the wine to shoot out of the bottle into the waiting glass. "Cheers. No, don't say anything else. I shall be fine."

Liz raised her glass. They each took a healthy swig before Mel refilled their glasses.

"So what happened with Brenda?" Liz hoped a change of subject would lighten things. She was in a state of shock, but did not want to pursue the matter against Mel's wishes.

"The blessed Brenda! Oh, it was only a minor bust up. She started off on one of her bloody crusades. You know, all that guff in the Bible about the witch of Endor? She's convinced I'm in league with the devil and should be burned as a heretic. It's my own fault; I can't resist riling her. She's so bloody pious. Donald had been asking me how business was and I happened to mention that the spirits were quiet at the moment. I wasn't going to explain that I've had to stop all that malarkey for now, but she wouldn't let it go. 'If the dead want to be contacted they don't need a medium...' well, you know the speeches as well as I do. I told her I hadn't expected the Spanish Inquisition and she said...this is Brenda, remember: severe lack of humour. She said: 'Well, it might have done you some good!' Honest to God, the woman's a lunatic."

They paused for a while to giggle at Brenda's expense. It was good to be relaxed again, enjoying one another's company.

"What you said before, Mel... did you really want children?"

"No way, I can't stand the little buggers!"

"Seriously? You'd have made super parents. Why didn't you have any?"

"I couldn't, simple as that."

"Did you want a family?"

"I suppose so, but we have to accept what is given and it obviously wasn't meant. Bob never seemed to mind so it's worked out OK in the end. How about you? Do you want more?"

"Gosh. I don't know. I took it for granted that I would have kids. Do I want more? Yes. I hadn't thought about it but, yes. I do want another one. Wow. That's a revelation, isn't it?"

"Maybe you should tell Edward?"

"Hmm...maybe, maybe not."

The subject hardly seemed appropriate so they reverted to picking poor Brenda to pieces.

CHAPTER 15

The waiting began. Mel had her surgery, a mastectomy and the removal of the lymph nodes from under her left arm. It was extensive and invasive, but she never complained or bemoaned her lot. Every day for two weeks she had radiotherapy, then three weeks of chemo, during which her mane of magenta hair thinned drastically. In solidarity with her new-found sisters in the oncology department she shaved off the remains of her hair and flatly refused to wear a wig. She wore her baldness with pride, only resorting to a hat when the temperature plummeted well into April. Late frosts had turned the wisteria buds to grey powder and spring nearly did not bother to appear at all it was so cold. Then suddenly it was May and the twin's tenth birthday loomed large.

Mel was still poorly, but insistent that the twin's tenth birthday was too important an event to be shelved because of a "bit of cancer". Throughout the ordeal Mel was strong and defiant. She had shown Liz her scar just a few days after the amputation. Liz had mumbled something about how neat it was, but inside she was horrified. If that happened to her she would die. Her breasts were an important part of who she was as a woman. How could one ever come to terms with losing one? Edward would never cope with it, not like Bob. Edward would be repulsed. He would see her as deformed and incomplete. His instinctive reaction would be to pretend it had not happened. She could never again undress in front of him or walk around in the nude. He would see it as a thing of shame, a failure. Oh, he would never say so in as many words, but she would always know what he was thinking and have to hide herself so as not to offend or hurt him. Bob was unbelievable. He gave nothing but full support. It was obvious that he felt his wife's pain and her loss, but that did not alter his feelings for her in any way. She was still the sexy, crazy girl he had married and nothing would change that. He adored her.

Harriet witnessed all this from her discreet distance. She was full of admiration for Mel's courage and ability to put on such a brave face. Try as she would Liz was not capable of being as stalwart. She had been terrified at the thought of losing Mel and found it impossible to hide her emotions. Although she tried not to cry in front of Mel she was always on the brink of spilling over or just mopping up after having done so. Mel forgave her, of course, but congratulated herself on having had the foresight not to reveal too much too soon. Liz swore never to take her friendship for granted again, while Mel just swore. Old-fashioned profanities kept her going in times of crisis and the air in the hospital ward was still blue as testament to her determination to win through. Brenda turned a deaf ear to these and adopted a professional objectivity while offering up a great many Hail Mary's to her Catholic unforgiving God.

*

As the late spring gave way to an early summer, life was bursting out everywhere including Mel's head. Her new shoots were straight and silver. They lay close to her head, forming an urchin cap that suited her amazingly well. Her feisty personality bounced back with a vengeance and she embraced her renaissance with a verve that left the rest of them exhausted. Jenny was the first to remark on the new Mel and in her usual forthright way suggested it was probably the fact that she had stared death in the face and beaten him that had brought about such a splendid transformation. Of course she was right. Harriet knew that better than most, but Mel was not ignorant of the facts either. She had come close to discovering that greatest of life's mysteries; death. She also knew that her battle was the first skirmish of what would be a long, hard war.

The consultant told her the cancer had moved to her lymph nodes. So far it had not shown up anywhere else and it was possible that they had caught it in time. Mel knew she had more chemo to face, but was determined to face it alone. She had seen the drama friends had made of her plight. Their concern and misplaced good deeds made her resolve to get on with things in her own way. Even Bob did not know. Only her guides and unseen helpers were allowed this privileged information. It was to them that she turned for strength and healing. She was not going to die; not for a long time; but her life might be very different for a considerable time.

She sought counselling from a psychic medium in whose circle she had sat for many years. This now elderly woman offered Mel all the reassurance she needed. They meditated together for long quiet hours during which Mel felt safe enough to allow her spirit the freedom to release itself and lose the baggage that weighed it down to the physical world. She emerged rejuvenated and cleansed by these sessions. They gave her not only the confidence to trust in, but also the strength to return to her own psychic work, with a renewed energy and increased insight. Her body's capacity to heal itself and the speed with which it did so astounded her doctors. By May she declared herself a cancer-free zone and defied anyone to say otherwise.

Having shed her magenta locks Mel decided to restyle herself. She became a creature of silver, adopting various shades of greys and silvery whites for her new spring wardrobe. Her jewellery was still heavy and flamboyant, the coral and jade replaced by silver and crystal. The clothes she chose wafted and drifted in chiffons and silks as she abandoned the velvets for a lighter, gossamer look. She had lost a good two stones in as many months and suddenly everything about her appeared lifted and freer. Mel had always claimed to "go-with-the-flow", but now she embraced the current with a resolute, almost manic determination.

*

This year, the twins' birthday fell on a Thursday, so it was decided to hold their party the following Saturday. In the past Mel, Sue, Brenda and Liz had helped with the children's parties. They enjoyed sharing the planning and the execution, with the three more able caterers keeping the fourth wild card out of harm's way. The wild card was, of course, poor Brenda. How she had become a Ward Sister was a wonder. There was nothing in the least domesticated or organized about her. She was a disaster waiting to happen and was usually assigned harmless tasks such as blowing up the balloons or folding napkins. Even then she had to be overseen with discreet diligence. "What can possibly go wrong?" was not a phrase one used around her as it tempted providence to the limit. This year everything was up for grabs. The circle had to be reinvented. Sue was far away in the West Country and Brenda announced rather unconvincingly that she was not sure what her schedule was. In reality she was still smarting from her contretemps with Mel.

Brenda was the only one of the group who could harbour a grudge for any length of time. She wore her Catholicism like a coat of armour. It shielded her from evil but also shut her away from the real world, predisposing her to misinterpret others' motives and emotions. Beneath this armour-plating she was extremely soft-skinned. As a nurse she had learned the art of clinical detachment; unfortunately it had become an intrinsic part of her make-up. Her faith was important to her, but she had a tendency to take it literally. Mel said Brenda had been born into the wrong century; Mel had actually called her a leftover from the dark ages. This remark had never been forgotten, as both parties knew there was a great deal of truth in it. The difficulty was that while one found this a good thing, the other saw it as a definite flaw. Mostly they managed to contain their differences to light-hearted banter. But with such a fundamental disagreement between friends it is not surprising that every now and then jihad broke out.

Mel had no formal religion to quote from. She had been born seeing angels and spirits, a benefit or burden hard to refute. One might consider the accompanying gift of clairvoyance as delusional, but Mel's trust in her spirit world was every bit as solid as were Brenda's Catholic beliefs. The differences, however, were profound. Mel knew what she knew and did not rely on faith. She had no way of proving anything to anyone else and proselytizing was not her thing. If her readings gave someone the surety that their loved ones were still near and still cared, all well and good. She knew why she did what she did and the fact that it helped people in times of need was enough for her. Admittedly the church offered comfort to many, but it came with too many conditions for a free spirit like Mel. Her persuasion left no room for man-made creeds or rules. Fat bishops and dissolute clergy were not her idea of feet planted on a spiritual path, so until she met an actual saint she was content to follow her own convictions.

Liz had never thought hard about her own beliefs. Life had not tested her enough for her to discover who or what she would call upon as a last resort. Her Church of England upbringing had been tame and conventional. She had worn a cross as a teenager, but only because it was a gift to her and was very pretty. In fact she still had it, keeping it out of sentiment. Someday she would give it to Jenny. Every little girl should have a silver cross to wear if she so chose. Liz had been married in church and the twins had been christened. It was the thing to do, so she had done it. Mel and Bob were godparents even though they were not churchgoers. The occasional spats between Mel and Brenda upset her as she had no understanding where they came from. She was not the stuff of martyrs and was glad of that. Religious fervour bordering on mania seemed to cause little joy for poor old Brenda. Mel's beliefs were weird, off the wall at times, but it was fascinating to watch her read those damned cards, although of course they meant absolutely nothing. Why the two of them could not agree to differ was baffling. It was not something to fall out over and it was messing with her plans, which made it serious.

Instead of her usual euphoric excitement at the prospect of a party, Liz was plunging into depression. Belief in luck was all very well when life was fine and dandy, but now she was experiencing a strong feeling of foreboding. Although she had come to terms with Edward's transgression and forgiven his appalling behaviour, it was not forgotten; it was stored as ammunition for any future battles. She tried to keep it out of her thoughts, but it had shaken her core belief in their charmed life, begging the questions: was luck a renewable source that one could recharge by displaying prudence, like turning off lights to save electricity? Or did it come in a finite pot, once used never to be refilled? Was everyone given the same amount, which some squandered and others buried like the talents in the Bible? She began to dread that her luck was running out, but she could not for the life of her think how to conserve it. No one had told her where the switch was.

Chapter 16

Thursday dawned and the twins were up long before they needed to leave for school. Edward blindfolded them and frog-marched them down to the jetty. They squealed with delight every step of the way. Liz had grave misgivings, strengthened by her forebodings, about Edward's choice of present. These he dismissed as trivial, insisting the twins were old enough. So, knowing they would love it, she had capitulated. But now the moment was here, her motherly instincts told her she had been right. Edward had succeeded in whipping the twins into an uncontrolled frenzy, which Liz knew only too well could end in tears. They were jumping up and down screaming in anticipation while Edward urged her to get a move on. It was too late to do anything but go with the flow, as Mel would say.

The early summer day made Liz feel churlish to let such negative vibes dampen the atmosphere. Arum lilies flanked the margins of the beck and yellow water irises stood tall, commandeering the best view. Nestling among the conifers and laburnums stood the newly built boathouse, in a coat of green paint as soft as moss and complementing the wooden tiled roof and dovecote in which two white doves had already taken up residence. It would make a splendid painting. Maybe later if she had time.

After a great deal of argy-bargy the twins were assembled on the jetty. Their blindfolds were removed and their surprise was facing them. Moored beside the jetty lay a small wooden boat. The little craft bobbed, dipped and rolled, tugging at her ropes.

"Well, what do you think?" Edward was almost as excited as the twins.

"It's wicked. Thank you, Daddy." James threw his arms around his father's waist in a rare physical demonstration of affection.

"She's phenomenal!" shrieked Jenny, leaping up and wrapping her legs around her father as she hugged his neck and showered him with kisses. There was nothing reticent about Jenny. "She's the most phenomenal vessel that ever sailed. Thank you, thank you, thank you."

Edward looked at Liz standing quietly holding an agitated dachshund in her arms. "I think they like it." He reached out his hand to Liz. The Pote growled and Liz laughed.

"Look, have you seen what's written on the bow?" Her voice trembled slightly and she hoped they would interpret this as excitement rather than fear. The children shared none of her forebodings. They rushed to the edge of the jetty. There on both sides of the bow, in bold red and black letters was the name, *The Olly Ro*.

"Wow!" screamed Jenny.

"Double wow!" echoed James.

Liz looked at Edward and deposited the wriggling Pote onto the decking as she announced, "I think it's a success!"

"Told you," he replied, looking a little too smug.

The dinghy was Edward's idea from the start. He had persuaded Liz that ten was the perfect age to start messing about in boats. Both children were good little swimmers and they would learn new skills, how to take responsibility, and have a whale of a time into the bargain. He had learned to sail at a similar age, out with his father on the high seas, not on a tame little lake, and what was good enough for him was good enough for his kids. The twins needed no such assurance. They were already clambering on board as their mother yelled out:

"Hey, hang on a mo. You've forgotten something. The rest of your present is over there."

She ran to collect a parcel which lay beside the boathouse. In it were life-jackets the colour of daffodils. "Now, listen to me, you two, you are never, ever to go on the water without those on. Do you hear me?" As she tightened and tested the straps her voice sounded uncannily like Aunty Sue's, but the children were hardly listening. They were already scrambling off the jetty answering her, rather too glibly, as they dropped down into a new world of adventure:

"Cool."

"Yeah, cool."

The dinghy wobbled and bobbed beneath them and for a moment their exuberance turned to trepidation. Once settled, their father gave them a few basic instructions then launched them into open water, calling out further instructions from the bank.

They ran aground twice, hit the jetty several times and put the fear of God into the water fowl which fled to the safety of the willow, keeping a sidewise eye open for the dog. Fortunately for them he was more interested in the mariners than any stray ducks. The unwieldy oars went in all directions, jumping out of their hoops and hitting the gunwales with frustrating regularity. Slowly, painfully but always accompanied by great hoots of laughter the little dinghy was manoeuvred around the lake with a modicum of seamanship and a great deal of luck.

Feeling prematurely competent and showing off to his sister, James stood up. "Look at me! I'm able seaman Jessop!" The boat lurched, throwing him backwards, his bottom hitting the seat hard as he landed. The *Olly Ro* lurched again, more heavily this time. Then she rolled and lurched again, taking in a fair amount of water each time. He had let go of the oars and one of them slid out and disappeared into the water. Leaning precariously over the side he made the little boat dip at a crazy angle as he fought successfully to retrieve it. Liz turned ashen. She was sure they would capsize. She screamed, her voice trembling, as for a fleeting moment she thought she saw a tall figure standing on the far bank. That wretched card could still turn her blood to ice.

"You'll be a disabled seaman if you don't sit down at once, you idiot." Jenny grabbed the loose oar and climbed into the centre of the vessel. Pushing her brother to one side, she took both oars firmly in hand and settled the craft on a straight course as if she had been doing this all her life. Liz smiled a watery smile and tried to look relaxed. But she knew she could not be there to watch them every time they were out in that wretched boat.

Harriet had positioned herself by the willow and she too was icy cold. She had watched until it seemed inevitable that James was going overboard. Unwilling to witness any more she had covered her eyes and leant against the tree to steady herself. Images flashed on her inner eye. They came rapidly and relentlessly, making her giddy. She could see the boat spinning, caught in an imagined whirlpool as it was sucked deeper and deeper into the cold dark water. Someone was calling to her but she could not make out their voice above the sound of swirling water and the blood rushing in her ears. She was drowning; her lungs were filling; and then she heard it. Laughter, carefree childish laughter. The unexpected sound broke her dream and she opened her eyes to see James and Jenny safe and well, rowing side by side, taking one oar each. Their laughter rang out across the lake and brought back those few happy memories of childhood. The old woman placed her hand on her heart, patting it to calm its beating. She sighed and rebuked herself for being stupid, yet as she looked across the lake at Liz she knew they were both gripped by similar doubts and fears. Whether these came from the past or the future was immaterial.

*

The *Olly Ro* was a great success as a present. By Saturday's party the twins were ferrying their friends around with confidence. It gave them enormous kudos and they readily showed off their newly-acquired skills. Liz kept her uneasiness to herself. It would be unforgivable to spoil such delight with her unfounded fears. She did not want to seem an over-protective mother obsessed with health and safety. She had, however, bought several life-jackets and insisted that anyone entering the *Olly Ro* without one would be keel-hauled. This allayed her fears to an extent, but secretly she hated the boat and the dangers it exposed her children to. She did not confide these fears even to Mel, not wanting to cast a shadow on her friend's recaptured exuberance. Mel approved of the boat and was a good rower, but since her operation had restricted the use of her arm she declined a turn at the oars, conceding, reluctantly, that she was not yet completely fit.

Facing death had increased Mel's love of life, regenerated her belief in the psychic world of spirit that surrounded and entwined itself in her earthly existence. Her wretched illness might have given her greater insight but it had denied her the chance to explore her friend's capabilities when it came to all things psychic. However, Liz's ability to access this hidden world had not been forgotten by Mel. That amazing evening before Liz's birthday remained unexplored and, not one to leave a stone unturned, Mel wanted to explore it now. For Liz, the whole experience had been shelved and she hoped it had been forgotten. Mel had her own plans; with the sainted Brenda not present this was an ideal opportunity to pursue them.

*

Once the party was over and the last of the stragglers had been collected the four friends settled down for the evening. The men took themselves off to watch a recording of the cricket, armed with copious bottles of ale and a large plate of bacon sandwiches, leaving the two girls free to amuse themselves. Liz lit a fire in the Fourth Room, intending to play some soothing music and chill out, as James and Jenny would say.

She manoeuvred the conversation around to Mel's health, determined not to be fobbed off with platitudes this time.

"I'm fine now. I promise you. The cancer's gone. I've to put it all behind me."

"But you must have thought about dying? Did it change what you believe?"

Mel laughed. She had no doubts as to her own beliefs. This life was a continuation of a spiritual path that we would join up with once we pass on through death. It was Liz who needed to examine her own philosophy or lack of it.

"But you must have been scared of dying." Liz betrayed her own fears by persisting with this line of enquiry.

"Of course I was. I'm psychic, not stupid. Dying can be a nasty business. But death is pretty natural. We all manage to do it and all have to face it at some time. Don't get me wrong: I love life and don't want to go just yet. I can't bear the thought of leaving Bob even though I know it wouldn't be for ever. But I get quite excited at the thought of what's waiting over there. Don't you? I can't imagine not believing in anything. It must feel very empty and pointless."

Liz had never thought of herself as being without a faith, but now that Mel mentioned it, she realized she had none. She was one of those predictable middle-Englanders, Church of England without thinking about it. Did it matter? Where did she think her parents were? What would she believe if God forbid, anything should happen to Edward or the twins? And was there a god who could forbid it? Mel's resolve was enviable and Liz decided she wanted some of it for herself. She would go to church, lots of churches, mosques, temples whatever, until she discovered where her own path lay. Mel's reaction was to laugh at her friend. This was so typical of Liz. To jump in at the deep end before dipping her shell-pink painted toenail in to test the water. Liz was about to defend herself, but before she could find the right words Mel had taken her Tarot cards from her bag and had begun to shuffle them.

Mel's illness had forced her to "close down" for a while and Liz had never fully explained the effect the last reading had had on her. She was in no doubt that her own bout of poor health was a direct result of dabbling with the occult. That last encounter had put the fear of God in her. This fear lived on in her subconscious, as her experience by the lake this very morning had illustrated. The occult carried so many connotations of witchcraft and black magic that, although she knew Mel was in no way associated with such dark arts, Brenda's warnings resonated in her ears. No, she decided, the cards were absolutely not for her. Anyway a believer in luck had no need for psychic intervention.

The unexpectedly eerie chill of the room was at odds with this warm summer evening. This had become her favourite room and no longer held any of the gloomy vibrations it had given out when she first discovered it. So when they entered on this particular evening it came as a shock to feel they were not welcome. She had assumed that funny business with this room was in the past. She knew that the turmoil she had felt watching the children in that blessed boat had something to do with it. That old rowing boat was still nagging at her to solve its mystery. It was far more than any natural maternal instinct that was urging caution. Part of her said, *"Leave it alone,"* but another, stronger part was urging her to finally unravel the mystery.

Harriet was also reconciling herself to the fact that the time had come to sort things out. She had little faith in those awful cards but recognized that they might have some significance. If they could unlock her memory, then she could be reconciled with her past. She needed to find out exactly how David had died and whether she could have prevented it. But, like Liz, she was in two minds. Knowing was one thing, being strong enough to face the truth and the consequences of such knowledge was another. A moment as propitious as this might not present itself again. All three of them were in tune, even the room seemed to be waiting for something. Harriet decided to put an end to the waiting.

"Doesn't it scare you?" They were seated on the sofa by the window. The fire was dull, refusing to burst into flame. It barely took the chill out of the air. Liz poked at it, trying to get it to liven up a bit. Mel was concentrating on the cards. She stopped shuffling and began to spread them face down in a long fan. She heard the question and replied without looking up.

"Doesn't what scare me?"

"All this," Liz indicated the cards but she meant much more.

"What's to be afraid of?" Mel said. "They're only bits of paper; or do you mean our spirit friends? Spirits are only people who have moved a little further along the same path we're on. I treat them exactly the same as I do anyone else. Anyway, some people are a damn sight more spooky than most spirits." Her eyes never left the cards, which she was tweaking at with the long silvery nail on her index finger. Liz was pleased to see Mel had begun to paint them again. It was a sign that things were returning to normality.

"What if you don't like them?"

"The cards?"

"No, what they might conjure up… the spirits."

"I tell them to get lost."

"What if they don't go?"

"Then I tell them to piss off! They soon get the message. Spirits can't hurt you unless you let them. Let's see if we can find out what's going on around you right now, shall we?"

Maybe this was what they both needed. Something was telling Liz to go for it.

The women looked at the face-down cards, then at each other. Liz nodded and Mel told her to take three. Liz chose one from each end and one from the middle. She placed them face upwards in a line and studied the pictures for clues. Was it possible that these painted bits of card could hold information about her innermost thoughts, even those that were locked away in her subconscious? Could they probe into the past or even predict the future? The first card showed a handsome young man in a romantic, somewhat over-dramatic pose. He stood high on a hill, almost in the clouds, and held his great sword in both hands. He looked like a bit of a poser to Liz. His head was turned away as he stared down and away from the king who filled the second card. This king was dark and complicated. He was seated on a throne, the corners of which were decorated with the heads of bulls. His elaborate coat was embroidered with vines and he held a sceptre and a pentacle. Liz felt sorry for him. He seemed tired and worried, a man who carried a heavy burden, in complete contrast to the third card, who looked like a joker. This man was dressed all in red, balancing two pentacles much as a juggler would. He wore a ridiculously tall red hat on his head and he was dancing. Then she noticed two tiny ships in the distance both tossed on huge waves; one riding on the crest the other half-hidden behind the great wall of sea.

Mel chuckled, coughed to compose herself, then began her reading. The three cards facing her were the Page of Swords, the King of Pentacles and the Two of Pentacles. These three cards showed Liz's immediate past and how she had dealt with it. Liz felt exposed. Was it possible she would learn something about herself that she would rather not know? Her doubts were plainly written on her face and Mel's wry expression let her know she was aware of her friend's anxiety. Without hesitating she jumped right in. She described a dark-haired man, a business man skilled in mathematics, a man willing to speculate in order to accumulate, powerful and in control. She never named him, but it was so obviously Edward. He felt pestered by someone demanding attention, vigilant and intrusive. His privacy was being invaded, he was spied on. But the spy was in danger of misjudging situations, blowing things out of proportion, with a dangerous tendency to create awkward situations by worrying at problems often more imaginary than real. Liz was being told to let go and look to the future. Mel was on a roll.

"That all seems pretty clear to me. Take three more. Let's see what the present holds."

Liz felt uncomfortable. So far the picture Mel was painting was quite accurate, though it certainly did not show her in a good light. She took three more cards, this time from the centre, laying them in a second line just below the others. The High Priestess sat between the Eight of Pentacles and the Wheel of Fortune. "This is now, and this," Mel prodded the centre card with her shiny nail, "is you, my lady. It's a great card. The priestess, signifying the wisdom of silence; she holds the secrets and mysteries of the future. On one side is luck, destiny, whatever you want to call it, and happiness. The wheel brings happiness. It's yours to turn. It's within your grasp, Liz. You were born lucky." Mel nudged the picture on the Eight of Pentacles: an artisan chipping away with hammer and chisel. "This is you and your talent, your painting. Craftsmanship, commission; skill in craft and business... it's there waiting for you to grab, kiddo!"

Liz had forgotten her initial disappointment and was becoming quite impressed and excited. The second trio of cards were much more to her liking. Why had she been so against all this before? It was spot-on even, if she did not like to admit she had gone over the top about Edward's dalliances. But it was good to know that luck was still with her.

At Mel's bidding she took three more, less concerned where they came from this time, the three nearest her. First was the Six of Swords, followed by the Page of Cups. As Liz paused, Mel smiled at her; then she took the final card and held it close without looking at it.

"Are you ready to glimpse the future?"

"Yes. Look, I've gone all goose-pimply. You can't stop now. I'm hooked."

Liz turned the third card and both she and Harriet gasped. Liz began to wish she had not started all this, but Harriet wanted to see it through to the end. These were her cards. They were not Liz's and she knew exactly what they meant.

Harriet knew the boatman, the Six of Swords, she had met him before. But where was he taking his passengers as he skilfully steered his craft with his long wooden pole? He was the ferryman, Fate, and it was his task to take the living away. Harriet noticed the water surrounding the boat: smooth and safe on one side yet rough and dangerous on the other. The middle card, the Page of Cups was her brother, David. A fair young man, beautiful to look at, just as Harriet remembered him, with his cinnamon hair and his fine features. There was no mistaking it. She saw a gentle bright youth, scholarly and keen. In his right hand he held a golden cup, which contained a fish. A fish out of water, just like Davy, vulnerable and emotional, staring back at her as clearly as if it had been a photograph. The last card was Death.

Harriet sat on the edge of her chair. Was this what she had been waiting for? During the reading she had warmed towards Mel. Could she really be a psychic? Could she contact David and give her the assurance that his soul was resting in peace? Harriet took a deep breath and challenged Mel to begin. The skeletal figure clad in black armour sat astride a white steed. He held a banner in his left hand, a black flag with a white rose on it, like the Tudor rose in the rose window outside. There were other figures, but Liz saw only the figure of Death staring straight at her with his eyeless, all-seeing sockets. It was chilling. There was a timeless quality to the image that made it all the more menacing. Harriet knew these cards were for her and had been expecting this one to be among them. Nevertheless Death always comes as a surprise.

"It's strange, but I don't see these cards as the future. They are reaching back, way back. They point to another life, another death. It must be connected to you since you chose them. At times like this I really miss my hair." Mel rubbed her hand over the fine silver stubble that was beginning to sprout from her head, enjoying the tickling sensation in her fingers while buying time to think. "This is all about him, this young man in the centre." She prodded the Page of Cups as she spoke. "He is trying to give us a message. He is telling me to read the cards like a book. Well, what can I see? Two children in a boat, on a journey. The Page has a cup with a fish in it and Death is turning away from him. I don't know what it all means or who the cards are for." Mel stopped speaking and a thick silence gathered around them.

But Liz did not need Mel to read the cards; they were speaking to her by themselves. She took over from Mel and began to tell the story so graphically displayed in front of her.

They were telling her the secret of the boat. They showed her two children, also twins, but not her twins. This was long ago, in another life. There had been an argument, a fight which led to a tragic accident. One of them, a little boy had drowned. It had happened long ago, but it had never been resolved. There was still a lot of blame and guilt that had never been dealt with. The tragedy was continuing and it was linked to Beckmans. It was as though her finding this house was for this reason: to lay the ghosts of the past to rest. The secret that had haunted her since she first came to Beckmans was contained in these pictures.

*

Harriet was frozen to her chair. Her heart was filled with the memory of her little brother. Every fibre of her body ached to reach out to him, to be with him again and hold him close. She had not held anyone in her arms since the day he died. Her presence was fading rapidly as her strength was leaving her. She could feel it floating out into the ether. Her body was shrinking and soon she would be gone. David was here; she could see him ahead of her, beckoning her, calling her to follow him. How could she refuse, having already failed him once? She watched as he began to float away. He was entering a swirling mist, and beyond the inky confusion shone a light of such intensity she was forced to shield her eyes. He was calling her name. He held out his hand for her to take. She saw her own arm outstretched and felt her hand burning as it drew nearer to his. It was time to surrender and go with him.

"Don't go!" The voice came loud and clear from the other side of the room.

Shining out against the dark stood a figure in a long white gown, framed by a dazzling halo of light. Its hand outstretched, it too was reaching out to Harriet. The sensation of being held enveloped her, making her feel secure. Warmth gushed into her cold veins, restoring her strength and rekindling her staunch desire to live. The tunnel began to fade and she waved farewell to her brother, who smiled back with resignation and understanding. Then he turned and went.

Mel and Liz nearly died of shock when the door shot open. Jenny was standing there in her nightdress. Light from the hall radiated around her, giving her the appearance of an angel.

"What are you doing out of bed, sweetheart?" Liz wondered for a moment if Jenny was quite awake. Jenny was rubbing her eyes and yawning as she peered into the unlit room.

"Someone called me." She wandered across to Harriet and snuggled up on the old woman's lap, their eyes saying all that needed to be said. Any lingering doubts Harriet might have had about staying behind vanished.

Liz meant to suggest that Jenny went back to bed but instead found herself inviting her to stay. She could not believe she had just asked her own child to take part in a séance. Mel seemed relaxed about it and Harriet was delighted. At last she would have a valid spokesperson, a kindred spirit. Jenny looked at the line of cards Liz had just read. Her forehead wrinkled as she narrowed her eyes thoughtfully. Then with total conviction she began.

"These three cards cover the past, the present and the future, which, of course, are all the same anyway. The boy is youth. He is a messenger reminding us that we are all connected in life and beyond. He has filled his cup from the sea on which the boatman travels. The boatman is not only carrying his passengers through life, he ferries them from life to death, through rough water to smooth. His passengers don't know he is there. We think we forge our own paths through life but we don't really. And eventually we must face Death. But he is not frightening when you see him next to this young man. He is just telling us not to get too fond of material things. They don't last. Life is too short to waste on things. He also says that as one life ends another begins. We should embrace change. Shall I cross the cards, Aunty Mel?"

Mel nodded and explained to Liz that by laying one card across the others you confirmed or denied the rest. Jenny picked her card and laid it down. Harriet and Liz both shuddered, Liz because she saw again that tall, haunting figure in black and Harriet because she recognized herself. Liz could not move. She wanted to run from the room, to scream out, shout for help, but she was paralysed. Of all the cards she could have picked, Jenny had chosen the Five of Cups.

As she laid the card down Jenny smiled at her mother. "I know you hate this card, because it frightens you, Mummy, but I really like it. It is quite special. It's sometimes called the mourning card because it can mean loss. But it means lots more than that. Look, three of the cups are lying down. Two are spilling a red liquid on the ground, it might be wine or it might be blood. It could be both, a reference to Holy Communion. They could represent a sacrifice. The third one held water. Is it a libation to the gods or an accident? None of them are broken. Have they simply fallen over, or could they have been tipped over on purpose? They held the past, which is over and gone. The other two cups are still standing because they hold the future. They are still full. They represent hope and redemption. Look, there behind the figure, do you see a bridge leading to a house? There's been a homecoming and there'll be lots more. You know this card also depicts inheritance. Beckmans is a part of us now and we'll always be part of its history. Isn't that an incredible thought? It may be just a house and we must all move on at some point, but our souls will be linked for ever. Don't you find that fantastic? That a house has a soul, I mean."

Liz stared open-mouthed at this amazing young person in front of her. Where had she been not to notice how grown up Jenny was? When and how had she developed all this wisdom and knowledge? Who had been teaching her such things? From the look of incredulity on Mel's face she was not the culprit.

"Well, I think that's a pretty good confirmation. I appear to be redundant in this house. I may as well go to bed!" Mel gave Jenny a resounding kiss and stretched her back as she stood up. They had been bending over the cards for several long hours although the time had flown by. The fire was looking brighter than it had all evening and Liz placed the guard around it as she too stretched her limbs. Jenny scooped up the cards and replaced them in their box. There was nothing more to say. She blew a kiss to Harriet and the three of them left the room leaving the fourth on her own to enjoy the last embers of the fire. Out in the hall, Liz put her arms around Jenny and held her close. She had never felt closer. Both knew that this was the start of a fuller understanding between them. A bond had been created tonight tying them together for eternity.

"However long that is," mumbled Harriet, settling down for the night.

CHAPTER 17

It rained solidly for most of that summer. July had been a complete wash-out and August showed signs of being worse. It had rained all Saturday and now, Sunday, it was raining even harder. The beck rushed through the garden, taking with it any marginal plants that failed to cling to the rapidly eroding banks. The bergenias lay face-down in the black wet silt, as less robust plants floated away to join the torrent that was the River Medway. The little bridge disappeared beneath the flood and the *Olly Ro* strained at its moorings. The lake shivered and quaked, no longer sure of its boundaries. It spluttered and surged onto the banks, where it lay as thick, smelly mud. The ducks took to the leeward side of the willow for shelter and watched aghast as their island home drowned in the rising tide. Only the boathouse stood tall, its turret silhouetted against the blackened sky, wallowing in the Gothic weather.

All weekend the twins had remained in the attic making a skull-and-crossbones flag for the *Olly Ro* and they were desperate to fly it aloft. Permission to set sail was flatly refused as the rain was bucketing down through the driving wind that lashed at the beck, whipping it into an unrecognizable maelstrom. Tempers were fraying. They were getting cabin fever. James was idly throwing a tennis ball at the wall; it thumped annoyingly at the sofa each time he failed to catch it.

Jenny was curled up on this sofa, trying to listen to a new CD of a song Harriet wanted her to learn. These activities were hardly compatible and a skirmish was in the air. Liz brought their supper up on trays and told them to watch a film or at least do something together before they drove everyone mad with their bickering. She had installed a baby alarm in the loft when they were a lot younger and the habit of plugging it in had never left her. Back in the lounge she heard them stop arguing and settle on a film they both liked enough to watch together. James slotted it into the DVD player. It was *Moby Dick*.

The twins became engrossed in pizzas and adventure on the high seas alongside Ishmael, tattooed natives, an obsessed peg-legged captain and the great white whale, while Edward and Liz, enjoying the peace and quiet, lit a fire. So much for summer! What light there was outside was fading fast. The long windows shook as the wind blew in from the lake. Liz drew the curtains and settled beside Edward, snuggling close as the strains of soft music floated over her.

Suddenly she sat up. "Listen, Ed."

He turned the music down. "I can't hear anything."

"Exactly: there's no sound from the kids." She crossed to the windows and drew back the drapes, cupping her hands against the glass to peer out into the dark. "Ed, did you leave the light on in the boathouse?"

"Not guilty. Maybe the kids are down there."

Before he had finished speaking Liz was out of the door. She ran slithering and slipping across the sodden grass. She kicked off her shoes and sprinted over the lawn, swearing at the darkness that hindered her speed. The mud splattered and stuck to her stockinged feet and legs.

"Hang on. You'll need a torch!" Edward yelled after her. "Bloody kids. I bet they're still upstairs in the warm."

But Liz did not hear him. She had seen the black rider, felt the hot rank breath from his stallion's wide nostrils as the great head shook and snorted against the night storm. His armour was sounding a death rattle in her ears as that piercing gaze from eyeless sockets held her mesmerized. The black cloak turned and beckoned. The cards had tricked her.

Upstairs the children had been slumped on cushions watching the movie. James was glued to the screen, but Jenny was bored. She pestered him relentlessly as only a sibling can. The remote control was her main weapon and having taken possession of it she proceeded to stop and start the disc at will. When finally the screen froze and adamantly refused to budge, tempers snapped. James jumped up with full force hit his sister around the head. They both froze. They had scrapped many times before. They had pulled faces at each other and name-calling was commonplace, especially in the attic, their adult-free zone. But violence, until this moment, was unknown. Jenny rubbed the side of her face. The blow had left a bright red blotch on her cheek. Refusing to cry, she shouted, "That bloody hurt!" and looked accusingly at her brother.

"Don't swear, Jenny," James taunted, using a particularly patronizing tone. "You deserved a good thump. You ruined my film. Just at the bit where…" He must have seen *Moby Dick* a hundred times. His well-thumbed copy of the book was dog-eared from page-turning.

"Where they catch the stupid old whale!" she taunted back.

"They don't catch him, Stupido, that's the point! He is Captain Ahab's nemi... nema..."

"Nemesis," she said impatiently. "Now who's *stupido*?" Jenny stood with hands on hips. Her jaw was set and her body language left no room for doubt. "You bloody hit me, Apeface!"

That was it. Within seconds they became one rolling, kicking, shrieking mass, eventually dissolving into a hysterical ball of laughter. One of them wriggled free and cried, "Let's go and catch a real whale!" It was James. Grabbing a handful of felt pens he set about tattooing himself. "I'm Queequeg; where can I get a harpoon? I need one to shoot that pesky whale."

While he hunted for a suitable weapon Jenny scrambled in his wake, busy with more pens, transforming him into a wild Polynesian whaler. Soon every inch of his face was covered with weird and wonderful symbols. In the general fracas no one had noticed that the baby alarm had been pulled from its socket.

Within minutes James had engineered a functional weapon from a water cannon, adapted to fire a pen. It flew a meagre six inches on its maiden flight but after a minor adjustment or two the pen shot across the room with a terrifying force, embedding itself in a bean bag. Moby Dick's days were numbered. Meanwhile Jenny was attempting to turn the table upside-down.

"What are you doing?" asked James rather disparagingly.

"This is the *Pequod* and I'm Captain Ahab. Hoist the flag and climb aboard, Queequeg."

"Excuse me, Captain, but this is a crap boat. Why don't we use the *Olly Ro*? She's as fine a vessel as ever went a-whaling,"

The idea filled the room with the smell of adventure. James waved the harpoon above his head and marched towards the door, only to find Jenny barring the way. She stood holding on to the doorframe, her legs spread wide. "We can't, James. Mummy would be furious."

"Remove yourself, scurvy scum! You might be captain but you're a lily-livered coward."

Jenny hesitated. She knew exactly what she should do, but to tell tales seemed so awful. She could not stop him now, not on her own. Someone responsible had to go with him. Anyway they knew how to handle the boat, so what could possibly go wrong?

"OK, I'm in if we wear our life-jackets."

"Yeah, yeah." He was already busy far out at sea, battling the storms and tempests as they searched for the great white whale. As they crept down the backstairs James muttered to himself,

"I've seen that film a hundred times and I've never seen anyone in a stupid yellow jacket!"

They jumped down, missing the last creaky step, and crept on through the kitchen and breakfast-room on tiptoe. They could hear the CD playing on the other side of the tall lounge doors. By the back door James grabbed a broomstick, to which he tied the flag.

"We're whalers, not bloody pirates!" snapped Jenny. Then as her brother's face crumpled she added: "I suppose it's better than nothing. Bring it along and don't cry, your tattoos will run."

They carried their waterproofs and Wellingtons to the jetty before donning them, for fear of alerting their parents, so by the time they reached the water they were already soaked to the skin. Jenny climbed into hers and watched as rain dripped off the end of her brother's nose.

She knew this was all wrong. Twice she thought she heard her mother call to them to come back, but she ignored it and when James exclaimed, "Isn't this the best night ever?" she had to agree. He was shouting, but his voice became a tiny whisper, made even smaller by the howls of the wind.

The night was wild. The wind blew from the East, cold and cruel. Their oilskins flapped, refusing to be buttoned until they hunched their backs against the gale. Sou'westers had to be strapped on; even then the wind lifted them from beneath their broad brims and tugged at the chin straps. James pulled the craft alongside and held her fast for his captain to board. It took all his strength and, for a moment, he thought of calling an end to the adventure. But it was too late. He could not be made to look cowardly in front of a girl. Ahab climbed in behind him and took the oars. Queequeg stood in the centre of the *Pequod* holding the broomstick as his mast. The pirate flag clung on with grim determination as the gale, equally resolute, tried to steal it. His legs worked hard to maintain his balance as the boat lurched and rolled in the swell. At last he was forced to sit and hold fast to the gunwale, annoyed at himself for giving in.

Ahab pulled on the oars, being the strongest rower, and with skill and determination the dingy was manoeuvred away from the jetty and deftly turned, heading straight out to "sea". Another quarter-turn and the *Pequod* headed into the wind, set fair to pursue her quarry. The rain stung the two small faces. Even when they turned away it continued to lash them raw. The storm was relentless. It was time to abandon the game. Jenny tried to point the vessel homeward, but it refused to obey. Her arms were tired and she could not turn it.

The boat was no longer under her control. As the horror of the situation dawned, Queequeg stood up in the bow, defying the elements and oblivious to the danger. He clung to the broomstick mast and pointed into the wind. "There she blows!" he yelled. His voice was lost in the wind that buffeted and battered them.

Without warning, he let go of the mast and aimed his harpoon at his prey. He fired. The missile shot forward just as a mighty crash of thunder filled the crew's ears and drowned out his cry. Seconds later jagged bolts of lightning lit the screen. Queequeg had gone.

The blackness stretched out and down, above and below, surrounding and consuming everything in a conspiracy between the night and the water. Jenny could see nothing but black.

"Oh, God. Oh, Christ, where are you? I can't see you?" Jenny was peering over the side, willing the dark waters to part and let her see her brother. What moon there was remained obscured by storm cloud. The lightning struck once more then it, too, put out the lights on the lake. Jenny was tearing at her boots and coat. "James? Hold on, James!" No reply. The blood drained to her feet, turning them to lead. Her head was light and empty. In her stomach a heavy mass was heaving ready to be spewed out into the blackness. She continued tugging until she was finally free of her boots, all the while yelling: "I'm coming James. I'm coming!"

Then she too had gone over the side into the pitch-black liquid. It was colder than death. She thought nothing could be colder than her own blood when she realized James had gone. Rising to the surface, she gulped in air, choking and spluttering on the mud and water she had swallowed. What should she do? There was no one to ask, no time to think. Then from the far side of the boathouse someone was calling her name.

"Jenny, can you hear me?" It was Harriet. In her hand she held a long wooden boat hook, which she aimed towards Jenny. "Grab the pole. I can see him. He's caught in the reeds on this side. I'll guide the pole to him. Swim down holding the pole and put the hook through his coat. Can you do that, Jenny?" Her calm voice steadied Jenny's erratic heartbeat.

Jenny took a long, deep breath. Feeling her way down the length of the pole she did as her friend said. Down she went into the inky blackness. She reached the end of the pole and felt the slimy water and reeds swirling silently around her. As she frantically searched for James, the only sound was her heart banging against her ribs. The air in her lungs was used up; she was desperate to breathe. She willed herself to stay below where the waters were horribly quiet and her brother was drowning. At last she felt his hair, his strong dark hair. Her lungs were bursting and her ears hurt with the pressure of the water and the blood pumping through her body.

He was held fast in the tangle of weeds. Her fingers felt down to where his coat was and grabbed at it. Thrusting the metal hook in through his collar and back out through the hem, she secured his body to the pole. Then, turning her own body around, she grabbed at her brother, wrapping her legs around him. If she did not save him she was prepared to drown with him. Her legs gripped tightly, so cold that she could hardly feel them. Her head was bursting and her lungs were empty, almost useless. Head-first she dragged herself up the boat hook, hand-over-hand climbing a wooden rope. Her fingers were numbed by the cold and she had no sensation in her legs. Was James still attached? She dared not let go of the pole to check. In a final burst of determination she pulled hard on her life line. Her fingers were slipping but the notches on the end of the shaft gave her purchase.

Harriet felt the tug and heaved at the pole until she could see Jenny. Leaning flat on the decking she reached into the lake and grabbed at the child's sodden sweater, hoisting the girl onto the walkway. Then she stood tall and called on all her strength to pull the pole out of the water. Jenny was gasping, her lungs burned and her head was pounding. She watched as Harriet tried to lift James. He was in the water face-down and too heavy for Harriet to pull ashore. The *Olly Ro* had been swept back towards the jetty and lay tossing freely between her brother and safety. By the meagre light from the boathouse Jenny could see him bobbing on the surface on the far side of the boat. She filled her painful lungs and dived in again, down under the boat, feeling her way beneath the keel until she burst through the surface to gulp in the cold night air. Cupping his chin in her hand she swam with his head held above the waves until they reached the bank. Jenny pushed him onto the grass, where he lay motionless in the dark. He was alive, but only just.

As she breathed, hot needles stabbed her chest, causing her body to shudder and heave. She was sure she was dying. It was all right to be dying. To lie down here beside her twin and let go would be almost a pleasure. The thread between life and death was very fine.

"Jenny." The deep voice was commanding. Harriet stood beside her. She knew the thread was fine, but she also knew it to be strong.

"Come on, my dear. You know what to do." The assertive tone prompted the girl into action. She positioned James flat on his back, tilted his head and opened his mouth, clearing it with her numb fingers. She listened to his chest. There was no sound. She took a deep breath as though about to sing, held his nose and pushed her own agonized breath into his lifeless body. The pain did not matter now. She would happily continue to breathe for him for ever if it meant he could live. Then he coughed loudly, spewing out a mixture of mud, bile and water. Jenny turned him on his side and lay down beside him, holding him while rocking him to and fro. The will to live had returned and she was daring him not to give up.

From the bridge, Liz could make out shadowy forms by the boathouse. A knife cut through her as she saw her two children and from her throat she let loose a howl that reached the gates of Heaven and the doors of Hell: a prayer and a curse that only a mother's agony could produce. As she reached them, she sank to her knees and Jenny finally let go and passed out.

CHAPTER 18

By the time the ambulance arrived, Edward had got his family back to the house. Liz sat by the Aga, silently rocking James, both of them wrapped in the duvet that Edward had thrown around them. James was like a statue, his eyes fixed and unblinking. Apart from an involuntary shudder occasionally racking his being, he was motionless and mute. His father kept one arm tightly around his wife and son while the other held the limp unconscious body of his daughter. All four of them huddled together by the stove as the steamy air filled the room with an unnatural silence. Edward was listening hard to this silence until he realized it was being broken by a voice. It was his voice. For the first time in his life he was praying.

That night was the longest Edward had ever experienced. Liz had been unnaturally quiet throughout the whole wretched business. She stared into space without speaking or crying. If she moved she was like a zombie, existing somewhere between life and death, like her children. At one o'clock Edward called Bob. The strain of facing all this alone was too much. He needed his friend and his friend's forgiveness. Real fear raced through his veins and he felt lost without Liz's cool strength beside him. The doctors said it was shock. He knew it was, but it still frightened him. He was afraid she would blame him for everything: for buying the boat, for letting the children out alone, even for the storm. Was this his punishment for infidelity? How would he live with the guilt if the children died? If he could not forgive himself, how could he expect his wife to forgive him? He wanted his family back. He wanted to turn back the clock and be washed of his sins. "The sins of the father..." - is this what it meant?

Mel and Bob arrived in time to hear the doctor pronounce that both James and Jenny would live. Jenny had regained consciousness, but needed to be assessed to see that no permanent damage had been done to her lungs, which were described as remarkable for a child of ten. With complete rest and warmth a full recovery was likely. They needed to keep her in to run a few tests, then if all was well she could come home. James was more complicated. He had been unconscious for a long time and had ingested large quantities of muddy water. X-rays showed no obvious signs of permanent damage, but once again, only time would tell. He was no longer critical, but not out of danger. He had been lucky to have someone who knew first-aid on hand. The doctor said that had he not been resuscitated so quickly he might have died or suffered brain damage. The young woman doctor looked at Edward:

"Was that down to you or your wife, Mr Jessop? Or could it have been Jenny? She did mention a lady. She said it was this woman who saved their lives. It might have been a dream. Trauma does strange things to the mind. Anyway, well done whoever it was."

Edward looked at his wife. What did she know about first-aid? And Jenny was a child. As for a mystery woman, that was plain silly. As the doctor said, it was probably just a dream.

"You can see them if you want. We've put them next to each other. Remember they've had a nasty shock, so tread carefully."

"Would you mind if I come too?" asked Mel.

"You must be the mysterious lady. She's been asking for you. She says you saved them."

Mel shrugged and gave a quizzical look before following the doctor, who turned and added: "By the way, don't be alarmed by James's colour. It had us worried at first. Then we realized it was paint, felt-tip pens actually, all over his upper body and his face; quite amazing. Anyway, don't worry if you spot a tinge of green around the gills. It will wear off." She smiled as she led the way to the children's ward.

Edward returned home alone and spent what was left of the night with just The Pote for company. It was the first time he had been alone at Beckmans and he found himself pacing the house, the dog trailing him. There was no way he could sleep. His conscience was stabbing at him as he relived his indiscretions over and over again. This was his punishment for taking his charmed life for granted. How could he have been so bloody stupid? If anything happened to the twins he would never be able to look Liz in the face again. How could he live with himself? When he collected his family the next day he was a very contrite man. He had vowed to every deity he could conceive of that if his family was spared he would change. No more liaisons, no more absentee fatherhood, no more reticence about Liz's plans for their home. It was their life and he wanted nothing more than to be in the thick of it, taking an active part. By the time they were safely inside Beckmans he had talked himself into sainthood.

*

It was weird. Nobody mentioned the accident. The children were tucked up in bed, having been told they should rest for at least forty-eight hours. Liz faffed about, making hot drinks and food that no one wanted and no one ate. James slept and chatted alternately, unimpressed when his father promised to teach him the art of the definitive googly. Jenny just lay there. She did not cry or smile, she did not speak. She did not even sleep. She stared straight ahead, registering no emotion at all. She had not said one word since regaining consciousness. It was as if she were somewhere else where nobody could see or reach her. She behaved as if she had stepped onto a different level, slipped into a parallel world. The doctors said there was nothing physically wrong with her, it was just delayed shock. But it was painfully obvious that something was very wrong indeed. Jenny was withdrawn. Her normal effervescence and exuberance had gone.

They tried to restore life at Beckmans to normal but Jenny's behaviour made it impossible. Her altered state cast a shadow over the house and its occupants. She grew noticeably thinner and paler and her face exuded a haunted look. She declined to eat and shunned company. Instead she would take herself off, only to be found, hours later, sitting alone, silently rocking to and fro. One Sunday morning Liz discovered to her alarm that Jenny had locked herself in the Fourth Room. Liz begged her to come out, but no amount of pleading could persuade her to unlock the door or simply let them know that she was all right. Edward and James tempted her with treats, goaded her with threats. Neither tactic worked. Jenny did not answer or open the door. Nothing anyone said could penetrate the barrier Jenny had built around herself. In desperation Liz phoned Mel.

Alone in her sanctuary, Jenny sat curled in the small armchair by the inglenook. Her jaw was set; her eyes had dark circles beneath them. They remained fixed on the child's sampler that hung on the bird-shaped hook. Her arms wrapped around her knees, hugging them as she swayed rhythmically back and forth. She hummed to herself, rocking in time to the music in her head. In her mind's eye she was the girl in the photograph. Perched high on her father's strong shoulders nothing could touch her. Up above the rainbow she flew with the bluebirds. This was the time she had chosen. This was her time and no clocks or calendars could alter that.

"I know this sounds fatuous, but have you simply asked her for her version of what happened, for a blow-by-blow account of the accident?" Mel suggested. "Because, like it or not, that's what is at the root of all this. OK, it was a stupid bloody accident that could have turned into a tragedy, and thank God it didn't. But all we know to date is what James told us and that isn't much. Jenny probably, almost certainly, saved his life. But there must be more to it. Maybe they had a fight and Jenny blames herself. Guilt is a powerful emotion. Those useless doctors, why haven't they tried to get to the bottom of this? You'd think they'd have offered her some counselling or something. We need to hold an inquest. One way or another we will get to the truth. Well, are you coming with me or do I have to do this on my own?" Mel was on a mission.

Not waiting for an answer, she approached the door to the Fourth Room, brushing past Liz, who sat slumped in the chair by the hall table. Why had all this happened? How could life suddenly turn so upside-down? Nothing made sense. Liz rose, arranged her cardigan fastidiously on the back of the chair and followed Mel into the Fourth Room.

Her daughter's behaviour put the fear of God in Liz. This was more than shock. Being made to feel so powerless, so useless, was hateful. She was a mother and yet she was redundant; the rejection was more than she could bear. She was willing to take the blame for everything that had happened and to accept the consequences if she thought it would help. But how could she begin to make amends when she had no idea what she had done wrong? She should not have listened to Edward. They never should have bought that blasted boat. And she of all people should have made sure her children were safe, whether or not they were at home. It was her fault. If Jenny pointed the finger at her, it would be justly deserved. That was her worst fear; that Jenny would judge her culpable. She would never be able to shoulder the guilt. To lose Jenny's love would kill her. Her heart was racing erratically yet outwardly she appeared calm and in control as she approached the door: a swan gliding towards the rapids.

The first move was to coax Jenny out of the Fourth Room. Visions of that sad, little girl by the lake would not leave Mel's mind. Was that whole incident by the stream a premonition? Had the Tarot predicted the accident? She too was feeling guilty. She had not been honest enough in her reading of the cards. In her mind she tried to recall them, to see them differently. Even if she interpreted them as a prediction, the tragedy had been averted, so why the Five of Cups? Two cups standing and three lying down; three lives at risk, whose was the third? Was it her own? Was her cancer going to win after all? Or was the card telling her of a past tragedy? The more she thought about it, the more convinced she became they had been foretelling the future. They had been showing her this accident. She had not read them accurately enough. One thing she did know. Jenny was instrumental in determining the final outcome. Jenny held the key.

Mel knocked on the oak door. There was no answer, so she tried the handle. The door was locked. When she called Jenny's name there was no reply. Mel concentrated her inner mind, letting her breath come in steady and controlled measure. Then she put her lips close to the door and whispered. "Is Jenny's friend there? Please could you open the door for Jenny?"

Harriet was leaning heavily against the banisters. Since the accident she had been feeling weak. Her head was still throbbing, accompanied by a persistent droning in her ears. The family's flight to the hospital had alarmed her. She had been left alone, not knowing what had happened to her precious children. She did not know if they were dead or alive. The past, the present and the future crowded in on her mind until she could no longer distinguish one from the other. Lightning flashes and startling explosions came at her from all directions, leaving her nauseous and giddy. This was how her father had described his fits to her. First he described rapidly flickering shadows of awareness, then an impenetrable dark into which blinding darts of light hit his eyes like rockets piercing his brain. They lit up scenes of terrifying visions, but never stayed long enough for him to define or describe them. This was what she too had seen: glimpses of reality swamped by obscurity before she could grasp them; and all this accompanied by stabbing pain and despair. Now she was being asked to face it yet again. How many times had she tried to fathom the mystery of her brother's death? Why should this time be any different?

But it was different. This time it was Jenny who was hurting. The pain had been transferred. Harriet had no choice. Stepping into the Fourth Room, stepping into Jenny, she took the griffin key in both hands and turned it.

The door opened. Jenny's sunken eyes peered out at Mel from the gloom. The room was dark; the child had drawn the curtains, blocking out natural light. She was not crying, but Mel could feel the weight of tears all around her. The room was crying and the pain of such distress invaded Mel's psychic self, causing her to tremble with received emotion. Jenny had returned to her chair. She did not speak or move; she simply stared at Mel with no flicker of recognition.

"Hello."

The child continued to stare.

"May I sit down?" Mel took the silence as tacit approval. "I'm a friend of Jenny's too. She's asked me to help you."

The child got up and moved to the window, deliberating on what to do. After some time she spoke. It was Jenny's voice and Jenny's eyes that pleaded with Mel for absolution.

"I have done something dreadful."

Mel smiled and waited. It was not the response the child had expected. There was no anger or accusation, just silence.

"I'm a murderer. They're going to hang me. I've killed my brother."

"Did you mean to?" Mel spoke quite normally and rationally.

"Oh, no," came the instant and definite answer.

"Then I don't think you're so evil. Who told you that you should hang?"

"Mama. She says I'm a murderer and the police will take me to prison and hang me. I have to wait here for them to come."

"I promise nobody is going to hang you. Will you let me help you?"

"You can't."

"Maybe not, but Jenny could. You trust Jenny, don't you?"

"Yes." The eyes that searched Mel's were no longer Jenny's. Physically they were those familiar green lasers that had twinkled at her for the past ten years. Today they burned with an amber fire, flamed by a torment that grabbed Mel's heart.

"Will she help me?"

"Oh, yes."

That was all she had to say for the child to run into her arms. Was it the lost child or Jenny she hugged so tightly? It was Jenny who Liz saw leaving the room with Mel, an hour or so later, and that was all that mattered.

Mel never told Liz what had transpired between the two (or was it three?) of them. Jenny made a remarkable recovery and seemed to have little memory of the whole business. Liz was relieved to have her daughter back again. The jigsaw was still incomplete but every fresh episode allowed another tiny piece of the picture to emerge.

CHAPTER 19

Harriet and Jenny met a week later. Harriet was leaning on the hand rail of the walkway around the boathouse as Jenny approached. They had not arranged to meet but their unfailing telepathy drew them together. For a while they stood in silence, the older woman resting her elbows against the rail while the other held it tightly and swung on it with her feet planted firmly on the decking. The *Olly Ro* was still floating free, unaware of the trauma surrounding her.

"Don't do that. It makes me feel giddy."

Jenny stood up and pulled her jeans up, yanking her T-shirt down at the same time.

"I can't sing yet. My lungs still hurt."

"I know. It goes in time."

"How long did it affect your voice?"

"You know what happened to my brother, don't you?"

Jenny had forgotten Harriet never answered a question directly. "I do. I'll tell you if you feel you are ready."

"I think – no, I *know* I am."

Hand-in-hand the two of them walked slowly across the bridge and round to the other side of the lake until they reached the willow. There they sat on the bench and Jenny began to tell the story that Harriet had been afraid to face for sixty-five years. She told it as though reading from a book and the old woman sat riveted, not passing any comment until Jenny reached the end.

*

It was Christmas Eve and everyone had gone to church except for Harriet and David. They had decided to hold a conference to try and find a solution to the horrible problems they were facing. They climbed aboard the *Jolly Roger* and Harriet rowed to the centre of the lake so that no one could overhear them. She pulled the heavy oars on board. They drifted and bobbed as David read and re-read the letters Harriet had brought with her.

"I think what it means when you cut out all the gibberish, is that Father is to go into a nursing home. Maybe that would be good for him?" David screwed up his eyes as he spoke and his pale face scrutinized the wind-tanned one opposite him.

"Good for him, my foot. They'll just stick him in a corner and forget about him." Harriet was angry. This was all her disgusting mother's fault. "I hate them. I hate the fucking bastards. How dare they interfere? We'd be fine if only they'd leave us alone. You know what they'll do next, don't you? They'll split us up; put us in separate homes or farm us out to horrid, boring old families so we'd never see each other again." Hot tears of fear and anger poured.

"They can't split us up and send us away, can they? Not if we refuse. Can they?" David's voice revealed his sudden realization of the awful reality they faced. "What about Mummy?"

"Mother will be taken to the nut house where all the drunks go." Harriet spoke the words angrily and without thinking of the consequences.

David jumped up, screaming now: "No! No! Don't let them, Harriet. Stop them! Please. Please stop them!" He was throwing himself around in a blind fit of panic, causing the *Jolly Roger* to lurch and roll, taking in water as she did.

"Sit down, Davy." Harriet grabbed the oars to try to steady the craft, but her brother's fear was fast becoming hysteria and he could not hear her. "Watch it, you'll have us over."

David was thrashing about in the bow. He climbed over to the seat and lunged at his sister. For a split second Harriet let go of the oars and watched as they slid into the water. She grabbed and missed. "Now what am I supposed to do? This was a stupid bloody idea of yours!" David lost his temper and pushed hard at Harriet, forcing her to fall backwards into the bow. Her legs shot up and her head hit the deck. When she came to, she turned to face the bow. It was empty. Her brother was not there. She clambered to the front and peered over the side. The winter sun was setting and bounced off the water's surface, leaving it dark and impenetrable. She called out, knowing it would prove futile. Then, she jumped over the side, upended and dived like a duck. It was frighteningly dark and silent and cold, so very cold. Fronds of weeds waved as she thrashed about searching for David. Strong fingers tore at her, wrapping themselves in fiendish knots around her limbs. Then in a thick clump of blackness she caught a glimpse of blue and yellow. It was his Fair Isle pullover. Instinctively her hand reached out to him, but her lungs needed air. She forced her body upwards until her head broke the surface. She kept her eyes closed against the light as she gulped air into her body, then turning a somersault she kicked her sandalled feet high in the air and plunged in again, fixing her eyes to where David lay trapped.

Her determined arms could not free him from the persistent reeds. With each attempt the vicious plants closed in behind her like bars on a slippery, living cage, as determined as she was to hold on to their victim. She needed a pole, something to act as a lever. She looked for the oars but could see nothing except the upright supports of the boathouse. She swam to them and pulled her body heavy with waterlogged clothes onto the walkway. As she ran she wrenched off her sandals, her skirt and sweater, her coat was already lost in the water. An image of her mother and *the bastard* flashed across her brain. Swearing loudly she dismissed them and entered the boathouse. It was leaning against the wall, the boat hook that Tom had made for them. She grabbed it in both hands. Seeing with relief that the boat had drifted towards her she leapt on board. Using the pole, she manoeuvred the boat to where she had last seen David. She shivered with cold as she braced herself to jump in once more. It was pitch-black now as she pushed the hook under and dived in. She could see nothing. The mud was churning up and the water turning to thick sludge. Her ears were bursting and her lungs ached to be filled; their emptiness pressed at her until she could think of nothing but her pain. The water was rank and fetid. If she swallowed or breathed it in she could stay down here with her brother; the fearful future would be over before it had a chance to hurt them. She saw David's quizzical expression. The distorted screwed-up face he unwittingly adopted when thinking hard was pleading with her. She knew what she had to do. She thrust the boat hook down and swam down, following its lead. David was facing her, his eyes staring, glassy and expressionless, challenging her; his familiar face a strange ghastly white, asking why? His arms which he had wrapped around his body were bound firmly in place by the reeds. Only his hair moved as it followed the motion of the undercurrent pursuing some macabre dance. Skilfully she guided the hook into the folds of David's duffel coat. Then she pulled it with all the strength she could muster.

She was much too close. It was impossible to get any leverage. Hating to leave him, she rose to the surface again. She hauled herself into the boat, filling her tired lungs with the freezing air. Standing tall with the boat hook firmly in both hands she heaved at it with all her might. Nothing happened. She tried twisting the pole, fighting the weight of it, turning it desperately to wrench the boy free of the weed. Then, swirling up through the thick brown water it came, a thin mist of dark rust, reddening as it spread, and billowed until the surface of the water was crimson with blood, her brothers' blood.

The smell of death permeated the dankness of the night. Harriet sat back in the boat. She had killed her brother. She had meant to save him but she had killed him. A sharp pain rose up from somewhere deep inside her and it carried her soul with it as it emanated from her body, taking the form of a long thin howl. The agonized sound filled the garden, encircling the lake and floating across the lawns, entering the house until it reached her father's room, piercing his wretched body with its unnatural pitch. His daughter was calling him. He had to reach her if it was the last thing he did. Using his wasted arms, the weight of his sparse body working against him, he inched his wheelchair through the door and into the hall. At the kitchen doorstep the chair pitched forward, hurling the invalid onto the terrace, his body spread-eagled on the flagstones. Crawling forward, he pulled himself upright holding on to the balustrade until he stood for the first time in months. Then walking, crawling, he dragged his useless limbs over the grass towards the cry.

From nowhere a policeman was running across the lawn, his whistle cutting the silence in regular high ear-splitting blasts. He hit the water in a running dive from the jetty and climbed aboard the little boat where the girl was still leaning over the bow, her arms stretched beneath the water towards her brother. Manoeuvring the boat to the jetty he handed the child to her father and dived in to where she was still pointing. Harriet sat with her father's arms around her, reddened eyes never leaving the exact spot where David was. The young policeman dived in again, rising through the surface like a seal to shake his head and gulp in a deep breath. Down and down the policeman went until he emerged at last with his quarry. Harriet's wide amber eyes were glazed and fixed, staring in disbelief as the limp little body was placed on the jetty. Her tears poured out, cold, silent tears filled with horror and shame, and the guilt hit her throat like a tidal wave attempting to drown her too.

David looked as if he was asleep; his white skin shone with the translucent quality of an angel. The large purple wound in his chest did not seem to bother him. His face was peaceful and he smiled quietly as if his final question had been answered satisfactorily. People appeared from nowhere. Old Tom had called the police and they had sent for the ambulance. Bells were ringing, whistles were blowing and men were running, carrying stretchers and blankets, shouting orders to one another. Suddenly

Harriet was sitting in the kitchen with her father, holding mugs of hot, sweet tea in their hands and cold, bitter tears in their hearts. From somewhere in the garden came the long, low howling of a dog.

*

When Jenny had finished, she slid closer to Harriet and put her arms round her. Harriet was crying the bitter, salty tears of childhood.

"You didn't kill him. He was already dead. You did everything you could to save him and he knows that. I was lucky, my brother lived. Yours died. But you didn't kill him. I know how awful it must be for you. When I thought James was dead I wanted to die with him. I would willingly have died for him. David wanted you to live, to live for him. Now he wants you to be together again. He loves you."

Harriet stood up and patted her hair down where the wind had lifted it. Then she took out a large white handkerchief and blew her nose loudly. Straightening her cloak she turned, her face radiant and smiling as she looked at Jenny. The telling of the story, the truth about the accident had not brought it back to her; it had instead taken it away from her. It had erased the guilt. Every day, for each one of those painful years, she had lived with the belief that she killed her brother. She was sure she had speared him with the boat hook, and had remained unpunished for her crime. She had lived in fear of the retribution of the law, that one day they would come for her and she would be hanged as a murderer. Worse, she had lived with the retribution of the Furies. Now, thanks to this child's love, she could face her past and accept it. She knew her brother had forgiven her and was at peace. Now she needed to forgive herself. Hope and redemption, wasn't that what Jenny said were in the last two cups?

Jenny expected to feel tired after such a taxing ordeal. Instead she was revitalized and full of energy. "Let's go for a walk and you can tell me what Beckmans was like when you were my age. I want to see it through your eyes, Harriet. I want to hear about your father and your brother, your time in hospital…. And that dog we heard, what was its name? "

Harriet held up her hand. "Whoa. Steady on. I'm not as young as you, my little one. I need to rest now. It must be five o'clock. Time for my nap! The barking dog was Tess, old Tom's Labrador. She was black as the ace of spades, a shiny rascal. We thought Tom used spit and polish on her because she gleamed like his Sunday shoes. Speaking of which, where's that errant hound of yours? He keeps me company while I snooze."

The Pote appeared as if by magic and the two of them took themselves off to the Fourth Room for forty winks, leaving Jenny alone by the willow.

CHAPTER 20

Harriet woke up at five-fifteen, refreshed and eager to start. The Pote stretched his long body and nimbly leapt to the floor, stretched again and bounced out to the hall. She had dreamt of her father: how he had been before he became so ill, before he was an invalid. In her dream he was singing to her and even now his voice was clear and strong in her memory. There on the wall beside her hung her pathetic attempt at embroidery. She smiled and rubbed her fingers, which tingled as they recalled the pinpricks they had been subjected to in its making. Taking it from the bird-shaped hook she examined it more closely. There just below the small "w" of the alphabet was a faint blood stain. How she had rubbed at it to try and remove it. The horror as she had watched the deep-red blood seep over her masterpiece came instantly back. This was the same blood that had run through David's veins, but it was not her shedding of it that had killed him.

Lifting the sampler to her lips she kissed it. Even through the glass she could smell the past. That pungent tobacco smell that hovered around her father, the sweet smoke filling the air, it was still here. *The past never leaves us it simply merges into the present and becomes the future, before drifting back into the past again. Like that tiny stain it will never fade. Something will always remain, a vibration resonating for as long as we choose to listen.* Thoughts filled her mind as her fingers were removing the sampler from its frame. Behind it lay the small black-and-white photograph, her past captured in a frozen second, released into the present with one swift glance.

She recalled making her father a cup of tea, his favourite Earl Grey, and she put a couple of Garibaldi biscuits on the saucer. There were rosebuds and forget-me-nots painted on the china and she had removed the silver teaspoon to stop it rattling against the cup. There had been no reply when she knocked on the door. Balancing the tray on her arm, she turned the clasp and opened the door. The room was empty. His wheelchair was there and his pipe and slippers were neatly in place. Propped against the table lamp was a brown manila envelope with the words, "To my little nightingale" written in his shaky but distinctive hand. Placing the tray carefully on the bed, Harriet had opened the envelope and pulled out a small photograph. It was this same picture, a memory of her perched high on her father's shoulders. She was leaning over to look at him, her wild hair cascading around her beaming face. His head was turned towards his shoulder so that their eyes could meet as they shared a forgotten joke. It was only a small black-and-white snapshot, yet it contained all the colours of the rainbow. Nervously she had turned it over. On the back were the words: "To my little nightingale x"

*

George Marchant had taken an overdose the night before. No one told Harriet. No one had explained that he was gone for ever. They had taken him away before she could say goodbye. For a brief second Harriet burned with the rage and betrayal she had felt that day. Then as she looked again at the photograph the anger melted away. It was her past but only a part of it. There were parts it was wise not to remember, but this was not one.

It was her birthday and the sun was shining. Everyone else had gone out and she was alone with her father. They had been walking round the garden collecting leaves and bugs to study later under their magnifying glass. Tom was working in the vegetable patch with Tess half-sleeping, half-watchful, stretched out on the hot flagstones by the greenhouse. Her father asked him to take a picture of the two of them and while Tom went to find the box Brownie her Daddy hoisted her high above his head. She was flying. All that existed above her was endless blue sky. Sitting high on her father's shoulders she was far safer than she would ever be again. To her these were the broadest shoulders in the world and the arms that wrapped around her brown gypsy ankles were the strongest, kindest arms of any man. She had bent down to give him an Eskimo kiss and he told her she smelt like a Munchkin. That was the joke they were sharing. As this memory returned to her Harriet laughed again, not with her usual snort, but in a giggly, childish way, as she would have done all those years ago.

And here they were together, still smiling, sharing the magic, in blissful ignorance of the fact that within a year he would be confined to a wheelchair, unable to raise his arms above his head, or that soon that happy little girl would be robbed of her childhood and thrown into a future where blue skies seldom featured. Nothing could alter the fact that once upon a time this was her life. Nothing could take it away. It would still be hers when what will be had become what was.

CHAPTER 21

The revelations by the lake had left Jenny far from exhausted. She was energized, euphoric, her head exploding with questions. Curiosity ate away at her. Who was Harriet? When had she lived at Beckmans and for how long? Already she had been given snatches of a life so different from her own. It was as though she had completed the outer edges of the jigsaw, but the inner picture was still missing. She needed to do some serious research. Maybe she should recruit James. He was a whiz with the computer. How much should she tell him? He would never believe she had befriended a ghost. What about her mother? Should she confide in her? She decided to operate on a need-to-know basis. Tomorrow she would visit the local churchyard to begin her investigations. Pleased with her decision, she discovered that she was extremely hungry. Whistling loudly, she raced back to the house demanding food, to her mother's delight. It was exactly five o'clock.

The next time Jenny and Harriet met it was to continue with their singing lessons. Jenny's throat and lungs had taken quite a bashing, but her voice now rested was back as clear and strong as ever. Scales were the main item on the agenda and Harriet was delighted to find that Jenny shared her own enjoyment in striving for the technical perfection required to master them. For hours they would run up and down musical stairways,

changing keys at a given signal or modulating from
major to minor at the lifting of a finger or the raising of
an eyebrow. The teacher's eyes never left her pupil,
picking up on each tiny glitch or deviation from exact
pitch. Only laughter was allowed to interrupt these
sessions and then only for the briefest of seconds either
when tension needed lifting or a real howler sent them
into paroxysms of giggles. Mostly the time was spent in
deep concentration and rapt absorption of the task in
hand. And they were always enjoyable times. At the end
of a lesson they would wind down by singing together.
Jenny's repertoire was considerable for a ten-year-old
and the speed and ability with which she mastered new
works never failed to impress Harriet. She never said as
much to Jenny. Not given to praise, she never told her
pupil that she had a truly remarkable gift; she would
simply say if the work was good or there was room for
improvement. Miss Bunting had taught her well.

Jenny adored her teacher, but there was much she did
not know about her. Asking questions proved pretty
futile, so the only option was to play detective. She had
already made two visits to the churchyard without
telling anyone apart from the sexton, who found her
rooting around the headstones. "Acting suspicious" was
the way he had described it and for one awful moment
she thought he would throw her out or have her arrested.
Of course, when she explained what she was looking for
he could not do enough to help. He apologized for
misjudging her, but told her "one could not be too
careful with all the young vandals rampaging around,
bent on no good". He knew of two graves bearing the
name Harriet. One dated from 1794 and the other from
1971. The first stone was very worn and offered no clues

264

linking it to her Harriet. In fact the name was so eroded that she would not have recognized it had the good verger not pointed it out. She began to wonder if the project was doomed before it had started.

The second grave had a simple granite stone without ornamentation, with the words: "Harriet May Marchant. 1931–1971". 1971. Jenny noted that was the same year her mother had been born. The grave stood in a family plot next to a more elaborate stone bearing the inscription: "David Edward Marchant. 1931–1942. Beloved son. Cruelly taken. R.I.P." This was it. A boy and a girl born the same year, only the boy died at the tender age of eleven. The likelihood of any other twins named David and Harriet being alive in 1939 when the sampler was embroidered was too incredible. The modest grave was Harriet's, resting beside that of her brother. Poor Harriet, the horror of losing one's father and twin was unimaginable. Jenny flinched at the thought. Her blood ran cold as she realised the horror of Harriet's loss. As she wiped her eyes with her sleeve she wished she too always carried a clean white handkerchief just like her friend.

The twins' graves lay side by side in the small family plot, separated by thirty years. The graveyard was tended, but it was large and there was an air of neglect about the older graves. There was no sign of flowers being left; it was many years since a tear had been shed for any of the occupants. Two larger stones dominated this site. The first was inscribed, "George Alfred Marchant 1884–1942. Devoted husband and father". The second simply read: "Alice Mildred Marchant 1909–47". Jenny wondered what would be written on her headstone when she died. The idea of being buried was horrible but the alternatives were almost worse.

This was not a subject she had thought about until now and it opened up a whole new scary dimension to be explored, but later.

Thrilled at her discovery of the Marchant family grave, Jenny made a note of the inscriptions in her notepad, thanked the sexton and left. She returned a little later and laid a small bunch of primroses on David's grave and a posy of violets for Harriet. It felt hypocritical kneeling at the burial place of a friend who was still so alive. Try as she might, she could not imagine Harriet mouldering in the grave. According to this she had died in 1971 at the age of forty. The woman she knew was much, much older. It did not seem so awful if you looked at it as a new leaf in an old book. But how unusual was Harriet? Do we all have the choice of going or staying? This was something she needed to discuss later with Mel. It was not the reason for her being here right now. This was the beginning of a quest. Now the research could start in earnest. Harriet was so alive for her that it was incongruous to be researching into her death. She felt as though she was playing a part in a film that she was also directing and watching. There was no way she could explain this to anyone else, she did not even understand it herself. She even doubted that Harriet would.

She was proved right. Trying to explain this bizarre situation to a ten-year-old brother proved impossible. After several attempts Jenny found herself lying. It was easier to call it a school project: "Choose a headstone in the local church and build up a history of the person's life." This involved researching old newspapers and parish magazines. She might have to visit the Coroner's Office or plough through church records and hunt for birth, death and marriage certificates. James's face lit up.

This was right up his street, exclaiming this was exactly what the internet had been designed for. He was off rattling away at the keys before Jenny could blink.

It took some time, but eventually the two sleuths amassed a thick dossier on the Marchant family: copies of house deeds, certificates concerning every possible landmark between life and death. They had extracts from local newspapers, photographs from *The Lady* and *Tatler*; they had even traced group portraits of the family posed in their Sunday-best. James managed to track down the photographer who had printed the snapshot in the sampler. Miraculously it was a family business that still existed and they had negatives dating back to the beginning of time. They generously allowed the researchers access to a wealth of information, adding a visual dimension to the nearly completed and fascinatingly detailed jigsaw that was the Marchant family.

*

Meanwhile Liz was preparing for her exhibition. The timing was perfect. Jenny jumped at the chance to take and fetch things from the printers, often adding a small unnoticed consignment of her own. It also kept their mother out of the way. She had been very dismissive of Harriet's existence whenever Jenny tried to raise the subject. Everyone had. It was disconcerting to be disbelieved so vehemently by so many whom one expected to believe you. Harriet was explained away as a figment of the imagination; an illusion conjured up to explain the inexplicable; or (and this Jenny found hardest to swallow) a projection of her subconscious mind concocted to enable it to cope with the traumatic complexes of guilt and fear induced by her ordeal!

Harriet's reaction to these "professional" opinions was a loud snort. Jenny was dying to tell her how far her research had got; how close she was to proving Harriet's existence, but she recognized the need for caution. She did not want to blow the whistle too soon. Her work was nearly completed. It took the form of a scrapbook, following the lines of a narrative piece with each entry backed up by, or justified by, actual data she had collected. It was a masterpiece of detection. There was only one identifiable fault and Jenny did not yet know how she was going to overcome it. Even when presented with all this evidence a sceptic could still deny Harriet's presence. There was no denying a woman named Harriet had lived and that she had lived here in Beckmans. The story of her brother and the tragic circumstances of his death were recounted in newspaper articles and coroner's reports. But how could Jenny prove her claims to have had prior knowledge, to have been told the whole story first by Harriet? They could simply say she had seen this information somewhere and registered it subliminally. How could she prove Harriet had played a central, integral part in rescuing James? How does one prove that a ghost is physical? Too much was left unanswered.

Jenny was an exceptionally open child, endowed with considerable psychic gifts herself but not yet tutored in the fine details of mediumship. It had not occurred to her that what she was doing was communicating with the dead. The barriers between life and death had not yet touched her. She had not lost anyone close enough for her to ask the most difficult questions. She believed in right and wrong with the fervour of a caring ten-year-old, but good and evil were not qualities she had really tried to explain. To her innocent mind what was happening was a simple question of fairness. It was not fair that Harriet should go unacknowledged by those people she had helped. Her mother's forthcoming exhibition was a case in point. Jenny could spot Harriet's hand in the paintings. She had personal proof of Harriet's gifts as a teacher and a guide. Why should they take all the glory when Harriet had been denied so much in her own life? Now Jenny had the facts about the Marchant family she felt it her duty to give Harriet the credit due to her.

The only person Jenny knew who might understand was Mel. Since her cancer, Mel was already taking a less prominent role in young Jenny's life. The incident in the Fourth Room had caused her to step back even further. It had taken a lot out of her. Over the years she had been taught to ration her psychic work so that it never exposed her to the limits of her ability. This had been her first encounter with a total "possession". The "sad little girl" had been so desperate to get through that she had taken Jenny's body as a means to communicate. She had tried it before with Liz with a modicum of success, but with a child of similar age the result was a resounding hit. Mel's knowledge of possession was that it was safe and containable, so long as the spirit was benign. If the intent was malignant, or if the spirit decided to stay in possession of the body it was using, that was altogether a different matter. It was no longer a simple case of asking the spirit to leave. The person possessed was in danger of losing their claim to their physical body, leaving their own spirit to wander homeless and defenceless, vulnerable as a snail without its shell. A lost soul. Mel had never had to deal with such a dilemma.

She had heard of it happening extremely rarely. Nevertheless, such things were not to be ignored or made light of.

Knowing the occult to be a potentially dangerous place, Mel was in no doubt that this was nowhere for a child to wander at will. It posed no fears for Mel, but then she was a shrewd cookie, an old soul who had been around the unseen world since long before she had been born. Nobody outside her closest circle of practising psychics had ever heard her talk about this side of her work. Just as a priest never admits to tapping into the power of the occult to anyone but his fellow clergy, a good medium keeps her counsel. It had been Mel's experience that as soon as she started to explain her beliefs beyond the safe shallows of clairvoyance and healing, the shutters slammed down and she would be declared a "nutter". This did not worry her; her spiritual skin had grown thick and fitted her well, but she was tired of explaining herself to a brick wall of scepticism. Better to go only as far as she could be followed, then leave the disbelievers behind to travel on alone. She had nothing to lose. If at the end of the day she was proved right then she would be laughing. Should it transpire that she had been wrong, then the joke would be on her and she would still be the one laughing. Mel never took her self too seriously.

So when young Jenny came to her with her story, Mel was intrigued but unsure how to approach it. It occurred to her that it might take her into realms of which she had little or no experience. She had no doubt about the truth of the existence of the Marchants. That was clearly documented. But as she understood it, Jenny was claiming that the spirit of Harriet was alive and well and living at Beckmans. The existence of a spirit was not the problem. She had already encountered the entity that had possessed Jenny and had previously taken over Liz. But that was the spirit of a child. In Mel's experience a spirit that remained earthbound took the same form it manifested at the time of its physical death. Jenny was claiming knowledge of an older woman, one who was aging in real time and could effect physical change. Never before had Mel been offered such compelling evidence of interaction between the physical and spirit worlds. In her experience, a spirit might work through a living being but had no power to manifest actual physical phenomena, apart from the odd twitch of a curtain or a clock stopping and starting. To believe Jenny's story she would have to revise her whole philosophy. The project excited her. And should it prove to be beyond her capabilities she could always call in the help of a more experienced medium. Either way, it was thrilling.

First, Jenny described how she had met Harriet. She talked about their shared passion for music and how Harriet had been training her voice to prepare her for the Royal College of Music once she left school. Mel could accept all this. Guides from the world of spirit often worked through others, sometimes altruistically helping a kindred spirit and sometimes to satisfy their own thwarted ambitions. Mel was convinced that Liz was receiving guidance with her painting and there was no reason to doubt Jenny was being helped too. It was Jenny's insistence that Harriet Marchant was her tutor that Mel found difficult to accept. It was her opinion that all the research, the wealth of facts Jenny had accumulated about this family, had filled her head. She was obsessed with Harriet, rather than being possessed by her.

The outcome was disappointing. No matter how Mel put it, Jenny knew she did not believe in her Harriet. It was not enough to describe her as a spirit. Surely, Jenny argued, we are all spirits but some of us have bodies too. Harriet was a real, tangible person. As far as Jenny was concerned Harriet was no different from herself. But Mel made it clear that she could not accept this. She resolutely clung to her conviction that Harriet was a projection of Jenny rather than someone who existed independently. For someone who had sat with her and spoken with her, had sung with her, been held by her and held her in return, this was not at all satisfactory. Jenny concluded that Mel might as well call Harriet an imaginary friend and have done with it. Jenny's opinion of Mel plummeted. But then, thinking back, there had been the business with the Tarot. Those last three cards had obviously been chosen by and for Harriet. If she could see that then surely a trained medium would have. The Page of Cups was poor little David, a fish out of water, desperate to communicate. The ferryman who carried them out to meet their fate was describing Harriet's accident, not hers. Death took one of the children while the other drifted alone throughout life, waiting for a chance to find hope and redemption. The Five of Cups was Harriet, who else? The homecoming, the inheritance: it was all there plainly for everyone to see - if one chose to look. The cards can be read in many ways and they can lead away from the truth if one dares not face it. Jenny decided it was time to tell the whole family the truth about the accident exactly as she remembered it. They could hardly dare to deny Harriet's existence then.

CHAPTER 22

Only Jenny and Harriet had ventured near the lake or the boathouse since the accident and the *Olly Ro* still drifted free of tethered ropes or moorings. Three months had passed and the storm would have been long forgotten had it not been for the near-drowning of the twins. All the murkiness had gone, leaving the lake and stream clear and innocent. A few ducks had returned to the safety of their island, dismayed to find their house in ruins. The water level remained abnormally high for weeks and when it finally subsided, the silt left behind on the bridge and the decking bore testament to the heights it had reached. Debris littered the far bank and there was a large muddy slick on the near side. Today the boathouse stood out against the sunshine, a couple of loose tiles being the only sign of any storm. There was an eerie stillness in the air, which mirrored the atmosphere of the little party gathered on the walkway beyond the bridge. The Pote remained in the house. Since all the drama he had taken himself off to the security of the armchair in the small sitting-room, seizing the opportunity whenever he found the door open.

"How do you guys want me to do this?" Jenny had assembled her mother and father, and James down by the boathouse. It was one week before Liz's exhibition and she was alarmed to be retracing a nightmare that, she felt, was best forgotten. The children had been reluctant to talk about it when it had seemed the obvious thing to do. Now the drama had died down, surely it was wise to leave it there, buried in the mud, where that wretched boat belonged too. No, Liz was convinced they should all look forward, face the engine, as her father used to say. Actually she was terrified of what might be dragged up. Inquests were morbid affairs best avoided. However, she could not ignore Jenny's request. Maybe there were issues her daughter needed to face and although Jenny had made a remarkable recovery, she had never talked about her experience, which was odd. It also left the nagging fear that the trauma could emerge as an emotional crisis at a later point in time. Better to deal with it now, once and for all. So Liz gathered with the others to listen to Jenny's story. A part of her was curious to know exactly what had happened on that awful night, nevertheless it was with some trepidation that she listened as Jenny began. Liz watched her daughter stand up tall and take a deep breath to compose herself. She felt amazingly proud of her children, especially Jenny. Her strength was phenomenal. Her voice was deep and there was an air of confidence about her that had only become apparent since the trauma of the accident had lifted. She described the night in graphic detail with no hint of fear or doubt. The squabbles in the attic were not touched on, nor James's refusal to wear his life-jacket. She concentrated on the accident itself, which she relayed with an eerie detachment and faultless accuracy. She described how she had wanted to turn back and how it was only at that point that she realized she had lost control of the boat. She told how one minute James was standing in the bow and the next he was gone. As she spoke, the full horror of the night was relayed, clearly and without emotion, almost as though she was watching a film.

Her family listened, amazed at the fluency with which she recalled the events of that dreadful night. Her rescue attempts, her fight for air, her lungs bursting and burning as the last atom of oxygen expired; the darkness and the freezing water; the agony of thinking her brother was lost. This was not the relaying of a child's experience. This was a studied heartfelt account by an eyewitness of maturity and understanding, which belied Jenny's ten short years of life. When she had finished she turned to the boathouse and a glimmer of a smile flickered across her pale drawn face.

"How did you get James out, Jenny?" her father asked gently, probing not challenging.

"She pulled him out." The sudden use of the third person was baffling. Liz and Edward began to feel uncomfortable, listening to this vulnerable child speaking with such detached control. It was as though by distancing herself from the whole ghastly business she could release her memory without reliving the pain.

Liz wanted to call a halt to the proceedings when Edward posed another question. "I don't understand, darling. If you and James were in the water, how did you, or 'she', pull him out?"

Jenny paused, thinking hard. She closed her eyes to remember in more detail. This time she spoke with considerable emotion. Again she told of the cold, the blackness of the water recounting flashbacks that brought her near to drowning. The searing pain in her lungs and ears the voice calling to her from where they stood now. It all flooded out. Harriet, the boat hook… she freed herself of every detail. When she had finished she was drained. Her hair stuck to her head, wet with perspiration, and her young body shook with spasms, causing her to gasp for breath. Red-hot tears streamed from her eyes and she clung to the rail as she sobbed. Her parents sat transfixed. Liz's thoughts were racing. *Why is Jenny talking as if all this happened to someone else? Has she concocted this bizarre rescue story to ease her feelings of guilt? Survivors can feel very guilty. Why didn't we do this with the help of professionals? What if Jenny has a relapse? And what is this nonsense about a boat hook? What boat hook? Why on earth did we drag all this up again?*

Suddenly Liz was back standing on the bank beneath the willow. The weeping child was there too, only now she was taller and wore a long black cloak. The two were becoming fused in her mind. Were they one and the same? Was one her daughter and the other herself? The long, black shadow was casting its misery over everything. It had to be stopped before it was too late. Again she felt the emptiness, the total absence of love that she felt the day they raised the first horrid boat. Were there two boats or just one? To her they had merged until they were one and the same. She could no longer separate the past from the present. What was it Jenny said about the cards, something about time being all the same? Was this what Jenny felt now? It did not need a mother's instinct to know her daughter was in pain. This brave girl was being left to face these horrors alone, feeling abandoned by the one person who should be there whatever. A real mother gave her children the strength and comfort they needed, unconditionally and unbidden. How could she refuse to believe in Jenny's friend, this Harriet woman? She was obviously very real to her daughter? All this raced through Liz's brain at the speed of a dream. She scooped Jenny into her arms, hugging her until they lay in a heap not knowing whether they were crying or laughing.

Meanwhile, James ever the pragmatist had wriggled free from his father's vice-like grip and stood before his sister. He had adopted her stance: fists planted firmly on his waist and his powerful legs planted squarely, and for once there was no mistaking that they were twins.

"So? Who pulled me out?"

That was too much for Jenny. "How many times do I have to tell you? It was Harriet. She handed me the boat hook. I felt the funny marks on the end where Tom carved their initials. They were what helped me grip it. She pulled us both out: me first, then you. She told me how to give you the kiss of life. She made me keep going when I wanted to give up and die. She saved your life and she's my friend. Look, over there; the tall lady in the long cloak. She has thick white hair and wears it with a comb like Mummy's. She's my singing teacher. She paints like Mummy, in fact she teaches her. Look, she's standing over there. For Heaven's sake, there's only us and her!"

Jenny was pointing to the corner of the boathouse. She looked imploringly at her mother for help. While Jenny was talking, Harriet had been standing close by, encouraging and prompting her prodigy. Liz was torn. She had always tried to be totally open and honest with her children. Should she lie now to support Jenny? To claim she could see someone who was not there seemed hypocritical, but here was her daughter desperate for her to corroborate her story.

The girl threw a desperate glance to Harriet and said, "I'm so sorry. They can't or won't see you." She looked at her family in bewilderment and not without accusation.

With the bluntness of the young, James said, "There's nobody there, Stupido."

In all honesty Liz could not see any woman, let alone an imposing white-haired one, yet the words of gratitude that tumbled out of her were addressed convincingly to the empty spot by the boathouse, surprising herself as much as the others:

"I don't know who you are, but from the bottom of my heart I thank you. Because of you my children are safe. You've given them back to me and I shall never forget that. If I can repay you in any way I will." Then she too blew a kiss into the ether. Had she spoken in solidarity with her daughter, or was it a subconscious desire to believe? It hardly seemed to matter, nor did she feel a complete idiot for doing it.

A falling leaf brushed her hair and she raised her hand to catch it. It felt as light as a kiss.

CHAPTER 23

Liz's Private View was a resounding success. She sold three and took five commissions. One of the buyers was a dealer from London, a friend of Mel's, and the other two were neighbours; but even so it augured well. The cards had been right. Her career was taking off. The whole family was swept up with the euphoria of the occasion. The gallery was delighted and agreed to hold another show in a year's time which meant Liz would be kept occupied increasing her portfolio. When Edward voiced his doubts as to the viability of the project he was quickly shouted down. The idea had never been to make money, which as he justly pointed out was lucky, because actually they hadn't. More champagne was passed around and eventually even he had to concede it was a successful night. Her paintings hung for three weeks and although no more sold there was always a chance of more commissions.

The accident was done and dusted, as far as everyone was concerned; everyone but Jenny. For her, there were still issues to be resolved. Her mother's address to Harriet had helped her contain her anger, but it was not yet a closed book. Then there was the other book and the small matter of the presentation. Harriet was completely in the dark as to Jenny's secret sleuthing. She was unaware of all the time and effort that had gone into researching her life, her family and her death. All the gathered information had been assembled and compiled into a large red book on which were embossed in large gold letters the words: "This Is Your Life, Harriet Marchant: 1931-1971." Jenny did not feel guilty about having commissioned this (at some considerable expense) from her mother's frame-maker without telling anyone or offering to pay for it herself; it seemed fair recompense for being doubted. She was still smarting from the fact that no one believed her. Worse, no one believed in Harriet. As for Harriet, she found it amusing to be considered an imaginary friend and dismissed it without a second thought. To Jenny it was an insult. Harriet resolved to think up a scheme that would exonerate Jenny, as an act of solidarity and to prove once and for all that she was very much alive. But that might take time.

*

Their lesson ended as usual with the two of them singing together. As often happened, Jenny would come with a request but this time she did not know the name of the piece or even the composer. As she began to hum it, Harriet took up the melody and performed it with such emotion that Jenny knew she must learn it too. Harriet was more than willing, for it was one of her all-time favourites. Originally a French peasant song, it had a pure, untainted quality that perfectly suited Jenny's voice. It was one of Canteloube's *"Songs of the Auvergne"* and although she was not yet aware of it, this would become Jenny's signature piece.

Exhilarated by the discovery of such a musical gem, Jenny deemed the time right to present her friend with the book. She had left it in the boathouse, wrapped in gift paper with a card that had a picture of a boat on it, in which she expressed her heartfelt thanks for a valued friendship. As Harriet opened it Jenny could hardly contain herself.

Harriet read the card and smiled. It was so long since she had received a gift, she had forgotten the thrill of tearing at ribbons and paper to get to the treasure inside. Her eyes read the inscription and she visibly stiffened. Her back upright and proud, she exuded a terrifying power. Her white head lifted to an even higher plane as she breathed in and turned to the opening page.

Jenny began to doubt the wisdom of her project. Harriet was a very private person and here before her was her life laid out for all to see. Jenny swallowed hard. The first page showed a photograph of Harriet's mother before her marriage, when she was still Alice Weatherby; a beautiful young woman in her debutante dress of white satin, a corsage of orchids on her pale, slim shoulder. Her long, silky hair was swept up into a simple chignon and held a discreet diamond tiara that shone beneath the studio lights. She had clearly been a real head-turner and Jenny was thrilled to have found this photo, albeit black and white, in an edition of *The Queen*, published in 1928. Harriet snorted loudly; not the reaction Jenny had hoped for. The page was turned roughly and the reader found herself staring at her parents on their wedding day. She began to flick through the book with an almost frenzied attack, pausing haphazardly to give an aggressive grunt. Then her eyes rested on a recent photo of the four local headstones, one of which bore her name and the dates of her birth and supposed death. It was too much for her. The book was hurled to the floor and Harriet's eyes met Jenny's. The disdain that shot from them terrified the child. Jenny bent to retrieve the book and straighten the pages, buying time for her confused brain. When she finally dared look up, there was no sign of Harriet.

Liz heard her daughter's song wafting across the lake towards the house. The clarity of Jenny's young voice rang in her ears and Liz put down what she was doing and went to the door. For some reason the tone switched dramatically, turning a sweet melodious tune into an angry bellow. This was matched by feet that kicked viciously at the unfortunate leaves in her path, sending them hurtling into the air, while an expression of hurt indignation burned on her face. At the back door Jenny kicked off her Wellingtons and vainly attempted to remove her woollen socks. One stayed gripping her ankle, having twisted to face the wrong way, while the other drooped off her foot, growing longer with each tug as though belonging to a far larger foot than hers. Swearing and cursing at the recalcitrant pair she noticed The Pote lying in a pile of leaves, his dark eyes full of sympathy and compassion. He too looked as though his heart was breaking. Jenny ran over to him, the stupid socks tripping her and gaining weight as they sponged up moisture from the grass. She slid to a kneeling position in front of her dog, buried her face in his warm coat and sobbed.

Liz stood in the doorway. She debated whether to interfere or leave them alone for a moment. Jenny was at an age when her hormones were raging and mood swings were common. When she was like this it was wise to leave her alone until she came round, which usually pretty quickly. She was not by nature a moody child and Liz wondered if it was the song that had brought on the tears. The music had reminded her of something distant, a long-lost memory. But that did not account for the tantrum; Jenny was very angry about something. Liz's thoughts were interrupted by a squeal of pain. Jenny had tried to lift The Pote and he had snapped at her, drawing blood. Jenny pulled away, more alarmed than scared. The Pote bit Edward at regular intervals, but never Jenny. Liz ran towards them and seeing the look of despair in the dog's eyes she realized he was ill. She carried him to his basket and Jenny covered him with his duvet. He licked her on the nose as if to say "sorry" and she tucked him in.

"What's wrong with The Pote?" Jenny asked as Liz stuck a plaster on her wound.

"He's in pain, that's why he bit you."

"I don't care about that. I just want to know what's wrong with him."

"I don't know, darling, he might have strained his back. He was chasing squirrels earlier and he does go a bit crazy. He's no spring chicken, although he tends to forget that. Let's leave him to rest for a while. He'll be as right as rain in a minute, you'll see. I'll call the vet if he doesn't perk up soon." Liz called James and served lunch. A familiar bark of greeting followed by a duvet with a wagging tail moved across the room to welcome James.

"It's amazing what the promise of food can do! James, get those muddy boots off now!"

Jenny ate her pasta with a disinterest that was not normal for her, then pushing her chair back from the table she made for the door. James had already bolted back to the shed to continue with his experiments.

"Hang on a mo," said Liz. "That was pretty amazing singing just now. When did you learn that song? Tell me what it is and I'll get a DVD. Would you like that?"

"Great, yeah, whatever, can I go now?" Jenny was itching to get back to the garden.

"I know I've heard it somewhere before. What is it?"

"Pastourelle. Bye, Mum."

"Who's it by?" Jenny was halfway out of the door as Liz caught her by the arm. "Hang on a minute. I hardly ever get to see you; you're either at school, messing about with the computer or you're mooching alone down by the lake. We used to be so close. What's up? Talk to me."

"OK, Mum, what do you want to talk about?" Impatience rang in Jenny's every word.

"Well, you never told me how your project went. You spent so much time on it. I'd love to see it. Is it finished?"

"Yeah, it's at school. Anything else?"

"God, Jenny, you are so transparent. OK. Go on. You've obviously got better things to do in the garden." Liz waved her daughter on and, as if to compound the hurt, Jenny headed for the Fourth Room. She had to find Harriet before it was too late.

She was half-expecting Harriet to be waiting. Hopefully by now she would have got over whatever had upset her and would be taking a nap in her usual spot. Sadly the room was empty. The Pote entered, immediately turned tail and left, without so much as a second sniff, confirming her suspicions that there was no sign or sense of Harriet. Pulling on her boots, Jenny whistled to the dog and slouched off alone across the lawn. The Pote stared after her, refusing to follow. To Liz's delight he came back in and lay at her feet. Someone appreciated her company. She picked the little dog up and he squealed with pain. She carried him into the sitting-room, leaving her guilt on the table with the dirty dishes, and settled down for an indulgent hour or two sprawled on the settee, lost to a soporific dose of afternoon TV, nursing the dog.

It did not take long for the warmth of the fire and the inane programme content to send Liz to sleep. When she awoke, The Pote was still stretched out across her lap. As she picked him up to place him on the floor his agonized crying told her his back problem was serious.

The yowls stopped Jenny in her tracks. As she burst in, Liz was on the telephone, her manner agitated. The dog lay immobile on the sofa and Liz signalled for Jenny not to touch him. As Jenny went to speak, her mother raised a hand in a gesture demanding quiet while she continued to speak into the phone. Jenny listened in horror. She sank to her knees and placed her head next to her dog. She was still there twenty minutes later when the doorbell rang.

James opened the door to the vet and the nurse. He showed them into where the The Pote was lying on the armchair with Liz. After a thorough examination, during which the poor little creature merely growled gently without even baring his teeth at his arch enemy, the vet had to admit that the back was severely damaged. They took him to the surgery where he remained for a week to undergo the most horrific operation on his spine. During the whole horrid business he remained meekly reconciled, but when it was obvious he was never going to walk again, the family had some serious decisions to make. Being paralysed from mid-back to his tail meant not only loss of mobility but incontinence and total dependence on human assistance. It seemed unfair to expect this proud creature to survive in such ignominious, reduced circumstances. It was deemed only fitting that he should be at home in familiar surroundings when the vet performed his unpleasant task.

So The Pote was brought back to Beckmans and carried into the Fourth Room. James ran upstairs so no one would see him crying, but Jenny determined to be with her dog to the bitter end. Liz nodded her approval and Jenny placed her best friend on Harriet's chair, kneeling beside it to be as close as possible. She had prayed that Harriet would be there waiting, but the chair was empty as she laid him down. The Pote looked up at Jenny and licked her on the nose. She felt her heart would break, it hurt so much. This was real pain, her pain not his. Her dog was calmly accepting his death. As the first needle went in he went to sleep. One more shot and he was dead. Jenny looked at her watch. It was exactly five o'clock.

*

They buried The Pote beneath the willow tree. The small congregation were in pieces. Harriet stood some distance off, unseen, holding him in her arms, remembering Tess who was buried in the exact same spot. The house was full of tears and emptiness for weeks after. The twins had not known life without The Potentate. This was their first taste of death. Jenny mourned the deepest as she was also mourning the loss of her friend. She had seen no sign of Harriet since the incident with the dreaded book. Jenny wished she had never written it, but for the life of her she could not see what Harriet found so offensive. It had, after all, been a gesture of love. There was no way of turning the clock back, but Jenny wished she could at least have a chance to explain her motives. The thought of never seeing The Pote again was hateful. To lose Harriet too was unbearable.

It hurt Harriet to watch Jenny in such misery. She knew how each new death brought back the memory of all the others. She too was missing her friend. She missed their singing lessons and the indescribable joy she experienced watching such a great talent grow and develop. And Jenny had a great talent, of that Harriet had no doubts whatsoever. In time maybe she would be able to forgive and understand, or understand and then forgive. Either way she was not yet ready. She was still smarting. It is hard to explain how it feels to see a gravestone bearing your name, to read a copy of your own death certificate and hold the coroner's report on your brother's death in your hand. It had been a shock. But when Harriet had calmed down she had to admit, reluctantly, that it was the photograph of dear Mama looking so beautiful and charming that really got up her nose. This was the picture her mother had always presented to the world, none of her cruelty or selfishness showing on that near-perfect face. It was unkind to punish Jenny. After all, she was still a child. How was she to know about the *"fucking bastards"* of this world?

CHAPTER 24

The winter of 2010 was an odd mix of delight and sorrow. Much of the delight came from the arrival of a new puppy, another dachshund: Google. The family soon discovered that pedigree dogs have similar traits within their breed. Dachshunds love to be covered, they hate to get wet and they would sell their souls for food. However, this shared gene was the only thing The Pote and young Google had in common. For one thing, The Pote was very much a dog and Google was a bitch. Whether gender played any part in the second difference was debatable, but from day one the puppy displayed exemplary manners. She never snatched food or became aggressively possessive. Her toys, her bed, even precious bones were willingly shared. She never snapped at or bit anyone, not even Edward; in fact she flirted shamelessly with him. It was predictable that in time her speed would match that of her predecessor, but she showed none of his hooligan tendencies. She was in no way a replacement but she was a great addition.

The children fell in love at first sniff and the feeling was mutual. They took Google to the willow where they introduced her to The Pote. She squatted by the small concrete headstone as James read in a pompous voice: "The Potentate April 1999 – November 2007. Beloved companion - Triumphant in death. R.I.P." They found this carved on a gravestone while researching the

Marchant family and thought it the ultimate in Victorian pomposity. They insisted on using it despite their father's disdain at its inappropriateness for a dog's grave. But they argued that it befitted a comedian of The Pote's standing to be given a suitably apt memorial. This was duly acknowledged and the stone was erected. Harriet watched the twins with their new puppy. Silently and unseen she observed them at play. They were just children. The same age her brother had been when…. Maybe it was time to step out of the shadows. *Life is far too short to bear grudges*, she thought. *Tomorrow. I shall be ready to meet Jenny tomorrow. After all, I still have my destiny to fulfil.*

Christmas loomed large and the aged fairy was hoisted aloft once more, having had yet more Araldite applied to her aching wings. In more ways than one, this year's festivities promised to be a trip down memory lane. David was returning from France on a much-belated visit, minus a bestseller as such, but with the first three chapters of his manuscript ready to take to an agent. Liz had succeeded in persuading Donald and Brenda to join them having warned Mel, under pain of alcohol deprivation, to behave. Young Robert was due home on a visit from Cambridge. Google was nearly house-trained and Edward had apparently recovered from his midlife crisis. Everything pointed to a splendid celebration. Liz shopped and cooked for England.

*

The book sat on the shelf in Jenny's bedroom. It remained unread, much to her disappointment. Wrapping her presents brought it all flooding back. Never had she felt so uncomfortable. She had completely misread the situation and could not find anyone sympathetic enough to confide in. There was little chance of discovering why it had been so badly received if nobody would talk it through with her. Her family made it very clear that the subject of the "imaginary" Harriet was a closed book, like the one sitting on the shelf. That hollow thank-you speech of her mother's had been exposed as just that, shortly after it was delivered, so eloquently after the post-mortem on the bridge. A dismissive, "Darling, don't you think you're a bit old for all this nonsense? Imaginary friends are babyish..." said it all. As soon as her mother uttered those uncharitable words, Jenny vowed never to mention Harriet in front of her again. Even Mel had betrayed her, reneging on all she purported to believe when presented with incontrovertible evidence.

Pressing her nose into the puppy's fur, Jenny poured out her angst and despair to her new confidante. Like her predecessor, Google listened attentively until her tiny brain was exhausted and she fell asleep, flat on her back, just like The Pote. Jenny kissed the soft pink belly and soaked up the milky, toasty smell of a young pup. The presents would not wrap themselves and at least they would provide a distraction from her morbid thoughts. The rustling of paper and ribbons and the novelty of sticky tape proved enough temptation to wake Google, and the two of them embarked on a splendid game of pass-the-parcel.

Jenny's salvation came in an unexpected form. Robert was in his third year at Cambridge, studying for a degree in medicine. Everyone agreed he would make the perfect doctor. He had decided to specialize in paediatrics and his comfortable manner with children made him ideally suited. Jenny and James had not seen him since he left for university, so this sophisticated, elegant young man was a complete surprise. Jenny had always loved being around Robert. He was sufficiently older to make him an adult in her eyes, yet young enough to operate on her level. Music was one of their shared passions and he came armed with a selection of old sheet-music he had found in a junk shop, which he presented to a very flattered Jenny.

They spent Christmas Eve at the piano surrounded by yellowing manuscripts that offered a selection of treasures, many of which were completely new to Jenny: Old Music Hall ballades and Edwardian favourites, which Robert played with great dexterity as they sang in turn or as duets, acting out the melodrama when not convulsed in fits of raucous laughter. If they discovered a number that particularly suited them they rehearsed it a few times, fine-tuning their act, honing it for their repertoire, to perform it later to a select audience. "In a Monastery Garden" had them in hysterics. It was new to Jenny, but Robert had heard it before and remembered the whistled birdsong that accompanied it. This was immediately adopted as their signature tune and they dashed off to the dressing-up box in the attic to kit themselves out in suitable attire for the grand recital the next day. They gave themselves the title of Cringe and Racket, which was lost on Jenny, although Robert assured her the old folks would get the joke.

These high jinks had not passed unnoticed by Harriet, who had been dying to join in. This was the music of her childhood. The covers of the sheet-music brought a lump to her throat. The illustrations and distinct style of printing belonged to the period between the great wars. Her father's music cabinet had been crammed full of similar copies and her earliest memories were imprinted on the pages with the notes. Had Jenny been alone, Harriet would have simply joined in, blending her voice with Jenny's. But this young man was a comparative stranger; one did not mix with young men without being formally introduced. He seemed very nice. His manners were immaculate, which was more than could be said for most of the youngsters who visited the house. She decided to remain in the shadows, to observe rather than participate. This was going to be a difficult Christmas.

Christmas Eve was the worst time for Harriet. The anniversary of her brother's death always hit her hard. Watching young Jenny with her new singing partner made her feel old and surprisingly resentful. Was this the beginning of yet another long stretch of loneliness? The prospect of living her life as an onlooker filled her with a cold ache. She began to wish she had gone with her brother when she had the chance. Would it be wrong to call him back from wherever he was and beg him to take her with him? Then there was the big question: where had he gone? Did she want to go to some unknown place? The after-life, passing over, beyond the grave, the other side, the spirit world, whatever one called it, did she really belong there? It sounded pretty grim when one could be among real people who were warm and solid. The thought of never holding Jenny's hand again, of no longer securing Liz's hair with the ivory comb was abhorrent to her. Somehow she had to conquer her fear and introduce herself to this young gentleman. Swallowing a certain amount of pride, Harriet stepped out of the shadows.

Jenny stopped what she was doing and ran to greet her friend and mentor. She had been trying to fix a large black ostrich feather to a headdress comprising a twisted length of silk. Harriet took it from her and deftly twined it around Jenny's head, creating a perfect turban.

"How on earth did you do that?" Jenny had rushed to the mirror and was admiring her reflection. Harriet stood behind, smiling. All was well, as though there had never been any hint of a separation between them.

"Aren't you going to introduce me?" Robert was looking straight at Harriet and by the neat little bow he executed Jenny knew he could see her as plainly as she could.

"Robert, this is my very dear friend and teacher, Miss Harriet Marchant. Harriet, this is Mr Robert Calder."

They shook hands and exchanged a few pleasantries then, the formalities behind them, they spent the next delicious hour dressing up.

At five o'clock Harriet took her leave, but not before assuring Jenny that she too had been with The Pote when he died. In fact she went on to describe the funeral, to make sure Jenny believed her when she said she had never really gone away. Then she took herself off to the Fourth Room and her much deserved nap, while Jenny off-loaded the whole story and her grievances to a very willing listener.

*

In the kitchen a different conversation had been taking place as the women busied themselves preparing supper. They swigged their champagne as they worked, laughing, talking and sharing as women do. Brenda's unexpected question took them all by surprise.

"Is Beckmans haunted?"

Liz looked at Mel. What constituted a haunting? Spirits, ghosts or vibrations; what was the difference? Liz always said she did not believe in them, but lately her whole belief system had been called into doubt. She was damned if she knew what she believed.

Mel's usual self-deprecation eased the situation as she said, "Of course it's haunted, but don't worry, ghosts don't drink much." Mel continued to lead the general banter that followed. Ghostly sightings and spooky happenings were related during breathtaking moments of reflection, before the silence would shatter with loud guffaws and hysterical giggles. Liz was occupied with a single thought now. Was Beckmans haunted? The incident by the lake, the sad little girl, the atmosphere in the Fourth Room, were these caused by ghosts? She comforted herself in the knowledge that she had never felt afraid in the house. It had always felt like home, from the first moment she had entered it. Ghosts frighten people; that's their job. No. Liz assured herself that there were no ghosts in Beckmans. Her parents would have explained the silly episode by the lake by recounting some long-forgotten incident from her childhood. How they would laugh. Any "ghosts" would soon be laid to rest. There was the Fourth Room, of course; and the boathouse; and the Tarot reading. But, *déjà-vu* and an old boat did not amount to spectral apparitions. Anyway the Fourth Room was beautiful now, her favourite room in the entire house.

Liz gave that snort of a laugh that was a familiar mannerism, as she brushed a stray lock of hair back from her face and adjusted her comb to hold it. In a suitably theatrical voice she said, "Oh, so you've seen the headless man who crosses the hall on the stroke of midnight and the trembling woman in grey who creeps up and down the back stairs every third Wednesday when there is an R in the month!" They were all laughing now, relaxed and close. The group had weathered many storms over the years. No one could accuse them of being fair-weather friends. When crisis struck, they mucked in together, pooling resources; whether money or moral support was needed, they shared willingly. Their accumulated sympathy had evolved into empathy, even at times an uncanny telepathy. Liz would lay down her life for them, unless one of them was being extremely stubborn. Which could happen, they were, after all, women.

Having raised a glass to good old Sue, they fell into the delicious indulgence of picking her to pieces. The conversation drifted to the subject of the men and they happily began to tear their beloved husbands to bits with the same tongue-in-cheek relish, but no malice.

The exchange was in full swing when Brenda announced, in her hospital matron's voice: "There is something I need to tell you."

"I knew it. Donald's got a mistress."…

"You've taken a lover."

"Two lovers!"

"You're pregnant - good old Donald!"

The quips came thick and fast. Brenda held up her hands to fend them off.

"This is serious, please." Her voice had a heavy tone that made the others pull themselves together. They sat around the table, all ears. Brenda looked at the eager trio. Embarrassed and nervous, unused to taking centre-stage she began:

"It's Robert."

Robert was her only son. A well-balanced and reliable twenty-year-old, he was the son every mother dreamed of. The women adored him.

"He's not ill, is he?" Mel voiced their fears.

"Not exactly." Brenda took a deep breath and announced: "He's gay, or at least he thinks he's gay."

The silence was audible. "And…?" coaxed Mel.

"Isn't that enough?" Brenda retorted, the tears welling up behind her glasses. Apart from Brenda's sobs the group remained speechless. They looked at one another, their eyes imploring no one to giggle. Brenda was obviously hurting badly. It needed someone to state the obvious.

Liz took the plunge. "But you knew that. Surely you did? You did, didn't you? We all did."

Heads nodded in agreement.

"No. Actually I didn't. I had no idea my only son was a homosexual; not a clue. Are you telling me *all* of you knew? Some friends you are. Not one of you told me." Brenda stared at them, incredulous. "How long have you known?"

Liz slipped her arm around Brenda's shoulder. "I think I've always known. Maybe when he was about five or six… oh, I don't know. Does it matter?" Liz was trying to give assurance, yet as she spoke she could feel Brenda's body stiffening.

"What Liz means," Mel said, coming to the rescue, "is that Robert is Robert. He's a great guy. Gay or straight, he's the same gorgeous creature."

"That's right, Brenda, you saw him today out there with my kids. They adore him. How many other guys of his age would be so patient and brilliant with those feral animals?"

"You're not concerned with him being around your children then?" The desperation in Brenda's voice was pitiful.

Mel threw back her head and laughed. "He's gay, not a bloody paedophile!"

"It's easy for you, isn't it." This was not a question. Brenda's voice betrayed a depth of fear that demanded recognition as to the seriousness of the situation. "He's going to meet all sorts of prejudice and be exposed to awful risks, you know what I mean." She paused, then continued: "Maybe I'm selfish but I always assumed I'd be a grandmother someday. Then there's his choice of career, his vocation. It hardly seems suitable." She chewed at her thumbnail. "And there's Donald. I'm not saying he's homophobic, but, well... He doesn't know yet and I don't know how to tell him. And then there is the church." She felt on shaky ground, unsure how much sympathy to expect. "Robert won't go to Mass. He says he hates the church. I can't tell you the awful rows we've had. It's not so easy when you have to live with it!" The tears were flowing freely now. Her eyes were red and swollen and her nose was congested. Liz produced a roll of kitchen paper and the heavy silence was punctuated by the sounds of sniffing and blowing of noses.

The women decided that talking to Donald would not help matters. Mel agreed to have a chat with Robert; he would talk freely to her, whereas his mother felt too close emotionally. It was left like that for the present.

Christmas proceeded as planned and was deemed a huge success. David and Edward slotted back into their friendship; all cutting remarks made in the past were forgotten. The recital was hilarious. Robert's dress was received with loud applause; even his father thought his son surpassed himself. Try as they might, the women could not tell if the men had realized the truth about Robert's sexuality. It would save an awful lot of hard work if they were as perceptive as their wives. Some rather politically incorrect remarks were bandied about during Cringe and Racket's performance, to Liz's and Mel's horror, but the sensitivity of the situation forced them to leave well alone and take their partners to task later in the privacy of their own bedrooms.

Eventually the Circus left, amid the usual parade and kerfuffle of farewells and kisses. For Brenda it had been a Christmas to remember. As she started the car she glanced back at her son, who was smiling at her from the rear seat. She blew him a kiss, sighed and started the engine. With a quick glance at her husband, another in her mirror and an even quicker one to the Almighty she drove off.

When later that night Liz told Edward about Robert she was relieved to find he had no problems. Challenging him about his bantering with Bob she realized his idea of being PC was different from hers. Much of it was about a pathetic need to be accepted as "one of the lads", but she was confident she could knock it out of him. It was James's reaction that worried her. He said the right things but she could tell he felt somewhat threatened. Jenny laughed and told her brother to grow up, which, Liz had to concede, was probably the right approach. He was, after all, only just coming to terms with his own sexuality, and the adult world could seem a minefield to an adolescent. A relaxed, positive attitude from his sister was exactly what he needed.

*

On Boxing night Robert returned with a friend. Liz was delighted when they asked if they could stay a few days. She showed them to the blue room, which had a king-size bed and an en-suite.

The following morning the breakfast table was abuzz with witty and youthful chatter. No one stood on ceremony. The toaster popped at will. Cupboards were raided for jams whose sell-by dates had long gone. By noon they were still sitting at table and they might have melted into the next meal had Jenny not declared it was time to go. The dishes were done at record speed, then Jenny, Robert and Mark donned warm coats and scarves and set off down the garden.

With the big red book under her arm Jenny led the way until they entered the privacy of the boathouse. Her burden was growing heavier and heavier. It was almost time for Robert to pass judgment on her work and then, if he thought it propitious, to confront Harriet with the consequences. The three of them poured over the contents for what seemed an age. Mark had heard all about Jenny's friendship with Harriet and studied the book with a genuine interest. He was reading history and had done a considerable amount of research of his own but this was something else. It had a personal quality to it. There was a warmth and concern for the people who appeared within its pages. These were not mere names to be examined then tossed aside. They leapt out from the pages, full of life, with clear personalities of their own, warts and all.

When he had finished reading he closed the book gently and stroked the red cloth binding.

"Do you know, Jenny, if someone had made this for me I'd be so flattered, to think anyone cared that much to go to all this bother. It's beautiful. It's not just a work of art; it's a work of love. This Harriet woman must have been tickled pink."

Harriet was, of course, hovering at the back of the boathouse. Being made to feel churlish did not sit easily on her shoulders. She was pink with shame. Had she really been so dismissive and unkind? What was she thinking even to suspect that Jenny had acted out of anything but the deepest respect and, dare she say it, love? Her embarrassment was acute. There was no way she could face Jenny without preparing herself. First she had to gather her wits about her and decide on the appropriate response. In the meantime she must let the child know that she understood and that there was nothing to forgive.

With a finger to her lips she approached Robert. This was a secret disclosure, one she did not want Jenny to know about. Slipping her arm through his she drew him apart from the other two and proceeded to whisper in his ear. He smiled in agreement and the two conspirators parted, but not before they had arranged another rendezvous.

When Robert addressed Jenny his voice was assertive and authoritative: "Right, young lady, this is too worthy a publication to put back on a shelf. I know if it had been made for me my first reaction would be one of shock. This friend of yours is a very proper lady, not used to casual kindnesses, and would probably have found it extremely difficult to accept something of this value without being forewarned. I propose that we hold a second presentation. What do you say to the Fourth Room at five-fifteen… better make that five-sixteen, this evening? OK?"

With that, he led Mark off for a tour of the garden.

Chapter 25

At four that afternoon, Mel and Bob dropped in for tea, which posed a slight dilemma for the conspirators. Should they let Mel in on the presentation or keep it a private affair? Mark decided for them, suggesting that it was better to have several points of view represented, especially if the hidden agenda was to prove the "existence" of Harriet to any sceptics. Mel could be a vital witness. At five-sixteen precisely, the four of them trooped through the wide oak door, on the pretext of listening to some new CDs.

Harriet was sitting in her chair with Google on her lap. She acknowledged the group, giving an audible "humph" as she spotted Mel among them. It was clear to Mel that Robert and Jenny could both see Harriet as plainly as they saw each other. Mark was happy to accept her presence, but claimed no psychic abilities of his own. Mel saw a chair and a small dog stretching lazily, having just woken from sleep. Her integrity would not let her pretend to a gift she did not possess, but it rankled that Harriet was not visible to her. Her reputation was on the line.

As Jenny approached, Harriet rose to greet her. She kissed her on the cheek and inclined her head to the two boys. She merely glanced at Mel, who was trying to induce a state of trance so she could at least feel the presence in the room. Harriet knew exactly what Mel was doing and mischievously moved about the room, hoping to block any energy that poor Mel might tune into. Sensing a possible clash of wills Jenny stepped forward and thrust the book into Harriet's hands. "Please don't take offence. I did this because I love you and it seemed a good idea at the time. But I do understand if it startled you."

Harriet placed the book on the table and gently passed her hand over the cover. The warmth that spilled out of it made the old woman smile. She closed her eyes. She had no need to scan the pages to know what they contained. Each photograph, every newspaper clipping, the certificates, the sketch of her sampler and the many and varied painstakingly hand-copied music manuscripts and poems Jenny had composed filled her inner eye. She studied the individual pages carefully. When, after an hour or so, she took her hand from the book, tears were flowing from her closed eyes. On opening them, it came as a surprise to find where she was. She had been on a long journey back through the life that was contained in such detail here beneath her hand.

"Well, Jenny, I don't know what to say. That is quite an accomplishment, and a considerable compliment. I thank you from the bottom of my heart and I apologize for hurting you earlier. I never meant to. But seeing the indisputable details of my death and the deaths of my family laid out so graphically was a shock, to put it mildly. Now I shall share something with you, something about me you did not know. I did not know I was dead until very recently. It is not an easy thing to come to terms with, but I am trying."

She paused and pointed at Mel, who felt a surge enter her as though she had been poked with a cattle prod.

"I know you tried to tell me ages ago. I didn't believe you. However, before you offer to 'point me to the light' again I have to tell you this. I am here for a purpose. My destiny is not fulfilled. I don't know exactly what it is but it concerns you, my dear." Harriet reached out and took Jenny's hand. For a brief moment she could not speak. Her eyes had filled again and her throat tightened. She swallowed hard then continued.

"At first I believed my task was complete when I saved you and your brother from the lake. It made sense to perform an act that would purge my memory of my brother's death. But now, thanks to your efforts, I have read the coroner's verdict, I accept that he was dead long before I stabbed him with the boat hook. What else is there for me to do? Teach. That is my destiny. You have a rare gift, a voice that will be spoken of until the next millennium, and I have been selected to train it. Don't worry, my dear, you will be guided over the coming years by many teachers far more competent than me. My task is to instil a permanent love of music in your heart. Your next years will be full of music, special schools, then colleges, in this country and abroad, all there for your benefit. And I shall always be here at Beckmans for you when you come home; as you said, Jenny, there will be many homecomings. I am tired now. I must rest. Tomorrow at the boathouse we have that Pastourelle to master. It is a difficult piece, perfect for your voice."

With that, she was gone. The book lay on the table unopened to those without imagination. The room was full of her presence even after she had gone. Where did she go? Had things changed for her now she was aware of being dead? Jenny had so many questions she needed answered. Sitting down in the armchair, Jenny thought back over her relationship with Harriet. It had begun when she first entered this house as a baby. That lovely voice that sang her to sleep each night, the soft light that came into her room when she was afraid of the unseen monsters of the dark, the comforting awareness that she was never alone, this was what Harriet meant to her. Even when The Pote had died, it was Harriet who had stopped his fear. It was her existence that brought the comfort of knowing he was well and happy. What had Harriet told her about pain? She could not become a great singer without touching pain. She had known its vicious touch when she thought she had lost her brother. She had hurt when Aunty Mel was threatened by cancer. Now she knew what she must do with all this and any future pain. She would pour it into her singing. If Harriet had stayed behind for her, she would not let her down. Her music would become her life and she would make her teacher proud of her.

Mel picked up the book. This was the first time she had seen it. Slowly she turned the pages, absorbed by the astonishing wealth of material. During the "presentation" Mel had been aware of a strong female presence in the room: a woman of a certain age, someone who knew the house intimately. Mel could not see her but she felt her to be tall and distinguished, a woman not to be messed with, someone who had known great sorrow and loss, a very determined person, tenaciously loyal, a woman with a mission. When Mel put this to Jenny she laughed. Mel had summed up Harriet's character pretty accurately. The child's account of what had taken place paralleled Mel's version of events although she was only working on feelings and shadowy glimpses, which were subject to misinterpretation. Poor Mel had the uncomfortable feeling that this ghost was playing with her. A gauntlet had been thrown down and she was not about to be called a coward or a charlatan. She too could be stubborn to a terrifying degree. Well, if this spirit wanted to challenge her professional reputation she had met her match. Let battle commence.

*

Mel's first challenge was her promise to Brenda, so when later that evening she found Robert alone rifling through some music, she came straight out with it. Robert was amused rather than annoyed. He had been waiting for some reaction from the Circus. Liz had been splendid, as had Jenny. Edward was reticent, not hostile, and he did not expect an adverse reaction from Bob or Mel. He was certainly not expecting their advice that he should address his parents' feelings.

After a friendly and frank exchange, Mel was assured that both his mother and father were aware of their son's sexual persuasion and had accepted it, albeit with reservation. What was not obvious was exactly where the animosity was coming from; there was no denying there had been quite violent clashes, especially between mother and son.

Eventually all became clear. The remaining stumbling-block was the church. Robert had been brought up Catholic, and like all good Catholic boys had served as an altar boy and chorister. He had always loved music, especially sacred music, which had kept him close to the church long after he began to doubt the Creed and the antiquated beliefs the clergy adhered to. As he grew older his sexuality was no longer a question for him, but it began to be seen as an issue by everyone else. Never had Robert considered his own God-given orientation to be anything other than natural; certainly not an "issue". But the Church in its infinite wisdom saw differently. His mother told him to keep quiet. It was nobody else's business. He could not help feeling she was praying he would see sense and, in time, become a "normal" heterosexual.

He was not wrong. Brenda's indoctrination was deeply entrenched. She believed that to be gay was a choice and an evil one at that. Knowing her son was in no way an evil person led her to the conclusion that he had made a few unfortunate choices along the way, which he should reverse as soon as possible. This simple application of a truly evil doctrine was a pretty fair description of the Church's attitude to homosexuality. It will all come out in the wash.

Robert could tolerate this attitude in his mother, but when lifted to the level of a dictate that ostensibly banned him from his own faith, he could not keep quiet, hence the rows. Donald had tried to keep his head down and adopt a low profile, but had exposed himself as weak. He tried to placate his son, also advising that he keep a low profile, which merely confirmed Robert's beliefs that his father was at heart a coward and homophobic. In his personal life he accepted his parents' stance. They were of the old school and were trying to be tolerant. Robert did not ask for tolerance. He wanted acceptance, equality and respect.

As he poured his heart out to Mel, Robert was at times tearful. His dignity and determination impressed Mel. He knew he had offended his mother by lashing out against her church, accusing it of gross hypocrisy, citing as evidence the many cases of child abuse and predatory priests. He had hated causing her such pain by turning his back on all she held so dear. She had pleaded on her knees that he come back to the fold for fear of eternal damnation, but Robert was quite prepared to chance his luck and accept his absolution elsewhere.

Mel agreed to report back to Brenda, suggesting gently at Robert's request that she should look to her own actions if she hoped to heal the rift between the two of them. With this rather unpleasant resolution made Mel switched subjects and pumped Robert for information about Harriet and they were soon engrossed in matters of a more metaphysical nature. It transpired that Robert had always had the gift of clairvoyance. He was convinced that we all have the same ability if we choose to use it. It came as a surprise to hear that Mel could not see Harriet, so calling Mark in as a rational, relatively impartial witness and Jenny, because there was no way she was going to be left out, they sat up late into the night discussing the various manifestations of the spirit world they had become aware of or been informed of. Mel and Bob stayed that night, which meant that the next day the four seekers were free to settle themselves in the Fourth Room to explore this fascinating realm even further.

That night Jenny fell asleep as soon as her head touched the pillow. Her dreams were rapid and colourful, filling the air with ghosts and demons, spectres and goblins. Hairy monsters breathing flames from their pulsating nostrils dived at her, making her twist and turn her head in a desperate attempt to avoid their suffocating swoops. As they spun around the room gathering speed with each diminishing lap, the drone of their vast wings drowned out the sound of her own breathing and the fire from their nostrils burned her face. As her last breath struggled free she woke to find Google spread-eagled across her face, panting in short hot bursts as her wrinkled dwarf legs chased imaginary foes pursued in her canine dreams.

By morning Jenny was glad to get up. Breakfast was another riotous affair with toast and croissants waving about as the hands that held them gesticulated wildly. The day was full of vitality. Things got done on days like this. Happenings were in the air. Bob, Edward and James had hatched a plan of their own, while the secret four were anxious to continue their research into the unknown. Liz had shopping to do, since the larder was empty and there were no signs of her rapacious guests leaving. She also had an appointment in town, which she was being pretty secretive about it. Edward assumed it was with the hairdresser. Mel, on the other hand, was intrigued. When her inquisitive pestering was met with a brusque "wait and see", her curiosity was aroused rather than sated.

CHAPTER 26

Edward, Bob and James were being equally secretive. Yesterday they had been discussing the accident. James had surprised the men by instigating the conversation. He was still not convinced by Jenny's explanation. After all, he was the one who had nearly drowned and he felt justified in wanting to find out exactly how his life had been saved. Of course Mel had told Bob every detail of the post-mortem, but forgetting that the two men seldom discussed anything but cricket and rugby it was never explored further. Minor matters such as world peace or life and death were left to the women. James had not yet reached the great age of enlightenment, where priorities are so easily identified. His curiosity was still a vital part of his motivation and he had succeeded in arousing a certain interest in the two older men. Ghosts were dismissed out of hand. The subject of the boat hook, however, still waited to be resolved. Bob recalled how agitated Liz had become when she first mentioned it, ordering him to "leave it alone". That was months if not years ago. They decided there must be a rational explanation, and resolved to find it before the various wild theories perpetrated by the women became even more fanciful.

The Jessops had never owned a boat hook, although Edward kept meaning to buy one. So what had fished young James out of the water? Edward was sure that a simple, if not obvious, solution would eventually come to light. Bob was less sceptical, having spent so much time with a wife who used her psychic powers in the everyday way most women use a dishwasher. He also believed the explanation might well fall into the category "not known" or "non-proven". Edward accused him of hedging his bets. Of course he had the additional advantage of having almost discovered something suspiciously fitting the bill when the old boat was salvaged. They decided to raise the *Olly Ro* and then see if they could locate the mysterious boat hook.

As they made their way to the lake equipped with a long rake and several lengths of stout rope, they had to admit this was a pretty stupid time of year to be embarking on an underwater adventure. A couple more beers and a flask of coffee were carried along in case the salvage took longer than anticipated. It was too cold for swimwear. Wet suits were dismissed as being over-the-top, and anyway they only possessed one. Waders were chosen as a sensible compromise. The boat was totally submerged now and lay deeper than they had expected, the level of the lake still being raised above the normal watermark. Edward regretted not having rescued it before it had sunk, but Liz had forbidden anyone to touch it. Eventually it succumbed to the constant tossing and turning and had shipped too much water to remain afloat.

As they approached it, Bob remarked that it was in almost the exact spot where the old *Jolly Roger* had lain all those years. Both men made light of the coincidence, bluffly speculating as to how much of a meal their wives would make of it.

Bob was decidedly uncomfortable about the whole business. He tried to appear casual but his arms were covered in goose pimples, despite the fact that he wore a thick oilskin coat.

"Where has Liz gone?" Bob was struggling with the rope, turning it into a large lasso.

"Shopping, I think. Then the hairdresser; she could be ages." Edward was already in the water and took hold of the lasso, feeding it around the submerged hull. "It's fucking freezing in here. Whoops, you didn't hear that, James."

James was taking up the slack on the rope. He had been told not to venture in the water and was not sorry, since it was indeed as his father described it. He was enjoying being one of the men. The swearing made it all the more exciting.

"Why did you ask about Liz?"

"Just making sure she's out of the way. I've already felt the wrath of her tongue. Not something I want to experience again, thank you very much."

The dinghy came up quite easily, reasonably intact and ship-shape, unlike her poor predecessor. But then she had not been submerged for anything like the same length of time. The salvagers inspected their loot.

"I can't see any signs of damage. She obviously just took in too much water and went down. God, the kids were lucky. It was a pig of a night." Bob shuddered at the thought of the children out in such a storm. His fingers were numb already. It must have been as cold as this that night. The water was not getting any warmer; water kills amazingly quickly and cold, sweet water is the worst. "Your Jenny must be one tough kid to survive in freezing water for so long and still function mentally and physically. I'm pretty strong, but I don't think I could have pulled a body up from the bottom of this lake, especially a lump like Jimbo here. You must have been tangled in weed, for one thing, and in the dark it's hard to tell up from down. How the hell did she do it?"

James felt someone pass over his grave and hoped the reluctant nervous grin that had fixed itself across his face masked his fear. He didn't want to appear a baby now that he had become one of the men. Bob was sitting on the bank with the rescued dingy upturned beside him. Edward was draining the last of the coffee from the flask. James began walking around the hull kicking it, mimicking his father checking the tyres of the car.

"James, go and get us some strong coffee, and put a splash of brandy in it."

James responded with a thumb's-up and a broad grin, turned and raced off up the garden to the warmth of the Aga.

Once his son was out of earshot Edward continued: "Jenny claimed… and bear in mind she has one hell of an imagination, but she swears that some woman called Harriet helped her. What a strange old biddy was doing in the garden at that time of night and in such fucking awful weather I don't know, but Jenny swears this woman saved them. Apparently she pulled Jenny out then pushed the boat hook in to show her exactly where poor old Jamie was. Jenny then went back in and fixed him to the hook, wrapped her legs around him (and she's got very strong legs for a girl) and inched her way back up the pole." Edward paused. "I couldn't have done it. To have the courage to dive back into that hell, having half-drowned already."

"You'd dive into a damn whirlpool to save your kids, Ed, I've no doubt about that, mate. The real question is where did this crazy old woman come from?"

"Well, in fairness, we don't know she was crazy," Edward remarked.

"Who in their right mind would be out on a night like that?" Bob laughed.

"I take your point. But, mad or not, the fact remains that Jenny swears she was there. I know things must have happened slightly differently, but it's a bloody good tale to tell the grandchildren."

Edward's face turned a chalky white and he sat down with a jolt. "At least we can have grandchildren now. Bloody hell, Bob, it's only just sinking in. I nearly lost my kids."

What might have been an embarrassing moment; a slight loss of manly bravado; was saved as James arrived with three steaming mugs of what tasted like hot brandy. Edward winked at his son and tapped the side of his nose, warning him not to let on to his mother. James glowed with pride. It was rare to be sharing secrets with his dad. He downed his mug of "coffee" in one. If this was what they called quality time, he was all for it.

Meanwhile Bob had been examining the hull. Edward's show of emotion had touched him. The Jessop twins were the closest he and Mel got to a family of their own; he could not begin to think what losing them would feel like.

"What do you make of these?" Bob studied the scratch marks, putting his large hands against them. "They are finger marks but they're much smaller than mine. They belong to a child. They must be Jenny's. They're quite new, and so is this." He was running his artisan's finger along the slimy length of the wooden structure. A long, wide scuff mark was visible where the framework of the hull had been scraped clean of its coat of algae and mud. Something had been dragged the entire length from stern to bow. It was as if someone had been keel-hauled.

"It makes sense. If she was on the decking as she claimed," he pointed across the water to the boathouse, "and the boat was somewhere here," he was thinking aloud now and pointing to where they had found it, "she would have had to swim under it to reach James and drag him ashore here." He indicated the mud slick next to where they sat. "That is one brave kid."

Bob sat back and took another swig from his mug then continued: "Clever girl, if she'd swum too near the island she'd have got tangled up, like poor old James. Round the boat would take too long, so she virtually keel-hauled herself to save her brother. She must have the lungs of a whale. All this in the pitch dark with a force nine blowing, it's a bloody miracle!" He emptied his mug with one long swallow and held it out for James to refill. "Your sister's nothing less than a heroine and if I were her father I'd be shouting it from the effing rooftops."

James tore up the garden, his drunken legs racing away with him, his arms swinging the three empty mugs and his voice hollering the triumphant phrase, *effing heroine* over and over again. Edward's mind was too busy to laugh at his son. It too was racing, trying to imagine the full horror of the situation. The fortitude and presence of mind shown by his daughter filled him with pride along with tremendous admiration and love for her. The enormity of it made him go cold with fear. Jenny, that wild, untameable, questioning hooligan, had grown into a fantastic strong young woman whose life was spread before her with every goal, every dream attainable, and it had nearly ended on that crazy night. He sat down next to Bob and wept. Bob wrapped his arm around his friend and they sat together in embarrassed silence.

That was how Liz found them. James was asleep at the kitchen table, drunk as a skunk. The other four were huddled together reading the Tarot as if their lives depended on them. She was bursting with news there was no one to hear it so she stood in the middle of the hall and raised her arms up to embrace the spirit of the house. Her house would listen. It always did.

She lifted her head and mouthed the words: "We're going to have a baby, in the summer, a little boy and it's our secret."

*

That afternoon, after a hot shower and a change of clothes, Edward set off for a solitary turn around the garden. He could hear the distant pealing of church bells and it dawned on him what a perfect garden his wife had created. The reality of the accident had brought the miracle and fragility of life home. He had been a selfish bastard and he vowed yet again never to take life for granted. He was standing by the beck renewing his vows when he heard Bob's voice.

"Tranquil, isn't it? Apart from the damned bells. Well, shall we finish what we started?"

"Why not? I hoped you'd come back. Sorry about this morning." Edward disappeared, to return armed with a miscellany of tools, and found Bob staring deep into the water.

"Are you sure you're up to this, mate?" Bob asked. "We could be opening a whole can of worms here."

Edward replied by donning his waders and throwing a spade to Bob. Together they climbed back into the freezing water. The current was still a force to reckon with and once or twice they had to hold on to each other to steady themselves. As they began to churn up the bottom the waters became thick with mud, forcing them to feel their way down into the thick sludge. Edward kept thinking this was what Jenny had faced, this black evil mud.

"Hang on. I've got something." Bob was pulling something from the grip of the slime. Already the walkway was littered with sticks and logs, each of which in its turn had caused the men to get excited, only to have their hopes dashed. This time Edward knew it was different. His nerve endings tingled with an electric force that was invigorating and scary at the same time. He joined Bob and together they felt their way along the length of the object. The thick silt was reluctant to give it up without a struggle. Using all their strength, they wrested it clear of the cloying mud. The wooden shaft had petrified in the alluvium and the metal had rusted away leaving just enough to give it an identity. The men lifted it on to the decking and climbed out. They were sweating from hard work and excitement and water had crept in over the top of their waders but it was worth it. Lying on the decking was a boat hook.

"That has been down there one hell of a long time." Bob wiggled the metal end and it snapped off in his hand. "Not exactly what you'd call fit for purpose, eh?" He was almost afraid to touch the frail object. "Well, this can't be the one the loopy old bat used, that's for sure."

He was clearing the pole of the mud and slime, trying not to get too close. The stench of stagnant weed was overpowering. His hands stroked the length of the shaft, disturbing years of fetid debris, which transferred itself to his fingers with the same tenacity that had held it in place for so long. Shaking it free with a series of determined movements, Bob continued his examination. As his fingers neared the end of the shaft they stopped. There was something chiselled out, deep gouges that he could sink his fingers in. He rinsed the pole in the water, swishing it around to expose the wood. At first he assumed it to be the work of animals gnawing at the rotting fabric. But, no this was man-made. It looked as though someone had carved it.

"What on earth do you think these are, Ed?"

Edward did not reply. He was staring into space. He felt his knees buckle and his head getting lighter. From somewhere far away he heard his friend's voice asking if he was all right.

"I could feel funny marks on the end of it," Edward muttered as he came round.

"What are you talking about?" Bob was confused; it was not every day his mate fainted.

"That's what Jenny said: 'I could feel the funny marks.' This is the same hook. I know it's impossible but there is your proof!" He was running his fingers over the notches. The two men looked at each other in disbelief.

Neither spoke. It was either an unbelievable coincidence or something very odd was going on. Edward was reluctant to entertain the thought of a supernatural explanation but, for the life of him, he could come up with nothing plausible. Here was an old boat hook that had lain at the bottom of the lake for donkeys' years, which fitted the description Jenny had given of the one used in the rescue. There was his stumbling-block. If he accepted the boat hook, and he wasn't sure he had yet, then he had to accept the existence of some fanciful old woman who hovered about round the boathouse. It was just not the way his mind worked. He was about to admit his confusion to Bob when Liz appeared, carrying two steaming mugs of coffee.

She placed the coffee on the decking and walked over to the boat hook. Instinctively she ran her hand along the water-smoothed wood until they rested on the initials carved at the end. Vibrations from the past connected to lives she would never know travelled through her body. So this was what had haunted her for so long. This rotting length of wood had been calling to her ever since she had moved into Beckmans. Its relevance to her life was now evident but the whys and the wherefores remained unanswered. How does an artefact from another age communicate emotions? Surely an inanimate object did not possess the power to reach out across time so compellingly? There must be a catalyst, a human element to join the threads, to make the connections. Liz turned to the two men and smiled.

"So, it was a boat hook. I was right. Well, I'm going indoors. It's freezing out here." She turned on her heel and hurried back to the house.

The boat hook was wrapped in an old sheet before being placed in the shed, and the *Olly Ro* was left upended on the bank, to dry out before it could be rendered seaworthy once more.

CHAPTER 27

Meanwhile, in the Fourth Room a heated debate was under way. It was Jenny's baptism into a full-blown intellectual argument, and much of the meaning was lost on her. Words soared over her head. The references and quotes sourced from works she had not heard of were tools she too wanted to use. She wanted all this knowledge at her own fingertips. The passion with which the speakers argued their points was a revelation. So much conviction, such conflicting views being discussed heatedly and vehemently yet without rancour, impressed itself on her young mind. Their vast vocabulary and dexterity of thought amazed her. They expressed themselves with an eloquence that made her long to be a part of this world. Argument and counter-argument rallied to and fro in a mixed doubles of the intellect. The conversation rose and descended in cascades, going over her head but permeating her brain by osmosis. She did not fully understand it all but she knew some essence of it would remain to nourish her mind, making it strong and flexible in the future.

By the end of the day the four diverse individuals had bonded into a homogeneous group. Their differences had been displayed and respected, shared and admired. Mel was pleased to find that she kept up with most of the reasoning without difficulty. Mark's knowledge of history was phenomenal and Robert had a firm grasp of theology. Never did they make her feel inadequate or inferior. They admired her work, despite approaching it from a completely different perspective. She had learned a great deal and although she had not radically changed her beliefs she had revised her thinking about the validity of certain other points of view. They agreed to differ as to what affected the ability to see or converse with a spirit, recognizing the degree of influence semantics played in one's rationale. No one claimed certainty about sentient life after death and they might have reached an agreement that at some point in the future they would find out, but Mark, being a confirmed atheist, argued that one needed to exist to realize that one didn't. At that point Jenny's brain began to hurt.

When they emerged from their conclave, they were starving. Liz had prepared a vast bowl of pasta and another of salad and the day ended as it had begun, with feasting and good company. Jenny went to bed too tired to dream. The young lovers went to bed to do what young lovers do and James was nursing his first hangover. Mel slept the sleep of the dead, feeling vindicated and reassured of her psychic gifts, while Edward and Bob shrugged off the day, agreeing not to discuss their findings and glad to rest their tired bodies. Only Liz was left in limbo. Inside her was a new life, forward-looking and full of promise. Outside was the nagging call of the past, ominous and threatening. She hardly closed her eyes all night, trying to decide when, how and to whom she should tell her news.

The boys left in the morning, Mel and Bob left after lunch. Liz had still not revealed her secret and was feeling miffed that the curiosity her visit aroused yesterday had vanished. One other person knew and that was Harriet. She had listened to some of the debate but got bored with the endless search for a non-existent answer. She had visited the salvage work, but could not stand by and watch what she considered an act of grave robbery. So when Liz returned, Harriet attached herself to her and resolved to spend a quiet domestic day free from any more startling revelations. She was therefore the only member of the house, apart from the house itself, to have heard the announcement. A new baby at Beckmans: now, that was surely a cause for celebration. She calculated that the baby was due in early September; Virgo, the sixth sign of the Zodiac, lying between Leo and Libra, bringing the ability to judge and a sense of fair play. And yes, the baby would be a girl, despite what those idiot doctors said. She persuaded Liz to tell Edward quietly once they were alone, sensing that a little private sharing between the two would not go amiss.

By the end of the month, the pregnancy had begun to show and Edward actually accused Liz of getting fat. He was exhibiting signs of stress again. This time work was to blame. The market had become a harsh environment in which it was necessary to swim like crazy just to keep one's head above water. They were not in financial difficulty, but even Edward could not remain unaffected by the global downturn. Liz was showing signs of restlessness; she was looking for another project, which would no doubt involve large sums of money. His spiritual vows, taken at a time of abject crisis, had been long forgotten and he prepared to tighten his belt. So it knocked him for six when he learned he was to become a father again.

By the summer, everyone knew. Pregnancy suited Liz. It was eleven years since she had had the twins and it had not escaped her that, at thirty-seven, things might prove more hazardous. The doctors assured her she would have a normal confinement and produce a healthy bouncing boy at the end of it. Her *laissez faire* attitude returned and Beckmans became an open house for the summer. The relaxed ambiance rubbed off on Edward, who talked himself out of his personal depression and resolved to let the global economy worry about itself. Life was back on an even keel again. The summer holidays stretched ahead, a seemingly endless span of carefree bliss.

David had not returned to France, confiding in Edward that the life of a semi-hippy author was not all it was cracked up to be. He was made welcome at Beckmans, at least until he managed to find a teaching job and a small flat near his new school. He assured Liz that he would finish his novel one day, and she believed him. Whether he ever mentioned it to Edward was debatable. Liz didn't mention it herself, knowing that Edward would be unable to resist crowing, which would do their newly rekindled friendship no good.

By the end of July Liz was enormous. The rumours abounded. It was obviously another set of twins. The thought of double trouble was daunting and Liz clung to the fact that her obstetrician knew more than the Circus did. Secretly Edward was praying for another son, preferably just one. Much as he adored James he longed for a son who would shine on the sports field, someone he could teach how to bend a football so that it swerved into the net, someone he could school in the art of throwing the perfect googly. James was a fabulous child and was growing into a brilliant young man, but shine as he might in the realm of quadratic equations it was on the games field that Edward sought his reflected glory and that was not going to happen. Jenny wanted a sister more than anything, and James himself wanted an Alsatian. Liz was content that whatever she was carrying would please one of them, so anything healthy was OK with her.

It was a gloriously sunny day and the Circus was sprawled on garden chairs around the long cloth-covered table that bore the remnants of a lazy lunch. The cheeseboard was still providing nibbles, and another bottle of Shiraz was being uncorked. Liz watched as the others fell under the influence. She felt rather superior in her enforced abstemiousness. The children had taken their food to eat as a picnic in the refurbished *Olly Ro* and were drifting effortlessly on the placid lake, leaving the adults free to talk. They had any topic under the sun to choose from and yet, to Liz's dismay, the business of the accident was paraded out yet again. It was Brenda who started it with an innocent enough remark:

"It was a blessed miracle no one was hurt."

That word "miracle" set the cat among the pigeons. The idea of heavenly intervention was introduced and the group were a couple of bottles too far down the line to skirt the unavoidable pitfalls. David prided himself on his atheism, which excluded any adherence to a superior power, and the Catholic camp would have no truck with any psychic nonsense. Edward saw it as an opportunity for some fun and mischief and Mel was more than up for it. Bob slipped into his role of peacemaker and Liz tried in vain to change the subject. The thought of that dreadful day being re-examined and dissected left Liz feeling her head would burst. She considered pretending to go into labour, but decided to keep that ploy up her sleeve in case of an emergency.

The discussion moved from the specific to the general, until the boundless question of the existence of the supernatural was left facing them. Like a bull at a red rag Brenda charged at the word. To her, "supernatural" meant one thing: spiritualism. That was enough to make her cross herself and utter a few Hail Marys. And spiritualism was a short hair away from Satanism, which literally put the fear of God in her. Like a reflex action Mel felt obliged to defend her beliefs and expound on the natural everyday intervention of unseen forces, citing the accident once more as a case in point. Some outside influence had definitely been at work, guiding Jenny in the rescue.

"Let's see what everyone else thinks, shall we?" A groan went round the table, followed by a series of deep sighs and a shuffling of chairs. "Just to see where we stand, that's all." Bob was doing his best to calm things. The group shuffled their chairs on the lawn and nodded or shook their heads but they did not leave or refuse to take part. "Right, those who believe in the existence of supernatural forces raise their hands."

"I'm out of this." David was too apathetic to physically abstain, so he pointedly pushed his chair away from the main fray and settled back to enjoy the show.

Liz's hand shot up, while Mel's hovered.

"Mel!" Liz's indignation was patently obvious. "You started this; don't back out now."

"Hang on a minute, I started nothing. You all know what my beliefs are. It's just that word 'supernatural'. I believe everything is natural." She was stopped almost mid-sentence by her husband's exasperated voice.

"Splitting hairs isn't going to help. I'll rephrase the question for you. Do you think that something... oh,

God, I don't know what to call it now… let's get straight to the point. Do you believe something spooky happened with the kids or not?"

"If you want my opinion as to whether I think spirits were involved, then, yes, I do. And I don't think it, I know it." Mel looked defiantly around the table, daring anyone to challenge her. Then she put her hand in the air.

"Now who's being dogmatic? Ha!" Brenda folded her arms and turned her body away. It was a hostile gesture, indicative of a battle to come. Before Mel could retaliate Bob jumped in.

"So, that's two for the spooks. Now, who thinks everything has a logical and rational explanation?" He raised his own hand and, seeing that the abstainer had also raised his, he retorted: "Oh, no, you're either in or out. You wanted out and out you stay."

"Does that exclude divine intervention?" Brenda asked before being shouted down by her husband. She raised her arm, waiting impatiently for Donald to do the same, which he did slowly and deliberately. Edward took a wry look at Liz but then raised his hand.

"Four!" Bob exclaimed, holding his own arm aloft. "I declare the non-spooks have it." He rubbed his hands together, pleased with his achievement. Then he caught sight of Mel's scowl.

"We should at least have a discussion, an opportunity to sway opinions or something; just taking a vote isn't fair. I'm not even sure what we were voting for. I think we should each have an opportunity to put our case." She looked at Liz and smiled. Liz slid down in her chair as far as her bump would allow, wishing she could disappear beneath the table. This was not what she had wanted when she had invited them for lunch. This was supposed to be a celebration of "closure" or whatever the Americans call it. A fresh start, or just a nice lunch, not another post-mortem; it was time to forget it all. Why couldn't they see that?

Meanwhile Bob was trying to assuage Mel. "What's the point?" he said.

"There's every point. Too many questions have been left unanswered. I take it we're talking about the accident, not just our general beliefs? In which case, we need to think it through before jumping to conclusions. That's all." Mel had turned back to face the table, every fibre of her being raring to take on the unbelievers along with the saints.

She was in her element. Bob recognized the signs and knew he had no chance of deflecting her. Too much wine had flowed.

"Yes, but you don't have a case." As he said it, he knew it was the wrong thing to say.

"Of course I do. How dare you say that! Explain yourself."

Bob sighed. How many times had he found himself in a similar situation? Knowing that whatever he said would sound patronizing, he added, "Because, my sweet little medium psychic, one cannot prove a negative."

"And arguing from a point of faith isn't valid. Well, not in my book." David, who was seriously slurring now, put in his tuppence worth.

"You keep out of this. You haven't even got a book," Bob snapped.

Mel grinned at him. She adored his sardonic wit and as far as proving negatives went he had a point. She did not intend to keep quiet, but he did have a point. And it certainly kicked the Catholic argument into touch.

The seeds of dissension were watered with yet more wine. Mel was placated and more than happy to let the summit continue. Arguments were batted to and fro, punctuated by hungry children drifting back for food, then beating a hasty retreat, not wishing to be part of any drunken row. More bottles were opened to further lubricate the proceedings and the debate continued.

When at last Bob stood up to put the case for the disbelievers, it proved a turning point for Liz. Bob was a persuasive advocate. He made his claims clearly and dispassionately. His exposition on coincidence was masterful and hard to dismiss. Liz found herself convinced that accidents of chance, or flukes, happen all the time and need no explanation. Had she not always believed in the forces of luck? It is only when they happen to collide with matters of vital importance to oneself that they mischievously get interpreted as "fate" or "destiny"? What happened on that dreadful night and with those wretched Tarot cards could be explained away as chance. When it came to the baffling question about the actual existence of Jenny's mysterious woman, Edward made some succinct points that she found could not be dismissed either. In fact, the more she listened to him the more she found herself agreeing with him.

He described his daughter as an original thinker; her innovative brain constantly experimenting with new ideas, words and emotions. Liz agreed. He described her as a natural visionary; choosing to see the whole in microcosms, each to be dissected and interpreted in her own fertile imaginative way. Liz agreed again. He felt that a mind so ahead of its peers might easily need to create or invent a mentor; a person whose cleverness was beyond question; someone who could be confidante and therapist; a sounding board; someone to dispense advice and guidance: an imaginary older friend. Liz was in total agreement.

Mel also saw the logic in Edward's argument, except for the fundamental question about the source of this guiding light. Why need this woman be a creature of Jenny's imagination? Why not an actual being, a spirit guide, a guardian angel? At this point Bob brought the meeting to order again. Mel was asked to provide proof as to the existence of such beings. When she refused to put her spirits to the test, her evidence was declared inadmissible. No one rose to her defence, so her argument was thrown out. Liz could not help feeling she had let her friend down, left her feeling betrayed and abandoned. She had forgotten of what stern stuff Mel was made. Mel had been on the receiving end of far worse than this many, many times. Being in a minority of one held no fears for her. Anyway, she was not alone. She had a legion of unseen helpers to call on should she need them. Proselytizer she was not, so she sat back, content to know what she knew.

The debate drew to a close and Bob got ready to count the final show of hands. Mel stood her ground but so did Bob, Donald, Brenda and Edward. Once again David's hand went up. Only Liz had switched camps and come down on the side of rational thinking. Then just as the verdict was being announced Liz asked the question they had all been avoiding:

"What about the boat hook?"

There was a deathly hush. Their faces registered confusion. Doubt was the spectre at the feast but no one would acknowledge it. It fell to Edward to dismiss it.

"I'm not kidding, but seeing that boat hook made me go cold. As for those notches, it was spooky. Sorry, wrong choice of word! I've given it a lot of thought; it may well have been the fashion to carve initials on them back then, who knows? The *facts* are these. It could not have been the same boat hook that Jenny claims was used. Ask Bob. It was buried under years of mud and gunge. No way had it been used recently. It was rotting down there for decades. That hook wouldn't support a minnow let alone a hefty lad like James!"

There was an irrefutable logic to what he said. The mood lightened, only to be brought down by Liz's next question: "What about the little girl? She still haunts me. If I close my eyes I can see her as clearly as I did then. Who is she? What did she want?"

It was practical non-believing David who answered: "Did you actually see her? Or did you just think you saw her? Who else has seen her? Nobody. You said yourself that you had a strong feeling of *déjà vu*. I bet you saw a film that triggered it off and, bingo, your imagination did the rest."

"Hear, hear!" exclaimed Edward. "You and Jenny are so alike. Nothing is simple. The obvious becomes a mystery and once you've got an idea you let your imagination run riot. All the business about that ridiculous card and the Fourth Room, look at it now. Is it haunted? Haunted my arse! No, Liz, sorry to disappoint you but I'm with David. You just got a bit obsessive."

Far from being disappointed Liz felt a surge of relief. Her subconscious had concocted the whole thing. It was easier and more comfortable to believe Edward and David.

"You are absolutely right," she declared. "It has been a weird and freaky set of happen-stances, coincidences, *déjà vu* and airy-fairy nonsense. Good. I'm glad that's been sorted out. Do you know, I feel quite light-headed; it's as if a great weight has been lifted off my poor brain, and I haven't had a single drink!" Liz shook her head and a stray lock of fine blonde hair swung loose; twice she tried to secure it and failed. Then her comb snapped in two.

Mel was on her feet, glowering at Liz. "Well, you've changed your tune. I defy you to come back into that room with me and face that sad little girl, then tell me she's a figment of your imagination. That poor little spirit came to us for help. Something's trapped her on this plane and she's asking for someone to guide her to the light. I've a good mind to go and release her now."

Brenda was incensed. If anything supernatural was going on, they should seek professional help, before something irreversible happened. She said as much to Mel, who took pleasure in pointing out that she was a professional. The wine was doing its worst. Brenda, who would normally have been asleep by now, was keeping fuelled by passion. She lashed out.

"If someone is possessed they need a priest. Only a priest can conduct an exorcism and exorcism is the only way. You must not mess with the devil. And he comes in many disguises."

She looked directly at Mel as she spoke and it was obvious what she was implying. Mel burst out laughing, her silver elfin head bobbing along with her earrings as she shook.

"If you think I'm the devil in-bloody-carnate then say so. But watch out. I might just cast the evil eye on you. Anyway, who's talking about possession? Get your facts straight, Madame."

"Mel, that's enough!" said Bob. "You two have been friends for years; you can't fall out over a bloody ghost that doesn't even exist."

"Isn't it interesting that one can 'know' someone for years and years without really knowing them at all?" Mel retorted.

"The church is quite clear. It's a sin to consort with spirits. I don't approve of what you do and I never have. All that business with the Tarot; it's the occult. It's an abomination and so are the witches that practise it." Brenda was leaning across the table, pointing her finger at Mel.

"Hello, hello, the Inquisition is alive and well. Maybe this time you'll finally work out how many angels can dance on the head of a pin. I'm surprised those deluded old men had time for such conundrums what with all that burning and torturing of innocent victims. They should have asked me. I know the answer. Shall I tell you? None! And why, I hear you ask? Because the poor fucking angels are too busy clearing up the misery and pain caused by self-righteous prigs like you to find time to bloody dance anywhere. God save me from hypocrites." With that, she turned her back to the table, lest she say something she might really regret.

"Listen to you. You're both deluded idiots. Can't you see this is it? When you die, you die. I hope to God there is no God and if I have to come back as a spirit, I'll be a single malt whisky, thank you very much." David poured himself another drink and raised his glass to Mel.

Liz listened horrified as the two women traded abuse. Now David was getting involved. She grabbed her glass and hurled it with all her might. It covered the length of the table, spraying everyone in its path with sparkling water, bouncing twice before landing, intact, but on its side, balancing and rocking on the table edge. "Stop it! I can't take any more. This family has only just got itself together. I will not let such a stupid row tear it apart again."

Meanwhile Brenda had been fumbling in her handbag for the car keys. She slammed the metal clasp shut with a loud snap and tried to stand. Meaning to steady herself against the table she mistakenly grabbed a handful of cloth. This last-ditch attempt to save herself sent both her glass and herself sprawling over the table, turning her face and the white cloth scarlet as she fell. Bob helped her to her feet, but without acknowledging him or his kindness she turned to her husband and said, "Are you ready, Donald? I'm sorry, Liz, but we're leaving. Our church is very important to us and I will not stay to have it ridiculed."

Donald remained firmly planted in his chair as he uttered his one word reply. "No." He did not look at his wife; he merely placed his glass in front of Edward to be refilled.

"What do you mean, 'No'?" Brenda glowered at her dissenting husband.

"What part of 'No' don't you understand, woman? I'm going nowhere. Your precious church has caused enough rifts in our own family. I'll not allow its medieval dogma to come between my friends and me. I'm with you, Liz." He was dangling the car keys provocatively at his wife as he spoke. "If you go, you're on your own." Brenda ignored the keys and sat down heavily. The tightness with which she kept her lips closed spoke volumes.

Mel was slow-clapping in a wicked act of provocation. Appalled at his wife's behaviour, Bob tugged at her sleeve to stop her, then watched in horror as his own glass tipped over.

"I am so sorry, Liz. Your poor table! What's the betting this wouldn't have happened if we'd been on white wine? Pass the fizzy water and some salt, it'll stop it staining." Liz was not looking at the cloth. All she saw were three cups lying down. Red liquid spilled from two and water had poured from the other. Beside them there stood two full cups, Edward's and Donald's. Behind them she could see the bridge that crossed the beck, on the far side of which stood a little house: the boathouse. What she did not see was Harriet, who had been standing silently at the end of the table. Her long black cloak fell closely around her tall figure. Her thick white hair shone in the setting sunlight and she was smiling. She had witnessed the entire proceedings.

Chapter 28

Harriet was smiling when, sometime later, Jenny met her for her lesson.

"We shan't have a lesson today. We shall just sing."

"You're in a good mood. Smiling suits you." Jenny kicked off her sandals and swung her legs over the edge of the walkway. Stretching her toes down, she could just reach the low summer water. She began to swing her long brown legs in a strict four/four tempo. Harriet picked up the rhythm and started singing.

"Somewhere over the rainbow bluebirds fly...." Her voice brimmed with emotion. It came from a very private place, deep within the old woman, and Jenny felt it would be rude to interrupt by joining in. When the song ended Jenny stopped her leggy metronome and watched Harriet climb down to perch beside her.

"Can I ask a favour of you, my dear?"

Jenny nodded.

"Could we go out in the *Olly Ro*? It's so long since I rowed in the sunshine."

For the next hour or so the two friends took turns to manoeuvre the little dinghy around the lake. They chatted and sang as they rowed and Harriet told Jenny of her plans for the future. The conversation over lunch had been a huge learning curve for Harriet, as she explained to Jenny; she had witnessed people at their best and at their worst. What amused her most was the fact that they were all saying the same thing. They just did not see it. They were coming from such different angles, that no matter how much they shifted their chairs around they could still only see their point of view. The actuality of what they were looking at was in fact one and the same thing. To some extent the whole thing could be dismissed as semantics, but choice of words was not all that separated them. Harriet realized that each one had a compass tuned to a very personal north. She reached the conclusion that although it might be possible to enable someone to see things from another perspective they can never lose their own bearings. It will always point them home in the end. That was what made life so wonderful, she thought. *How boring if we all sang the same tune. Singing from the same song-sheet still leaves room for a wealth of harmony. It's when we each choose a different key that discord begins.*

Jenny let Harriet ramble on. It was fascinating to hear this guardedly private person expound so freely her philosophy of life, but Jenny was more interested to find out the reason for this sudden openness. Harriet stopped speaking, looked at Jenny and laughed.

"You are quite right, as usual. I have had some major decisions to make lately and this mad rambling is my way of skirting the issue. All right young Jenny, let's cut to the chase. I was feeling a little upset that some people do not believe I exist. It hurt. Now, I no longer care. We see what we choose to see. Often we can only see what others choose to show us. So I have come to the conclusion that I have been taking it all too seriously. I know I am here. You know I am here; who cares about the rest?

"Hear, hear."

"I haven't quite finished." Harriet's tone changed and her smile was replaced by a more serious, though still benevolent, expression. "I have been thinking of moving on; passing over; going to the other side; turning to the light. Pick a euphemism, it hardly matters which. But for years I have been kidding myself that I still have a purpose here, a conceited belief that Fate or Destiny has not yet done with me. I was wrong. I realize now that none of us knows our fate. Life isn't that complicated. We are born, we live; we die. At least most of us do. What is so difficult? I have done what I wanted to do and I think maybe it is time I went."

Jenny stopped rowing and let the boat drift. She did not speak although there was a great deal she wanted to say. She sniffed hard. Harriet offered her a neatly folded white handkerchief. Trying to sound light-hearted Jenny said, "You must be the only ghost that always has a clean hanky." Then she made a desperate plea. "Don't go, Harriet. You can't leave. Who will teach me if you go? I don't want you to die."

"It's a bit late for that, my dear. As for your singing, there'll be teachers queuing up to train a voice like yours, people who know much more that I do. My methods are old-fashioned. I have always known I could only take you so far. Hopefully I have given you a glimpse into the wide spectrum of music and a lasting love of it. Keep that and I will have fulfilled my task."

Jenny was alone in the boat. She called Harriet's name but there was no reply. Slowly she rowed back to the jetty and moored the *Olly Ro*. She looked around the boathouse before dragging her feet back to the house. The Fourth Room was empty except for Google, who was stretching her long back on the armchair. She looked at her watch. It was five-fifteen.

She told her mother she had a headache and went to bed early. Clutching Harriet's book she sobbed for several hours. From the lounge she could hear the sound of drunken laughter. The Circus was in full swing, having sorted their arguments by agreeing to differ. It would not be long before they were going hammer and tongs again; that was the fun of being a family. Their loud competing voices drifted up the stairs, increasing Jenny's loneliness. This was how she had felt when The Pote had died; cold waves of horror stopped her heart each time she realized she would never see him again. She was mourning again, this time for her friend; and this time there would be no one to mourn with her. They could not grieve for someone they did not believe in. Her future spread in front of her like a desert, arid and barren. She fell into an exhausted and fretful sleep where she was alone, drowning in a sea of sand.

*

The next morning she appeared at the breakfast-room door dressed from head to foot in black. She refused to eat and drank only water. Liz thought she appeared taller than usual, or was that because she held herself very upright and moved more sedately than usual? Her mother watched as Jenny put her water glass in the sink and turned to take her leave. One side of her short brown hair was held back with a small comb, which Liz recognized as one of hers. She said nothing but her hand went up to her own hair and she realized that since yesterday her stray lock had stayed off her face unaided. Her ivory comb was still in pieces, waiting for Edward to glue it together for her. The whole scene would have been comical if the dark circles around Jenny's eyes did not tell a sad story. No amount of imploring would get Jenny to break her silence. Dramatically she threw her mother's black serape around her shoulders and swept out into the garden, pausing to take a walking-stick from the rack as she passed.

When she reached the bridge she stopped in her tracks. Harriet was waiting for her, emitting loud snorts of laughter.

"What do you think you look like?"

"I thought you had gone."

"Well, I did think about it but then I thought better of it. Where was I going to go? I don't know what it's like over there. It could be awful. I couldn't stand it if they only sang sacred music. I'd miss a bit of Cole Porter now and then. And I have no guarantee that my family will be there. Anyway, this is my family now. And Beckmans is my home. I love it here. Why should I leave? I think I'll hang around a bit longer, if that's all right with you."

"Good. Let's start with the Canteloube, it still needs a lot of work."

Harriet grinned. Jenny was learning more from her than how to sing.

"I would never leave without saying goodbye, Jenny. You should have known that." Her smile was returned and the lesson began. "Right, the Pastorelle. You're not standing straight, and will you remove that ridiculous get-up. You look like an eccentric old tramp."

Jenny shed her black clothes and returned to her usual bouncy self. The improved posture stayed and her manner became more refined. Liz approved. Life was good. Her family were safe and together, all her chicks in the nest, as her mother would have said. She felt more at one with herself than ever before. She was her own woman. The baby was due soon and she already knew it and loved it. This child would be her mirror as James was her joy and Jenny her pride. Jenny's chosen path was destined to carry her away for long periods at a time and her talent held Liz in awe. She would always regret that she could not believe in Jenny's friend, for this hovered between them as a ghostly, contentious issue. But she could not pretend; she still needed irrefutable proof. They would have to learn to live with it. There would never be an unbridgeable distance between them but Jenny's fame would keep them apart. She would have to share her with the world. She would do this willingly, but part of her already felt a loss. James would marry and she would become the second woman in his life. He would give her grandchildren and would always be her son, but she had to learn to step back.

This next child would be like her. She too would be a homemaker and would become a friend. She would have the relationship with her that she had been denied with her own mother. This would be the daughter she would watch walk down the aisle and whose children would spend every holiday at Beckmans. This little girl would fill her old age with the noise of young people. It was definitely a girl. The doctors had got it wrong, of that she had no doubt. She had already chosen a name, Persephone. It came to her out of the blue and when she looked it up it seemed perfect. It epitomized the late, fruitful summer. This baby would be a child of wisdom and judgement. A beautiful little girl, how lucky was that?

*

Today she intended to paint. The children were out, there was no noise, Google was at her feet and Edward had gone out with David. Today would be a time of peace and quiet. She waddled down the garden to her favourite spot, beneath the willow looking out across the water to the boathouse. Spreading the heavy paper on her board she secured it with masking tape and opened her paint-box. She dipped her jam-jar into the bubbling water of the beck and held it up to the light. It too was full of life. Feeling the baby kick she placed her hand on her belly. It was stretching and curling, exerting its wish to get on with the business of living. The fears of the lake, the dread of the twins taking to the water again, had completely gone. The accident was a memory Liz had learned to live with, locked inside her head. There were no nagging questions, no unsolved riddles haunting her thoughts. Today she marched to her own drumbeat, and woe-betide anyone who could not keep pace with her feet.

As she began to cover the paper she remembered her very first painting. Laughingly she recalled the scruffy old brush she had used and the children's limited palette. She remembered having been quite pleased with it, a long time ago. In comparison to her work now it must have been a pretty rudimentary effort. As usual when painting she lost all concept of time. Before she knew it her painting was finished. She screwed up her eyes to examine it. It was good. She could use it in her next exhibition, unless she kept it for herself. It might be interesting to hang it side by side with her first attempt. Tipping the content of her jam-jar into the stream, she waddled back to the house with Google leading the way.

There it hung in the stairwell, rather pretentiously mounted on moss-green card and set in a golden frame. She must have passed it hundreds of times but never actually saw it any more. She scrutinized it now. It was not bad for a first attempt. The misty edges created a feeling of transience; she liked that. Yes, she had caught some of the ethereal quality of the old ruin. It was hard to remember what it had been like. The new boathouse blended in so well it seemed it had always been there. Then she remembered; of course, she had taken a photograph of it.

She set off to find her box of old photos. It would be there somewhere among all her painting snaps, the one capturing that very instant when she first discovered the joy of painting. Her fingers rummaged through the prints, and suddenly there it was. The old boathouse; it was far more beautiful than she remembered. Her painting in no way did it justice. In the photograph it was taller, more imposing and, she hated to admit, not nearly as twee as she had made it. There were shadows and nebulous depths she had not managed to hint at, let alone capture. Around the dilapidated walkway hovered the contours of evocative shapes suggesting mystery and danger. Where were these in her painting? They were far removed from the fairytale image she had painted. Her eyes fixed on one such shape. Indeterminate and blurred, it resembled the form of a woman. In the dresser drawer she found the magnifying-glass and with uncontrollably shaking hands held it to the print to examine it more closely. Obscure, but definitely a woman: a woman carrying a walking-stick, a white-haired woman in a long dark cloak.

Her heart pounding and leaping erratically, she examined each photo in turn. The cobnut tree; the willow; the north side of the porch; the southern wall with the wisteria; on each print, in the background, there she stood. She was not lurking. On the contrary, she held herself erect and proud, a commanding figure wrapped in a dark cloak, a woman with attitude. She was not skulking in the shadows, she was watching, aware of all that was around her.

Liz left the photos where they lay and ran out into the garden. She was holding her belly. The baby was kicking, urging her on to the shed where Bob and Edward had placed the old boat hook. The rusty hook was already snapped off, but taking the band that had secured it in her left hand she pulled at the shaft. With one effortless tug the band came free.

There under the metal, trapped between the pole and the head, was a tiny strip of yellow. Carrying the remnant as if it were a sacred relic, she returned to the house. Hanging on two hooks behind the door were the twins' yellow oilskins. She spread James's coat on the table, scattering the photos to the floor. Examining it, she found what she was looking for: a small tear where a hook had pierced it. A tiny fragment was missing. Liz laid the remnant on the tear. It was a perfect fit.

EPILOGUE

It is the task of the many to enable the few to achieve their potential and allow them to shine, if only for the benefit of a good story. But who decides which of us is the angel and which the mere mortal? Are angels and saints chosen by divine destiny or are they created by chance? Surely all lives are of equal value. We are all woven into the book of life whether we choose it or not. If there is a great author in the sky there may well be a blueprint for life. If not and we get scrawled into place by a mere doodler, or a random ink blot, does it really matter? All we petty creatures can do is live out our span to the best of our ability and within the remit of our own conscience. To question it is as futile as pondering how many angels can dance on the head of a pin. Who cares? Only angels and saints hold the answers, and they will not tell us, not because they are too busy dancing but because they know we probably won't be listening. And so it will be for the rest of eternity. However long that is.

*

Lightning Source UK Ltd.
Milton Keynes UK
UKOW051430211011

180726UK00001B/2/P